THE LEGENDS OF OLD

GREGG ANDREW MURPHY

This book could not have been completed without Cori.

Eternally grateful

The Legends Of Old

Chapter 1: *Cute as a Fox*

It was 7:45am, and puddles of rain were scattered across the roads and paths of the small town of Tinree Island. Children were making their way to school huddled under umbrellas, rain jackets and even ponchos. It often rained in Tinree Island, which was a small peninsula in the southeast of Ireland. The area could have very harsh winters, with an icy wind that was described as God's punishment. They would also have glorious summers, with scorching heat and warm gentle breezes, referred to in the area as the reward.

Tinree Island was a very religious part of Ireland, which in modern days was hard to find. Ireland had evolved from a religious state to a thriving technological destination with many parishes and areas having such little religious interest anymore that the doors to the church would close forever. Tinree Island, however, was a religious haven in the southeast, with many pilgrims arriving to hike it's famous mountain: the Cnòc Mòr *(Knock More)*.

This impressive mountain was the highest in the southeast and overlooked the sea from a staggering height to outstanding views of the mighty Irish Sea. Another reason why Cnòc Mòr attracted so many pilgrims and interests is because it was supposedly the spot where the mythological old heroes of Ireland – the Tuatha Dé Danann *(Too-ah De Danan)* – fought and vanquished the ancient demons of the land. The violent and oppressive Fomorians.

As with any tourist area, Cnoc Mor was once a place of true pilgrimage and worship. Nowadays, however, there is many a native to Tinree Island who makes their wage off simple tourists. There is still true and honest pilgrims who take the 3 hour plunge it takes to reach the top, but most arrive, take a picture at the bottom and float around the locals' gimmicky gift shops.

Maura Finnegan, a sharp-tongued teacher, would set up a stall during the summer holidays and sell broken bits of steel, claiming them to be shards from the sword of light. The sword of light belonged to the leader of the Tuath De Danann, King Nuada. Now the shards of steel Maura Finnegan were selling did not belong to the sword of light, or any sword for that matter. Her husband was a welder and would leave out sharp bits of metal that may look like sword shards. Mr. Finnegan was also in favour of exploiting tourists; especially during the summer months.

"Nowhere in any Bible does it say it's wrong to make a few pounds off people who are willing to give it," he'd say. "We haven't robbed anyone; it's a fair trade"

Mr. Finnegan would retort with that any time someone questioned his ethics, but all in all the town had a fair understanding that the money to be made off the tourists would be reinvested in the town, so no one had a real issue with it.

With the Summer over, the fine heat had subsided and the rain had once again made its way back to Tinree Island. Most of the school kids in the area would work locally during the summer. The area did have a particularly low amount of students who went off to college. The vast majority ended up working at their parents' tourist trap or starting their own. There was 13 different "guided tours" up Cnoc Mor, all with different little gimmicks. Some included a free sandwich, and others offered sporadic prayer sessions along the way. Mainly all of them made significant money, so when faced with leaving the area to study for four years to gain an entry level job to earn a fraction of what they earned in Tinree Island, most just stayed.

Students usually graduated at eighteen, once they had completed their sixth year of secondary school. On this particular September morning, only the third-years and sixth-years of Tinree Island secondary school were returning, as they were entering examination years. The third-years would be doing their Junior cert the following summer, and the sixth-years their final exams – the Leaving cert. The other years would return later in the week, luckily for them, as now the rain was pouring down.

Some girls were waddling like penguins up along the busy paths sharing one umbrella. School didn't start until 8:00am, but due to the rain everyone was rushing. Maura Finnegan drove by slowly, examining the children to find something on one of them that she could later bring up in class.

"I saw you holding hands with Tom Keane on the way in, isn't he a bit young for you Ms. Byrne? He's only in second year," she had said to an extremely embarrassed Lucy Byrne, who was a fourth-year, one Wednesday morning in math class.

As Maura Finnegan drove by, the rain intensified and the wind howled, causing a mini typhoon for the students as they crossed the road towards the unimpressive, small school gates.

All the students were rushing as the time creeped closer to 8:00am – all students bar one. A third-year boy was taking his time walking up the road. He was absolutely soaked to the bone. He wore no rain jacket, no umbrella, no poncho. The boy wasn't even wearing a hat; his mid-length, jet black hair was stuck to his face as the rain poured down. An average looking third-year boy of average height, average build and a less than handsome appearance sauntered through the rain.

The reason this boy was taking his time was that he didn't want to go to school. He figured his discontent of going to school there was so great that if he took his time there would have to be some divine intervention. Not only was it a rainy day of school, it was his first day at this school.

Gerard Fox had just been rehomed from the state system to Tinree Island. Gerard Fox, who preferred to be called Gerry by his friends, was always called Foxy in any home he had been in. The nickname had stuck so well, the social workers at the shared residential homes he would live in would all call him Foxy.

At fifteen years old, Foxy's chances of being adopted were essentially none. He had gone into the system at age ten, when both of his parents sadly passed away from a particularly strong case of the corona virus. His parents had no brothers or sisters, and Foxy's grandparents had long since passed away.

He still remembered the extremely small funeral. There were two or three work friends for both his Mam and Dad, the priest, and then the state-appointed carer for young Foxy. While extremely sad, Foxy never cried. He still thought about that. In fact, he had never cried in his life. Although it looked like he was crying now with the rain pouring down his cheeks.

He was looked after very well by the state, no gruel-serving grey brick orphanages. Instead, Foxy was placed in nice modern houses built for children who had nowhere else to go. The social workers who stayed there and minded the children were excellent.

Foxy was reserved and introverted, never really making a proper connection with a staff member, but always was polite, friendly and kind. Most children in his homes were kids who had lost their parents, but occasionally you could get a runaway, a problem child, orpeople from other countries who had also sadly lost their parents. While riddled in tragedy, Foxy had a relatively happy transition from his previous life with his parents when they lived near the midlands of Ireland to his new life in Tinree Island.

Foxy was pleased to hear that a foster home was willing to take him, as the other children he considered friends had all been taken into similar homes or adopted. However, he was remiss when he heard where he was going.

"Tinree Island?! The holy tourist place out by the sea? That's miles away from anything," Foxy mourned to the social worker one day.

The social worker looked calmly at him and replied, "Calm down, Gerry. There is an older couple who live down there who have applied to foster someone. Mr. and Mrs. Sullivan have a beautiful house near the beach. They own a little farm, so I expect they may be wanting some help on it."

Foxy was never shy of work, and always helped out around the homes. It was more so the remoteness of the area that was stressing him out, plus he had never been religious. He always thought the priest was apathetic the day of his parents' funeral.

"Well, they are willing to take you, but you will have to go soon; the school term starts a few days earlier down there than it does here. You will have to attend school before meeting your foster parents. We will drive you down, drop your bags off, and you can head off to school and then meet your foster parents after. School is extremely important!"

The social worker droned on and on, but Foxy knew it was better to accept than argue. These things very rarely, if ever, changed.

So at 5 am that morning, Foxy packed up the few things he had into the staff bus. He bade his goodbyes with the staff, who were adequately pleasant as Foxy always was. The driver headed up towards Tinree Island. Foxy and the driver barely spoke the whole way.

As they came over the crest of the road into Tinree Island, much to his own astonishment Foxy was in awe of the beauty of the place. Mainly, he was staggered by the sheer size of the Cnoc Mor mountain.

The driver pulled into a lane and up to a fine sized farmhouse. Indeed, the house actually looked too big for the relatively small farm out back of it. There were a few sheds, and what seemed like only two or three fields of wheat. There was a small porch at the front of the house, with a note up against the front door.

"Hi Gerard,

We won't be back until after school. The front door is open; you can leave your bags in the front hall. We have gone to town to get a few things for the house and for you. We hope you have a nice day at school.

Love, Linda"

Foxy's initial thought was that it was weird that she said 'love', since she hadn't actually met him yet. He was also overcome with a sense of feeling like a burden, that they had gone to town to get things for him. He hated receiving gifts more than anything else; he just couldn't fake sincere gratitude. He received a particularly nice scarf off one of the female staff members at Christmas last year. He'd tried it on and thanked her, but he thought his face must have looked dejected, as the staff worker looked upset. Foxy hated making anyone feel bad, but he just couldn't act surprised about gifts.

The front door was indeed open. He gave it a nudge open to a lovely, homely, clean house. The front hall was spacious and immaculately clean. The sitting room had a large, open fireplace right next to a large TV, and he thought to himself, *that looks brilliant.*

He took a quick peek into the kitchen. It felt rustic, homely, and strangely cool. Plants hung across the ceilings and walls, and a beautiful kitchen island was covered in the finest of fresh fruit. Again, he was stunned by the cleanliness. He had to have assumed this was because of him, which again make that burden feeling grow. They had a large clock in the kitchen, with the long hand in the shape of a carrot and the short hand in the shape of a turnip. He chuckled to himself, but he did notice the time and quickly left his bags in.

Foxy had assumed the bus driver would take him to school, but as he was leaving the bags inside and having a prolonged look at the place, the bus driver actually left. Foxy laughed and looked around, simply taking in the remoteness of the quiet farmyard he had been moved to.

"This might work out," he whispered to himself.

He got changed into the school uniform in the hall. The clothes had been provided by his social house back in the midlands.

Foxy quickly checked his phone, saw that the school was only a thirty-minute walk away, and off he went. Just as he hit the top of the driveway, the rain started.

Reflecting on the morning had taken more time than he thought, as now Foxy was standing directly outside the school gates. He just stood there, the feeling of "it might work out" having totally faded. The sheer amount of butterflies in his stomach felt like a fist. He saw that the time was 7:57 am. He knew he had to go in, but his legs wouldn't move. He also knew if he was late, it would be a bigger deal walking into the class and interrupting the lesson. Again, his legs just wouldn't move.

Out of the corner of his eye he saw a very posh-looking car arrive at the school gates. The driver had gotten out of the car in the rain, opened an umbrella, and held it over the back door. He opened the back door, and a pretty young girl got out. She was tall, with long, jet-black hair similar to Foxy's. Her uniform looked different. The skirt was a different colour, Foxy was sure. Then he realised it wasn't, it was just the first uniform he had seen that was dry! The uniform wasn't near as dull as he thought; it was somehow a vibrant black complimented by a deep red around the cuffs and seams.

 The girl nodded to the driver, who politely nodded back and then got back in the car and drove off.

The girl crossed the road, looking curiously at Foxy. She stopped in front of him, and very obviously looked him up and down.

"Oh my god, did you go swimming before you came to school? You'll get sick," said the girl.

She handed him the umbrella. Foxy took it, but was too shy to speak. He nodded quietly. The umbrella was large enough that both of them fit underneath it, but they were quite close, and it did make Foxy nervous.

The girl continued, "I've not seen you before, is it your first day? Follow me; I'll show you where to go and mainly where to dry off."

The two of them set off towards the school. The feeling in Foxy's legs had returned, and so had the feeling that everything may "work out".

Chapter 2: *The Lay of the Land*

Foxy and the girl walked into the large, grey, concrete courtyard at the front of the school. She was whistling a gentle tune, only stopping when a strand of her long hair got caught in her mouth. Foxy's looked at her lips as they walked, not in the usual way a teenage boy looked at a girls lips, but because he had strangely noticed how good of a whistler she was – easily going up and down the musical scale, holding long notes effortlessly.

"You're a good whistler," said Foxy.

The girl stopped and smiled at him.

"You know, that actually means a lot. No one ever compliments my whistling. My parents said I could whistle before I could speak. I do it all the time," she replied happily.

They arrived under the porch at the front door of the school, on the far side of the courtyard. Foxy handed the girl back the umbrella and muttered a gentle, "Thanks for that."

Foxy couldn't believe how long of a walk it was from the front gate to the front door; he was very glad for the girl's company. Foxy, not being a very smooth operator when it came to the fairer gender, was nervous about asking her name. He knew that's what he should do, but the words wouldn't come out of his mouth. Instead, he looked at her, smirked, and took a long breath. He did not exhale for a moment, and when he did no words followed as the girl expected.

She looked at him curiously, wondering why he didn't speak. The girl, however, was confident and forthright in her actions. She took the umbrella back, shook the water off it, and smiled at Foxy while confidently putting her hand out.

"My name is Naoise *(Nee-Sha)* Moone. What's yours?"

Foxy shook her hand, very aware of how slippery his hand was. He was thankful for the rain, as it hid how sweaty his palms usually got in nervous situations.

"My name is Gerard Fox, Gerry Fox, uh, I mean, Foxy. Call me the Fox," Foxy stumbled over his words, instantly mortified. Naoise was again looking at him with a curious look. "Please forget that last one. My friends just call me Foxy."

Naoise chuckled slightly. "Nice to meet you, Foxy."

Just as she had said this, Maura Finnegan poked her head out the front door. "Naoise Moone, you get chauffeured to school daily and somehow you're still late! Get inside, now!"

Turning her attention to Foxy with a snarl, she said, "Mr. Fox, I presume? Late on your first day. I mean my god, did your parents not teach you how to be on time?"

The teacher's face recoiled instantly. Mrs. Finnegan was aware of Foxy's past, and morbidly disgusted at herself for what she had said. She thought it best to pretend she didn't know.

Foxy, however, was well accustomed to the assumption that everyone's parents were alive. At most events and places he went, there was a question about his parents. Even meeting new people in the social houses, the first question was always regarding parents.

Foxy eventually stopped taking offence to when people assumed his parents had just left him or that he was a problem child. How were they to know? He also knew this very much made him the minority and different, as the vast majority of people his age did, in fact, have both parents alive.

Foxy just nodded at Maura Finnegan, accepting of her mistake.

"I'm sorry Miss, I got lost. Naoise here was kind enough to help me. She's late because of me," Foxy said, now finding his words more comfortably.

Naoise looked at Maura Finnegan, awaiting her reply. The teacher looked the young girl up and down patronizingly.

"Our Naoise, ever the Samaritan" said Mrs. Finnegan.

Naoise smiled back. "The story wasn't called *The Bad Samaritan*," she replied cheekily.

Mrs Finnegan gave a mocking smirk.

Finnegan stood back with the door open. "You're both in the same class, so hurry up, get inside," she said.

Foxy was happy to oblige. He was internally thrilled to find out that he and Naoise were in the same class. Naoise and Foxy stepped inside. Naoise could tell from Finnegan's face that she was no longer in the humour for stalling.

"Yes, Miss," Naoise replied, tugging Foxy by the jumper and pulling him down the hall.

As the two walked speedily down the hall, Naoise tried to fill Foxy in. "You've got double English first. Mr. Jordan is very kind and will help you settle in. Although, it's not the teacher you need to worry about."

Foxy speedily walked behind her, somehow trying to shake the excess water out of his hair. He was curious and nervous as to what he *did* have to worry about. Just outside the classroom door, Naoise stopped him.

"Some of the students here have no intention of ever leaving this town or venturing off this little peninsula. They can be a little closed-minded, and can make life hell for someone. I would suggest to try and keep your head down. Fly under the radar; don't do anything that will create buzz about you," Naoise said forthrightly.

Foxy was never really worried about bullies. He had a thick skin and a quick wit when he wanted to. He was brave, and never one to take abuse from other house members or anyone else, really. He would also say to staff after any disputes that just because he was introverted and quiet didn't mean he was weak.

Naoise could see he wasn't too stressed about it.

"Foxy, honestly, these people are horrible. Trust me, I know. Don't give them any ammo. They're well able to shoot already," she said with an air of concern in her voice.

Foxy could tell that she was serious. He nodded. "I'll do my best."

Naoise quickly knocked on the door and entered. "Sorry I'm late, Sir," she said, walking into the room.

Foxy was nervous, but Naoise being there made it nowhere near as daunting as it could have been for him. He put on a brave face and walked in. He saw Mr. Jordan, a middle-aged man with a kind face and a weak goatee. Just after he saw the teacher, Foxy looked around to see a bog-standard classroom – the usual posters on the walls and a clock at the front hanging above two large, white boards, one of which read, 'Welcome back students' and the other read, 'Salutations, returning scholars.' Underneath it, 'SYNONYMS' was underlined.

There were roughly eighteen students spread across twenty-four individual desks and chairs. There was what seemed to be a 50/50 split of boys and girls. Foxy realized that they were all staring at him. He was unsure if this was due to how wet he was, or if it was purely because he was new.

Mr. Jordan happily announced, "Everyone, this is Gerard Fox, a new student from the midlands. Now Mr. Fox, do you prefer Ger, Gerard or Gerry?"

Foxy looked at Mr. Jordan and calmly said, "My friends call me Foxy."
The kind teacher smiled. "Foxy it is then. There is a seat at the back beside Ms. Moone," he said, gesturing Foxy to the desks at the side of the room.

His desk was right beside the window, which made Foxy very happy.

As Foxy walked down towards his desk, he saw a burly, grimace-faced young man snigger to his friends. "Hiya Foxy," he said. All his friends laughed lowly.

Foxy heard them all laugh at his name, and for the first time in a long time, he felt small. He couldn't believe how small he felt over something as stupid as a few people he didn't know laughing at him. His stomach sank when he sat down behind Naoise.

She was kind enough to turn around and say, "I'm glad you're here, Foxy." This made him feel better.

The lesson continued. It began no different than any other English lesson Foxy had attended. Naoise whistled quietly throughout; it really was impressive how long she could hold a note. The class did drone on a bit, although Mr. Jordan did have enough enthusiasm to keep Foxy's attention from the rainy landscape he could see from the window. His attention was particularly attuned when Mr. Jordan was discussing the great Irish storytellers. Especially when he mentioned the Tuath De Danann.

Foxy knew it wasn't a good idea, but he really wanted to know. He thought to himself about when Naoise had said, *"Fly under the radar!"* but his curiosity had gotten the better of him.

He raised his hand. Mr. Jordan spotted him and gently asked "Question, Mr. Fox?"

Foxy cleared his throat "Who are the Tuath De Danann?"

The class erupted into laughter. Foxy was so confused. Even Naoise seemed to stifle a laugh.

"Quiet down, everyone be quiet!" cried Mr. Jordan, who also fought back a light smile.

Foxy had asked the question and wanted an answer. He continued, "So, who are they?"

Mr. Jordan sat down on his desk, leaning back into it stretching his back.

"Foxy, my boy," he said, settling in, "the Tuath De Danann literally translates to 'the tribes of the gods'. They served the folk goddess Danu. They were made up of powerful kings, mighty queens, mystical druids, enchanting bards, brave warriors, kind healers and expert craftsman, and all of the Tuath De Danann had powers."

Foxy was utterly enthralled by this story. Mr. Jordan continued

"The goddess Danu sent the tribe to Ireland to bring peace to the land, as Ireland was covered in darkness, and evil did indeed rule the land."

Some of the students' eyes were rolling, as they had heard the story an infinite number of times, but Foxy was fit to scream if Mr. Jordan did not continue.

"Ireland was once ruled by a large group of malevolent spirits named the Fomorians," Mr. Jordan continued. "The Fomorians arose from the nether regions of the Earth, and claimed Ireland as their own. They are said to dwell in the land beneath men. Fire ravaged the land; the Fomorians gained great delight in torturing the land by digging large craters and pits. Their goal was to connect their new home of Ireland to their old home of the land beneath men – the otherworld. They called this process 'the scourge'."
Foxy noticed that Naoise had started whistling again, her gentle melody only embellished Mr. Jordan's story as he continued.

"Danu, the mother goddess of the land, was distraught over the damage the Fomorians were doing to the beautiful land. So she sent forth the Tuath De Danann to rid the land of the Fomorians. The Tuath De Danann arrived in a ferocious thunderstorm. The battle commenced for a thousand years.

"The Tuath De Danann were far superior to the Fomorians, and their powers allowed them to connect with the land in a myriad of ways. The Fomorians' strength came from their leader, who was almost omnipotent with power and a savagely powerful seer: Partholòn *(Part-ho-Loan)*. Partholòn's seer powers made him impossible to find; he could see everything before it came to pass. He was a genius when it came to battle, as he always knew what was to take place. His sole goal was to cause the scourge."

"What exactly *is* the scourge?" asked a semi-interested girl from the back.

"The scourge," replied Mr. Jordan, "is a power that only Partholòn has. It is dark fire and twisted flames that burn and scorch the land. His ultimate goal is to unleash the scourge, but he never fully achieved it."

Foxy was nearly in Naoises's seat he was sitting so far forward as he asked, "Did the Tuath De Danann defeat the Fomorians?"

Naoises continued whistling, her tune turning more cheerful.

Mr. Jordan concluded, "You see, Partholòn was so powerful that no Tuath De Danann could defeat him." The teacher slowed down the story to build drama. The class, who was clearly used to his antics, were less than impressed. He raised a single finger. "There was one, though."

Foxy's eyes widened.

20

"The celestial King Nuada *(Noo-ah-dah)*, the embodiment of everything good and virtuous. Nuada was an imposing figure, the tallest of the Tuath De Danann, his broad shoulders covered by long red hair. Nuada was the leader of the Tuath De Danann, chosen specifically by the Mother Goddess Danu.

"He vanquished Fomorians all over the nation, and it was Nuada who came up with the brilliant plan to defeat Partholòn. He concocted a plan that, by using the four magical treasures Danu had gifted them, they could seal away Partholòn and defeat the remaining Fomorians. The four treasures were Dagda's cauldron, in which no company ever went away from it unsatisfied, the spear of Lugh, which no battle was ever lost against, the stone of Fal, which would glow under the new king of Ireland, and Nuada's incandescent sword of light, whose light no one could resist.

"The three mightiest – Dagda, Lugh, and Nuada – set off one day to a deep valley where Partholòn was residing. Lugh was a tall, lean man in impeccable physical condition with muscles bounding out of every area of his body. Lugh used his ancient spear, which held its own deep powers. In contrast, Dagda was as wide as he was tall, with a great big belly begging to break free from his tight tunic top. Dagda's treasure was a very special cauldron, which could feed all the Tuath De Danann, as it could grow to any size and shrink to any size. The cauldron also acted as a portal, and could appear anywhere within the realm of Ireland.

"By using Dagda's magical cauldron, they were able to step inside it and teleport to Parthelòn's location unbeknownst to him. When they surprised him, Parthelòn was sitting calmy on a rock in a blazing fire valley. He suddenly drew his long sickle. He threw it in a blaze of speed towards the Tuath De Danann, striking Dagda and Lugh. The two gods were immobilized. The plan then came to fruition as Nuada held up the stone of Fal, which emitted a glorious, blinding light that distracted Parthelòn. Nuada's sword of light then absorbed the blinding light, and the king of the Tuath De Dannan aimed it at Parthelòn and charged at the Fomorian leader, piercing him with the sword.

"Parthelòn laughed as Nuada stared at him. Nuada then quickly dragged the wounded Fomorian and forced him into the large cauldron. He fought back, until Lugh stabbed him back down with his powerful, mystical spear. Parthelòn was still overpowering them. Dagda then assisted his Tuath De Danann brethren and fought Parthelòn. The three tribal gods were able to force the Fomorian king into the cauldron, which then shrank instantly to the size of a gemstone which emitted a faint, golden glow.

"Nuada once again held the stone of Fal, which emitted the white light signalling him as the king of the land. Almost instantly Nuada, Dagda and Lugh left the cauldron gemstone at the base of the valley. Then Dagda placed his hands together and the fire filled valley suddenly went out, and above the large valley the hole began filling in with luscious, vibrant green grass. The valley then grew into a glorious, impressive mountain, and thick, flowy meadows filled the sides of the mountains.

"Parthelòn was buried beneath the huge mountain. Green grass filled the land as the Tuath De Danann defeated the remaining Fomorians, and what was left over is the beautiful country we are left with today. The Tuath De Danann, having completed their godly destiny, returned solemnly to the thunderclouds from which they came."

All Foxy could say was, "wow."

His eyes were almost in tears. He could not remember ever being so interested in a story. The next thing before he knew, the bell rang. The class quickly rose to leave the room in a busy cluster of noise.

Mr. Jordan loudly exclaimed, "Also, Foxy, if you are curious as to why this town is so famous, the hill that Parthelòn is buried under is right out that window."

Foxy turned to look out the rainy window and saw the mighty Cnoc Mor. He felt an obsessive interest about the Tuath De Danann and wanted to know more.

While leaving the class, the surly-faced boy who'd laughed earlier said to him, "Don't tell me you're interested in that rubbish?"

Foxy again felt very small, because he most certainly was interested in it.

The boy left the class, and Foxy turned again to look out the window. The whole class was gone except for Foxy and Naoise. Mr. Jordan gestured for Foxy to leave with Naoise. On his way out, Foxy stopped by Mr. Jordan's desk.

"Thank you, Sir, I really enjoyed that story."

Mr. Jordan kindly smiled at Foxy. "My pleasure."

Naoise and Foxy left the classroom as the wild rain that had pattered the windows finally stopped.

Chapter 3: *What Makes A Home*

Foxy made it through the rest of his classes that day dealing with the separate teachers' unique personalities, the snide comments from other classmates – which ranged from dirty looks to group whispers – and one encounter in a corridor where he was sure the groups of boys would do something. But Naoise had stuck beside Foxy all day.

Foxy noticed how Naoise received no grief from anyone. No male students said a word to her, and the female students acted like she didn't exist. As they headed for their last class of the day – math with the sharp-mouthed Maura Finnegan – Foxy couldn't quite figure out how no one was talking to her, as she was very friendly, and very pretty.

His curiosity got the better of him, and he quietly asked, "Where are your friends, Naoise?"

Naoise heard the question, but didn't look at Foxy. She just sort-of giggled to herself as they walked, turning her head towards him.

"I'm looking at him."

She laughed again and trotted on a little ahead of Foxy. He was thrilled to learn she thought of him as a friend, although another thought did cross his mind.

How am I her only friend? Is there something wrong with her?

He quickly corrected his thoughts, as everything she had shown him in the time they'd spent together so far would indicate there was nothing wrong with her. She was a perfectly lovely girl, and he should be thankful to her for helping him today.

The last class of the day whizzed by. Math class took place on the second floor, and Foxy sat by the window, where he had a great view of Cnoc Mor. He kept visualising a great battle taking place on the hill, and Ireland's three bravest warriors – Lugh, Dagda and Nuada – standing triumphantly on the top of the mountain, King Nuada holding the stone of Fal high in the air. Its glow signalled him to be the king of Ireland.

Mrs. Finnegan brought him straight back to math very quickly with a piercing, "Mr. Fox, is there a more interesting math class taking place outside?"

Foxy, slightly embarrassed just replied, "No miss, sorry," accepting that he had been looking out the window for far too long.

Just after he apologised, the final bell for the day rang. The class rose and began to exit. Naoise turned around to Foxy in her chair, twirling with her ferociously.

"Where do you live, Foxy? Would you like a lift home?"

Foxy very aware that Naoise must be very wealthy, and while very generous for the lift, he knew his foster parents were from a modest background and did not feel comfortable flaunting wealth on their first introduction.

"Ah, that's very kind, Noaise, thank you. But I think I'm gonna walk; it'll help me learn the area and think about what I'm gonna say when I meet my foster parents."

Naoise and Foxy both packed up, and as the pair headed out of school towards the front gate their conversation continued, Naoise brimming with curiosity.

"Foster parents?" Naoise replied inquisitively.

Foxy, having had this conversation ad nauseum with people throughout his life, gave his standard reply, "Yes, my birth parents both died when I was young. It was actually Covid-19 that got them. I've been in state homes ever since, moving from residential settings to temporary foster parents and so on. Six months or so the foster parents hang onto me, then they'll return to sender. Happens all the time, not just to me. Some people just aren't ready for a teenager to burst into their life."

Foxy had given this exact answer to anyone enquiring about his life or living situation. He had crafted it to perfection to leave no doubt and minimise any follow up questions. He also had his tone of voice for the response well crafted, so that they knew he missed his parents but understood he had come to terms with the scenario.

He had received every possible response to his cover all bases answer, Naoise's expression didn't change too much as Foxy explained. However, Foxy's expression changed to bemusement when she responded, as no one had ever asked him this question before.

"What were your parents' names?"

Foxy looked at her, stunned, and then let out a little laugh. He replied, smiling, "Thomas was my dad's name, and Bridget was my mother's name."

"What pretty names," Naoise replied sincerely.

Foxy now emitting the most honest smile Naoise had seen on him all day. The two friends reached the front gate of the school.

"I haven't actually said their names out loud in a long time," Foxy laughed heartily.

He had a wave of memories flood back to him, that he had not thought about in a very, very long time. He began to feel emotional as a lavish car arrived at the school gate. A sharply dressed man got out of the driver's seat and opened the back door.

Foxy looked at the car and then at Naoise. "Your chariot awaits," he said jokingly.

She returned in favour and jokingly curtsied.

"You sure I can't offer you a lift?"

"No thank you, you've honestly done too much for me today," Foxy responded.

Naoise understood the finality of the statement, and that Foxy would not be coerced into the lift home. Then, suddenly, she remembered something.

"Oh, I almost forgot!"

She reached into her handbag, took out her phone, and handed it to Foxy.

Foxy being bad at receiving gifts, he didn't really know how to respond to this gesture at all.

Trying to break it to her gently, he said, "Thank you very much Naoise, but I've already got a phone?"

Naoise rolled her eyes. "Put your number in it, Foxy."

Foxy was very much embarrassed, as he had thought she'd taken pity on him and decided to donate a phone. He turned tomato red.

"Oh my god, I'm so sorry," he awkwardly said, grabbing the phone and typing in the number.

As it seemed standard with Naoise's disposition, she laughed, taking her phone back. "I'll text you later. Best of luck meeting your parents."

She happily hopped towards her car. The driver shut the door behind her as she got into the back seat. The sharply dressed driver shot Foxy a damning look, then proceeded to return to the front of the car and drive off. Foxy was confused over this look, but it didn't take long to forget it as he walked back up the country road. Straight away Foxy got a text on his phone from an unknown number, it simply contained the emoji of a fox. He smiled to himself and saved the number as "Naoise"

As Foxy got ahead of the school crowd and was walking solo up the country road toward his foster parents' house, his mind was not full of angst and planned conversation with his foster parents. Instead, Naoise's question about his parents' name had been like breaking a dam that was holding back memories.

He was thinking fondly of a Christmas morning when he had been only a young child, maybe three of four. He had received a "warrior play set," which came complete with a helmet, shield and sword.

His mam and dad had played with him all morning by the roaring fire in their sitting room. The family dog, Chunk, was playing the role of a fierce demon that needed to be slain. His mother and father were cowering in the corner from the heavy, out-of-breath golden retriever. Foxy would then burst into the room to save the day.

"Begone, foul beast!" the young Gerry Fox would shout across the room.

He would charge down the obese beast and pretend to stab him with his foam sword. Chunk, having been already far over-exercised for him, collapsed to the ground.

Foxy would stand proudly over the slain beast and declare proudly to the room, "I have killed the monster and saved King Thomas and Queen Bridget."

The memory felt like a warm blanket draped over him. He wanted to bottle up that feeling of warmth. The pleasant feeling this memory had placed over him, he replayed in his head over and over again until he reached his foster parents' driveway. He couldn't believe how quickly the walk had passed by. He looked out across the land to see sun dip in behind a cloud.

He was now debating whether it was the memory or the sun that had warmed him so. As much he was cherishing that memory, he decided to store the memory in a neat shelf in his cognitive storage where it wouldn't be forgotten again. He knew he had to be open to accepting his new foster parents. He took a deep breath and walked up the driveway.

As he walked up the drive towards the small farm and the modest house, he noticed the smoke coming out of the chimney and did feel slightly giddy at the prospect of the open fire. His Christmas morning memory snuck back into conscious thought.

He drew close to the house and saw the front door open up. An extremely short, round woman opened the door. She waved enthusiastically, jumping up and down although never actually leaving the door. Foxy knew this must be Linda. His first impression was of her height, and she was only slightly old; maybe early sixties. He waved back awkwardly.

He reached the porch and found that he was significantly taller than her. Her head came up to just under his chest. She embraced him a vice-like tight hug.

"Welcome to Tinree Island, and welcome to your new home. I'm Linda," Linda Sullivan said in her warm, thick rural Irish accent.

Foxy was never partial to hugs; especially since the loss of his parents.

"It's very nice to meet you," Foxy said gently.

Linda stood back and looked up at him. "You must be so cold; we're so sorry we couldn't be here when you arrived this morning, but I hope we made up for it."

Linda dragged Foxy inside the house. Flustered she stopped. "Oh, do you prefer Ger or Gerard?"

He was pre-occupied looking in at the roaring fire in the sitting room. He turned back to Linda. "I actually go by Foxy, if that's okay?"

Linda smiled warmly, noticing the young man looking at the open fire. "Well Foxy, why don't you go grab a shower and I'll show you your new room."

Foxy felt somewhat sad that he didn't get to stand beside the fire, but didn't want to offend Linda in any way at all, so he followed her instruction instantly.

Linda led him up the stairs to a surprisingly big room. He was taken aback by the size of the bed in the room. A large, double bed, made perfectly with large pillows and thick duvets, stood in the middle of the room. He spotted in the corner a new television. He turned to look at Linda, who handed him a remote control as he turned.

"Now I don't know anything about TVs, but the lady in the shop said this one should be perfect for a boy your age."

Foxy was overcome with gratitude, but as was standard for him he felt extremely awkward trying to show it. He was already feeling empathy for Linda, so he tried his best smile.

"It's perfect," said Foxy in soft tones. "Thank you so much."

Foxy looked around the room again and saw the en-suite bathroom stemming off the main room.

Linda briefly stepped out of the room and returned with large, soft towels.

"Also, Foxy, I hope you don't mind but I took the liberty of putting away your clothes from the bags; they're in those drawers. Now I want you to get a long hot shower, put on some dry clothes, and then we'll have dinner ready for you when you come downstairs."

Foxy felt as light as a feather with the proposition of the shower and dinner. He actually felt like a lotto jackpot winner. Linda handed him the towels. Foxy took them gracefully, he couldn't help put them to his face. They were exceptionally soft.

Linda turned to walk out, but Foxy called her back. "Excuse me, Linda?"

She turned and looked like the world's most content woman.

"Thank you so much, truly. You really do have a beautiful home," said Foxy earnestly.

Linda smiled from ear to ear. "Foxy my boy, a home is only as beautiful as the people in it." She smirked at him one more time and left the room.

Foxy pondered that statement as he got into the shower. Eventually his thoughts washed away as the powerful, hot shower melted any stress or angst off him.

He didn't realise how cold his bones were from the rain until he got into the hot shower. He felt them warm up, and stood with his head under the steamy hot water until his brain went completely blank and just pure comfort took over.

Chapter 4: *The Dinner, the Dream, and the Drag Harrow*

Foxy stepped out of the steamy shower. He had lost track of time. When he looked at his watch, he realised he was in the shower for over half an hour. He hadn't felt as relaxed in years. He didn't think that much once the warm water and steam engulfed him. The towels Linda had givin him were large, fluffy, and very comforting. With one towel around his waist and another draped around his shoulders like a large robe, Foxy flicked through the presses and drawers to see that his clothes had all been impeccably folded and arranged in the drawers. He also spotted several new clothes that Linda had also purchased.

He perused the room and got dressed into comfortable wear – tracksuit bottoms and a jumper, both of which were his own. He didn't want to go downstairs in the bought clothes, but he made a mental note to make sure to say thanks.

Before he went downstairs, he did check if the TV worked. He never had a television in his room before. The first programme that came on was horse racing. He sat on the bed and smiled. He thought to himself, this was his. His own private space. Then his mind raced to, *I can't wait to tell Naoise*, but this thought was squashed fairly quickly, as he assumed that if she had a personal driver, a TV in his room would not impress her.

As he sat on the edge of the bed watching the tele, he heard a voice call upstairs, "Foxy, dinner is just about ready."

Foxy quickly turned off the TV, put on his runners, and went to go downstairs. He heard a man's voice downstairs.

"Well, what's he like, Linda?"

"You'll just have to see for yourself," Foxy heard Linda reply.

Foxy understood this man must be her husband, and his new foster father, so he put on his best polite face and headed downstairs. He had only taken one step down the stairs when he was taken aback by something.

What was this, he thought. It was an aroma.

A sweet, warm, heavenly aroma. It was wafting up from the kitchen. Foxy had never smelled anything like it before. Was this his dinner, he hoped. Each step he took further down the stairs, the more the smell penetrated his nostrils. He thought it smelled like happiness, family, and sunshine. He couldn't quite think of the correct adjective, but he did agree with himself that above all else it just smelled delicious.

He walked in through the door in the kitchen and saw Linda over a pot on the cooker. It was bubbling at the top and the vapour rising off the top was thick and smelled intoxicating.

"Come on in dear, your stew in nearly ready," Linda said cheerfully.

She took out a small wooden spoon that she was stirring the pot with and scooped up a bit of broth, capped with a bit of mincemeat and carrot. She held it out to Foxy.

"Taste this for me dear, will you? Let me know if it's ready."

Foxy awkwardly tried to grab the spoon and accept the food. He ate up the stew from the spoon. It tasted simply sublime. He smiled contently at Linda.

"Oh, that is amazing. It's definitely done. Also, thank you so much for the clothes and TV and everything, really, including this delicious dinner."

Linda accepted his thanks comfortably, and greeted him with a wide smile.

"Now please sit down, sit down," Linda shooed him towards the table.

Foxy walked closer to the table to sit down, but just as he was about to take his seat a man entered through the back door to the kitchen. A tall, strong looking man. He was similar in age to Linda, but he looked quite fit, muscular, even.

The man's eyes lit up as he saw who was in the kitchen, Foxy stood back up immediately. Linda turned around bursting with cheer.

"Foxy, this is my husband Macdara."

Macdara had a kind, inviting face. He had a strong presence to him. He cleaned his hands quickly with a nearby dish cloth and then bounded strongly over to Foxy.

Foxy, now realising that Macdara was indeed quite tall, looked up at the tall man.

"It is very nice to meet you, Macdara," said Foxy, somewhat shyly.

Macdara grew a handsome smile and looked down at the boy.

"Believe me, Foxy, the pleasure is absolutely all mine," he loudly replied.

Foxy noticed instantly that Macdara had a booming voice. He presumed it was necessary on the farm for shouting at animals or something.

"Thank you so much for everything," said Foxy.

Macdara sat down in the kitchen chair and relaxed into it, and he gestured for Foxy to sit down too.

"You are very welcome young man; we will do anything we can to make sure you are as comfortable here as possible," Macdara said exhaustingly as he flicked off his wellies.

"I want you, from today, to treat this house as your home, but remember nothing comes easy in life without hard work."

Linda spun around. "Honestly, Macdara, can you go one evening without discussing work?"

Macdara laughed back at her. "It's important! Do you think I'm out playing games on the farm all day?"

Foxy poured himself a glass of water from the jug on the table as he said, "I'll happily help out or work on the farm. What type of farming is it?"

Macdara's face grew distorted with excitement. Linda tutted and turned back to the pot. Macdara sat up in the chair now and excitedly began, "This here is a relatively small farm. We have a few sheep, a few beef cows, and a couple fields for grain. Now I love this farm almost as much as I love that woman." he nodded over to Linda, who blushed.

"The real work around here is, once I look after me own farm, I go and work on other people's farms who need extra help, and some poor auld divils around the area who have gone too old to mind their own farms, so they ask me."

He leaned in close to Foxy and quietly said, "Now don't tell Linda, but I do actually love working. I do play games and all in my head as I work. Hard work makes the world go round."

Foxy, who had never really worked a day in his life, questioned how much fun it could be, but was eager to find out. Internally, he had compromised too that he wouldn't mind the TV and new clothes if he was able to work back and help the Sullivans.

"When can we start?" said Foxy.

Macdara laughed heartily and slapped Foxy on the back.

"Tomorrow morning. Tuesday before school we'll put in two hours on the farm and I'll see what you're made of. How does that sound?"

Foxy smiled at the proposition "It's a deal."

Then all of a sudden there was a gentle thud in front of him. Linda had placed a beautiful looking bowl of stew in front of him. The steam rising off it warmed his face. She then placed a small plate beside the bowl of fresh, homemade baked bread and what looked like the softest butter he had seen.

Linda returned to ready Macdara's bowl and her own. When she came back with both of them and sat down, she began to scold Macdara.

"Honestly, his second day of school you're going to make him work the farm?"

Macdara pretended to look offended. "He offered."

Foxy, swallowing a decadent bite of buttery baked bread bathed in broth, nodded at Linda "It's true; I did offer.".

Macdara and Linda laughed. Foxy then joined in as they all tucked into his dinner.

He thought to himself, this might be the nicest meal he's ever had.

***

After dinner had ended, Foxy was stuffed. He couldn't possibly eat another bite. Macdara had gone into the sitting room while Foxy stayed to help Linda clean up. He was doing his best, but after the meal, dessert, and a cup of tea, he was ready for bed. He had been up since all hours that morning.

Linda spotted this and said, "It's nearly 8 pm. Why don't you go to bed and get a good night's sleep? I can finish this up."

Foxy smiled. "Are you sure?"

"Yes," she replied quickly. "Now off to bed with you."

Foxy walked out of the dining room and poked his head into the sitting room. "Goodnight, Macdara."

Macdara himself had nodded off on the couch beside the warm fire. Foxy thought he looked particularly comfortable.

He headed off up the stairs into his room, took his runners and socks off quickly, and then collapsed into the bed. Initially on top, he then crawled under the duvet. It was still semi-bright outside, but he didn't care. The second Foxy closed his eyes, he fell asleep.

***

Foxy opened his eyes. He was no longer in his room. He was looking at the sky – a crystal clear blue day. As he looked around, he spotted an occasional cloud trapsing across the deep blue of the sky. The sun beamed down on his face. It felt so pure to him.

Foxy sat up in the bed and looked around. He thought he was sitting on another sky, as it was a perfect reflection of the heavenly sky above. When a cloud moved along above, he would see the same cloud move along on the ground. He sat to the edge of the bed.

Foxy then realised the bed was floating on a shallow lake. he placed his feet in the water to find the lake water was warm. The water only covered his feet to his ankles, just below the hem of his tracksuit.

Foxy looked around to see that there was no end to the lake. He could only see the horizon. He looked around in a 360 degree motion to see only this beautiful, reflecting lake. He stood up and took a step into the lake. The warm water spread around his feet as he stepped. Only the ripples of his steps interrupted the otherwise perfectly still water.

An overwhelming feeling of emotion ran over him. He almost felt like he wanted to cry, but not tears of sadness. He continued to walk further away from the bed. As he took a step, he looked down, and in the ripples of the water he saw something.

The ripples subsided, he squatted down and gently broke with water surface with his hand. He saw a faint vision of himself as a child smiling eye-wide.

Once again, the ripples dwindled away. Foxy made a more staggering smack on the water. He could now see more clearly that it was a memory. It was him and his parents on the couch by the fire. How could it be a memory, though, Foxy thought. In the vision he was asleep. How could he remember it if he was asleep? He looked at it longingly, though, as the ripples washed away into the seeming eternity of this lake.

Foxy had now walked so far across the lake that the bed had faded from view. Occasionally, a warm breeze would blow through, creating a little stream of miniature waves. Foxy would smile as they trickled by him.

What is this place? he wondered as he walked, *How did I get here?*

He strode across the majestic lake until he eventually spotted something in the distance. He couldn't quite make out what it was, but the crystal lake was so flat he instantly recognised something.

He began to run towards it. As he was running, he noticed that he was not getting out of breath. He ran closer to the object until he realised it was a person – a woman.

Foxy stopped running and slowly approached the woman who was sitting cross-legged in the water. She was a young, beautiful woman who had gorgeous, thick, red hair. She was wearing a light, satin blue dress; it was almost like she was wearing a waterfall.

She turned around, unfased, to look at the young man. She felt warm, Foxy noticed; there was a feeling of sunlight coming off her. She gently looked at him and patted the water beside her, gesturing for him to sit down.

Foxy, now gawking at the woman, sat down slowly, cross-legged in the water, mimicking her.

She turned and looked at him while swivelling herself around so they were face to face. It was just the two of them from one horizon to the other.

The woman spoke in a soft, commanding voice, almost as if she was a tall flower who could talk, "I wasn't sure if you would find me."

Foxy went to respond, but no words came out.

He tried again to talk, then realised he had no use of his voice. The woman noticed he was beginning to panic.

"Relax, Foxy, this is no place for distress."

Foxy then did relax, quite easily to his own surprise. He then looked at the woman, who continued speaking.

"Nothing you ask me at this stage would be of any value, so I think it's best if you just listen this time."

She reached out and grabbed his hand. Her touch was radiant. He felt his very centre ease at her touch.

"Foxy, you have come to a very special place at a very special time. You do not know it yet, but you have a very important role to play."

Foxy embraced her hand with his own.

"I know this sounds confusing, but I need you to have faith. Not in me, or in anyone else. I need you to have faith in your convictions and judgements. You will have some difficult decisions to make in the near future, and I need you to follow your heart."

Foxy noticed his own eyes welling up, and then realised that the lake was no longer still and was beginning to shake. The ripples were rising, and the waves were beginning to crash.

The beautiful woman continued calmly, "Foxy, there is danger on the horizon."

Foxy noticed the water rising, and he began to panic again. He fell backwards. The lake was now extremely deep, and he was being plunged into darkness below the water.

He could see the woman look down at him and hear her voice clearly in his head.

"You have become too panicked to stay here at this time. I do look forward to chatting again."

Foxy was then swallowed by the darkness of the bottomless lake.

***

His eyes shot open, and he sat up sharply in his bed. Looking at the clock, he saw that it was 4:50 am. He was breathing heavily, and needed a moment to compose himself.

As he was taking a breath, he heard a gentle knock on his door.

"Hello?" Foxy called out, delighted to see his voice was working again.

The door opened softly. It was Macdara who, did not look even remotely tired. "Good morning, Foxy. Ready for a bit of work?" He said heartily. "I'll be down in the kitchen if you fancy it."

Foxy, now being totally awake, was, in fact, quite ready for work. He got up and dressed in some of his older clothes and followed Macdara down to the kitchen.

Macdara had a warm cup of tea ready for him, which Foxy graciously accepted.

They walked out into the yard, the residue of summer air lingering. It was a mild, windless morning. Foxy looked across the darkness and only saw a few spotlights attached to the sheds that were illuminating the grounds.

They walked out to the smallest of the fields. It was the size of maybe two tennis courts.

Macdara walked into the field, seamlessly climbing over the gate. He could have done it blindfolded, Foxy guessed.

The sun was beginning to peek over the hill when Foxy got into the field. He spotted a large bit of metal on the ground. It looked like it should have been attached to a tractor.

"What is that?" asked Foxy inquisitively.

Macdara gave the piece of metal a good kick and replied, "an old drag harrow. I'm real glad you're here, cause I usually have to do this myself or I get a donkey to help. You see this field is so small it's a real pain to get a tractor in it and to turn, so it's easier to just plough it myself by pulling this piece behind me."

Foxy couldn't believe he pulled this by himself, it was so big. Large claws sprung out of its diagonal shape. There was a bar at the front that kind of looked like a carriage rickshaw.

"Well," Macdara said, "are you ready?"

He hoisted up the bar easily and tucked himself underneath it.

"You can fit in here with me. We'll have the whole field ploughed before 7 am. Give you lots of time to get ready for school."

Foxy got in under the bar and the two set off to push it.

The drag harrow took unbelievable force from Foxy to move it, especially as he slipped through the soft ground, which was bogged from the previous day's rain. He couldn't comprehend how Macdara could do this by himself. They marched up the field. Foxy was utterly exhausted by the time he had done one length.

"Time to turn it now," said Macdara. "I need you to put lots of force on your side."

The sun was fully creeping over the hills now as Foxy pushed with all his might and his side reached out ever so slightly in front so that when they both pushed it turned to face back the way they came. Foxy was quite pleased seeing the ploughed lane he had left behind him on the way up, but he was nowhere near as pleased as Macdara.

"Hup ya boyo, Foxy! Let's see if we can make it back to the top of the field before the sun gets above that hill."

The two struggled on again down the field, and then up and then down.

By the time the sun had fully risen at 7am, they had finished. Foxy was utterly spent. He almost collapsed over the end of the drag harrow.

Macdara gleefully wiped sweat off his own forehead. "Is there any better way to start the morning?"

Foxy was exhausted physically, but mentally he was beaming. The morning had come and he had won, that's what he was thinking in his mind. He had one up on the day already.

"You'd better run in and shower up before school, young man. I've got work to do," Macdara said happily.

Foxy smiled and jogged off towards the house, although a little scared that Macdara didn't consider that work.

Foxy entered the house and saw Linda had started a breakfast. There were sausages and pudding sizzling away in the pan. Linda turned. "This is just for today, we don't do fried food everyday in this house."

Foxy thanked her and ran up for a shower. He was so utterly happy.

He quickly hopped in the shower, and in the reverse of his last shower which washed away his stress, this one somehow washed away his happiness. The water reminded him of falling into the lake.

He was not thinking of the dinner. He was no longer thinking of the drag harrow. He was focused solely on the dream.

"There is danger on the horizon," he thought to himself.

He washed that thought away as just a dream and then sank back into comfort as the warm water washed away the muck and soothed his blisters.

Chapter 5: *Four Short Days*

The morning had flown by for Foxy. He was out of the shower and dressed in his school uniform in very quick time. He had his delicious breakfast eaten and tea drank all before 7:15 am. While he was eating, Macdara had stopped in to sing his praises as a worker.

"He's not a bad lad to work. Good, even! However, let's give you a break for tomorrow, and if you want to work again in the morning just give me a shout," Macdara boomed across the kitchen.

Smiling over the praise, and very, very pleased to hear that the work was not to occur every morning, he replied, "Let's schedule another morning in for Thursday."

Macdara was delighted to hear this, and took his breakfast into the sitting room where he would relax into his big chair before he undoubtedly headed back to the farm for the day. He whistled a happy tune as he walked off. The whistled tune reminded Foxy of Naoise. He just realised he never text her, he wondered was that rude behaviour or would it have been ruder to text her just after getting her number.

While thinking on Naoise, he realised he would get to see her soon in school. Although again he was debating how best to play the situation. He knew he wanted to meet her before class, but he was deciding in his mind which was the stranger thing to do.

Text a girl he'd just met yesterday, "Hey do you want to meet at the front gate?" Or wait for her at the front gate. He thought both were strange, and didn't want to come across as too forward. Even though he did want to meet her before school and really didn't want to go in class and wait for her.

What if she didn't want to be friends today? Or maybe her friends were out sick yesterday, and today they were back and she wouldn't have any time for him.

Those wild thoughts raced through his mind as the clock clicked over to 7:20 am. Linda tidied up the table in front of him.

"Foxy dear, why don't you relax for a bit? and I'll drop you to school at 7:45 am."

Foxy drank down the last of his tea as he replied, "Oh thank you very much, but I had planned to walk if that's okay? I really enjoyed the stroll in yesterday and it only takes half an hour."

Linda smiled at this response "No problem at all; we always walked to school. Nothing like it to get you ready for the day, and time to wind down in the evening."

She looked at the clock. "You'd better head off now; it's a lovely morning for a walk. Just be mindful of the cars, dear."

"I will, don't worry Linda" Foxy replied earnestly.

He stood up, got his bag and prepared to exit. He popped into the sitting room to say goodbye to Macdara as he headed off for school, but again he noticed Macdara was having a snooze. Foxy could see how he slept so much as the man really was a glutton for work.

Foxy waved goodbye to Linda as he stepped out the door into the glorious morning. The first feeling he had outside since the sun had taken its place high in the sky was a warm breeze on his face. He inhaled it deeply, his dream from the night before flooding back. He could now clearly visualise the place he had met the red-haired woman. Although he only thought on it for a moment as he took to the road walking to school.

The road the Sullivans lived on was quiet, away from the main road and relatively remote for the area. Foxy was beaming as he strolled up the quiet country road. He reflected on the night and the morning he'd just had and really was grateful to whatever power had graced him with such a lovely setting. Even the stress of dealing with the less than desirable classmates didn't bother him, as the hassling wasn't too bad yesterday and he assumed it would dwindle today.

The closer he got to the school, the more in-depth he internally debated how to play what he was referring to as the Naoise situation. He decided that ultimately it would be weird to text. Maybe if he'd texted last night it would have been okay, but it was too late now to text, according to Foxy. He also took heed of her advice to fly under the radar, and committed to the fact that the decision waiting at the school gate would be weird and would draw eyes and attention from people he didn't want attention from.

The solution that he came up with as he increased his walking pace was to arrive early enough so he could hide out of sight and then just casually arrive as Naoise was dropped off. He assumed her car would be easily enough identify due to the size and luxurious nature of it. The more he thought on this plan, the more sense it made. It wouldn't be weird if they just both happened to arrive at the same time.

"Oh hey, fine morning isn't it, Naoise?" Foxy said out loud, practicing, then he looked disgusted with himself.

"That's stupid, please be normal," he uttered to himself. He then composed himself as he walked and just calmly said, "Good morning, Naoise."

A little more content with his introduction now, he smiled a little to himself "Okay, that's better."

Foxy then turned the corner over the hill, leading him to the main road to school. He was looking forward to this road, as he had a clear view of Cnoc Mor. The mountain looked imposing on this sunny morning. With the clouds gone, he could really see the height of it and when the wind subsided he could hear the gentle crash of waves.

His imagination was running wild as he envisioned a battle taking place on top of the hill. He could see the white light slashing from Nuada's sword and Partholòn's sickle flying around as Lugh fended it off with his spear. He could see Dagda's giant form swinging a hefty hammer around, dismembering Fomorians all around him.

Foxy then realized that Mr. Jordan had never mentioned Dagda using a hammer, but Foxy was happy to see his own imagination taking the story by the reins. He wondered if there were other stories about the Tuath De Danann. He made a mental note to check out the school library on lunch.

The school was now on the horizon, and Foxy spotted the perfect wall. It was far enough away from the school that he could hide behind it while still maintaining an eye on the school gate. Unbeknownst to him, Foxy was now surrounded by school students. He was thinking so hard he didn't realise all the other students were getting dropped off as their parents continued onto work.

Instead of heading down towards the school gates, Foxy just slid out of the crowd behind the wall at the corner of the school's front gates and barriers. He pretended he was on the phone, so other students didn't pay much attention to the boy behind the wall. There was a large hedge bush further down, but he didn't want to appear too mental, so he just leaned against the wall on his phone, trying to look as nonchalant as possible. He looked at the time and it was 7:50 am. With each minute passed by, he would survey around the wall to see if Naoise's driver had arrived.

7:55 am. Still no sign. There were essentially no other students on the roads now, as they had all gone in to the school building. Foxy was starting to panic. He began to realize Naoise may not be coming to school today. He thought about texting her again, but quickly eliminated that idea as it would be ever weirder to text her now.

7:57 am, no sightings. He knew he would have to go in soon, as to go in late alone would draw several jeers and looks from others in the class. He decided he would give it until 7:58 am and then rush in.

He closed and reopened his phone screen, alternatively changing his gaze from the phone to the school gates and the realization was clear. She wasn't coming. He opened his phone again and somehow his phone had skipped 7:58am, and it was now showing 7:59am. He was swept up in a panic realizing he was late unless he began sprinting now.

Just as he was about to begin the race to the school, he got a tap on the shoulder.

He turned around and his jaw dropped.

"I was so curious to what you were doing, I had to stay looking," said Naoise softly.

Foxy was simply lost for words. A few noises dripped out but calling them words would be generous. Naoise continued to look at him, confused.

Again, more stuttering sounds slung out of his mouth, but no actual words.

Naoise waved her hand gently in front of Foxy's face, which did draw a reaction.

"Hi Naoise, fine morning isn't it?" Foxy said, cringing at his own words.

Naoise looked around at the sunny hills. "I suppose it is," she replied, admiring the morn.

"Foxy," she said inquisitively, "What were you doing behind the wall?"

Foxy stuttered and stammered for words, and – having always been a particularly bad liar – just exhaled and said quietly under his breath, "I was waiting for you."

Naoise continued to look and raised her eyebrows, waiting for a longer answer.

Foxy sighed. "I didn't want to go into school by myself, and you're the only person I know so, and I wasn't sure if I should text you first. Then I decided that would be weird. Then I thought waiting at the gate was weird, so I chose to wait here and then whenever you got dropped off I could just arrive as you arrived and we could go in together."

Naoise started laughing. "Aww, that's cute."

Foxy then composed himself slightly and asked, "Where did you come from, though?"

"From the bushes," Naoise replied calmly, as if it was a run of the mill reply.

"From the bushes?!" Foxy exhaled. "What were you doing in the bushes?"

Naoise jogged on ahead, her hair bouncing as she ran. Foxy noticed how shiny it was. He called after her, "What were you doing in the bushes?"

Naoise shouted back as she ran, "Hurry up, we're going to be late."

Foxy gave chase after her as the school bell rang in the background. Once he caught up beside Naoise he turned around as they ran and asked, "Why were you in the bushes?"

Naoise's hearty smile was beaming as they ran, her hair streaming behind her. "I was waiting for you, she replied."

They were approaching the school's front door, the sprint shortened to a jog and then finally a brisk walk. Foxy looked at her, wide-eyed.

"You were waiting for me?" he asked.

"Yeah, well, I wasn't sure if it would be weird to text you or not, and I didn't want to wait alone at the gate. So I got the driver to bring me early, the bushes seemed the best hiding place. When I saw you walk past, I'd pop out and catch up to you. Except when you walked past you just hid behind the wall. I had to wait and see what you were doing, but when you looked like you were about to run, I popped out."

Foxy began to smile. He felt an honest connection. A similar connection he had felt to Linda during dinner, and Macdara during work that morning. Naoise was a genuine friend.

"In future, let's not do this and just text each other," Foxy said lightheadedly. He turned to walk into class and his phone buzzed. He took it out to see a text from Naoise with nothing else but a smiley face emoji.

"Now, the first text is sent, so just continue the chat later on," Naoise said as the school door flew open. It was Mrs. Finnegan, and she was enraged.

"Fox and Moone!" she bellowed.

Their eyes and posture sharpened immediately. Mrs. Finnegan continued as she glared at them.

"Two mornings in a row I have found both of you late and chatting. This school runs on its own time, not yours. That's twice you two; do not let there be a third."

Both Foxy and Naoise understood this as a serious warning as they skulked past her towards Mr. Jordan's English class.

They arrived late, but not too late, considering. They were able take their seats as Mr. Jordan was setting up for the lesson. Much to Foxy's dismay, this class was nowhere near as interesting as yesterday's. Rather than epic tales of ancient warriors battling evil, the class discussed how to format a stanza for long-form poetry.

Foxy's eyes and imagination kept drifting to Cnoc Mor out the window. The class went by without event, as did the next. Foxy had realised this was just school now, the buzz and nerves of the first day had gone, and it had returned to standardized curriculum.

Lunch time came, and instead of heading to the canteen, Foxy asked Naoise where the library was. When questioned, he stated, "I want to see if there's a book about the Tuath De Danann."

Naoise smiled delightedly. "Oh, I'm so glad you said that. I'm something of an expert on them. I actually have lots of books on them, anything in the library would be rubbish. I tell you what, you can come over to my house on Friday after school; we finish at 1 pm on Fridays anyway. I can have the driver collect you and drop you off at home. I'll give you a lend of the books then?"

Foxy's mind blanked everything about the books and just heard "You can come over to my house."

"Yeah, that would be great. Thanks very much," he said.

Naoise replied, "Alright, but be warned, I'm really into them. Anyway, lets go eat."

The two went off to the canteen and ate standard school lunch fare. The rest of the day was as uneventful as the morning.

At the end of the day, Naoise and Foxy said their goodbyes as she hopped into her car. Foxy had again declined yet another lift. On his walk home, he was excited about Friday. One week in and he had a date with a girl he liked. Then he corrected himself.

It's not a date, its two friends, he clarified internally.

***

He arrived home to pleasantries by Linda and Macdara. Instead of going up to relax, Foxy headed straight for the yard to give Macdara a hand, as he was loading cavity blocks into a small trailer.

"Bejaysus, atta boy. Sign of a good lad when ya don't have to ask; they're just happy to help," Macdara basically shouted to Foxy.

"Happy to help," replied Foxy.

The two worked away on the yard for an hour or so doing odd jobs. When they had cleared all the blocks, Macdara said, "Foxy, I owe you for that one. I tell you what, don't worry about working in the farm Thursday morning. We'll ease you into it bit by bit. I don't want you resenting me for making you work."

Foxy replied, "Honestly, I like it. It's no trouble."

"You're a good lad, now go in and enjoy your evening. I'll finish up out here," said Macdara stretching his back.

Foxy took his advice and headed in. He had a lovely evening. A gorgeous Shepard's pie was presented to him when he arrived down after his shower. He joined Macdara in the living room after dinner to watch some of the classic hurling matches that were being shown. Once Macdara nodded off the sleep, Foxy went to the kitchen and said goodnight to Linda. Then he jaunted upstairs. He watched some TV by himself in privacy. He found it exceedingly relaxing. He wondered if he would dream about that place again as he nodded off. He did not.

***

The next day as he was walking to school, he texted Naoise.

"Hey just left, should be there round 7:50 am."

A reply came through almost instantly:

"Cool, I'll be there around then too. Let's get in before Finnegan goes mad again."

Foxy smiled as he saw this.

Once again, he turned down the road with the clear view of the Cnoc Mor and imagined the mighty battle taking place again and again. Each time, he could see Nuada piercing the sword of light through Partholòn.

Wednesday and Thursday went by pretty similarly to Tuesday. Both days Foxy and Naoise met at the front gate, slipped into class on time, and chatted amongst themselves, avoiding the other students as the pair of them just got on so well.

Each day when Foxy got home, he helped Macdara around the farm to some degree, and each evening Macdara insisted that Foxy did not have to help everyday, but he was very grateful for the assistance.

Then Friday morning came around. Foxy was standing at the front gate when Naoise's luxury car model pulled up. The driver got out and opened the door. He once again gave Foxy a glowering look. Once Naoise got out, she said, "Vincent, this is Foxy. He is coming back with me after school today."

Vincent nodded indignantly, hopped back in the driver seat, and motored off.

Foxy noticed that there was a certain buzz in the school on a Friday, as they got half days. The day felt very short, and by the end of Mr. Jordan's English, there were only three hours left. These classes went by very fast for Foxy, although he did not learn too much as he was more focused on Naoise's house and discussing the Tuath De Danann. It was after school that he had his first incident with Connor Sweeney.

As Naoise and Foxy were walking out of school, happily chatting and joking about Mrs. Finnegan, who had been so irate at a student getting a simple multiplication problem wrong she snapped a ruler on the teacher's desk, they saw a small crowd in the school yard and went over to investigate.

As they nudged through the crowd, they noticed the large, surly-faced boy who'd made comments on the first day was holding down a very small boy on the ground. There was a litany of phones pointed at the situation.

They were chants of "Get him, Connor," and "Do it now before the teacher comes."

Connor was a large, heavy boy who was kneeling on the smaller boy's chest and had his arms pinned to the ground. He was squeezing the smaller boys wrists tightly as the young boy on the ground hollered in pain.

"Get off me! Stop!"

Connor Sweeney yelled back in the boy's face, "I warned you not to rat me out! I warned ya, didn't I?" He grabbed the young boy by the head and jerked it into the ground. "Didn't I?" he roared again.

Foxy was in awe of how many people were just watching. Nobody was helping.

Naoise had just opened her mouth to say something, when a collision occurred in the middle of the shouting students. Foxy had charged down Connor Sweeney and shouldered him at such speed that he went flying off the smaller boy and into the crowd. Foxy stood up quickly and looked at Connor Sweeney, who was also rising, quite flustered.

Sweeney looked at Foxy. "You're that new freak. Who do you think you are? This has nothing to do with you. Do you want it as well?" He threatened, wiping the blood from a scratch on his face from the collision."

"Who am *I*?" replied Foxy bravely. "Who are *you*? Jumping on a chap not even half your size; think you're the big man?"

The boy on the ground was indeed very small, but he had moved himself out of the circle, and now it was just Foxy and Connor in the circle.

Connor Sweeney threw a punch at him. Foxy dodged it and tackled Connor to the ground. Holding him down in a similar way, Connor had held the smaller boy.

Foxy shouted at him, "Not nice, is it?! To be made to feel small."

Foxy was astounded by his own strength. He looked around and saw Naoise with her hands covering her mouth. He also saw Mrs. Finnegan charging over roaring so loudly that Foxy couldn't distinguish words, but knew he had to stop. He rose up off Connor Sweeney, who quickly stood up beside him.

The two boys stood frazzled in front of the teacher. The small boy who was initially the victim had snuck into the crowd and away from the teacher's gaze, which was firmly fixed upon Foxy and Connor Sweeney.

"Would someone care to tell me what was happening here?" demanded Mrs. Finnegan.

Naoise's eyes glanced from Foxy to Mrs. Finnegan, to Connor Sweeney and back to Mrs. Finnegan.

Before Mrs. Finnegan could roar again, Connor Sweeney jumped in, "We were just messing around, Miss."

Her eyes darted to Foxy, whose body language would have you believe this was not the case.

"Is this true, Mr. Fox?" she asked.

Foxy looked at Naoise, who subtly nodded.

"Yes, Miss, just having a laugh," Foxy said acting as if it was just a game that got a little out of hand.

Mrs. Finnegan, clutching her car keys, stared at the crowd. "Well, schools over. Go on, get out of here."

The crowd dispersed as Mrs. Finnegan left herself.

Connor Sweeney picked up his school bag and walked off. He turned to Foxy. "Enjoy the weekend, freak; keep an eye out."

He stormed off, leaving just Foxy and Naoise.

She turned to Foxy. "Are you alright? That got out of hand real quick."

Foxy looked at his own hands and checked himself. He had actually taken no damage at all, and besides a declining adrenaline rush he felt perfectly fine.

"I'm actually great," said Foxy. He was proud of how he'd acted; he felt brave.

Naoise exhaled slightly. "That's good. Oh, there's Vincent, let's go." She spotted her driver's and car outside the gates. He had gotten out of the car and stood out waiting for Naoise and Foxy.

Naoise and Foxy walked over to the car, Vincent smiled and nodded at Naoise, then looked begrudgingly at Foxy as Naoise entered the car and beckoned him in. The back of the car was spacious, with smooth sleek leather seats.

"How was your day, Ms. Moone?" Vincent asked politely

Naoise looked at Foxy and smirked. "Oh, just a normal Friday," she sniggered.

"Glad to hear it, Ms. Moone," Vincent replied.

"Straight home?" He asked, once more looking in the rear-view mirror.

"Yes please," said Naoise.

Foxy was too nervous to speak, as he had a strong sense that Vincent didn't like him, but he couldn't figure out why. He spotted Vincent shooting him a damning glance in the rear-view mirror before the car took off.

"What sort of food do you like, Foxy? I usually order fast food on Friday for lunch." Naoise said, turning to Foxy.

Foxy was still a little nervous and just whispered, "Whatever you like, Naoise, is fine."

Naoise understood that he was nervous about Vincent, and just let them enjoy the drive through the sunny countryside. They both headed off towards Naoise's house, Foxy wondering what it was like.

Chapter 6: *The Lonely Manor*

As the car cruised comfortably through the scenic hillsides of Tinree Island, Vincent remained stoic and seemingly annoyed in the driver's seat. Foxy couldn't quite place what he could have done to upset this man. Naoise sat content in the back seat of the car looking out the window at the undulating hills and cliffs. Foxy noticed how they were all dwarved by Cnoc Mor. He built up the courage to talk as the uncomfortable silence attributed to Vincent's discomfort had grown too large.

"It must be the biggest mountain in Ireland?" He asked in a soft tone, as to not sharply break the silence.

Naoise continued looking out the window. "One of them anyway," she replied. "It's pretty quiet outside of summer, but if you saw it during the summer holidays all you could see would be swarms of people hiking it. If you climb it September to May, you're most likely the only person on it."

Foxy leaned a little closer to her side to get a better view. It looked smaller as they were heading away from it.

"That's crazy. Do the locals not go up it regularly?" Foxy asked out of genuine interest.

Naoise smirked a little bit. "Some do," she said as Vincent threw a damning glance in the rearview mirror.

Foxy moved back over to his seat.

"I'd like to go up it someday," he whispered to himself, not really intending for anyone to hear.

"That would be a bad idea, my friend," a voice sounded from the front of the car.

When Foxy looked up, he could see that it was Vincent who had spoken, and he was staring directly at Foxy through the mirror.

He continued, "It's quite a difficult climb, and it's extremely dangerous in the wet."

Vincent's stern voice intimidated Foxy, but the feeling of intimidation was wiped away when Naoise jumped in. "Oh, Vincent, I think he could do it? He seems pretty brave" she winked at Foxy, referring to his earlier altercation with Connor Sweeney.

The stern voice rippled back again. "I disagree, Ms. Moone, I don't think your parents would want you or him going up the mountain in the wet."

Foxy looked confused. He wondered why her parents would care what he was doing. They didn't even know he existed for all Foxy knew.

"I'm pretty fit. I reckon I could give it a go," Foxy said, objecting to Vincent's claims.

"I strongly recommend against it, my friend," Vincent said strongly.

Naoise grimaced, letting Foxy know not to push the topic any further. Foxy simply wondered why Vincent would call him his friend, when it seemed like he really had taken a dislike to him. The great mountain was falling out of sight as they turned up the rural roads into a wooded area.

As the car drove through the woods, the trees became so dense that the light was dwindling. The car eventually came to a halt when it turned to face two giant gates guarding a long drive through the forest. Either side of the gates was attached a long, high, iron fence. Foxy could not believe the size of the gates, clad black iron with strong golden spikes along the top. He could see the driveway disappear into the deep woods with no sign of a house.

He spotted Vincent clicking a button beside his steering wheel, and the giant gates made a loud noise and they began to move. They were quite slow to open. They dragged large piles of leaves on the ground as they swung inward, opening the driveway. Once the gates had fully opened, the car drove through them gently. On the far side of the gates, the car stopped once more. Vincent clicked the button once more and stared at them in the mirror in full determination. While waiting for the gates to close, Foxy looked out the window into the deep forest, and what he saw made his eyes light up and jaw drop.

A very large stag was strolling through the forest, with wide, majestic antlers. The male deer was grazing on a small grassy hill. Foxy was so excited.

"Look, Naoise, there's a deer over there! I've never seen one before. He's huge!"

Naoise was looking at her phone unenthusiastically while the large gates closed behind them. She lifted her head from her phone and was clearly happy to see how excited Foxy was about spotting the deer. She looked through the window herself to spot the deer.

"Oh, that's just Fallow," she said.

"He has a name?" Foxy replied, puzzled.

"Well don't you always name your pets?" Naoise said, almost offended.

"Well, yeah, but I've never heard of someone having a pet deer, and oh my god, look!" He almost shouted, much to Vincent's dismay.

As Foxy was quizzing Naoise over the name of her pet deer, a crow landed on Fallow's antlers. When the crow landed, Fallow lifted his head and looked towards the car. Foxy could have sworn it looked like the crow had told the deer to look up.

"That's amazing! The crow landed right on Fallow," he exclaimed.

Naoise smiled. "That's Morrigan."

Foxy turned away from the window and looked at her in amazement. "Don't tell me you have a pet crow, too?"

Naoise began to laugh loudly "Oh no, Morrigan isn't a pet; but her and Fallow do get on really well. You see…"

She was interrupted by Vincent. "Ms. Moone, I don't think young Foxy is too interested in your expanding list of animal friends."

Naoise knew to stop talking. There was a large, heavy thud behind them as the gates shut, the car then began to zoom up the driveway.

The dense leaves rose on the driveway as the car tore through them. The driveway was impossibly long, and to Foxy it appeared like they were going uphill. After a short while, Foxy could see daylight beginning to burst through the trees, as the car reached the end of the wooded tunnel the sunlight was blinding as they emerged out of the forest. They had come out to a large clearing on top of the hilly forest, and placed right in the centre of the clearing was the biggest house Foxy had ever seen.

The driveway went right up to the house where there was a large circular road for cars to turn around on. Vincent stopped the car and got out to open the door for Naoise. Foxy, in absolute awe, got out of his side, never assuming that Vincent would open his door. He looked up in astonishment at the staggering size of house.

Naoise got out on the other side and shouted, "Welcome to Tryst Manor!"

Foxy had to move his head from left to right to take in the manor, which looked like it was split into an east wing and a west wing. The manor was white, with conservatories bursting from both sides. Ivy covered the very front of the house, complimented by the heavy foliage around the staircase to the front door – booming flowerpots with the most colourful, vibrant flowers. Vincent turned to Naoise.

"I have a few jobs to do, Ms. Moone, I will be back in a short while, and I can take Foxy home then."

Naoise nodded to Vincent, who then got in the car and drove back down the forested driveway. Naoise walked up the white stone staircase to the front door. She got to the door and turned to Foxy, who was still staring at the house.

"Well come on, aren't you coming in?" She chuckled to herself and then opened the front door and walked inside.

Foxy went to follow her, but just as he took his first step on the staircase, a crow landed on the pillar beside him at the base of the stairs. The bird looked at him. This surely was a different bird, Foxy thought. The crow cawed loudly at him.

Foxy made a quick sudden movement to scare the crow away. "Shoo," he said in hushed tones, but the crow remained unfased. Foxy thought it was weird, but was not too concerned with it and moved on up the stairs. The crow continued to caw as he made his way inside and shut the door behind him.

A beautiful open foyer stood before him, with a large stone sundial in the middle that was lit up by a parallel skylight above it.

"Your house is amazing," Foxy said earnestly.

"My family's house," Naoise said softly. "My family has lived here a long time; I'm the youngest of the entire lineage! So I had the least to do with this house."

Foxy motioned to the sundial "Is that a sundial?"

Naoise walked over to it, tracing her finger along the shadow on the sundial. "Yes, my family likes old-school things to say the least."

"That's so cool" Foxy said as he walked around looking at not just the sundial, but the whole house and the dual staircases heading upstairs.

"Right!" said Naoise, capturing Foxy's attention. "Let's find you that book! Now I just need to remember which library it's in…"

Foxy nearly collapsed. "Did you just say *which* library?"

Naoise snapped her fingers and ran off down one of the halls, Foxy heard a distant echoey, "Follow me."

He didn't take long to jog after her. When he caught up with her, she was outside a door. He spotted a painting of a family – two parents and two daughters. One looked like Naoise, but he couldn't be sure. The other had fiery blonde hair and was a few years older. Foxy looked at the two imposing adult figures in the painting and asked,"Naoise, where are your parents? I don't want to be running in their house."

She looked at the door handle she was holding. "They're not here right now. They're rarely here," she replied with sadness in her voice.

Foxy, being quite versed in questions about absent parents, knew to leave well enough alone. It wasn't his business, and he often hated when people pried into his short answers about his parents.

Naoise turned to him through light sadness and put on a big smile. "Vincent minds me most of the time; he cooks most of my meals and drops me off everywhere I need to go. He also helps me with homework and that stuff!"

Foxy now understood Vincent's dislike of him. It wasn't personal, he was just protective of Naoise.

Naoise went on, "Vincent doesn't have any family or friends either, so until I met you he was my only friend. He was the only one here, and went to the pharmacy for me when I needed certain lady products for the first time."

Foxy felt awkward at that comment, but quickly corrected himself.

"Well, he gave me a lift in his fancy car, so he's a friend of mine," Foxy said.

Naoise beamed at the thought that Vincent had a friend.

"So now you're a friend of Vincent's and mine," Naoise said, finally opening the door to a small, cosy library. It had only about four bookshelves. Foxy thought it was small in comparison to the size of the house. Naoise flicked through the books until there a loud "Ah, here we are."

The two of them sat on a couch against the wall and placed the book on a small coffee table in front of them.

The book was old, a purple leather cover bound in what looked like heather. There was no title, and the pages looked very worn and old. This was no schoolbook, Foxy thought to himself.

Naoise opened the book and turned the pages carefully until she landed on a chapter in which Foxy could see the title.

"Falias," he said aloud.

"Correct," Naoise said. "Falias, is where the Tuath De Danann lived before Danu summoned them to defeat the Fomoriams. There were four ancient cities: Gorias, Findias, Murias and Falias, which is where the Tuath De Danann come from. You should read this chapter."

Just like Mr. Jordan's story, Foxy was once again fully enchanted. He asked, "is that where the Tuath De Danann went back to after Partholòn was defeated?"

Naoise slowly shook her head. She looked like she was suddenly overcome with sadness.

"The Tuath de Danann could only return to Falias once the stone of Fal had declared a new king and the Fomorians were defeated once and for all," she said somberly.

"But they were defeated, weren't they?" Foxy said. "I mean, in the story," he reiterated.

"Mr. Jordan's story is slightly different than the one I've heard," Naoise said quietly.

Foxy looked at her for a moment, he could tell she was thinking deeply.

"What's the version you heard?" he asked.

Naoise thought for a second, then shook the sadness from her face and the smiling girl was back. She closed the book swiftly.

"That's enough history for one afternoon. You must be hungry?" She picked up the book and jolted out of the room. Foxy, more confused than anything else, followed her.

They arrived in the large kitchen. It looked like it was equipped to feed an army. A huge table was in the middle, with two bowls and a small plate on it wrapped in clingfilm. There were two portions of vegetable soup, and the plate held brown bread. There was a note that said:

"For you and your friend. Vincent"

Foxy realised Naoise must have told Vincent earlier he was coming, even before he got to the car. Foxy, realising, he was actually quite hungry, said, "Oh he didn't have to do that, but it looks lovely."

Naoise said, "I'll heat up the soup. You go into the sitting room and put on the TV I'll bring this in."

She pointed Foxy in the direction of a room off the kitchen. He went in and, to his surprise, this sitting room was extremely modern – sleek white furniture with a very large flat screen TV on the wall. This room felt so different from the rest of the house. He sat down on the couch and suddenly felt bad that he wasn't helping Naoise with the food.

No sooner had he felt bad than Naoise arrived in the room with soup and bread. The two of them happily ate the food while they watched light-hearted TV for an hour. They joked about school teachers and what horrible comeback Connor Sweeney might have for them.

**

After a very pleasant evening, Vincent arrived back and Naoise told Foxy to "hide the book," so he put it in his school bag.

As Vincent arrived in, he announced "Foxy, I'll drive you home now."

Naoise said to Foxy "You'd better go, I'll see you on Monday!"

Foxy smiled at her and thanked her for the food and book. As he walked back to the front door, he looked at Vincent directly and said, "Thank you for the soup, sir, it really was lovely."

Vincent's expression didn't change, but he did grunt a, "You're welcome."

Foxy gave one more wave goodbye to Naoise as he and Vincent exited the house. To Foxy's surprise, the crow was still on the pillar staring at him. Foxy made awkward eye contact with the bird as he went down to the car. He also spotted Fallow the deer on his way out. Fallow was resting by the side of the driveway.

Foxy arrived back in the Sullivans' home shortly after, he thanked Vincent for the lift.

As Foxy got out at the end of his driveway and was about to walk up, Vincent let down the window and shouted after him, "Be careful with that book!" then he drove off.

Foxy felt like he was caught red-handed, but Vincent was gone. He walked into the house to the wonderful smell of a lit fire and fresh vegetables boiling. Linda met him in the hall.

"Hello, Foxy dear, you're home later than usual," she said.

Foxy smiled at her "Yes, I was just up at a friend's house after school – Naoise Moone."

Linda was in shock. "You were in the Moones' house? Oh my goodness, I've heard it's enormous and built all from marble." Then a look of sadness quickly washed over her face.

"Did you speak to anyone there, Foxy?" Linda asked.

"Just Naoise, really," Foxy said, on account that Vincent didn't really speak to him, so he didn't think it worth mentioning.

Macdara poked his head out of the sitting room. "Did I hear you say you were in the Moones' house? Some amount of work must have gone into building it, I hear? Well, go on Foxy, tell us what's it like."

Linda quickly washed away a sense of sadness from her face.

"Oh, it's stunning I bet," said Linda.

Foxy looked at both of them extremely contented and said, "This house is much nicer, and smells better, too." He meant it too.

Linda nearly burst into tears she was so happy to hear this.

"Oh Macdara, did you hear that? Our house is as nice as the Moones'!" Linda squealed.

"Not as nice my love, but *nicer*!" Macdara joined in.

Foxy was very pleased to see how happy they both were.

"Go in and get your tea, good man," Macdara said as he went back into the sitting room, undoubtedly for an early snooze.

Foxy was relatively full from the bread and soup at Naoise's, but he ate every bite of Linda's chicken and vegetable dinner. He would rather burst from being too full than ever possibly insult her by not eating her food.

He thought on how happy an evening he was having, then, as he retired to his own room and began watching TV, he thought of Vincent and Naoise up in that lonely old manor all by themselves.

Chapter 7: *The Forbidden Hike*

Foxy was really settling into his time in Tinree Island. School was going by pleasantly. He and Naoise met outside the gates every morning and ate lunch together each day. Connor Sweeney had thrown him dirty looks and unintelligible comments, but there was never any major reaction from the fight outside the school. However, Foxy always thought Connor was planning something, but seeing that there was only one week left of school before the Halloween mid-term, he assumed he could get by.

He worked with Macdara the odd morning, and he would hang out at Tryst Manor with Naoise every Friday after school. As the calendar marched towards Halloween, a shocking heatwave had hit the region. An 'Indian summer', they referred to it as on the news. Macdara was thrilled with the news; he adored working in the heat. While it wasn't melting heat by the rest of the world's standard, twenty degrees Celsius in Ireland in October was certainly odd.

Foxy had been reading Naoise's book on the Tuath De Danann. Falias sounded like an amazing city. A vast and highly built-up ancient city, hidden – it's location only known to the Tuath De Danann. The book described it as surrounded by water, with huge waterfalls pouring around it. In the centre of the city there was a palace, where the prized treasure was the stone of Fal, which was said to emit a blinding light when the next King of Ireland held it.

Foxy recognised it from Mr. Jordan's story. It was the stone Nuada had used to blind Partholòn and defeat him. The stone was said to have unimaginable power, and that only Nuada could have held it.

Foxy was so enthralled by the Tuath De Danann currently, that his desire to learn more was frothing. He had read the book almost entirely, and it was a thick book. The next morning, he woke up and went through his morning routine. Macdara and himself cleared out a particularly messy shed and then enjoyed a hearty bowl of porridge and a scalding hot cup of tea. That morning Foxy had a proposition for Naoise.

After thanking Linda for breakfast and saying goodbye, he hopped out the door to the extremely warm morning. It was extremely dark at 7:20 am in October; the clocks had just gone back an hour a few days before. The warm air and dark sky was a strange feeling for Foxy, but either way he began to walk, as he knew it would be bright very soon.

Sure enough, by the time he reached the end of his driveway and turned out onto the main road, there was enough morning light that he was very confident a car would see him. So, he strolled gently to school.

As he was walking in, he heard a car approach from behind. He would always make sure he was as close to the ditch as possible when they passed. However, this one slowed down, he turned to see who it was, and it was Vincent driving his fancy car. Naoise was waving frantically at Foxy from the back.

Foxy waved, and Vincent begrudgingly nodded through the windscreen. Foxy could see that he and Naoise were discussing something. No, they were arguing. After a moment, Naoise got out of the back of the car and Vincent drove off.

"Sometimes, he makes me so mad," Naoise echoed down the dawning road.

"Good morning to you, too," Foxy said, very happy to see her.

Foxy had never seen her this frustrated.

"Is everything alright?" he asked.

Naoise launched into a tirade. "We had to leave early because Vincent said he had work to do somewhere else, so I said fine, I'd just wait at the school for thirty minutes. Then, when we passed you, I said 'Great, let me out so I can walk.' He said 'No, you can offer him a lift.' So I said, 'But if we both walk from here we won't have to wait thirty minutes at the school'. Then he said, 'It's dangerous to walk the roads.' Then I said, 'But Foxy does it every morning and he's safe.' Then he said, 'I strongly recommend against it'. Then I said, 'I strongly recommend you let me out of the car.' Then he said—"

"Woah, relax," Foxy interrupted. "Look you're out of the car, and now we can walk to school. He's only trying to look out for you."

Naoise's irritation had slightly subsided, but she did huff as she began to walk.

Foxy followed after her. "No need to be upset, Naoise. It's Friday; no danger now, we're all safe."

She looked annoyed at him. She began to whistle as she walked. It was a more laborious tune than ones he had heard before.

Foxy was trying his best to not further aggravate the situation. The sun was beginning to rise, and the morning was heating up as they turned the corner than provided the best view of Cnoc Mor.

As they walked, Foxy said aloud looking towards the mountain, "I wonder if people will start climbing it again now that its dry?"

It was as if a lightbulb appeared over Naoise's head. She turned to Foxy suddenly. "Let's climb it now!"

Foxy was stunned. He looked at her and replied, "What do you mean *now*? We've got school."

"Oh come on," Naoise said, "We haven't missed one day all year. Plus, it's the last day before mid-term. Loads of people don't bother going in."

Foxy's initial feeling was guilt. Linda and Macdara had looked after him so well. He had a feeling that by doing something that would certainly get him in trouble with the school, he would be letting down the Sullivans.

"I don't think so," said Foxy. "Perhaps tomorrow? We've got nothing planned, and it'll be Saturday."

Naoise rolled her eyes and began walking the road toward school. She began to whistle again.

Foxy was having another internal dilemma. On one hand he knew it would be wrong to skip school, but on the other hand he felt as if he most certainly owed Naoise one. She had, after all, been his only friend, and had really made the move to Tinree Island much more enjoyable and bearable. When he thought about doing a favour for her, the decision came naturally, albeit one he knew was wrong on some level.

Naoise heard a call from Foxy, "Where are you going?"

She turned around and glowed with glee. She saw that Foxy was standing on the other side of a fence off the road.

"I think Cnor Mor, is this way?" he said, laughing and pointing toward the big mountain.

He was getting a buzz off breaking the rules, something he wouldn't have done usually.

Naoise ran back towards the fence and threw her schoolbag over it for Foxy to catch as she climbed the fence.

"I knew you'd come around," she said exuberantly.

Foxy smiled at her, trying to look cool. "Well, I have been talking about it for so long, let's pretend we're Tuath De Danann and climb the mountain ourselves."

Naoise smirked.

She took her bag back off Foxy and said, "Let's do it. We can be back on this road by 3 pm, then back at the school by end of day! Vincent will collect me and will be none the wiser."

Naoise strode off across the dewy grass of the glistening field. Foxy was just about to take after her when he spotted a very similar looking crow. He looked at the bird for a second, then the crow took off into the sky.

Foxy and Naoise walked across the fields, taking in the glowing scenery and basking in the warm morning sun. They spoke constantly about people they knew, with Foxy doing a crude Vincent impression which made Naoise laugh so loud she snorted. This made them both laugh very hard.

The more fields they crossed, the larger the mountain became. Foxy was really understanding the height of it the closer he got, and nerves were creeping in.

"I wonder how big Mt Everest is in person?" Foxy asked.

Naoise responded, "There's so many things I'd love to see in person." Her tone had become laden with sadness.

"I'm surprised you haven't seen the world," said Foxy. "I mean, your family must be quite rich."

"If I had money, I think all I'd do is travel. I don't want to go to the tourist locations, though; I want to see the hidden treasures. To be the only person there. Or to be the first person to find something."

Naoise smiled at him "My parents don't really believe in leaving Ireland. They don't usually let me think about my future, either. They mainly just tell me to focus on the now."

Foxy said, "Well, they may be correct. I mean, just look at this."

They were just one field away from the mountain overlooking the sea. You could hear the waves crashing, and the smell of the sea was wafting by. Cnoc Mor was so high it was blocking the sun from the angle Foxy was looking from. So, when he looked up it was as if the mountain was wearing a halo. Foxy noticed in the field they were in that there was a very large drooping tree. The centre of it rose very highly, and the branches fell around it.

"Perfect," said Foxy, as it was beginning to get hot. It provided quite a bit of shade for them as they took a short break.

"This is a weeping willow," said Naoise. "We only read about them in biology last week. Can you remember why they are called weeping willows?"

Foxy was like a deer in headlights. He had been in that class, but could not remember the answer. As he hemmed and hawed, Naoise saved him by saying, "No worries, I can't remember either." She hopped up quickly.

They took a quick drink of water from their schoolbags as they got ready to head towards the base of the hill.

"I'm so excited," said Naoise. "I've never climbed it."

"No way?!" replied Foxy happily, "At least we can do it together for the first time."

Naoise laughed. "Let's hike first." She walked toward the mountain trail.

Foxy didn't really get the joke, but walked behind her. Suddenly, Naoise pulled Foxy behind a nearby bush and gestured for him to shush.

Foxy, confused, did just as she suggested. He mouthed, "What's wrong?"

Naoise replied in a voice that was barely even a whisper. "There's someone in a school uniform following us."

Foxy peered over the bush and saw a student wearing a uniform, but before he could look anymore, he was pulled back by Naoise.

"I'll be killed by Vincent if he finds out what we're doing. What if this student tells on us? I bet it's Connor Sweeney trying to get back at you," Naoise whispered.

Foxy looked around and whispered back, "Well, we can't walk anywhere without him seeing us now. We can't hide behind the bush all day."

Foxy looked up behind the bush again, carefully. Then his worries eased, and he stood straight up.

Naoise, half-whispering half-shouting at him, said, "Foxy, what are you doing? Get down!"

She could see Foxy waving. Then he shouted, "Hey, what are you doing here?!"

Naoise then stood up and saw the other student nearing them. Her worries vanished, too.

A small, skinny boy was approaching them. He was carrying a schoolbag that looked far too big for him. He was panting.

He reached them as Foxy and Naoise stood facing him.

"Hi," he wheezed.

Foxy recognised him straightaway; it was the boy who was being attacked by Connor Sweeney. Naoise realised this too.

Naoise walked over and handed the short boy a drink of water.

"Thanks," he gasped.

"What are you doing here?" Naoise asked.

The boy caught his breath again. He had been following them at a quick pace for a long time. Plus, he had much shorter legs than they did.

"I was cycling to school when I saw you too hop the fence. When I saw it was you, I realised I never thanked you for helping me that day, so I thought I'd see where you were going. Also, I really hate school; everyone is so mean to me," he said with his breath back.

Foxy stuck his hand out. "No need to say thanks. I'm Foxy. This is Naoise."

The boy grabbed Foxy's hand and smiled. "I'm Cathal Lowry."

Naoise then shook his hand. "Nice to meet you, Cathal."

Cathal took another drink of water from the bottle Naoise gave him.

"So what are you guys doing heading towards Cnoc Mor?" Cathal asked.

Naoise smiled at Foxy, then turned to Cathal, who had a gentle aura around him. "Well, we're actually going to climb it."

Cathal gasped slowly. "Outside of Summer? Are people even allowed do that?"

Foxy smiled at Cathal. "No one knows we're doing it, so you can't tell anyone, okay?"

Cathal replied, "I won't tell anyone, but can I ask a question?"

Foxy nodded.

"Can I come it up with you too?" Cathal asked with bated breath.

Foxy and Naoise both smiled.

"Well, I don't see why not," Foxy boomed across the field, trying his best to mimic Macdara.

Cathal gave himself a little fist pump, Foxy held out his school bag, which was miniscule compared to Cathal's.

"Let me carry yours; it looks a little heavier than mine," Foxy said.

Cathal handed over the bag, looking emotional. "I'm so excited. My life is pretty boring, so some excitement will do me good. I've always wondered how many exciting stories the Tuath De Danann shared on the mountain after the Fomorians were defeated," he said.

Naoise and Foxy shared a look of mutual acknowledgement that they'd made the right decision in bringing Cathal with him.

The three set off up the trail with Cathal in the middle, flanked on either side by Foxy and Naoise.

Very early on into the hike, all three of them knew they had vastly underestimated the climb. Very quickly, the fun chat between them was exchanged for breathless grunts as the incline became greater and greater.

"Macdara would love this," Foxy said to himself breathlessly.

Naoise was trying to whistle, but only exasperated bits of spit came out.

Cathal looked as though he might have collapsed at any moment.

The top of the mountain somehow looked further away now than it did when they were at the bottom.

"How long have we been going for?" Foxy asked under severe pressure.

Naoise stopped for a second and looked achingly to the sky, lifting her watch.

Her heart sank. "Oh my god," she said. "We've only been walking for twenty-five minutes."

Cathal tried to curse, but did not have enough air in his lungs to make enough noise to support the word.

Foxy took a moment and took a quick drink of water. "Only one way up. Let's keep going."

Naoise groaned and then followed, realising it had been her idea. Cathal asked, "Can we still be friends, even if I don't make it to the top?"

"No," Foxy shouted back jokingly. "The whole team needs to make it to the top."

Cathal, enthused by hearing he was part of a team, felt determined. They marched on.

They struggled on for another hour before taking a break. Naoise reckoned they were nearly halfway up. It was 10 am on the watch; time was their friend. They drank water, regaining their breath. As they looked up, they could see that the trail was becoming steeper.

"Just think of the view," Foxy said, exhausted.

"I can see why this would be so dangerous when it's wet," Naoise said, surveying the hilly mounds that surrounded them.

Cathal threw his bag on the ground and looked around "There's no one else on the mountain. Can't we leave the bags here and just get them on the way back down?"

Foxy, who was physically exhausted from carrying Cathal's impressively heavy bag, agreed with the idea and dropped the bag. They nestled the bags behind a large, jagged rock on the side of the mountain. You would not spot the bags unless you looked closely. Naoise left her bag down, too, as the three marched towards the top of the mountain. Feeling much lighter without the bags, the next hour was manageable.

The next break they took was really short, as they felt the summit was near. The day was really heating up now. There wasn't a cloud in the sky, and the autumn sun was fighting with all its might to burn them. Foxy was now wearing his school jumper around his waist, and had his sleeves pulled up. Naoise had fashioned her jumper into a headband of sorts, while Cathal never took off his school jumper and never seemed to struggle with the heat.

Foxy figured he was so thin, he was always cold.

All of a sudden, the trail was levelling out. Then, so gradually that none of them believed it, they arrived at the summit. The view was simply breathtaking. The top of the mountain was wide and flat, but the view was otherworldly.

Foxy just uttered a breathless, "Wow."

Naoise and Cathal didn't even have words.

The sun was bedazzling the calm sea, and from this height it looked like an infinity of diamonds. The expanse of the sea seemed to go on forever, and the small town of Tinree Island looked truly minute from this vantage point.

Foxy sat on the ground and began to take in the view. Naoise came over and sat on one side of him, then Cathal on the other.

The three of them stared out into towards the horizon, their breath came back.

"It's the most beautiful thing I've ever seen," Naoise said.

"I agree," said Cathal. "I feel like I've seen nothing in the world, but I don't think anything can beat this."

Foxy just stared. He looked at the glimmering diamonds on the sea and a memory returned to him. It was him and parents at a lake, and he could see the glimmering light on the water again. His mother was jokingly splashing him, while his dad emerged from the water in the lake pretending to be a monster and then jokingly attacked a very young Foxy.

Foxy laughed out loud. Naoise noticed his eyes well up with tears, but she chose to ignore it.

"I think you're dead right, Cathal," said Foxy. "I really don't think it can get any better than this."

Naoise took out her phone and said, "Let's get a picture."

She stood beside Foxy and held her phone out, Cathal went to take the phone from her to capture the moment.

"Don't be silly, Cathal; I want you in it too. It'll be a nice memory," she said.

Cathal was overjoyed, and almost burst into tears but held it back. The three friends smiled as Naoise took a selfie, with Foxy beside her and one arm around Cathal.

After the photo they sat on the side of the cliff.

The three of them sat in silence for almost twenty minutes just watching.

Chapter 8: *The Fomorian*

The morning nipped by in the most beautiful fashion. It had taken a couple of hours to reach the top of Cnoc Mor, and the group knew that journey time would be far shorter on the descent. With no time constraints, they basked in the morning sun. Foxy had a feeling of particular contentment. In the short time he had been in Tinree Island, he had found two new friends, been welcomed into a warm, welcoming family, and was now gazing on the most stunning view he had ever seen.

"I wonder what they're doing in school now," Cathal said, very relaxed.

"Most likely watching a film or playing silly games" replied Naoise.

Foxy remained silent, looking at the sea. he picked up a stone beside him and tossed it out over the edge of the cliff. It shortly fell out of sight as he was trying to catch the stone with his eyesight again. He thought he saw a bird swooping by the water really low down. He thought it was black; a crow perhaps.

Foxy stopped looking at the sea and fell back into look directly at the sky. the odd cloud grazed easily across the vibrant blue October sky. It reminded him of the sky in that dream he'd had.

"There is danger on the horizon," Foxy heard the woman in the dream lake repeat in his head.

He sat back up and looked out at the horizon, but indeed he saw no danger, just a soft glimmer of light.

Naoise stood up, grabbing the attention of both Foxy and Cathal. She brushed the dirt off her uniform.

"I'm starting to get hungry now; I left my lunch in my bag," she said, holding her stomach.

Cathal also stood up and agreed, looking a little unsure. "Yeah, me too. Maybe it's time to head down. What do you think, Foxy?"

Foxy stood up himself, took one last look over the cliff, and took in a deep breath of the fresh air.

"Yeah, let's get back. By the time we get down, eat, and then walk to the school for Naoise to be picked up it'll be perfect timing," Foxy said.

The three of them started to make their way back across the summit of Cnoc Mor towards the path that would lead them back to the bottom. About halfway across the flat summit, they could hear gentle humming. The sound grew closer, and then they saw something.

There was a shape ascending the path.

Naoise stopped instantly in her tracks. Foxy went to speak, but Naoise shushed him instantly.

"Hide," she said in a tone that Foxy had never heard before. He could clearly tell that she was being serious. He assumed it was the fear of Vincent's scolding if they got caught.

The three of them quickly got behind a nearby cluster of rocks. Cathal looked at Foxy as if to ask, "What's going on?" But Foxy just had to give a shrug of unknowingness. Naoise's face had lost all its humour and charm. She was staring with great intensity from the side of the rock.

Cathal had ducked down, and Foxy crept silently around him. He poked his head out the other side of the rock. What he saw didn't fill him with fear, but rather just curiosity.

The shape that had climbed the path was an older man. He was very thin, with wispy hair. Foxy noticed the older man had an extremely gaunt face and horrifically rotten teeth. He looked back over at Naoise, who had not taken her eyes off him.

When Foxy looked back at the man, he noticed that he was carrying three bags. He was carrying *their* bags. Foxy was about to walk out and confront him, but Naoise grabbed his leg. When he looked at her, she stared at him with such a look that he didn't dare move.

He could tell she was serious. Moreso, he could tell there was an emotion on her face he was not familiar with. What was it? He thought. Then he realised what it was. It was fear.

"Hello?" The man's cold voice called out across the summit.

A bead of sweat broke from Naoise's brow and dripped down her face.

The man threw down all three of their bags.

"I know someone's up here. I found your bags. Come on out, and I'll give them back," the cold voice rang out again. There was a tone of mistrust in the voice. Foxy was now beginning to get a bad sense about this individual.

The man gave one of the bags a kick and laughed to himself as it flung up in the air.

"I can wait all day," the voice called, a bit more aggressive in tone.

Cathal and Foxy were exchanging glances behind the rock, unsure of what their next step was. Naoise's intensity had not wavered an inch.

"I know," the voice called out. "If you're not here, you must have forgotten your bags, and I am not carrying them all the way back down."

He picked the three bags back up and said "I guess I'll just have to throw them over the edge."

Cathal panicked behind the rock whispered "My phone is in the bag, I can't lose it"

Naoise grabbed him and gestured him with her finger to shush.

"On the count of three, the bags are gone," the man said.

Cathal went to get up and Naoise grabbed him down. The man heard the scuffle and looked toward the rock.

"Ah," he said, relieved. "So you are here."

He dropped the bags and began walking toward the rocks.

"There's no point in further hiding, just come out now. We need to have a little chat," he said, smiling

Foxy could see that Naoise was absolutely terrified, but he had no fear for a random old man, although he could tell he was far from trustworthy.

Foxy then just bit the bullet and walked out from behind the rock. The man smiled and bowed slightly to him. Foxy gave an awkward wave and said, "Hiya, we just want our bags back and we'll be on our way."

The man looked at him, then the smile washed away from his face.

"You're not the one I expected behind the rock. who else is there?" he said coldly

Cathal ran out from behind the rock and shouted, "Just give me back my bag!"

The man sneered coldly, then took a few steps away from the bags and pointed at them.

"Here you go, boys, take them. I wasn't expecting you either, little man," he said to Cathal condescendingly.

Cathal ran over to pick up his bag. The man never moved a muscle toward him. Foxy remained motionless and was beginning to sense some danger in the current situation. What could possibly be going on, he thought.

The man then turned his attention back towards the rock, "There's one more behind that rock, and I bet it's the one I want," he called louder than before.

"Get out here now!" he bellowed.

The sense of urgency was building, Foxy knew something bad was about to happen, but he simply couldn't figure out the situation.

The man, who was wearing old, tattered pants and a long jacket, took off his jacket to reveal an impossibly thin torso that was horrifically pale. It looked like it had large scabs across it. some that had been picked, and some were dry and scaly. The man threw his jacket on the ground with great anger. What happened next made Foxy's stomach shrink with an enormous sinking feeling.

"Right!" he shouted, "I'm bored of this."

The man then pounced to the pile of bags, where Cathal was standing. He grabbed Cathal by his collar and dragged him abrasively over to the cliff edge. Cathal being so light made for easy luggage. Foxy sprang into action and tried to run toward them, but the man and Cathal were already near the cliff edge.

"Stop now, boy!" he roared at Foxy.

"Stop now or he goes off the edge."

Cathal was in such disbelief of the situation that he was actually too numb to cry. Cathal was indeed very close to the edge now, with the man's tight grip around his collar holding him at arm's length.

The man was now screaming. "Stupid child! I know you are behind that rock! Get out here now or this boy is going flying."

Foxy could sense the conviction in the man's voice, and knew he meant to do it. His heart was in his mouth. Foxy looked at the rock, then back at Cathal.

"Naoise, get out here, now!" Foxy shouted.

There was a moment of silence where Foxy thought Naoise might have run off the other direction or something. Then the girl stood slowly from behind the rock with such great intensity that Foxy had to doublecheck to make sure it was the same girl.

She glared at the man, but didn't say a word. The man's cold eyes glistened as he smiled.

"There she is," he said, smiling. "I haven't seen one of you in forever!" He cackled.

Cathal had his two hands gripping the man's wrist tightly, trying to remove it, but it was to no avail.

"What on earth is going on, Naoise?" Foxy asked.

But it was as if he hadn't spoken. She remained laser focused on the older man and never acknowledged Foxy.

"Help me," Cathal managed to muster a few words together through his fear. The man had ignored Cathal as though he'd made no noise at all.

"You know what I want," the man told Naoise.

She just looked at him, her eyes never so much as blinking.

"Well?" the man asked with increasing menace. "Where are they?"

Foxy was astounded by Naoise's response. She didn't reply with words. She slowly pursed her lips and began a very faint whistle.

The man looked enraged, frothing with anger.

"Have it your way," the man said, devoid of feelings.

Then what happened made Foxy scream. The man had changed his grip from Cathal's collar to his throat. His squeezed his neck tightly, Cathal gasped for air. The men effortlessly lifted Cathal off the ground, looked at him as if he was nothing, and then threw him off the edge of the cliff.

Foxy screamed as he sprinted towards the cliff where Cathal had been thrown off. He failed to notice the man sprinting past him towards Naoise as he sprinted the other way. He reached the edge too late; Cathal had fallen. Numb with shock, emotionless, he turned to see something that had no rational explanation to Foxy. It all happened so fast.

The man sprinted towards Naoise, who crouched into a stance to withstand a tackle. Then, like he had fallen asleep, all the ambient noise was lost. All Foxy could hear was Naoise whistling a soft tune. The man sprinting towards Naoise then leapt towards her, about to grab her, when suddenly there was noise again. It was wind. Howling, gale force wind.

As if it formed around her, Foxy saw what looked like a giant, powerful tornado materialize around her. It was so high Foxy could not see the top when he tried to look up, awestruck. He saw the older man shooting up towards the top of the dark, windy funnel. The tornado grew wilder. The top of the windy funnel then bent and shot the vicious man out the top and over the edge of the cliff with mighty force.

Foxy was being blown back by the wind; he had to grab a nearby rock for support. While he clung onto the rock for stability, he saw that Naoise had not moved.

"Naoise," Foxy called.

Her eyes shot towards him. He could hear the whistling tune change. Then, instantly the tornado shifted direction and zoomed off the cliff. Foxy in total and utter disbelief could see Naoise whistling with the greatest concentration.

The tornado then rose again back to the top of the cliff. The wind was too strong and blew Foxy away from the edge of the cliff. He flew across the summit, bouncing on the hard ground along the way. He looked up, and to his sheer amazement, he could see that there was a figure in the funnel.

Foxy looked over to see Naoise then collapse. When she fell, at the exact same time the tornado instantly dissolved. To Foxy's huge relief, he saw that the figure in the tornado that emerged back on the summit was Cathal. He was white as a ghost, and unable to speak from shock, but for the most part he looked like he was okay. Foxy rushed over to him and grabbed him by the shoulders.

"Cathal, are you okay?" Foxy asked in a swirl of confusion.

Cathal gave himself a quick pat down, and, though stunned, managed to mutter, "I think so. What happened?"

"I really don't know," Foxy replied.

He stood up and ran over towards Naoise, who was unconscious on the ground. She was motionless, her eyes were shut, and her body was limp.

Foxy called to her, sat her up and tried to wake her up, but she remained unconscious. Foxy looked around to make sure that elderly man was gone for good. It appeared he was.

Foxy began to panic as he called Naoise's name, trying to wake her up.

"Cathal," Foxy called, "we have to get her down."

Cathal was only just coming to terms with the frightening experience he had just had, and now he was being thrust into another one.

"Grab the bags," Foxy shouted as he lifted up Naoise into his arms. Her dead weight was far heavier than he expected.

Cathal, sensing the urgency of the present situation, ran around the summit and grabbed the three scattered bags. Foxy was holding Naoise in his arms, while Cathal managed to cargo the three bags as they began to descend down the hill.

The hike down was extremely difficult; Naoise's weight was exemplified by her motionless state. Foxy and Cathal were practically running down the mountain now.

"Cathal," Foxy panted.

Cathal made a grunt to let Foxy know he had heard him.

Foxy stopped. He took Naoise's phone out of her skirt pocket. Holding it up to her motionless face, the phone's facial ID opened.

"Cathal, I'm going to run down with her. I need you to call a man named Vincent in her contacts. Tell him exactly what happened and to meet us at the bottom as soon as possible," Foxy said with conviction that this was the best plan.

Cathal nodded and took the phone off Foxy. Cathal slowed down his pace while he called Vincent. Foxy began to run faster, carrying Naoise, who remained asleep.

98

"Don't worry Naoise, we're nearly there," he whispered to her as he ran at near sprint speed.

After a very difficult period of time carrying her down the mountain, he realised he must be close to the bottom. His muscles were screaming, his back in particular was howling in pain. He fought with every ounce of strength he had, and then it happened. His back and legs gave up on him, and Foxy's legs failed momentarily. Enough for him to trip and stumble down the hill. He hugged Naoise tight to protect her from the fall, turning his back to the ground to take the brunt himself. He bounced and skidded for a short distance down the hill.

He howled in pain. He tried to stand back up holding Naoise, but his legs were in agony. This was far more difficult than pulling the drag harrow. Foxy then felt like he was about to pass out. He chose to give it one more effort and, through excruciating pain, he managed to make it to his feet. He most definitely could not run now; his speed had been reduced to something just shy of a walking pace.

"I'm sorry," he said to Naoise.

He could feel that he was about to drop again, then he spotted a shape moving toward him quickly. Foxy was scared that it was the aging man again from the top of the mountain. What he saw filled him with relief and fear.

He saw Vincent, sprinting at full tilt up the mountain. Foxy couldn't believe anyone was running up the mountain. Vincent looked like he was under incredible duress, but his pace never changed until he reached Foxy.

He ripped Naoise out of his hands, and roared at Foxy, "Where is he?"

Foxy shuddered from the shout. "Where's who?" he asked timidly.

"The Fomorian!" Vincent roared back. "Where is the man who attacked you?"

Foxy was stunned. He had to think for a moment of what a Fomorian was. Then he remembered. Surely Vincent didn't mean the enemies of the Tuath De Danann? Vincent moved closer to Foxy and stared into his very soul.

Foxy had never felt that intimidated in his entire life.

Through confusion and fear Foxy replied, "The tornado threw him off the cliff."

Vincent was looking furious "The other boy, the one who called me, is he okay?" Vincent said sternly.

"Yes, he's just behind me on the way down," Foxy replied.

Vincent looked like he was about to burst with rage "You and that boy, be outside the school tomorrow at 9 am."

"But there is no school tomorrow," said Foxy.

"9 am, boy," Vincent said with such ferocity that Foxy dared not disobey.

Vincent then took Naoise in a tight hug, cradling her head, and sprinted off down the mountain at such pace. He was out of sight very quickly.

Foxy, now fully certain that Naoise was in the best hands, let himself relax. He fell on the ground and let his body ache.

After a while, Cathal caught up to Foxy, and the two nodded at each other.

"Will she be alright?" Cathal asked.

"I don't know, really," said Foxy. He continued, "Vincent told us you and I have to be outside the school tomorrow at 9 am."

Cathal looked puzzled, but after the traumatic and shocking scenario he had just faced, he simply accepted this direction from Foxy.

Cathal and Foxy made it back down the hill. They didn't speak a word as they walked back across the fields to Cathal's bike.

"9 am, school, please make sure you're there," Foxy said.

Cathal nodded, hopped on his bike, and rode off. Foxy was certain he would not see Cathal the following morning.

Foxy looked at the time and realised if he walked home now, he could just say he left school early. He walked the road home, frequently looking back at Cnoc Mor to rethink what had just happened. Was it real? Was Naoise okay? Who was that man? Vincent said he was a Fomorian, but that couldn't be right, Foxy reassured himself.

When Foxy arrived back at the Sullivans' house, he wasn't in the door a moment before Linda noticed the state of his uniform and the cuts on his arms from his fall.

"Dear lord," she exclaimed.

"What happened, dear?"

Foxy was overcome with outstanding guilt as soon as he saw the sweet woman who had cared for him so well the last while. He lowered his head.

"Me and two of my friends skipped school and hiked Cnoc Mor. I had a fall on the way down. I'm really sorry," Foxy said sincerely, although he didn't tell her everything.

Linda was in shock, she certainly looked sad, but quickly swallowed her tears.

"I'm glad you're okay, and I'm very glad you told me the truth, but my dear boy, what a stupid thing to do. I have to say, I'm very disappointed," Linda said with deep sadness.

Those words hurt Foxy more than anything else that day.

"Go, Foxy, clean yourself up at least. Get a shower and leave your uniform out; I'll have to wash it," Linda said with an authoritative tone Foxy hadn't heard before.

He sorrowfully made his way upstairs to his room. He took off his uniform, folded it as neatly as he could, and left it outside his door. He got a quick shower. He felt like he didn't deserve to enjoy it.

After he cleaned himself, he sat alone quietly in his room. He could smell dinner being cooked downstairs as the evening went on. However, he stayed in his room; he didn't feel like he was welcome downstairs that evening.

A feeling of being unwanted he hadn't had in a very long time.

Chapter 9: *The Night Before*

Foxy sat in his room amidst a whirlwind of his own thoughts and feelings. He was still trying to comprehend what he saw that day, also trying to battle his own guilt of disappointing Linda, and his stomach was in a knot over what Vincent was going to say to him and Cathal tomorrow morning.

The smell of dinner was wafting upstairs, but Foxy decided they would rather eat without him that evening. That thought was confirmed when he heard Macdara arrive. He could hear the murmurs of the two of them discussing something. He assumed they were talking about stupid he was. He then heard the clanks of plates and bowls, and now knew they sat down to dinner without him. This made his heart sink.

Foxy turned on his TV and watched some boring nature programme. There was a section on tornados in Kansas, and his mind raced back to Naoise and the top of Cnoc Mor. She couldn't have possibly created that wind, he thought to himself. Although, he could think of no other explanation for what happened. He knew for certain that without the tornado, wherever it came from, Cathal would have surely been done for.

Then who was that man, Foxy pondered. Vincent had referred to him as a Fomorian. He had the same thought as the wind, in that it couldn't have been true. He knew tomorrow would give some answers, but then he thought, what if Vincent didn't want to talk to them, but scold them; maybe make sure they never told anyone about what they saw. Then Foxy's mind drifted to Naoise.

"Is she okay?" Foxy whispered to himself aloud.

He was very concerned about her. Vincent had looked so angry when he took her.

Then Foxy's stomach groaned. He only realised that he hadn't eaten anything at all since his breakfast that morning. He thought about going downstairs, but his guilt and deep, guttural feeling kept him in his room.

As Foxy sat there on his bed feeling bad for himself, he could have sworn the food smelled stronger. There was a gentle knock on the door, followed by Foxy's bedroom door opening. Macdara slowly stuck his head in.

"Alright young man," Macdara said softly.

Foxy looked at Macdara's hands. He was carrying a big bowl of stew and a cup of tea. The aroma of it in the room was intoxicating.

Foxy looked at Macdara. His guilt was overwhelming.

"I'm very sorry; I promise I'll never skip school again," Foxy said sincerely at the time.

Macdara let out a chuckle as he left the stew and tea on a nearby locker.

"Foxy," he said, maintaining his soft tone, "Linda isn't upset that you skipped school. For god's sake it's the last day before mid-term; most students skip school. She's mad at you because you could have gotten hurt. She has been running over what could have happened to you all evening. She assumed you were with the Moone girl, which is upsetting her, too."

Foxy looked at the ground, saddened. "I'm sorry I made her feel that way," Foxy said.

Macdara's smile faded sharply, and a very sombre look took over his face. "You see, Foxy, Linda and I had a son before."

Foxy's eyes looked straight at him in disbelief. Most foster parents were people who couldn't have kids.

Macdara looked down at Foxy.

"I know we seem like pretty nice people, but we haven't always been nice. I was quite a strict man when my son was growing up. Linda was also a perfectionist and stickler for the rules. There was a day when our son came to us to tell us he was moving out. That he had gotten a job as a live-in assistant. Linda was furious; she thought the job was no different than a servant. You see, Linda worked as a housemaid when she was younger, and wanted so much more for our son. It broke her heart that he would be doing the same thing."

Foxy was stunned to hear that Linda and Macdara were ever anything but the nicest of people.

"She was angry over a job?" Foxy asked inquisitively.

"Oh, people around here can be very proud. There's a reason it's a deadly sin," Macdara said very seriously.

"What did you do about your son?" Foxy asked, interested.

Macdara smirked. "Oh we had a vicious fight. He told me he had to take the job. I argued that he was making his Mother sad, and he told me he didn't care; that he had to take this job. I never understood why it was so important. It is probably my greatest regret – when he said he didn't care about his Mother's sadness, I hit him. Hard. In the face. He looked at me through tears and walked out that driveway."

Foxy looked at Macdara. "And you never spoke to him again?"

"I tried," Macdara exclaimed. He then looked very sorrowful indeed.

"He never forgave me. Linda took my side in the argument because of her shame with his job. He never forgave her for that. Linda lived to be a mother; it killed her when he left. She made enough dinner for him every night."

Foxy asked, "How long ago was this?"

Macdara looked up as if he was counting "God, it must be six years ago now."

Foxy was shocked. "You or Linda haven't seen your son in six years?"

Macdara corrected him, "Oh we've seen him, but he has ignored us. We eventually came to terms that he would never speak to us again over me hitting him. We changed our ways. Went to counselling courses. Anger management courses. Therapy to deal with the guilt. Eventually, through all of this, we decided maybe we could repent or make good by fostering someone. Hence how we got you. So if you were to get hurt, Linda would feel like she failed as a mother twice, and she doesn't deserve that. So, promise me you'll stay safe?"

Foxy smiled and gave Macdara a nod of encouragement "I promise."

Macdara laughed and went to leave the room again. "Eat up young man, don't let that get cold."

As he was about to leave, Foxy asked, "What was his name?"

Macdara turned around and regretfully said "Vincent."

Foxy's jaw dropped.

"Does he work for the Moones?" Foxy asked.

Macdara nodded.

"They're a strange old bunch, those Moones. I'm delighted you have a friend; just be careful." Macdara laughed as he walked toward the door.

He left the room, and instantly Foxy understood why Vincent had taken such a disliking to him from the beginning. It wasn't because of his protection of Naoise. It was because he was the Sullivans' son! While processing this information, Foxy shot over to the locker and began to eat the soup. He was absolutely famished now. The first bite of brothy beef made everything seem alright for a brief moment.

He knew Linda and Macdara would be livid if they found out he was meeting Vincent tomorrow morning, but he also felt that it was a meeting that was impossible to miss. Had it not been for the tornado and the mention of the Fomorian, he would have skipped it, but he knew he had to attend it. He had to be at the school at 9 am. He wondered if Cathal would show up.

He continued to eat his stew, and the warmth and hearty taste of the food eased him. Macdara was obviously not good at portioning, as the bowl he had given Foxy was enough to feed three people. Foxy, however, was so hungry he ate it all. By the time he was done, he was already falling asleep.

He made himself comfortable and got into bed. He continued to watch a nature programme. He set his alarm to ensure he would make his meeting with Vincent, and then very quickly – and surprisingly without much stress – Foxy nodded off to sleep.

***

Foxy sat up in his bed and looked around to see that he was back in that place he had dreamt about before. The gorgeous, clear sky was reflected in the impossibly still water. He sat on the edge of the bed, more confident than he had been the last time he was there. He placed his feet in the lake to feel them land softly on the shallow ground. He stood up and saw gentle ripples spreading out.

Just like the first time he was there, a warm, gentle breeze blowed by him. He began to walk away from the freestanding bed in the beautiful lake. Foxy walked for a while, feeling the warmth of the sun on his face. He was aware that it didn't feel like a dream; the sense of peace he had in this place felt very real. Foxy bent down and cupped the water in his hands, then took a drink. This too felt like it couldn't be anything but real.

He strolled through the shallow lake until the bed had faded beyond the horizon. Again, he saw a shape sitting in the water at a distance. He rallied towards the shape.

When he arrived at the shape, he noticed it was the same gorgeous woman, with her shining dress and fire-red hair. The woman looked at Foxy.

"I think it's best you sit down," she said powerfully but softly. When she spoke, a wave of calmness flowed over Foxy.

Foxy sat down in the water beside the woman.

"How am I here again?" Foxy said the lady quietly.

She took his hand softly and said, "The how is not important; the why is the more pressing matter."

Foxy maintained eye contact with the woman. Her eyes were like crystal blue swimming pools. When she blinked, it was if the water in her eyes swished around. He was enamoured with her eyes. She never made eye contact with him, always looking slightly away from him instead.

Foxy looked around the lake. He ran his spare hand through the water, then lifted it up. He watched the drops fall off the end of his fingers and disturb the peaceful water surface.

Looking at the woman, whose eyes were fixed firmly upon Foxy's hand, he asked, "This isn't a dream, isn't it?"

The lady scooped up some water in her hand and poured it over the back of Foxy's hand, she spoke as she softly poured the water.

"The concept of a dream is vague. Our sleeping dreams and often very different to our waking dreams." She paused and raised her head, taking Foxy's hands in both of hers.

She said with a certain level of conviction, "This, however, is neither."

As soon as she spoke, Foxy and the woman fell through the lake floor. Foxy felt as if he was skydiving underwater; he was falling so fast he could only see brief, fleeting flashes of light. Anytime he began to panic as they traversed through this seemingly endless waterfall, the woman would squeeze his hands, and almost instantly the panic would wash away.

Once the speed of falling was slowing down, Foxy felt he needed to breath. How could he drown in a dream, he thought. Unless it wasn't a dream.

Suspended in the water at what appeared to be an infinitely deep lake, Foxy noticed at the bottom of the lake was light. He had to break away from the woman as he was struggling for air. He swam hard and fast towards the light with the lady swimming behind him.

Foxy was swimming as hard as he could, clawing for the light. His brain was getting confused. The light looked like the sun, but he was swimming downwards. He just reached the light and then he broke the water surface and took an almighty breath of air. He looked around to find that he had just come up from a lake, somehow the right way around.

The woman appeared beside him. She rose effortlessly and smoothly to her feet so that she was standing in a lake. Foxy thought it looked like a magician's levitating trick. She was standing directly beside where Foxy was treading water. She held her hand out to him, and he took it and was helped to his feet by her.

Foxy was then amazingly able to stand comfortably on the bed of the lake where he'd just emerged. He looked around in astonishment. The warm sun was nice on his wet face and skin. Surveying the area, he saw that it was an identical lake to the one he had fallen through, except for one detail in the distance. There was a huge shape in the distance. It was dark and very far away.

"Let's take a walk," The woman said, beginning to walk towards the shape.

Foxy followed behind her, and the two conversed as they walked.

"Last time I was here, you said there was a danger on the horizon?" Foxy asked.

"Yes, I believe it has arrived quicker than expected," she replied.

"Does it have anything to do with what happened on the top of Cnoc Mor? With the tornado and that man?"

The lady looked at him while walking with a serious expression on her face. "Do not insult your own race by referring to him as a man. You should refer to him as what he is."

Foxy looked ahead as they were getting closer to the shape and uttered, "A Fomorian."

For the first time in this place, an icy wind blew past, and Foxy shivered to his bones.

The woman nodded and said, "You are very lucky Foxy. If it were not for young Naoise, you and Mr. Cathal would have met a most gruesome end."

Foxy could begin to make out what the shape was. It appeared it was moving. Just when he was to make a full guess of what he was looking at, the woman spoke, "Fomorians are a horrid race of malevolent spirits – scourgers of goodness. They eternally dwelled in the otherworld beneath Ireland. They rose up once before, led by Partholòn."

"But the Tuath De Danann defeated them? They trapped Partholòn beneath Cnoc Mor?" Foxy interrupted.

The woman looked regretful and said, "Trapped and defeated are very different things. Soon, we are about to find out just how different they are. Foxy, you won't have much time left here. Be warned, Fomorians are huge in numbers. Where there is one, many will follow. They exist to burn."

"Were the Fomorians not all wiped out by the remaining Tuath De Danann?" he said.

"You've heard long-warped stories. What actually happened is far from the tales that have been told. Not only were the Fomorians not wiped out, but the Tuath De Danann were not all the godlike, virtuous heroes you have heard, either."

Foxy stared at the woman, waiting for her to continue.

"Be very careful of the Fomorians, young Foxy. They are not to be taken lightly."

"What can I do about them?" said Foxy.

"Make sure Naoise is alright. Defend her. Always defend what's important to you. Although I do foresee you playing a particularly important part in the story," the woman said.

Foxy could see the shape clearly now, and it made his jaw drop. An awe-inspiringly large castle was floating across the lake. It was tethered to what seemed like an island by a huge, iron-clad chain. Foxy could see that on the island, there was what looked like a town. Different buildings and small houses.

The castle drifted across the water, pulling the island behind by the huge rusted chain.

"My home," the woman said.

Foxy looked at her, surprised.

"It's been so lonely," she said.

A strong wind blew through and sent the castle off in a direction away from Foxy and the woman.

"I'm afraid it's time to go back. I do love our chats," she said.

"What can I do about a Fomorian?" Foxy asked as he felt the ground opening up around him and beginning to fall.

He fell into the water impossibly fast and dark. As he fell, he could hear an echo from the woman, "Bravery is a power itself."

***

Foxy woke up and saw the clock showing him that it was 8 am. He was drowned in sweat, or was it water, he thought. He sat up and got dressed. He knew where he had to go and who he had to see.

He got dressed with a level of determination and began to head towards the school to meet Vincent.

Arriving downstairs, Foxy met Linda, who handed him a cup of tea. She looked sad. Foxy really did want to speak to her, but he knew how important it was to be at the school for 9 am.

"Where are you going, dear?" Linda asked, concerned.

Foxy immediately felt a swell of guilt as he was about to lie again, but his trip to the lake last night had made his meeting with Vincent unmissable.

"I feel bad about missing school yesterday, Naoise. Cathal and I are going to do Saturday study just to make up," said Foxy in his most convincing tone.

Foxy knew by Linda's face she saw through his lie. She was sure to call him out for it. Then, suddenly, she was hugging him. Tightly, she hugged him. Foxy hugged back and said softly, "I really am sorry about yesterday."

Linda had her firmly buried in Foxy's chest.

"I'm sorry too," she said. "No matter how mad I am at you, please don't ever feel like you're not welcome to dinner. If you killed someone, I'd still feed you."

The two of them both burst into a little laughter. Just like that, the tiff between them was totally washed away.

She handed him a large sausage roll wrapped in kitchen paper.

"Here then, dear, you can eat this on the way to school," Linda said with a smile.

Foxy thanked her and headed out the door. He felt anxious on his walk to school, particularly as he walked past Cnoc Mor. Where was that Fomorian from yesterday? Had he climbed back up? Perhaps he was waiting to jump out and attack Foxy on the way.

As Foxy was walking and feeling anxious, he was shocked by a voice shouting from behind him, "Hey, wait up!"

It was Cathal cycling up the road behind Foxy, he was very surprised to see. Once Cathal had reached him, he slowed his bike and got off to walk beside Foxy.

"Do you think Naoise is okay?" Cathal asked sombrely.

Foxy accepted the company and replied, "I don't know, to be honest."

The two discussed the events of the day before as they approached the school. They arrived at the school wall. It was exactly 9:00 am. Cathal and Foxy exchanged small talk and were recalling yesterday's events when Vincent's car pulled around the corner. Strangely compared to other times he had parked around Foxy, he did not get out of the car.

Foxy and Cathal both knew they had to get in. Foxy could see that Cathal was extremely nervous. He was shaking.

"I don't foresee this being fun," Foxy said in an effort to lighten the mood.

"I can't believe I'm here," Cathal said. "To tell you the truth, I wasn't going to come."

"What changed your mind?" asked Foxy as he walked towards the car.

Cathal, then filled with courage, walked ahead of Foxy towards the car, opened the back door, and replied, "To be honest, I had a dream, and this woman said it was really important to make this meeting. It was really weird, but I just took it as a sign."

Cathal got into the car. Foxy was in total shock. He knew where Cathal had been. Although where he and Cathal were going today, he was not so sure.

Chapter 10: *The Lost Tuath De Danann*

The car ride to Tryst Manor was painfully quiet. Not one single word was spoken. Foxy could spy Vincent's knuckles whitening around the steering wheel.

Arriving at the massive gates that guarded the manor, Cathal was very clearly in awe at the size of them. Once they drove through the gates, Foxy looked frantically through the woods and saw Fallow the deer chasing through the trees alongside the car. When the car arrived at the front of the manor in the circular car park, Foxy spotted straightaway that there was another long luxury car parked at the house.

Vincent parked and got out. He stormed inside the house without a single solitary word to Cathal or Foxy. In the back of the car, Foxy and Cathal looked at each other.

"I suppose we'd better go in," said Foxy.

Cathal looked very scared. "Are you sure we have to? Maybe Vincent is coming back out?"

Foxy got out of the car and called back to Cathal, "I want to find out if Naoise is alright."

Cathal groaned and then followed him out towards the steps. As Foxy walked towards the house, he was blindsided with a pain in the back of his head. He then heard a loud cawing. A crow had swopped down and pecked Foxy hard on the back of the head. He called out in pain. The bird kept cawing but seemed to be happy with just the one peck. It was Morrigan, there was no mistaking. The crow perched herself on the pillar at the bottom of the entry stairs and screeched again and again as Foxy kept walking.

Cathal, meanwhile, was frozen in fear. A large stag was staring at him from the woods. Wide, powerful antlers were tilted down slightly towards Cathal. There was a snort from the stag, who glared at the short man.

"Come on Cathal, let's get inside," Foxy called back rubbing his head from where Morrigan had attacked him.

At the top of the stairs, Foxy and Cathal finally opened the front door and met an ominous sight inside.

Inside Tryst Manor, standing in the main foyer area was Vincent, who continued to look furious, although he was stood to the side.

In the middle of the room was a tall, imposing-looking man wearing long black robes. He was accompanied by a tall, slender woman with long blonde hair that fell like a curtain over her shoulders. They both stared at Foxy and Cathal without so much as a hint of a blink.

Foxy and Cathal simply looked at them, awaiting words to fall from their intimidating faces.

The tall man's eyes flicked between the two boys.

"I am Aengus *(Aan-goos)*, this is Aine *(Awn-Yah)*," the man said. The woman gave the slightest nod.

Foxy looked between Aengus and Aine, and yet he knew the answer he still asked, "Are you Naoise's parents?"

"That is correct," Aengus responded in a matter-of-fact tone.

"Is she okay?" Foxy asked.

Aine looked to Aengus, unfaltering. "Perhaps we should tell the boys?" she said in a soft, sweet voice.

Aengus began to walk down the hall towards the library where Naoise had given Foxy the book of the Tuath De Danann. Aine walked behind them.

"Vincent, perhaps some tea for our guests?" Aine said. Vincent politely nodded and went off into the kitchen.

"Hurry along now," Aengus' deep voice echoed through the hall.

Cathal and Foxy followed along up the marble hall, the clunks of each step ringing out from the marble floor against the high ceilings. There was a multitude of paintings strewn along the hall. Foxy hadn't noticed them the last time he was here. They all contained various regal-looking figures, from warriors to bards. They looked like characters in a fantasy TV show or film, Foxy thought.

After a short, slow walk, they arrived outside the door to the small library Foxy had been in before. Aengus stood outside the door, his wife directly beside him.

"I must warn you that what is behind this door is quite shocking," Aengus said coldly.

Foxy snapped and then yelled, "Is it Naoise? Is she alright? That's all I care about!"

Aine then cut across Foxy with a sharp tone, her soft voice remaining but the tone radiating a certain level of authority, "Do not interrupt, child."

Foxy rescinded into himself a little. Later he would think back on this and wonder why he didn't respond. Even later than that he would realise that it was fear of the woman that caused him to be silent.

Aengus cleared his throat and continued, "As I was saying, what is behind this door can be shocking. You must think of it as a large boulder placed across a river. What is behind the door will take you on a different path. One from which there is no conventional means of return."

Cathal and Foxy were both on the wrong side of curious, and didn't ask questions. They waited for Aengus to continue.

"The path behind this door is such a divergent, I tell you now, boys," his voice changed to a gentler sound, almost empathetic. "Listen to me very carefully. I will not make you take this path. Neither will Aine."

Aengus then looked at his wife and traced his hand through her resplendent hair.

"And neither will Naoise," he continued. "So, boys the decision is yours. If you want to go back to the car, Vincent will drop you back at the school and you will never receive any consequences. Neither Vincent nor us will ever contact you again. This agreement must work both ways. If you choose to leave, then you agree to never contact us again. Are we at an understanding?"

"Where is Naoise?" Foxy responded feeling stronger in his voice.

Aine smirked, and then broke into a little chuckle to herself. "I don't think he heard a word you said, Aengus."

As she laughed, she entered the library and shut the door behind her.

Aengus remained outside, totally ignoring Foxy's question.

"Cathal, Foxy, I have explained the rules should you leave. Now listen to me as I discuss what I expect from you if you enter," Aengus said.

"Is Naoise alright?!" Foxy called through the hall.

"BOY!" Aengus bellowed back at Foxy, losing all semblance of empathy, Cathal cowered from the piercing shout.

Foxy never flinched and stared directly at Aengus.

He and Aengus were locked in a stare for a moment, and then Aengus seamlessly switched back to his empathic tone.

"Foxy, I need you to listen to me. It is of the utmost importance that you have all the information before making your choice."

Foxy backed down, gesturing for Aengus to continue.

Aengus turned to see if Cathal was alright before continuing, "Now, listen to me very carefully. If you choose to enter this room, this is what I expect of you. I want you to open your minds to things you thought were not possible. Your lives will be far beyond the concept of normal, should you choose to enter. If you enter, you must believe what I say, and trust fully that what I ask of you is asked in the utmost of good faith. Do not take this decision lightly, my young friends."

Aengus stood up. His robes swished around as he turned and entered the room, closing the door with a heavy thud.

Foxy and Cathal stood outside the door without speaking for a minute.

Foxy eventually looked at Cathal and said, "Cathal, I knew what I was doing to do the minute he suggested it. To be honest, I am waiting on your decision."

Cathal looked back, almost in tears, at Foxy. "I mean, I've always had a fairly normal life, and honestly I'm lonely a lot. While yesterday was the scariest day of my life by far, it was the most I've ever lived! My life would have also stopped had it not been for Naoise. I suppose it would only make sense that I owe her one. So whatever is behind that door, and whatever Aengus asks us to do, I'll give it my best to try and make up to Naoise for saving my life."

Foxy nodded and smiled "Well then, I guess the decision's made."

The two clapped hands in a firm handshake. Foxy then took a long, deep breath, grasped the handle of the door, opened it, and both boys stepped through.

When they walked inside, Foxy looked around to see that the mood in the room was far lighter than what he expected. He could see Aengus and Aine in the corner. Aengus was clapping loudly, and he looked exceedingly happy.

"Well done boys, well done!" he shouted across the room.

Aine was lightly clapping her hands, but looked pleased. Foxy was now most confused. He and Cathal stood side-by-side in the room, then he felt as if he was being attacked.

An armflung around his chest and neck, and the next thing he knew he was being squeezed beside Cathal. He turned his eyes to the left to see that Naoise had grabbed both he and Cathal in a tight hug. She squeezed them both tightly.

"Oh, I knew you'd do it, I just knew it!" She said, bursting with excitement.

"Naoise, you're alright?" Foxy said.

"Thankfully, Vincent got me back here and my Mother was here," She said with a beaming smile.

Aine nodded graciously in the background, but Foxy didn't know what she was being thanked for.

"It's good to see you," said Foxy.

"And great to see you," Naoise replied quickly, giving Foxy an individual hug.

Then Naoise quickly turned to Cathal. "And how are you? I'm more surprised to see you in here, but no less pleased!"

Cathal swallowed loudly and said, "I'm fine. Thanks for saving me yesterday."

Naoise's happiness sank a bit. She looked down.

"You should be thanking me. I should be apologising. I knew that was a possibility yesterday, and I still risked going up the mountain." She bowed her head apologetically. "I'm so sorry, please forgive me."

"There is nothing to forgive; you saved us," said Foxy.

Naoise looked up not really believing him, but grateful to hear it.

"I do have one question," Foxy said inquisitively.

Naoise nodded and said, "Of course, because you chose to enter, no questions are off-limits."

"Vincent said that man… he said he was a 'Fomorian'?" Foxy asked quietly.

Naoise nodded again. Just as she was about to speak, Aengus cut her off.

"Yes Foxy, he was a Fomorian. A weaker one, but yes."

Had Foxy not seen the tornado conjured from seemingly thin air, he would have not believed this answer, but between what he saw yesterday and his dream, he actually took this information in his stride. To his amazement, so it seemed had Cathal, who was listening intently beside him.

Aengus walked to a bookshelf at the back of the room as he spoke, "The reason Naoise was able to save you yesterday is this."

Foxy and Cathal were both about to burst with curiosity. Naoise looked nervous as she stood waiting for the answer.

Aengus himself took a deep breath. "Naoise is one of the Tuath De Danann."

The room was overcome by silence for a moment. Naoise nervously looked at Foxy and Cathal to see their reactions.

Cathal was stunned and did not speak.

Foxy was also stunned, however he turned to Naoise and smiled. She was relieved and smiled back.

"How come you never said anything before, when I spoke about them all the time?" Foxy asked in a kind voice.

Before Naoise could answer, Aengus spoke sternly, "It is forbidden. It is a cardinal sin for Tuath to expose who they are. We are here as protectors; not as celebrities."

Aengus now walked towards Cathal and Foxy holding a large book he'd taken off the shelf.

"We have told you the truth as you were exposed to it in a situation that could not be helped, and you chose yourself by your own free will to learn more. It is of the gravest importance that you tell no one of Naoise's true nature. There will be grave and dire consequences should this rule be broken. Are we understood, boys?"

Both Foxy and Cathal nodded. They clearly understood the gravity of Aengus' demands.

"Are you two both Tuath De Danann, too?" Cathal asked like a child talking to Santa Claus.

Aengus nodded and Aine chuckled.

Aine stepped forward to speak. "We are descendants of the original tribe of the Tuath De Danann. Our strength is miniscule compared to what they had. Naoise is our child. We are long-distant descendants of Dagda, one of the three Tuath that fought Partholòn."

Foxy asked, "But didn't they defeat Partholòn?"

His mind was then snapped back to his dream the night before, where the woman had said, "Trapped and defeated are very different things."

Aengus glowered at Foxy as he opened the large book on a table in the room where they gathered round.

"The stories, and tourist trappers here would have you believe that. However the truth of that story is sadly much more bleak" he said

Cathal sat down on a chair at the table and looked interested as he said "What is the true story?"

Naoise sat beside Cathal and said quietly to him "Shush, just let him tell it. He'll get there himself"

Foxy and Aine then also sat down at the table

Aengus continued "The true story is what you need to hear. Focus closely on the book"

Foxy then looked at the book and couldn't believe what he was seeing. The two pages Aengus had opened on were a large colourful map. The longer Foxy looked he could see the hills and mountains more clearly, they were coming off the page. Spectral version of hills and mountains and lakes filled the room. As Aengus spoke, small wispy human shaped figures arose on the page, and began to act. Aengus was narrating their story as all the hills and mountains caught fire in the holographic tale.

"The Fomorians scarred this land, they ruled and burnt it for many an age. Danu then sent forth the Tuath De Danann."

Foxy saw the whisp of a woman speaking to a few other spectral beings. He thought she looked familiar

Aengus continued "This was not a simple decision for the Mother goddess. You see the Tuath De Danann were her family. They lived together in Falias. By choosing to send the Tuath De Danann to save Ireland, Danu was leaving herself alone. When Partholòn and the Fomorians were defeated the Tuath De Danann would be free to return to Falias."

Aengus paused, both Naoise and Aine looked at him waiting for him to continue. Foxy was less patient and coughed to get his attention. This did the trick and Aengus began narrating again as the whisps acted out the story he was telling.

"The part of the story you know where Nuada, Dagda and Lugh fought Partholòn is true, and he is indeed buried beneath Cnoc Mor. However, it is not as triumphant as you are led to believe. The truth is Partholòn defeated the three of them."

The ghostly story showed Partholòn and his sickle easily and swiftly strike down Nuada, Dagda and Lugh.

"How did they trap him then?" Cathal asked.

Aengus' face was beginning to look sad. Aine placed her hand over his in support.

"The popular story is that Nuada pierced him with the sword of light and they trapped him in the cauldron. The truth is Nuada was struck so badly by Partholòn that he was immobile. Lugh was battling Partholòn as best he could when he also received a devastating blow. Partholòn was such a powerful seer, he could see what they were going to do, so it made fighting him basically impossible. There was one thing, though, that he never saw coming."

Aengus' voice began to burst with pride as a tear rolled down his grizzled face. "My descendant, the head of this family! Dagda! He made the ultimate sacrifice. When Partholòn was about to deliver a fatal blow to Lugh, Dagda grabbed him and without a moment's hesitation threw his cauldron over both he and Partholòn, and then he shrank it to the size of a gemstone."

Naoise and Aine both had tears in their eyes now.

Foxy looked at Cathal and then at Vincent.

"You mean…?" Foxy said but before he could finish, Aengus cut him off.

"Yes," said Aengus. "Dagda knew they could not defeat Partholòn, so he trapped himself and Partholòn in the cauldron. Forever."

"What about Lugh and Nuada?" said Cathal.

Aengus snorted at their names. "They buried the cauldron beneath Cnoc Mor and began to wipe out the rest of the Fomorians."

Aengus then shouted, scaring Cathal again, "They never even tried to save their friend!"

Cathal shuddered. Aengus spotted this straightaway and apologised.

The spectral whisps of the story rescinded and reverted back to the pages of the book, and once again became an ordinary map.

"Just one more thing, though," Foxy said. "You said Nuada and Lugh wiped out the Fomorians?"

"Ah yes, well-spotted, Foxy," said Aengus.

"They were wiped out for centuries," Aine said. As she spoke, she spotted a deep graze on Foxy's arm from the fall the day before.

"You see, Danu had sent the Tuath De Danann to Ireland, and they were to remain here until Partholòn was defeated. With him never truly being killed, the Tuath De Danann were unable to go back to Falias."

While she was speaking, she had plucked one of her extremely long golden hairs. She grabbed Foxy's arm and tied the hair around it. The graze amazingly began to heal at an extraordinary rate. Foxy was stunned, watching his arm heal. He now realised how Naoise had been in such good spirits.

Aine continued talking,"With the Fomorians gone, but Partholòn only trapped, the Tuath De Dannan were trapped here, no longer able to return to their home. They were here so long, and some raised families, but even beings with long life eventually return to the earth. Many of the original Tuath De Danann lost their forms over time, and just became part of nature."

A crow then landed on the windowsill outside and cawed.

"Hey, it's Morrigan," Naoise said.

Foxy looked up at the crow and had a sudden realisation, but Cathal got there before him.

"Morrigan? Wait a minute! I've read before Dagda's wife's name was Morrigan," Cathal exclaimed.

Naoise smiled "Yes, that crow is Dagda's wife. She promised she would wait for him. So she has stuck around for as long as possible; she found herself in the form of a crow. Their son, Fallow, got a much cooler form, I think."

"Naoise!" Aine corrected her daughter quickly.

"So the deer is the son of that crow and a legendary hero?" Foxy asked genuinely.

Naoise and Aine looked at each other, then, at Foxy, and simultaneously said, "Yes."

Aengus then took over from Aine and continued the story, "As Aine said, with the Tuath De Danann fading into the land. Their descendants were losing touch of who they were themselves, until many centuries later Fomorians started showing up again. They were very few in numbers, but as time went by more and more began appearing.

"A few of the Tuath Descendants began to harness the power of the original tribe and launched into an eternal battle against the Fomorians. We believe that Partholòn has been creating them in his trapped state, although it was decided eons ago that it was safer to deal with the Fomorians as they came than risk releasing Partholòn again. Most of them are weak enough."

Foxy responded inquisitively, "Most of them?"

Aengus took a deep breath. "Yes. Although, there are three we believe to still be out there. Partholòn had three very close friends. He had promised each of them an ancient city of Gorias, Findias, and Murias, and he would keep Falias for himself. These three Fomorians are the ones we are primarily concerned about."

Vincent then arrived in the room with tea and biscuits. He left the tray on the table.

"Ah, thank you, Vincent," said Aengus.

"Boys, Vincent made a similar decision many years ago, and he too chose to enter the room. Although, Vincent was not a descendant of a Tuath De Danann."

Foxy and Vincent exchanged a heated glance. Vincent then turned his eyes away from Foxy.

Aengus said, "Vincent could not aid us in the fight, so he swore to help us in any way he could."

Vincent lowered his head. "It was the least I could do."

"None of that," said Aine, and Vincent's head rose immediately.

"You said anything you asked of us, we had to accept in good faith?" Foxy asked.

Aengus slammed the book closed on the table. "Yes. You see, one of Partholòn's core three has been rumoured to be in Achill, on the West of Ireland. Far from here. So Aine and myself need to leave. We only returned because of Naoise's accident. She is unable to control her power."

Naoise looked embarrassed.

Aine held her hand, and that seemed to make the embarrassment pass.

"Stand up, boys," Aengus said to Cathal and Foxy.

They did so. He stood them side by side and put his arms on their shoulders.

"Aine and I will leave tomorrow for Achill. Vincent will begin your training every day after school. It is time. It is time for you, too, Naoise; I fear great danger is on the horizon. Boys, Naoise already knows, but it is of the utmost importance that our existence remains secret. Any word about our existence is fuel for the Fomorians. Promise me you will keep our true identity between us," Aengus said.

Both Foxy and Cathal agreed to that. Neither of them had planned to tell, regardless.

"Great danger is on the horizon," Foxy heard this in his head again.

Aine began to cry a little as she hugged Naoise tightly.

Aengus stood up and looked at Vincent. "Should you complete this, your debt is paid."

Vincent nodded intensely.

"I trust you wholeheartedly," Aengus said as he embraced Vincent in a tight hug.

Aine hugged Naoise very tightly and whispered in her ear. She walked past Cathal and Foxy, smiling at them.

"Best of luck, boys," she said as she left the room

Aengus began to laugh heartily. "I have a good feeling about you two, and I know Naoise will be amazing. Through this training regimen, lads, we will find out if you are descendants of Tuath De Danann. We will see if there is ancient power to be unlocked. I am very glad that Naoise has two good friends to go through this with."

He looked at Foxy and nodded. "Maybe one is more than a friend," he said, then he laughed loudly.

Naoise turned bright red with embarrassment, and she slunk into her chair in the background.

Aengus then turned to leave. "Vincent, these lads are in your hands. Train them well."

"I will." Vincent nodded, and the two once again shook hands.

Aengus kissed Naoise deeply on the forehead before he left. "Travel well, my little flower," he said, then he left the room.

Foxy and Cathal's brains were on overload. The amount of information they had just received was incredible. Foxy felt totally burnt out. Naoise walked over to the two boys and put her arms around them.

"Don't worry, lads, this is going to be so much fun!" Naoise squealed.

"I've also been alone with this stuff; I'm so glad you know about it all now, too."

Foxy hugged her back "I'm glad you're here, too."

Then Foxy looked at Cathal and gave him a friendly punch in the arm. "I'm glad you're here too, Cathal"

Cathal blushed a little. He really did feel like he was wanted there.

"Training regimen has spooked me a bit," Cathal said.

Vincent then spoke, "I will bring Cathal and Foxy home shortly. We will begin training Monday morning. There is no school, so it gives us plenty of time to begin. Training will commence in the Tryst Manor courtyard at 9:30 am. I will collect you at the school at 9:00 am. Do not be a minute late."

Foxy nodded. He had been thinking a lot about Vincent since Aengus had mentioned his debt would be cleared. What was the debt, he wondered, although he assured himself now was not the correct time to ask. Vincent left the room, leaving the three of them alone. They all shared a glance. Morrigan cawed loudly on the windowsill and then flew away.

Foxy turned to Naoise and Cathal, smiling now with the excitement of learning. "Well, where do we begin?"

Chapter 11: *The Long Morning*

Foxy, Cathal and Naoise remained in the library after Aengus and Aine had left. They discussed the events of the day prior.

"Did you know you could create that tornado?" Foxy asked.

"I didn't even see it," Cathal stated. "One second I was falling, and the next I was on land. It all happened in a flash."

"I could also control the wind in small amounts through whistling, but I've never conjured anything like that until yesterday. It's why I collapsed; I was drained," Naoise said. Then she looked at Foxy and a beaming smile broke across her face. "But you saved me. Vincent told me how you carried me down the hill."

Foxy replied, "I didn't even have time to think; it just kind-of happened."

Naoise then joked, "Well, if Cathal couldn't carry the bag up, thankfully you were able to carry me down."

Cathal feigned offence and the three of them laughed. They joked for a short while. Amazingly, Foxy and Cathal were taking everything in stride with all the news – the training that was going to begin to try and unlock their powers, even the fact that Naoise was a Tuath De Danann. This information was all just accepted at face value.

It seemed when adventure called those who were willing, there would be no hesitation.

Vincent then entered the library once again to inform the two that they would be taken back to the school.

"Monday morning, 9 am. You will be collected from the school. You have all day tomorrow before beginning training. I suggest taking it easy," Vincent said darting a look at Foxy.

Naoise hugged both Foxy and Cathal tightly before they left. The two boys made their way back through Tryst Manor and out to the car in the courtyard.

Fallow the stag was standing on the edge of the forestry staring at them. Morrigan was perched on a nearby tree, cawing loudly.

The drive back was just as awkward as the drive there – utter silence in the car with intangible tension emanating from Vincent. They arrived back at the school. They never received a goodbye.

As they got out the car, all they heard was, "Be here Monday morning. 9 am."

Then Vincent drove off as quickly as possible it seemed.

***

The time was reaching midday as the two boys made their way back home.

As they passed Cnoc Mor, Cathal said, "I wonder what my power will be?"

Foxy laughed and replied, "What would you like it to be?"

Cathal pondered for a moment, then said, "Well, if I could fly then I would never have to worry about being thrown off anything again."

Foxy laughed as Cathal mimicked himself flying. "How about you, Foxy?"

Foxy again thought deeply, then said "Well, before I moved here, I would have definitely said invisibility. I always wished no one could see me when I was younger. However, I have been looked after so well since I've been here that I think I would take strength so I could protect everyone, and help Macdara on the farm as much as possible"

Cathal paused and looked at him. "You have the possibility to achieve ancient power, and you want to use it for farming?"

Foxy shrugged. "It seems that way, doesn't it?"

The two both shared a hearty laugh. When they reached the turn for Foxy's road, they agreed to meet here at 8:30 am Monday morning so they could begin their training.

They said goodbye, and Foxy walked back up to the Sullivans' house. He could spy Macdara grooming a small donkey to the side. Foxy felt gracious for the chat with Macdara last night, so he walked over and offered to help him. Macdara was delighted for the company, and the two shared a funny experience as Foxy held the donkey's tail in the air as Macdara sheared its backside.

"You're a good lad, Foxy. This donkey will remember you," Macdara laughed. "Go on get inside, enjoy your weekend."

Foxy entered the house to that intoxicating smell he'd first experienced back when he arrived. He knew stew was for lunch.

Linda popped her head out of the kitchen "Foxy dear, lunch will be ready shortly. You can go relax for a bit. I hope you're hungry."

Foxy went into the kitchen to steal a smell. While inhaling the hearty aroma, his thoughts surrounding training, the Tuath De Danann, and the core three of the Fomorians were a million miles away.

Foxy, in a particularly excited mood – a traveller on the verge of adventure – went to his room and relaxed watching television.

As he was in his room, he began looking at himself in the mirror over his dresser. After a moment, he took his top off. He tried to flex his muscles and was throwing shadow punches, pretending he was a warrior. Even though he was alone, Foxy was feeling pretty embarrassed.

He looked at his body and a great sadness fell over him. He was in decent shape – skinny, but not scrawny. Looking at his body, he focused in on his lack of large muscles. He thought of Aengus, who was a large, imposing figure. Even the Fomorian on the top of Cnoc Mor would have easily been able to physically thwart anything he may have tried.

The body in the mirror did not reflect what he envisioned an ancient warrior to have. He had gained some muscle definition from working the farm with Macdara, but he had a long way to go to transform his body to what he believed it should look like.

His excitement then transferred to anxiousness. How could he be protect anyone, he thought, replaying the events from the top of Cnoc Mor all over again in his head. He could only see himself freezing while the Fomorian held Cathal. Disappointment hit his gut like a shotgun blast.

He didn't have time to dwell on it, as Linda had called him for food. He put on a brave face, feigning a happy mood. He went down and shared a deliciously filling meal with Linda and Macdara. They shared light, happy chatter. Cnor Mor, the Moones, nor Vincent arose as dinner conversation.

Linda told a story of how when she was working at the post office as a young woman, Macdara joked that he sent many letters as an excuse to go down and speak to her. Foxy found the story quite charming, but his mind was whirring away with what Monday had in store for him.

While they were chatting at the table, Foxy received a text notification on his phone. It was an alert letting him know that Naoise had added him to a group chat. The WhatsApp group was named, 'The Legends of Old'.

He knew it would be rude to open his phone at the table. So, as the food was finished, Foxy did his best to hurry through the post-dinner chat. He then drank his tea and helped tidy up the kitchen. Foxy was quite keen to see what was in the group chat. As quickly and politely as he could, he excused himself and said that he was going to go watch TV for a while.

Once back upstairs and feeling quite full from the gorgeous stew, Foxy sat on his bed, turned on the TV, and opened the phone to see that Naoise and Cathal had been having a good chat.

The first message in from Naoise read:

"Hi Lads! This is an easy way for us to chat as I guess we're going to be in contact for a long time (yay). I've named the group the legends of old, cause (hopefully) we can access the powers from the you know who (let's not mention anything obvious in the chat), and naturally because the three of us are all legends!"

The message was capped off by a plethora of various emojis.

Cathal had stated that his parents had never noticed he had left that morning, so he reckoned there would be no issue when it comes to the training. He and Naoise had been discussing what the training could entail. Naoise ensured Cathal that while it would be fun to spend time together, the training would be difficult, as they had to be pushed very hard to see if there was any power there.

Foxy was ecstatic reading the messages; he had never been in a group chat before. He penned his response:

"Hi guys, sorry, was eating dinner! I like the name, Naoise! The Legends of Old, it has a good ring to it. To be honest, I was super excited at the manor, but since I got home I've been really nervous about training Monday. What if we're not able to do it?"

Foxy felt a bit stupid pouring his emotions out in a first message when he knew Naoise and Cathal were having a laugh, but his feelings of stupidity were eliminated with Cathal's response:

"I'm nervous too, Foxy, but the alternative is doing nothing and worrying about school! The way I look at it is as an adventure, which is the reason I joined you two in the first place!

Foxy smiled and laughed looking at the phone. He kept chatting with the other two all evening and watching TV, occasionally popping downstairs for a cup of tea and a quick chat with Linda.

He had an extremely relaxing evening, and as nightfall crept in he fell into a wonderfully deep, dreamless sleep.

140

***

Waking up on Sunday morning to an almighty stretch, Foxy felt every muscle in his body expand in blissful comfort. He knew this would be the last day of normality, so Foxy tried to enjoy it as much as possible.

He had a terrific breakfast with Linda and Macdara. He then worked on the farm with Macdara for a few hours. The field he had previously ploughed with Macdara needed to be cleared of rocks, so Foxy had to walk up and down the field with a wheelbarrow, loading loose rocks into it.

It was exhausting and tedious work, but Foxy did feel a sense of accomplishment when he finished. After another filling lunch, Foxy then sat in the sitting room with Macdara, as there was a hurling match on TV. Foxy was never much into sports, but he could tell Macdara was quite passionate about the teams playing, so Foxy played along that it was of the utmost importance to him that Macdara's home county team won.

He was also hopping in and out of his group chat all day. Cathal had mentioned that his father was also watching the hurling match, but Cathal told them he was not allowed in the room while his Father was watching the match.

Dinner was a light toasted sandwich and a cup of tea. Before he knew it, Foxy checked his watch to see that it was after 9 pm. He couldn't believe where the day had gone. Now his nerves rattled in quick and hard.

He said his goodnights and went off to bed. Suddenly, the realisation of what the morning held was very real. He had already pre-explained his absence in the morning, stating that he and Cathal were going to start going to the gym together, Macdara and Linda were happy to hear he had a friend that wasn't a Moone.

Foxy lay awake most of the night. Sleep did not come easy, and when it did, it only lasted for short spells. He didn't receive more than two hours consecutively all night. Tossing and turning, imagining what could possibly take place at Tryst Manor in a few hours, by the time he had mentally grasped what could potentially happen it was 8:00 am, and he had agreed to meet Cathal at 8:30 am.

He was up and dressed in a flash, eating breakfast so fast he was barely able to speak with Linda. In the blink of an eye, the morning had passed, and he was at the end of the drive waiting for Cathal. At exactly 8:30 am, Foxy saw Cathal cycle round the bend and dismount his bike.

Cathal looked as nervous as Foxy felt.

The two began to walk towards the school.

"Right. No matter what, we stick together," Foxy said.

Cathal agreed, albeit a bit shakily.

After an impressively silent walk, Foxy and Cathal arrived at the school, though they did not see Vincent. Instead, they saw Connor Sweeney and a few of his friends smoking behind the wall that Foxy had hid behind the day he wanted to meet Naoise before school.

Connor and Foxy shared a look. Foxy stopped and noticed how frightened Cathal was. Connor Sweeney, spotting them, informed his friends and then flicked away a cigarette.

"Well, it seems the two best friends have also got detention on midterm. Not as perfect as they think they are," Connor said boastfully, to the laughter of his three friends.

Cathal didn't want to speak.

"We don't have detention," Foxy said calmly.

Connor then snapped in anger and got in Foxy's face. "Do you think you're better than me, Fox?"

Foxy remained calm and stared into Connor Sweeney's eyes.

"Relax, Connor. We don't need a repeat of what happened the other day."

Connor pushed Foxy hard, and he fell back and tripped. Connor Sweeney and his three friends then were about to pounce on Foxy on the ground when Cathal stood in front of them.

"Stop!" Cathal shouted, putting his arms out to protect Foxy on the ground.

Connor Sweeney began to laugh, but just as he was about to punch Cathal, they heard a car horn go off.

Cathal looked over to see that Vincent was parked and now looking directly at the altercation from the driver's seat.

"You're a very lucky little boy," Connor said as he gave Cathal a push, but Cathal stood his ground and didn't budge.

Connor and his three friends reverted away from Foxy and Cathal and headed into the school.

Cathal helped Foxy up. "Thanks Cathal," Foxy said sincerely.

"No worries," replied Cathal, "I think I owed you one anyway."

The two shared a quiet laugh, the morning was off to a rough start, and was only going to get more challenging.

Without so much as a good morning, Foxy and Cathal got into the car with Vincent, who began driving towards Tryst Manor the second Foxy shut the car door behind him.

They waited for the large iron gates to close behind them, and then Vincent drove up the long, winding, wooded driveway into Tryst Manor. Naoise was sitting on the steps that led to the house. Foxy was happy to see how healthy and happy she looked. Then, to his amazement, he noticed Morrigan the crow sitting on Naoise's shoulder. It looked like Naoise was playing with her. Then, even more amazingly, at the base of the steps, seated, was Fallow the large stag. Neither Morrigan nor Fallow reacted to the car driving in.

When Foxy stepped out of the car, there was a head rise from Fallow. This was the closest Foxy had been to the deer. His antlers were staggering.

"Hi guys!" Naoise shouted, quickly followed by a loud squawk from Morrigan.

Foxy and Cathal waved back, but were clearly frightened to approach due to the utter size of Fallow.

"it's okay," said Naoise, "they won't do anything."

Foxy wasn't so sure, as he had received a severe peck from Morrigan before.

Cathal began to walk and turned to Foxy, "Come on, how can we possibly train if we're afraid of a deer and a crow?"

Foxy agreed with Cathal, and they faced the trio of Dagda's family.

Foxy and Cathal carefully walked towards Naoise and her two animal ancestors, once they were close. Fallow slowly stood up. He was as imposing a figure as either Cathal or Foxy had seen before. He was towering over the two boys with his antlers reaching impressive spans on either side.

Then, to Foxy's relief of, Fallow lowered his head to the two boys.

Foxy was in awe until he heard Naoise say, "You can rub his head; it means he acknowledges you."

Foxy put his hand out and gently stroked Fallow's large, hard head. This filled Foxy with extreme joy and eased his heart. Cathal could barely reach the top of Fallow's head, even when bent, but he gave a few timid pats. Vincent then strode over in total seriousness.

"Right you two, off please. You are not required this morning," Vincent said humourlessly.

Morrigan cawed as she quickly flew off into the wooded area. Fallow raised his head and looked at Cathal and Foxy. The deer let out a loud snort, and then pranced off towards the woods, eventually evolving into a tremendous sprint.

"Change into these and follow me," Vincent said, handing each of them a generic sporting t-shirt and tracksuit, then he walked off to a side lane aside the manor. Naoise went inside and changed, while Cathal and Foxy got changed to one side of the house. When Naoise emerged, she looked like she was buzzing for this.

"This is the first day for the legends of old, lads," Naoise said with latent excitement.

Cathal's fear was front and centre. Foxy, on the other hand, had been comforted by Fallow's seeming approval.

"I'm ready," Foxy said confidently as the three followed Vincent. They were now motivated to face whatever the rest of the day may bring.

Around the side of the manor lay a large, open grassy area surrounded by the most beautiful and colourful plants – dazzling arrangements of large, yellow, blue and purple flowers. The large, open, grassy area was sloped down on all sides by immaculately cut grassy hills. Foxy reckoned Vincent was the one who cut the grass. On one side in particular there was a huge steep hill that had a small clearing at the top too.

Foxy could see stuff at the bottom, but he couldn't make out what it was.

The three teens arrived in the middle of the clearing, where Vincent was waiting. There was a series of different things laid out across the ground. Wooden swords, medicine balls, balloons, and large sandbags along with a multitude of other items.

"Training will differ between you. Naoise, your goal is to control your power. Foxy and Cathal, our goal is to see if you have any. To determine that, we have to put you under severe duress, and then try manifesting that into an ability." Vincent spoke in a manner of great authority now.

He handed Naoise a balloon. "Please blow this up, Ms. Moone."

Naoise, who was slightly confused, complied and began to inflate the balloon.

Cathal went to grab a balloon and begin to blow it up too. Vincent slapped it out of his hand.

"You do not do anything you are not asked to do," Vincent snapped.

He bent over and picked up one of the large sandbags, seeming to struggle to lift it.

"Hold out your arms," he muttered under the weight of the bag.

Cathal put his arms out, Vincent immediately dropped the sandbag into Cathal's arms. Cathal collapsed to the ground under the weight of the bag.

"Now you," he said to Foxy, raising another bag.

Foxy held his arms out, determined not to give Vincent the pleasure of seeing him fall. Foxy held strong when the bag hit his arms. Vincent was clearly displeased by this.

Cathal had managed to stand back up under tremendous pressure from the heavy sandbag.

Vincent's demeanour changed drastically when he turned to Naoise. "Ms. Moone, I want you to try and control this balloon. I want you to practice blowing this balloon up and down the big hill."

Naoise nodded emphatically, fully believing in her ability to do just that.

Vincent's body language and expression switched back rapidly as he spoke to the two boys. "Right lads, let's get the spirit under pressure. While Naoise controls that balloon up and down that hill, you will carry those sandbags up and down that hill."

Foxy's mouth dropped open. He was shaking from holding the heavy bag already; he would find it extremely difficult to carry the bag up the hill. He assumed Cathal would have almost no chance.

Cathal dropped the bag in protest. "I can't do that," he said, exasperated.

In the meantime, Vincent had picked up the wooden sword, and in swift reply to Cathal's protest he gave Cathal a swift whack on the head with it. Not enough to damage or really enough to leave a mark, but enough to definitely draw attention. Cathal fell to his knees when whacked on the forehead.

Foxy, outraged, then dropped his bag and went to confront Vincent, but was also greeted with a lighting-fast whack on the head. The blow stung him.

"Care for another?" Vincent asked, pointing the sword at Foxy.

Foxy recoiled in anger.

"You said you would do anything asked of you in good faith," Vincent said. "You swore to Aengus you would train. This is training. Now get that bag up the hill."

Foxy stubbornly lifted the bag, flung it over his shoulder, and walked towards the large hill. Cathal couldn't lift the bag and walk at the same time, so he had to drag it.

Naoise quite easily carried her balloon, she felt bad at how seemingly easy her task was.

Foxy, Naoise and Cathal all stood side by side at the base of the hill.

"Three, Two, One, go!" Vincent shouted, swinging his sword down in a motion as if to start a race.

Foxy began to sprint up the hill with the sandbag.

Naoise began to gently whistle, and a faint gust of wind softly carried the balloon to the top and back down. The tune was particularly joyous.

"Excellent Ms. Moone," Vincent called across.

Foxy was halfway up the hill when his feet slid out from underneath him. He tumbled under the weight of the bag, and the next thing he knew he had fallen back to the bottom.

"Weak footwork Foxy; that won't get you far," Vincent said mockingly.

Cathal was now further ahead than Foxy; he was pulling the bag along the hill with him. He groaned under the severe pain his back was in.

Foxy, meanwhile, had started up the hill again at a slower pace. He passed Cathal quite quickly and eventually, after a mighty slog, made it to the top.

"Now carry it back down!" Vincent roared.

Foxy trudged his way back down the hill. Naturally it was significantly easier going down than up. The moment he reached the bottom, Vincent shouted, "Again!"

Foxy, who was exhausted and breathing heavy, saw Vincent walking towards him with the wooden sword. Foxy once again threw the bag up on his shoulder and began to make his way towards the top of the hill once more.

Naoise was still comfortably whistling, and the balloon was being guided by her wind up and down. Then the balloon was blown drastically off-course. Naoise had a severe and sudden pain in the back of her head.

While walking back, Vincent had struck Naoise in the head with the wooden sword. "You lost control of your object the moment you were hit. You must do better, Ms. Moone. Get your object back."

Naoise was stunned. Vincent had never been anything but impeccably well-mannered and protective towards her.

"The balloon, Ms. Moone," Vincent said again.

Naoise noticed that the balloon was caught in its own drift from the natural breeze. She began whistling again and was able to redirect its course. Foxy had just made it to the top for a second time and was making his way back down. Sweat was pumping down his forehead.

Then, to make things much, much worse, an almighty rain shower began.

The hill became very slippery, and Foxy took a nasty fall down the hill and into the muck at the bottom.

"Get up, Foxy," Vincent said.

Foxy needed a moment to catch his breath. He was exhausted, and the fall had winded him.

"Get up, Foxy, or we're done here. I will finish this right now. You can go back to that ignorant fool and we'll be done!" Vincent roared.

Foxy now filled with a deep-seated rage he had not felt before in his life. Thate rage gave him the determination to stand up and throw the bag on his shoulder. Through muck and rain, Foxy turned to Vincent and said, "He may have made mistakes, but he's a kind man and he's certainly no fool."

Foxy then turned and started dragging his feet through the mucky wet hillside to the top again. Cathal had just reached the top for his first time. They shared a glance while at the top.

"Keep going, Cathal. Don't you dare stop. Do not give in to him," Foxy said.

Foxy held out his fist as a sign of encouragement. Cathal looked ready to collapse.

"Move it, lads!" Vincent screamed from the base of the hill.

Cathal looked back at Foxy and stuck his own fist out. Both boys' fists touched, and this gave them a burst of encouragement. Cathal began to slowly make his way down the hill. He tried to hold the bag going down to varied success.

Foxy spotted Vincent whacking Naoise again with the stick and the balloon going off-course. The rain was making it cold, and Naoise was trembling, which made it difficult for her to maintain a whistle.

"You can do it!" Foxy called from the top of the hill.

Naoise looked up at him. Foxy shouted again, "We can all do it!"

Naoise focused and corrected her whistle, and the balloon was once again on track. It was becoming more difficult to control her breathing. Foxy once more loaded the bag on his shoulders. This would be his most successful stint with the bag. He made it down and back up three more times before having to drop the bag from sheer exhaustion.

The rain was passing, and the sun was breaking through. Foxy's entire body screamed in pain. Naoise looked as she did on top of Cnoc Mor – very weak and seemingly at her limit. Cathal was sticking to his own pace, but was also on the verge of collapse.

Then, in a stroke of music to their ears, Vincent called, "Once more and we're done!"

Foxy was halfway on his way up the hill, Cathal was just at the top, and Naoise's balloon was just ascending. All three reached the top at the same time, and instantly turned and made it back down the hill. The three of them embraced in an exhausted, faltering hug. Cathal couldn't raise his arms, Naoise collapsed into the other two held up only by Foxy.

Breathing beyond heavily, the three of them held each other up for a moment. Then something happened that Foxy never really could explain. Either out of intuition or perhaps he'd heard it coming, he turned around at the last second and caught Vincent's wooden sword in his hand just as it was about to strike him. Vincent stared at Foxy in disbelief, and Foxy stared back indignantly.

The stare-down between the two was quashed when Naoise asked, "Can we get showers now please?"

Foxy let go of the weapon and Vincent pulled back.

"Yes, Ms. Moone, please go get showered. Can you show the other two where the showers are?" Vincent said reluctantly.

Cathal and Naoise walked off while Foxy and Vincent shared an extended glance.

Foxy then turned to walk away and catch up to the others. Out of earshot, Foxy heard Vincent say, "Hey, Foxy."

Foxy turned around to see Vincent seething over something.

"What" Foxy asked from a body that was ready to crumble.

"He wasn't always kind," Vincent said morosely.

Foxy just looked at Vincent. He then turned away from him and, in as light a jog as he could muster, he caught up to Naoise and Cathal.

"Day one, eh?" Foxy said, laughing.

Cathal was nearly in tears. "Surely day one is the hardest?"

Naoise laughed. "Somehow I don't think so. I imagine we'll be having a few long mornings this week."

Foxy looked back over his shoulder at Vincent, who hadn't moved. He remained soaked, standing in the garden. Turning back to Cathal and Naoise, Foxy said "I can't wait for all of them!"

Chapter 12: *A Midterm*

Correspondence

The sleep Foxy had that Monday night was extravagant. He crawled into bed shortly after 8 pm and slept soundly and dreamlessly until 8 am the following morning. He woke to his body in screaming pain and aches from Monday's training. In the midst of internally coming to terms with how much pain his body was in, he realised in a very short while he would be back out at Tryst Manor training again. He groaned in pain as he got to his feet.

When he met Cathal that morning, the two shared a conversation which almost turned into a competition of who was in the most pain. They dreamt up what new and innovative horrible ways Vincent would torture them today, but never once were they close to the actual training that awaited them on Tuesday morning.

Same as the day before, once they arrived at Tryst Manor after a silent car trip, they greeted Naoise, who seemed to be in great spirits, and then changed into their training uniforms. They walked out to the grassy area again, and Foxy's stomach sank when he saw what was waiting for them.

There was two large sandbags and a balloon.

Foxy realised they were going to be doing the same task again.

The three of them groaned, and the motivation was lost from them entirely until Vincent spoke. "Only when you are at your limits, may we see if you are descendants of Tuath De Danann."

Vincent loudly whacked one of the bags with his wooden sword and said, "Let's get to it. Also, just to squander any hopes, this training exercise will continue each day this week, with the bags getting slightly heavier until Friday. Then we will test to see where we are as we continue into our evening training when school returns. Let's go."

Foxy rolled his eyes. He felt like he had now accomplished nothing yesterday.

The three of them began training again, Naoise concentrated hard to keep the balloon on track with an occasional thump on the head from Vincent. Foxy slogged up the hill with the sandbag, his body agonised with each step. What almost hurt Foxy more was that Cathal was going faster than him today. Cathal had kept the same dragging style as yesterday, but he consistently kept passing by Foxy.

Foxy began to worry that Cathal had unlocked his power already and he hadn't. As the morning passed by into the afternoon, Vincent could tell that the teens were about to collapse and gave the sweet call of "one more rep".

Once they had finished and were making thier way back to the manor, Foxy asked Cathal, "How did you do that so easily? I was dying."

Cathal swiftly looked around to see Vincent was far away, then he whispered, "On the way over to the hill, my bag snagged on a rock and was leaking sand for the whole morning. I was just pretending it was heavy so Vincent wouldn't catch on!"

Foxy didn't know whether to laugh or cry. He was caught between laughing at Cathal's ingenious or crying at his own stupidity for never letting any sand out of his bag.

Naoise was fainty again; using her power seemed to make her quite weak. She turned to the two boys and said, "Friday is Halloween. Can the three of us go for dinner or a massage or something?"

Foxy nodded in agreement. "A great idea, Naoise. Friday evening, we'll go for a Halloween feast! However, I'm not dressing up."

Cathal agreed with Foxy about no fancy dress.

Naoise laughed and said, "Why do you both assume I want to dress up?"

Cathal and Foxy shared a glance with each other and knew they were better off not answering.

***

The schedule for the week remained the same, with long sleeps and long mornings carrying bags up hills. Thursday was particularly bad for Foxy, as when he came back from Tryst Manor Macdara needed help barbing a new fence. This took several hours of hard graft That evening Foxy was in bed by 7 pm.

Vincent informed them Friday morning that there would be time to rest Saturday and Sunday, and then training would resume Monday after school.

"But before we break for the weekend, I must test Cathal and Foxy to see what progress has been made," Vincent said.

"Ms. Moone, join me please," he said, beckoning Naoise to one side of the grassy area.

Vincent began to walk around the three of them, tracing a circle in the grass.

"Foxy and Cathal, your goal is to knock Naoise down. You may use any of the tools in the circle."

Foxy and Cathal looked confused, but no more confused than Naoise, who was standing in the middle of the pseudo-circle. Then Vincent turned to Naoise.

"Ms. Moone, your goal is to use the wind to throw both boys out of the area."

Cathal, looking hesitant, said to Vincent, "You want us to fight each other?"

Vincent ignored him and shouted, "Begin!"

There was a period of silence. Neither Naoise nor the two boys moved. Cathal then eventually picked up a wooden shield. Foxy just looked at Naoise and shrugged.

Naoise started to smile "Are you afraid you can't do it?" She said in a playful tone.
Foxy now understood that no one was going to get hurt too badly, and it was all in the name of competition. He looked at the various wooden items across the lawn and opted for a javelin pole.

Just as he picked up his javelin, he heard a playful tune being whistled. Then he felt the wind rise.

He looked at Naoise, who was smiling as she whistled, the grass ruffling around her as a gust forced its way from her towards Cathal and Foxy.

Cathal ducked down behind the shield, taking the brunt of the wind and holding his ground. Foxy was able to stand through the gust.

He shouted back to Naoise, "is that all you've got?!"

Through an aching body, Foxy began to run towards Naoise, who, through her whistles, continuously knocked him off course with various gusts. He was getting close to her, and a slight pitch change in her whistle shot Foxy a few feet up in the air. He landed hard on the ground.

While Foxy was down, Naoise noticed that Cathal had creept up behind her. She whistled loudly while Cathal was running. To his own misfortune he was holding the shield at a bad angle, and when a mighty gust caught the shield it acted as a kite and sent Cathal zooming across the garden well and truly outside the area Vincent had outlined.

With her attention turned she felt a hand land on her shoulder, Foxy had gotten up and got his hand to her. Breathing heavily, he said, "I got you."

Naoise smiled and said quietly "The goal was to knock me over, not catch me"

Foxy's eyes sank as he heard a sharp whistle and then felt an almighty strong wind force him back. He managed to stick the javelin in the ground. He was holding onto it like a flag for a moment before the wind forced him back and well outside the circle.

The three of them laughed when they rejoined, all enjoying the training exercise and mainly just happy to see a change from the hill.

Vincent walked over and spoke intently, "Plenty of work to be done."

His eyes then flicked to Naoise. "From all of you."

She felt quite disheartened over this, as she'd felt she did well in the challenge.

Vincent's tone slightly lifted then as he said, "You are free for the weekend. Boys I will drop you off at home shortly."

Then he walked off.

Naoise turned to Cathal and Foxy, shaking off the bad feelings she'd just received. "I'm going to go with Vincent and get dropped off with you. I'll go to your house Foxy, and Cathal, when you're ready you can meet us back there and we'll go for food together then?"

Foxy found it strange how his first thought was, "Is my room clean?" about Naoise going to the Sullivans' and not the complexities of the relationships between the Sullivans', the Moones', and Vincent. Foxy nodded in agreement with Naoise. "Sounds good."

"Great," said Naoise. "I'd better go tell Vincent, 'cause I just know he won't be happy." She ran off towards the manor.

Shortly after a shower and a quick change, the car ride back to the school was not silent, as it was filled with Naoise's observations on trees and other passing cars. When they arrived at the school, Vincent spoke very seriously.

"Naoise, I will collect you from the restaurant at 11 pm. You are to go no further than the restaurant or anywhere else. Understood?"

Naoise understood and let Vincent know. The three of them got out of the car and it was then that Foxy noticed Naoise had a large bag with her.

"What's in the bag Naoise?" Foxy asked, worried.

"These are our costumes," said Naoise.

Cathal and Foxy began to argue the whole walk back to the Sullivans' that they would not wear them. Somehow, Foxy was never sure exactly how, by the time Cathal had headed home to get ready, both of them had agreed to wear the costume. Cathal took his collection of costume items off Naoise.

"Okay, meet back here at 6 pm," Cathal said.

Naoise and Foxy nodded and then turned to walk into the Sullivans'.

Naoise said quietly, "I told Vincent we were going to Cathal's for the afternoon. I knew he wouldn't let me come here. See, I know the Sullivans are his parents."

Foxy showed little reaction to this being said. He had assumed that Naoise would know.

"He told me the first time you and I were together. I guess he keeps tabs on what his parents are up to," Naoise continued.

Foxy stopped walking as Naoise began to look worried. She looked up at him reservedly.

"I am worried your foster parents will dislike me," she said.

Foxy smiled and replied, "I don't see a world where they possibly couldn't like you. They seem to honestly like the nicest people. I'm sure it will be okay."

Naoise took a deep breath and then began to walk toward the house.

Foxy and Naoise entered the house to a warm and hearty, "Hello dear!" from Linda.

When Linda popped her head out, she gasped.

"Oh, Foxy dear, I didn't know you had company."

Linda eyed Naoise up and down. "Well aren't you a pretty thing!" she said cheerfully.

Naoise smiled shyly. This was the first time Foxy had seen this side of her.

Foxy looked between them and said, "Linda, this is Naoise Moone."

Linda gasped again. Naoise looked to the floor. The Vincent connection was obvious. However, Linda met all of Foxy's expectations of her. She walked over to Naoise and gave her the tightest, warmest hug she had ever had.

Naoise embraced Linda back.

"Any friend of Foxy's is always welcome in this house, dear," Linda said lowly, specifically to Naoise.

Naoise stepped away. "Thank you so much, you have a beautiful home," Naoise said looking around.

At this time, Macdara burst into the hall. There was again a moment of fear that was quashed quickly as he stuck his hand out towards Naoise almost instantly. "Macdara Sullivan," he said.

Naoise placed her small hand in Macdara's massive hand. "Naoise Moone, Sir. Nice to meet you."

Macdara nodded acceptingly, then looked at Foxy "So what have you kids got planned this Halloween?"

All of the awkwardness was then washed away as Naoise reverted to her happy, quirky self. She explained that they were heading to the local diner *Teach Bia (CHOCK BEE-AH).* That the diner was having a halloween party, and they were dressing up.

Macdara was obviously very tickled by this, and he looked directly at Foxy and said, "I never pegged you for the fancy dress type."

"I wasn't until about ten minutes ago," Foxy retorted, somewhat resentfully.

Macdara laughed heartily "Well I tell you what, when you're ready to go I'll drop you both at the diner."

"And Cathal," Naoise stated quickly.

Foxy had been so enjoying the fact that Naoise, Linda and Macdara were getting along that he had actually forgotten about Cathal.

"No problem at all," laughed Macdara as he returned to the sitting room. The second half of the hurling match was starting.

Linda caught Foxy looking at Naoise, and the smile on her face was about to exceed her ears. Foxy then noticed Linda had caught him looking, and he got slightly embarrassed. Linda, realising this, removed herself back to the kitchen.

"I'll make you two tea while you go get ready," Linda said beamingly.

Naoise and Foxy headed upstairs to his room, which wasn't particularly tidy. There were bits of clothes thrown across the floor. Foxy internally was ecstatic that there was a girl in his room. This was a situation he had never come across before. As he looked at her, Naoise looked at her watch.

"Okay, it's 5 pm, let's get ready now." She exclaimed excitedly.

Foxy was confused by that. "It doesn't take an hour to get ready. What are we even going as?"

Naoise's jaw dropped. "Maybe it doesn't take boys an hour. It will certainly take me an hour. I'll go to your bathroom and get ready, and you get ready here."

Naoise then grabbed some unidentifiable clothes from the bag and nipped into the en-suite. From behind the door, Foxy could hear her calling, "I left your outfit in the bag."

Foxy walked over to the bag and pulled out a pair of tight black pants that had large silver boots sewn over the base of them. There was also a silver long-sleeved top with golden bracers around the wrists. He was beginning to put the costume together when he took out a long tunic with a house crest in the middle. The last two items were a long red cape and a cheap plastic chainmail hood. Foxy now realised he was going as a knight. He never thought the costume would be this big.

"Do I have to wear the whole thing?" he asked to Naoise.

All he heard back was a frustrated, "Yes!"

Much to his dismay, he began to change into the costume. It was far heavier and bulkier once it was on than it looked. He was just about ready, and it had only taken him a few minutes.

"Will you be much longer, Naoise?" Foxy said again with a feeling that perhaps asking this wasn't a smart idea.

His assumptions were confirmed when he just heard a loud "Tut" from the bathroom. Foxy then realised it was perhaps best just to wait. He began to watch some TV.

Some time later Naoise called, "Are you ready?"

Foxy then quickly popped to his feet and placed the last item on.

Once he put the chainmail on, he spotted another item in the bag. He took it out to realise it was a large, Styrofoam sword. Forgetting to answer Naoise, Foxy then caught a glimpse of himself in the mirror in his room. He was quite enjoying the look of being a knight. He began to swing the sword as if he was in battle. It reminded him of playing dress up as a child with his parents.

As he was swinging the sword, Naoise walked out and stunned Foxy, who was caught enjoying the costume he was so previously opposed to.

Foxy was then further stunned when he properly looked at Naoise. She had obviously planned their costumes together. She was dressed as a maiden in a gorgeous, long, green velvet dress. She was wearing an old-fashioned corset around her waist. Her hair was tied in long, thick braids, and then those were interwoven together. He thought to himself no wonder it took that long. She then had a classic looking medieval headpiece on like an inverted tiara.

"You look nice," Foxy stuttered.

"You looked like you were enjoying being a knight," Naoise quickly replied.

Foxy then got quite embarrassed until Naoise broke the embarrassment with a laugh.

"Right you two, I'll drop you off now if that suits you," Macdara shouted up the stairs.

Naoise and Foxy shared a moment looking at each other in their costumes. When they walked downstairs Foxy noticed that Linda had her phone out. The woman looked like she was about to burst with love.

"Jump in there real quick for a picture together," Linda squealed.

Foxy awkwardly stood beside Naoise for a picture. Naoise, not typically the person to be awkward, hugged Foxy tightly from the side as the flash went off.

"Oh dears, don't you just look gorgeous," Linda said, fighting back tears.

"Right, come on you two, out we go," Macdara stated.

They left the house and got into the car. Just as they were driving down the lane, Macdara uttered, "What in good heavens is that?"

At the end of the lane there was a short man with a very long tall pointy hat. He was wearing long blue robes and was holding a staff of some sorts. He also had a very long bushy beard with thick glasses on his face.

Naoise began to laugh out loud in the back. As Macdara got closer, Foxy could see that it was Cathal. Dressed as a wizard.

Foxy too couldn't help but let a laugh out. Macdara slowed to a halt. The short, bushy wizard got in the backseat of the car beside Naoise.

Cathal did not look impressed with the laughing. "Do you know how many people shouted at me on my way here?" he asked.

"I think you look the grandest, son. Finest wizard on this side of the Shannon," Macdara said.

Naoise and Foxy then burst into laughter. Cathal then shortly joined in, realising this was the simpler option than to be angry at them. They had a pleasant drive to the town, where they parked outside *Teach Bia*. They could see all the other kids from school entering dressed in a variety of costumes ranging from Halloween classics to some girls just wearing their normal clothes with cat ears on.

"Do you need a lift later on?" Macdara asked kindly.

Naoise went to speak, but Foxy got in before her. "No, Cathal's parents had said they'd collect us later on."

Naoise initially was a bit taken aback by this, but also thought maybe this little white lie was for the best.

"No worries at all kids, go have fun," Macdara said as the kids got out of the car. The evening was just brimming to darkness as the sun settled in for the night behind Cnoc Mor.

Cathal, Foxy and Naoise all looked at each other and laughed.

"We make quite the little adventure party, don't we?" Naoise said, very pleased with herself.

"Well how come Foxy gets to be a strong powerful knight, and I'm a bushy old wizard?" Cathal argued as they walked towards the restaurant.

"At least people can't see who you are," Foxy replied. This was seemingly the first time Cathal had realised that those who shouted at him most likely didn't know who he was. This made the costume more at ease on him.

They got to the door of the diner amidst a cavalcade of other costumes. They were greeted by a waitress when they entered *Teach Bia*. Naoise asked for a table for three, and the exhausted looking waitress who had little more than some fake blood on her escorted them to a small booth in the corner of the restaurant. The woman was no older than twenty, most likely just out of school, and did not seem impressed about having to work tonight.

Foxy examined the diner, which was classically designed. It had a hint of an American 50's diner mixed with old Irish pubs. Foxy found the place quite charming overall. At the far end of the restaurant, Foxy spotted Connor Sweeney and his friends. He noticed them taking out a small bottle of Vodka and pouring it into their drinks at the table and then laughing obnoxiously loud. They were all dressed normally, with stupid sunglasses and even more stupid hats.

Foxy turned his attention back to his own table.

"I am so hungry, I don't think I've ever burnt as many calories as I have this week," he said.

"Tell me about it," said Cathal. "I wonder if there is any benefit to carrying that bag to that hill, besides Vincent torturing us," he continued.

Naoise seemed to be thinking, and then she said, "Well, after I whistled on top of Cnoc Mor and collapsed, you had to carry me down, didn't you?"

Foxy nodded.

"Well, I'm not that much heavier than those bags, at least I hope not anyway. Plus, didn't you fall on the way down, too?"

Foxy conceded to this fact – that he had fallen and he could have endangered her.

Naoise spoke again, "I'm just thinking, that's the only real-life situation we've faced. So maybe Vincent is just trying to use that example as a way to train us up."

Cathal seemed very impressed by this observation. Foxy looked more deflated that he couldn't draw that conclusion himself.

"You'd have quite a few marks, if I used my technique on you coming down the hill," Cathal said, and then fixed his large wizard spectacles to look at a menu.

Naoise then burst out laughing, Foxy didn't feel much like laughing, but faked one to move past the topic.

"But anyway, I am starving, so let's order" Naoise said scanning the menu

"Let's get starters and everything," Cathal demanded.

The other two complied, the fed-up waitress returned to the table and the three of them ordered a colossal amount of food. Everything from chicken wings to hotdogs, and then from sliders to milkshakes. The food had no sooner arrived at the table, than it was gone. The three of them all laughed sincerely throughout the meal and were deeply enjoying each other's company. Foxy found Cathal eating with the beard pulled down around the chin particularly funny.

"I really am starting to think you'd make a great wizard" Foxy said to Cathal as they finished their meal.

They were absolutely stuffed. Cathal could barely get words out.

"Me too, if only I could magically pay for the meal, we could do this every week," Cathal joked as he pretended to use his wizard staff to cast a spell, but as he waved t, the staff was snatched from his hand. He looked around to see Conor Sweeney with his friends.

"Having a nice dinner?" Connor asked in a mocking voice. It was clear to Foxy, too, that he had had more than a little bit of vodka.

The three of them just stared at Connor, who was smiling as he looked at the wizard staff. Then Connor looked at Cathal.

"I'm astounded to see you dressed as a wizard. I always saw you as more of a dwarf!" He exclaimed, to the laughter of his friends. Then, in a vicious move, he snapped the wizard's staff over his knee.

"Now it's the right size for you," he said in a nasty voice.

Cathal looked distraught. He had always been self-conscious about his height. This was one factor that Connor Sweeney continually picked on Cathal for.

Cathal went to sadly take off his wizard's hat when Foxy grabbed his hands. "Don't you dare take off that hat, Cathal," Foxy said in a deadly serious voice.

Foxy stood up face-to-face with Connor Sweeney. He could smell the alcohol on his breath. Connor Sweeney looked ravenous and said, "You and I have an issue to sort out. Why don't we sort it out now," while he poked Foxy hard in the chest.

Foxy knew this situation was beyond saving, and felt like he owed Connor one for what he'd said to Cathal. Foxy poked Connor back in the chest hard and said, "Yeah, why not? Let's me and you sort this out outside, now."

Foxy was seething with anger. To his surprise, Naoise seemed to be backing him too.

"You're a nasty little boy," she said through gritted teeth while simultaneously checking on Cathal.

Connor Sweeney looked at her and then winked and blew a kiss at her. This disgusted Naoise right down to her core.

Foxy drew his attention back to him, fists clenched. Foxy was bursting with anger. "Let's go."

Sweeney laughed and gesturedFoxy towards the door. Foxy stormed out while Naoise and Cathal followed. Both were determined, like following a leader into battle. When they got outside, Foxy took off the chainmail headpiece and the cape.

A large amount of other students in the diner had realised a fight was about to take place and, in typical fashion, they rushed out. Soon there was a large circle of various costumes surrounding Connor and Foxy.

Connor Sweeney seemed to be playing up to the crowd, but none of this was any joke to Foxy. For the first time in his life, he actually felt strong ill will towards someone. He wanted to cause pain for Connor. Although, Foxy's own body was already in massive pain from the week of excruciating training.

If Foxy had learned anything this week, it was that waiting around usually lead to a whack. So, without hesitation he walked face-to-face with Connor Sweeney, who was about to say, "What are you going to do?"

He was unable to finish the sentence because Foxy had punched he square in the face as hard as he could. Connor Sweeney stumbled back, holding his nose, which was gushing blood. The crowd fell silent. Sweeney's friends were stunned. Connor himself, he looked incensed. Sweeney sprinted at Foxy, arm cocked and ready to punch him.

Foxy stepped deftly to the side, dodging the punch that was aimed towards him. He quickly hit Sweeney with a sickening left hook in the body, followed swiftly by a right hook to the jaw which floored Connor Sweeney.

Foxy stood over him, knuckles clenched but in total control. He was able to relax his breathing. Connor Sweeney was rolling around on the ground holding his stomach from where Foxy had hit him. It was at this time that Foxy felt a ferocious pain in the back of his head. A very small point at the back of his head was pulsing in white hot pain. Quickly he felt it again. He turned around to see that one of Connor Sweeney's female friends was swinging a large stiletto high heel at him.

Just as the girl was about to swing it down again, she was tackled out of Foxy's field of vision. He looked to the ground to see Naoise had charged this girl down and was wrestling with her on the ground.

Foxy went to go help but was pulled back. Two of Sweeney's group had grabbed his arms. Then taking advantage of the situation, Connor stood up and punched Foxy right underneath his left eye. He was about to strike again, when Cathal ran in and walloped Sweeney in the face with half of his staff as hard as he could. It didn't do much damage, but enough to stall him. Foxy wrestled free of the other two, taking one down with a windmilling elbow. The other boy gracefully removed himself from the situation.

Cathal was trying to tackle down Connor Sweeney in vain. Sweeney was too big and easily threw Cathal to the side. Naoise was still wrestling, and winning against, the other girl who also stank of alcohol.

Just after he rid himself of Cathal, Connor Sweeney was dealt a thundering right hand from Foxy. He knocked him to the floor and left him seeing stars. He tried to get back up, but stumbled around, his legs constantly falling out from underneath him. More of Sweeney's friends surrounded them. Cathal stood back-to-back with Foxy. Once Naoise had finished with the other girl, she stood back-to-back with Cathal and Foxy as well.

Sweeney's friends were circling them like wolves. Connor had just got his mobility back. They were closing in on the three friends, strangely to the jeers and applause from the large crowd, who was receiving their entertainment in abundance.

At the very moment, the circle of encroachers was about to strike, the loud revving of a car roared into their surroundings. Bright, beaming lights pointed at them, followed by a staggeringly loud car horn. The watching crowd dispersed immediately, running off and back into the diner as kids were wont to do.

Sweeney and his friends, however, did not run off. They stared at the car and faced it. To Foxy, Naoise's and Cathal's simultaneous delight and dismay. They saw that Vincent step out of the car.

Without a moment's hesitation he walked over towards Naoise. Connor went to confront Vincent.

"Who are you?" Connor bellowed in an exhausted, breathy voice.

Vincent shoved him out of the way with tremendous ease. Connor's friends weren't sure what to do. They simply looked at Vincent, who had made his way to the three friends.

"Come with me, now," Vincent demanded.

The three of them knew that tone, and they knew there was an air of seriousness they had not yet heard. They obliged.

As they were following Vincent, Connor shouted back at them, "You won't have your babysitter to save you next time."

Naoise ignored this comment and looked at Vincent. "Is everything alright?" she said, concerned.

Vincent kept walking. "Not here; we must get back to Tryst Manor. Boys, you're coming too."

In a matter of moments, Foxy had gone from a ferocious fist fight to sitting in the back of Vincent's car. He was very confused. Each of them gained their breath back, but each time Naoise tried to speak, Vincent told her to wait.

Cathal and Foxy knew better than to speak out of turn, so they remained silent, exchanging inquisitive looks at each other. They arrived at the large gates blocking Tryst Manor, waited for them to open, and made their way up to the manor courtyard.

When they got out of the car, Vincent walked into the house. "Follow me please," he said in an unusually kind voice.

The evening was dark, but as Naoise began to walk towards the house, Foxy noticed that Morrigan was perched on one pillar at the base of the stairs. The crow's head was bowed slightly. Foxy then saw Fallow the large stag on the other side with his head bowed. Naoise walked between them.

Cathal and Foxy followed, both of them realising that this was not going to be a joyous occasion. This was also the first time Foxy remembered Morrigan not cawing at him. They walked between the two ancient animals and entered the manor.

Vincent seemed extremely flustered. Foxy thought it looked as though he had been crying. He was always extremely composed; he had never looked dishevelled.

"Right," he said, trying to regain a measure of composure. "Boys, I want you to wait here. Naoise, can you follow me please?" Vincent said in what was most definitely a sympathy-laden voice.

Naoise looked at the two boys and nodded to them. They returned the favour. Naoise and Vincent walked off into a nearby room. Cathal and Foxy then sat down on the large stairs in the foyer disrobing from their costumes back to their regular clothes underneath.

They sat there in total silence for a very brief moment. Then they heard noise from the room where Naoise and Vincent went. For a moment, they weren't sure what the noise was, as neither of them had heard it before. Foxy was sure of exactly what it was after listening intently. It was Naoise, crying.

She was crying loudly and painfully. The sound echoed through the halls. This was exemplified by a screeching squawk coming from outside, and then a piercing, hollow scream from a deer.

"Fallow and Morrigan," Cathal said softly.

"They're crying," Foxy added.

The two boys waited in the hall for the crying to ease. It took a while. Vincent then emerged from the room by himself. He walked over to the two boys.

"Thank you for waiting lads," he said, visibly upset. His eyes were raw.

Foxy and Cathal didn't need to ask, they knew he was about to tell them the same news he had just told Naoise.

Vincent looked at the two boys on the stairs and said, "I received a correspondence this evening from an ally in the west. It contained news most harrowing, about one of the Fomorian core three that Aengus and Aine were hunting."

He voice stuttered, caught by a lump in his throat. The moment just before he cried, Vincent was able to swallow it and continue, "It pains me to say that the Fomorian known as Tethra found Aine and Aengus first and…"

The lump in Vincent's throat overpowered him, and a large tear leaked out the side of his eye. He let it slide down before he finished his sentence, "And killed them."

Foxy and Cathal sat there in silence. Foxy's eyes shifted to the room where Vincent had come from, his concern lying firmly with Naoise.

Cathal was also visibly upset, Foxy stood up, looked at Vincent, and stuck out his hand "I am very sorry for your loss. May I go speak to Naoise?"

Vincent wiped the tears away from his face, he looked at Foxy's hand for a moment, then shook it andnodded slowly.

"But Aengus seemed so strong," Cathal choked.

"I know," Vincent said as he was finding it impossible to hold back from full-on crying. He excused himself and left down one of the corridors.

"You'd better go in to her alone," Cathal said.

Foxy agreed and walked towards the room where Vincent had told Naoise the news. When he entered, she never looked at him. She was curled up on the couch, miserable, with tears pouring down her face. She was looking out the window at the bright full moon.

"Naoise," Foxy said. It was all he could think of to say.

She turned to look at him, then ran into his embrace. She hugged him tightly and began to wail uncontrollably again. Foxy then hugged her back, tightly. Foxy consoled her in the moonlit room for a while. Every time she would cease crying it would begin again.

Foxy would not have reacted to trauma with tears, but he knew all too well the devastating feeling of being parentless. After a long while the crying did subside, and they were able to speak. Cathal then joined them tentatively. He hugged Naoise, too. It did not have the same comfort for her as when Foxy hugged her.

"I always thought he was invincible," Naoise said through raw tears.

"I hate the Fomorians. They live to scourge," she said again.

The three of them sat in the moonlight, Foxy and Cathal saying very little, just listening to Naoise as she spoke through her grief.

After a while Vincent came back to say that he had a very important announcement.

"I need you three to listen to me very carefully. I have a very important task to do." he said.

Naoise's eyes were raw from crying, but she was listening.

"Naoise," he said "I am devastated about this news. However, this news brings about a horrible omen. If Tethra has acted, that means the other core Fomorians are also acting. They are most definitely heading here to try and raise Partholòn again. We cannot allow that to happen."

The three of them looked at Vincent, open-mouthed.

Vincent grabbed Naoise's hand. "Naoise I need you to be brave and strong like your parents. I am going to be leaving for a while. I have just made the most difficult phone call of my life."

His eyes then shot to Foxy as he said, "The Sullivans have agreed to take you in for a while."

Foxy realised that Vincent must have called Linda or Macdara. He knew how difficult that must have been.

Naoise started crying again "What do you mean, you're going away?"

Vincent leaned towards her empathetically and said, "It is a grave matter that I must attend. In the event of your parents' death." Those words stung Naoise.

Vincent went on, "There were specific instructions left. I am not the only one with an important task."

The three of them stared at Vincent. Naoise was going to scream if he didn't hurry up.

Cathal was overcome with curiosity and knew it wasn't the time, but he asked, "Who are the three core Fomorians?"

Vincent, still holding Naoise's hand tightly, said, "They were the three most powerful in Partholòn's army. There was Conann (Ko-Nan), the oppressed. Cethlenn (Kehlen) of the crooked teeth, and then Tethra, the chief of the Fomorians. He was Partholòn's right-hand man."

"I'll kill them," Naoise muttered under her breath with great distinction.

Vincent grabbed her hand even tighter.

"I need you to listen to me Naoise," he said. "I understand your anger and emotions. Trust me, I do. Our next days are extremely important."

Naoise grabbed back his hand and said, "What is needed, Vincent? What can we do?"

Vincent acknowledged the call to action and said to all three of them, "We each have a person to find. If the Core three Fomorians are returning to Tinree Island, then it is imperative we gather the strongest Tuath De Danann here too. I need to travel north; that is where I believe Lugh is residing. We know where Dagda is. All that's left is you three."

Cathal and Foxy looked at each other in total confusion. Naoise knew what he was going to say.

Vincent let go of Naoise and stood up. He looked out the window at the moonlight, too, and said, "I need you three to find King Nuada."

Foxy and Cathal's jaws hit the floor.

"How on earth can we do that?" Foxy asked with the greatest concern "We've only trained for a week."

"Training is cancelled, I'm afraid," Vincent said. "I understand this is a whirlwind of information, but Nuada is residing somewhere around Tinree Island. I need you three to find him and inform him of everything that is happening."

Vincent looked at Naoise. "Naoise, my dear, I'm going to need you to go pack a bag. When she is ready, I will bring Cathal home, then drop Foxy and Naoise off at the Sullivans'. Then I must head North. I could be gone for a long time. Keep your ear to the ground and search the entire area for Nuada, and watch out for the Fomorians."

Naoise ran off to pack a bag. She was crying again.

"Go wait in the car, you two," Vincent said without room for reply.

Foxy and Cathal sat in the back of the car for a long time. It was very late at night now, and Foxy was locking eyes with Fallow. Eventually, Vincent came out of the manor carrying two large suitcases. Naoise, who was visibly shaken, came out behind him. She got into the front of the car as Vincent loaded the luggage.

Once they were all in, they drove and dropped Cathal off. Before he got out, Vincent turned around in the car and said, "I wish you the best of luck, Cathal. I mean that. Sincerely."

Cathal thanked Vincent, then got out of the car and headed to his house.

A short time after that, Vincent drove up the lane of the Sullivans. He gave the house a hefty stare, then got out to unload Naoise's suitcases. Linda and Macdara had now come to the front door, both wearing heavy expressions on their faces. Vincent continued as if they weren't there.

Naoise and Foxy got out of the car. Vincent dropped the bags off at the door and stood face-to-face with Linda and Macdara – his parents.

"Mind her please," is all Vincent said.

180

Linda began to cry. Macdara nodded at his son.

Vincent quickly turned around, walked to Naoise, and hugged her tightly. "It'll all be okay, Ms. Moone. I promise."

Then Vincent turned to Foxy and said, "I think you have a bigger part to play in this story than you realise, boy. Stay sharp."

Vincent shook hands with Foxy for the second time that evening. Then, in a flash, he had gotten into his car and drove off.

Linda was escorting Naoise into the house, holding her in a warm embrace.

"Come on in lad, the fire's on," Macdara said to Foxy.

Linda gave each of them a cup of tea "Naoise, I have a spare room made up for you. If you need anything, dear, please just ask, anytime of the night."

"Thank you," Naoise managed to reply without many tears, "but if it's okay, I think I'll just go to bed."

Linda nodded and showed her the way to the room.

Naoise was so exhausted she never thought to say goodnight to Foxy or Macdara.

"You too, lad. Bed will only do you good," said Macdara.

Foxy agreed. His body was so sore from the training and the fight, he would have slept on a bed of nails.

"We can discuss the Tuath De Danann in the morning," said Macdara to Foxy's utter disbelief.

"You know about the…" Foxy replied, stunned.

He never got to finish the question. Macdara just brushed him off. "Yes, yes, we know. We can chat in the morning. Off to bed with you, lad."

Foxy didn't need to be told again for bed, he went straight upstairs. No sooner was he in the bed than he was asleep, and no sooner was he asleep than he had awoken once again in the lake of Falias, with a soft female voice calling in the warm breezy distance.

"Come, let us speak."

Chapter 13: *Death Over Life*

Foxy sat beside the gorgeous red-haired lady in the still water of Falias lake. Foxy noticed all of the pain from the fight and training had subsided. The woman's waterfall-like dress caught his attention as it refracted in the strong sunlight.

"They have begun to act," she said in a sombre tone.

"The Fomorians?" Foxy asked.

"Yes." The woman nodded. "They have struck and taken two of my children. Tethra is a venomous being. I fear the core three may be heading to Tinree Island"

"To try release Partholòn?"

The woman nodded again "You have become quite knowledgeable, Foxy." She paused and looked across the lake. Far in the distance; the castle of Falias floated by, the town being dragged behind it by the massive chain.

"Tethra, Cethlinn and Conann will have been building their own defences around the land, readying an attack."

She placed a hand on Foxy's shoulder and said, "Sadly, I don't believe you, Naoise and Cathal are able to defeat them when they do come."

"When will they come?" asked Foxy.

"I don't know. They may not come all at once. I just know that they will arrive eventually, and we must be ready to defend Cnoc Mor," she said.

"The only way to do that is to find Nuada," Foxy replied. "That's what Vincent told us to do. He said he's going to find Lugh. How can we start looking for Nuada?"

The woman looked at Foxy, as if she was about to weep. "Nuada was my strongest and most vibrant child, but ever since Dagda and Partholòn became trapped together, he lost himself."

Foxy sat back on his hands helplessly and said, "But if he's lost himself, how can we find him?"

The lady eked out a smirk on her sad face. "I have not seen him for a very, very long time. However, I know he would not have left Tinree Island. He blamed himself terribly for Dagda's sacrifice, and I'm sure has waited there for the day he might be able to save his brethren. However, it has been so long, I wonder what fragile state his mind is in."

"What if we can't find him?"

The lady's face suddenly became very serious. "Then I'm afraid the land of Ireland and everyone in it would be at risk of another violent scourging."

Foxy felt that uneasy sinking feeling he had felt before just before he was about to leave the lake and wake up.

"Please," pleaded Foxy, "where should we start looking? Any clues at all?"

A single tear escaped the lady's eye as Foxy fell down through the water again. The only echo Foxy could hear as he woke up was, "Follow the sadness."

***

He awoke in his bed. The pain from the fight and training was all too real now. He winced in pain as he got out of bed. He could hear noises down in the kitchen, and when he ventured downstairs he saw Macdara and Linda were cooking breakfast. There was no sign of Naoise.

"Morning lad," Macdara said.

Foxy was more concerned with Naoise's current wellbeing than how Macdara knew about the Tuath De Danann.

"Is Naoise up?" asked Foxy.

"She was earlier, now she's gone back to bed," said Linda. "You let that girl have her rest."

"Give us a quick hand outside, Foxy, will you?" Macdara asked kindly.

Foxy obliged and followed him outside. When they reached the yard, Macdara leaned against the tracto, very relaxed looking.

"Let's me and you make a deal, Foxy," Macdara said.

Foxy looked at him, very keen to hear what he had to say next.

"Linda detests all the Tuath de Danann, Fomorian, Cnoc Mor business. Right, she hates it. She blames all of that for Vincent leaving us years ago. So the less said about them the better. Now me, I understand what those Moone folk were trying to do. My family has lived in Tinree Island just about as long as theirs has. Linda ain't from here, though. She doesn't like to think about it. I'm going to have a little chat with Naoise later, too, and I'd like you to be there for that also."

Foxy was stunned to hear Macdara talk so casually about it.

"You see, I have no doubt Aengus Moone has given you and Naoise and that other young fella a task. Probably an impossible task," Macdara.

Foxy went to speak in Aengus's defense, but Macdara cut him off quickly. "Don't worry, Foxy, I won't ask what it is. I also won't try to stop you from doing it. That's what happened with Vincent, and look what happened there. All I ask of you, Foxy—"

There was a deep pause from Macdara and then he said "All I ask of you, Foxy, is that you don't put yourself in danger. I don't think Linda could handle it, if something happened to you."

Foxy went to say how much danger there was involved, about the Fomorians on top of Cnoc Mor, but he changed his mind. He decided just to give peace to Macdara.

"I won't. I promise," said Foxy.

Macdara smiled. "That's a good lad. Now go on, get in and have your breakfast."

Foxy went back inside and had a gorgeous breakfast of crispy fried bacon and homemade soda bread. The morning tipped by very fast, and still no sign of Naoise getting up.

"Should I go wake her?" asked Foxy.

"You will do no such thing," screeched Linda. "That girl is going through a very traumatic time. You will let her rest!"

Foxy felt foolish for asking. The day passed by, and Foxy helped Macdara sporadically, constantly going back inside to see if Naoise had woken up. Each time, Linda would throw him a scalding look.

Foxy, Macdara and Linda were just about to sit down for dinner when a very tired and very sad looking Naoise gently walked into the kitchen. She was still wearing her pyjamas. Foxy couldn't tell if she was about to cry or had just finished crying.

Linda quickly rushed over to Naoise and gave her such a warm, loving hug that Foxy actually felt jealous.

"Oh hello dear," Linda said. "Sit down, and we'll get a bit of dinner for you. You only have to eat what you want, okay?"

Naoise nodded like a wounded puppy. Linda led her to a seat at the table.

Foxy looked at her with complete empathy. His initial reaction was guilt for wanting to wake her up. If he could have it his way, he would let her sleep for a month. Naoise's eyes were blisteringly red from crying and rubbing them.

Linda placed a small bowl of soup with some fresh baked bread in front of her.

"Thanks," said Naoise in little more than a whisper.

"Eat as much as you like, Naoise, but don't feel like you have to eat it all," Linda said with a gentle hand on Naoise's shoulder.

Foxy looked at Naoise, who hadn't yet made eye contact with him. When she looked up, he wasn't quite sure what to say. He eventually reached his hand out and rubbed her arm; he smiled at her and said, "The bread is really good dipped in the soup."

Her reaction made Foxy's heart swell, as through Naoise's raw eyes and exhausted face, a smile crept out. Naoise then took a slice of bread, spread a thick layer of butter on it, dipped the bread into the steaming vegetable soup and took a bite out of the bread. You could see the hot and hearty food warm Naoise inside as if someone had given her a loving hug right to her stomach.

The four of them then shared a conversation-light dinner. Naoise didn't eat all of her bread and soup, but she did eat enough to feel full. They spoke about meaningless things to best try to distract Naoise from the recent trauma. At the end of the dinner, Linda began to clean up the dinner table. Macdara went back towards the yard through the kitchen back door. He turned back to the kitchen.

"Foxy and Naoise, could you give me a quick hand in the yard, please?"

Naoise was most certainly not expecting this request, and it showed on her face. Foxy quickly jumped in, "We'd happily help."

Although Foxy knew there was no way this chat Macdara had planned could go pleasantly.

Foxy handed Naoise his jacket, which she put on and looked quite comical in with the large jacket over her pyjama's. She placed on a pair of large wellies near the door, again to Foxy's delight. Naoise took a look at herself and let out an endearing chuckle. Foxy laughed with her.

"I think I found next year's Halloween costume" Naoise said.

"I ended up being quite fond of mine," Foxy quickly replied.

"I'm glad" Naoise said. "I had planned on those outfits for a while. I had to get Cathal's late in the day to match ours."

"That was a very kind thing to do," said Foxy.

They both walked out into the yard. Macdara led them both to the spot where he'd spoken to Foxy earlier.

Naoise and Foxy hopped up on a fence near where Macdara was as the sun drifted behind the mountains.

Macdara turned to both of them, and, wearing his best sympathetic face, he said, "Naoise, I'd like to ask a favour of you, if that's okay?"

Naoise, who had been smiling looking into the wild roaming hills which were fading from sun-kissed to black turned back to Macdara.

"You want me to not talk about my parents in front of Linda?" She said with an unenthusiasm-ladened voice.

Foxy couldn't believe her response. How could she have known that's what he was going to say? She had only met Macdara for the first time the day before.

Macdara was smiling. He reached deep into his jacket, into what looked like a secret compartment, and took out a pipe, nonchalantly packing it with tobacco and taking a match to it. Foxy had never seen Macdara smoke. He had never smelled it either.

Before Macdara took a puff from the pipe, he looked back towards the house to see if the kitchen was empty. He saw Linda had left the kitchen, he took a couple of quick puffs in succession and blew the smoke out into the thinning night air.

"Very wise, Naoise," Macdara said, smiling.

Naoise actually smiled back.

Foxy felt very left out. It was as if there was an unspoken conversation going on between the two of them.

"I didn't know you smoke," said Foxy to Macdara.

Macdara took another few puffs of the pipe and then tossed the tobacco out and stored the pipe again deep in his jacket pocket.

"I stopped smoking six years ago" Macdara said to Foxy's bemusement, but Naoise was apparently ahead on the conversation as Macdara continued,"Linda truly believes in her heart of hearts that I quit smoking six years ago. The truth is I never stopped. I sneak a few puffs every now and then, and we both get on quite happily. The reason I'm telling you this is because much like this pipe. I want this conversation to be a secret between the three of us."

"You have my word," said Naoise.

Foxy also agreed as Macdara sat down on a nearby haybale.

"Naoise," Macdara said calmly, "how did you know what I was going to ask?"

Naoise looked down as she kicked her hanging legs back and forth on the fence. "Vincent spoke about you a lot," she said gently.

Macdara's smile slowly drained away from his face.

"He used to tell me how you and Linda hated us. How you hated my parents."

Foxy was looking between Macdara and Naoise. He quickly realised this conversation had very little to do with him, so he knew it was best for him to stay quiet.

Macdara looked earnestly at Naoise, not as an adult talking to a child, but with that look in which they were on the exact same level of authority.

"I did hate them, Naoise," Macdara said, "and so did Linda."

Naoise knew this was coming, and both her and Macdara seemed ready and gunned for an argument.

"We both blamed your parents for Vincent running away."

Naoise responded angrily with, "Vincent chose to help our family; he was never made do anything."

Macdara help his hands up and said, "I have conceded that I will never truly understand what happened. Why a happy, young, intelligent fella would leave his family, his house, and his gorgeous girlfriend to run off and become a butler." There was venom at the end of Macdara's sentence, but he tried his best to contain his anger.

Naoise retorted quickly, "Vincent felt like he had to come to us. He felt like he owed a debt."

Macdara's voice rose sharply, "He owed *us* a debt, we raised him!"

Naoise stood her ground firmly and replied, "He felt the debt he owed my family was greater!"

Macdara remained seated, but Foxy could tell his feet were beginning to mount pressure on the ground, as if he was going to burst into a rage.

"What debt is greater than life? That's what me and Linda gave him," Macdara said, holding back as much anger as he could.

Naoise didn't respond immediately. She was thinking. She looked back at the hills and said in a low voice "Death"

Macdara's anger and stance rescinded quickly. "What did you say?" he asked.

"Death," Naoise stated again. "Death owes a greater debt than life."

Foxy was looked at Naoise more in a confused state opposed to Macdara's awed state.

"Do you remember my older sister, Evanna?" Naoise asked strongly.

Macdara seemed as if he was kicked by a mule over this question "Of course I do," He responded abruptly.

Foxy never knew Naoise had a sister. He had never seen her, although when he thought back he had seen a family painting in Tryst Manor with two girls in the painting.

"Do you remember how she died?" Naoise asked.

"It was a car crash. She was cycling home and got hit by a drunk driver," Macdara said with full certainty.

Naoise's response was heavy and sure. "No," she said, "She was killed by a Fomorian. Six years ago."

Foxy almost fell off the fence.

"What?" Macdara said, exasperated.

"You were right," Naoise continued, "she *was* cycling home. As she was cycling up towards the woods, there was a Fomorian standing in the middle of the road. Evanna knew the danger right away. Evanna's powers were amazing. She would freeze things with her hands, but before she got a chance to fight the Fomorian, he attacked her. He knocked her off her bike and began assaulting her."

Both Foxy and Macdara were enthralled by this story.

Naoise continued, "Evanna was such a beautiful girl. She minded me so much growing up. My Mother and Father were gone a lot of the time. My earliest memories are of Evanna, make little ice statues for me. In the Summer when it was hot, Evanna would make ice and I would blow it across the garden to made snow in the sun. My parents were there too. When I think about it, it's probably my favourite memory."

Foxy could tell Naoise was beginning to feel emotion again, but he noticed how well she held it at bay.

"What happened Evanna?" asked Foxy politel.y

Even though Naoise herself assumed she had none left inside her, a single tear leaked out onto her face. She looked up at Macdara. Foxy was sure if she had more tears, they would be bursting out of her.

"They never blamed Vincent," Naoise shouted. "Not Once! And neither did I."

Macdara was literally too stunned to speak, in the midst of confusion and anticipation that he may finally find out why his son left him all those years ago.

Naoise spoke again and, "It was never his fault, it was just…" She stuttered to get the words out, "it was just a horrible accident."

Naoise held her hands to her face to try hide her raw eyes, trying to wretch out tears.

Macdara asked calmly, "What wasn't his fault?"

Foxy was also in the depths of curiosity to find out what happened.

"After the Fomorian attacked Evanna," Naoise said, regaining her composure, "she tried fighting him off, but he had wounded her badly in the stomach. The Fomorian attacked her again. While they were fighting on the road, a car drove by. To the car driving by, it looked like a man was attacking a woman.

They slowed down to stop. It was Vincent's car. He was with his girlfriend at the time. Vincent stopped the car immediately. When he got out, the Fomorian screamed at Vincent to get back in and leave. His girlfriend also encouraged him to get back in. 'We're only playing,' the Fomorian said, as he held his hand over Evanna's mouth." Naoise choked out a dry cough.

"Vincent knew what was happening, but hesitated, got back in the car and was beginning to drive away when Evanna got her mouth free and screamed for help. Vincent's car then screeched to a halt hearing the scream. His girlfriend tried to hold him back, but he got out anyway and went to his boot and got a hurl.

"Vincent sprinted back down the road to where the Fomorian was attacking Evanna on the ground. Before Vincent got there, Evanna was on her back, face-to-face with the Fomorian. She had got both her hands on either side of the Fomorian's face. She used what power she could muster and froze the Fomorian's head solid. Vincent couldn't see exactly what was happening; he was just trying to protect her."

Naoise's voice suddenly went very cold. "At the very moment Vincent reached them and swung at the back of the Fomorian's head defending Evanna, the Fomorian's head shattered from the frost. So Vincent's hurl swung straight through and missed him... instead hitting and killing Evanna."

Foxy was stupefied, he had no words. He looked over to Macdara to find a startling sight.

Macdara was crying. He was caught between fighting the tears and letting them out.

Naoise continued, "Vincent knew who Evanna was. Stricken with guilt, he carried her to Tryst Manor. He instantly blamed himself, and I don't believe he ever really stopped. He always said if he'd gotten out of the car the first time... My Father always told him, 'If is a wonderful word for dreamers, but it has no place in reality.' It was that day that Vincent swore to repay the debt he believed he owed my family. My Mother and Father loved Vincent very dearly. So do I."

195

Macdara was wiping his tears away with his leathery, worked hands.

"Why didn't he ever tell me?" Macdara wept.

"I assume he felt too guilty about what he deemed to be his own mistakes," Naoise replied.

"I would have understood. He came back and told me about the Tuath De Danann and Fomorians, but he never mentioned Evanna. I would have understood, wouldn't I have, Foxy?" Macdara's saddened face turned toward Foxy.

"I'm not a bad Father, am I?" cried Macdara.

Foxy had never felt such gut-wrenching sympathy for someone.

"No, you're not," said Foxy.

"I agree," said Naoise. "It would take a good Father to raise someone as honourable as Vincent."

Macdara cried heavily.

"Mr. Sullivan," said Naoise, "I understand you and your wife's disdain for my family, but please know that my family only ever had the highest respect for yours."

Macdara looked in awe at Naoise.

"Should I tell Linda?" he asked, seeking genuine help.

"Perhaps," said Naoise. "You could go have a private talk with Mrs Sullivan. Then tomorrow we can wake up and let us not allow guilt to reside in us and move forwards."

Foxy couldn't believe how eloquently she was speaking. This was a great deal of maturity he had not seen from her before, although he knew that the death of one's parents created a great deal of maturing.

Macdara nodded. "This will be a hard conversation," he said, and he walked inside.

Naoise and Foxy sat out on the farmyard fence in the moonlight.

"I'm so sorry, Naoise," said Foxy.

"I know. It's okay; I'm sorry too."

The two of them looked up at the dark rolling hills lit dully by the moon.

"I will grieve," said Naoise, "but I feel wallowing in sadness would not honour my sister or parents. Vincent gave us a task to stop the Fomorians. I believe completing that task is the way to honour them."

"Right. Together, I think we can do anything," said Foxy, placing his hand gently on hers on the fence. She looked at him and smiled in the lunar shine.

"I actually got a clue," said Foxy.

Naoise looked at him, perplexed. "Really?"

"Yes, a woman in a dream told me," Foxy said.

"Ah, I have seen her too. Last night, in fact," Naoise said.

Foxy had now confirmed in his head that this woman had visited he, Cathal and Naoise.

"What did she say to you?" Foxy asked.

"She just comforted me. She held me while I cried. What clue did she give you?" replied Naoise.

"'Follow the sadness.' She said we should follow the sadness," said Foxy.

"Ironic," said Naoise. "That's what I thought I should be running away from. Perhaps I *will* take some time to grieve. You go to school next week. I will take the week to reconnect. Then we can see where we are"

Foxy understood this rationale. Maybe the woman meant that by Naoise embracing her sadness there would be another clue to Nuada's location. All they could do was hope. Exhausted, they both went to bed and heard Linda crying all night.

Chapter 14: *The Forlorn King*

The next week of school was monotony incarnate for Foxy. The morning after Naoise, Foxy and Macdara's heavy chat, they never spoke about the Fomorians. It was a trend that followed throughout the week, and further on. Linda had a brave face on the next morning. In typical Irish fashion, she pretended nothing was bothering her and busied herself with chores.

Naoise dedicated her week to grieving in an effort to follow the advice of the woman in the lake. She sat out in the farmyard with the animals for long periods of time, helped Linda with housework where she could, and helped Macdara with the sheering of some sheep. As the week continued Naoise's sleep improved drastically, which reinvigorated her youthful, pretty face. Her eyes no longer looked dry and sad. Instead, they started to carry the sweetness and fullness Foxy had noticed the first time he saw her.

Naoise was still grieving in her own time. Foxy was quite content to allow her to grieve, and he would go to school for the week. Naoise and Foxy would chat each evening about their respective days, and whether any clues surrounding "follow the sadness" had appeared. While Naoise spent her time at home during the week helping Linda and Macdara, Foxy went to school as normal.

On Monday morning, he walked into the kitchen to a strange sight. Linda was sitting down having a cup of tea. He did not know this woman to ever be sitting down. When he peered around the corner in the kitchen, Naoise was actually cooking breakfast.

"Good morning dear," Linda said cheerfully as she sipped her tea.

"Good morning Linda," Foxy said. He then turned to Naoise. "Good morning Naoise."

"Shusssshhhhhh," Naoise quickly whipped back "I'm in the zone."

She was trying to manage about four pans in the one go. There was a strange aroma of burnt smoke and eggs at the same time. Linda smiled and laughed. This was a very different sight in this kitchen, as Linda's cooking was meticulous and mess-free. Naoise's cooking seemed to be more of a disaster relief area.

Foxy sat down at the table beside Linda, who whispered to him in quite a strict tone, "Whatever that girl serves you, you'd better say how much you like it."

Foxy smiled. "Smells good, Naoise," he said, winking at Linda. They both shared a content smile, and Foxy knew that Linda was going to be her normal lovely self while Naoise stayed there.

After a few flames, wild hot oil splashes, and a split pot of tea. Naoise served up breakfast.

She placed a plate down in front of Foxy. He felt special that she gave him his food first before Linda. The breakfast was made up of one piece of burnt bacon, one piece of seemingly raw rasher, and two sausages that looked okay to Foxy. There were two eggs that looked like they had been hardboiled then whisked, and two puddings but Foxy couldn't tell if they were black or burnt white. There was a grilled tomato that had the edges burnt off, and a few bits of smoking toast.

"Voila," Naoise said, happily grabbing a plate of the same for her and Linda.

Without thinking twice, Linda tucked in straightaway, biting a sausage "Oh it's lovely, Naoise," she said.

Foxy, following suit, did the same, except he went for the pudding, which was like hardened turf, but he put his best face on and convinced Naoise he was enjoying it. "Oh that's really good, thank you so much, Naoise."

Naoise looked thrilled; she was in need of a good feeling.

Macdara then burst in through the door in and looked at the mess and smoke surrounding the kitchen. Just as he was about to speak, Foxy cut him off, "Macdara, come try this breakfast Naoise made. It's delicious."

Macdara looked over. He was confused by Foxy's tone, but when he saw Linda glaring at him he knew exactly what the ruse was. Linda was staring a hole through him, and Macdara knew better than to cross Linda when she made that face.

"You know what?" said Macdara. "I will eat my breakfast right after I finish my little bit of work in the yard. I just came in to get a jacket." He quickly looked around and grabbed the first jacket he saw. He smiled at Linda "That does smell tasty though, Naoise, well done!"

Naoise turned back to Foxy, chuffed with herself, as Macdara headed out.

Linda, Foxy and Naoise shared a lovely breakfast. Linda questioned Naoise on her cooking technique and where she'd learned it. To quite literally no one's surprise, Naoise replied, "I've actually never cooked before; Vincent always did it."

Linda winced a little at Vincent's name, but composed herself to say "Well you did a great job."

Foxy looked at the watch "Oh I may go now, actually; I told Cathal I would meet him at the end of the lane."

"Say hello to Cathal for me please," Naoise said.

"I will of course," replied Foxy.

"Go on dear, get going," Linda said. "Naoise and I are going to bake bread and cook lunch. I'll show her some of my cooking techniques."

Foxy knew Naoise would be in great company for the day, and left with zero second thoughts over leaving her there.

"I hope you two have a nice day. I'll see you this evening, Naoise. I'll tell the teachers you won't be in this week," Foxy said.

Naoise smiled sincerely at him. "Have a nice day, Foxy."

He smiled back, grabbed his coat, and left out the door.

Foxy and Cathal walked to school together that morning, and Foxy brought him up to speed on everything he had learned over the previous weekend, including the clue, the tragic story of Naoise's sister, and Vincent's debt to the Moones.

"So that's why he works up there," Cathal said morosely on the walk to school. "I kind-of feel bad now for what I said about him during training."

"I don't remember you saying anything about him during training?"

Cathal replied, "Oh I said some things you couldn't repeat, but they were said to myself."

They both shared a quiet laugh as they walked. The last bit of warmth was leaving the air as undoubtedly Tinree Island was winter-bound. There was the emergence of a biting breeze. Foxy wondered how Vincent was faring on the North Coast; he figured it must be far colder up there.

Foxy and Cathal discussed the entire situation before they arrived at school.

"Please don't let Connor Sweeney be outside the school today," Cathal said as they approached. the school on the Monday morning.

"Me too. I don't think I have the mental space for him and his idiot friends today," Foxy replied.

No sooner had he said that than Connor Sweeney and his entourage of goons emerged as Foxy and Cathal turned the corner. Connor Sweeney had some distinct markings on his face from the fight. Foxy locked eyes with him immediately. Connor Sweeney also upset to see him, too. Foxy actually thought he looked exhausted.

Foxy and Cathal paused, looking at the large group and anticipating another physical encounter or some verbal abuse. Connor Sweeney looked remiss, and had consigned to do nothing until one of his smaller friends shouted, "There they are Connor! Go on."

Connor looked disgusted to hear this. He now knew he had to act, as his friends had instigated it. He made his way towards Foxy and Cathal. The two parties stood outside the school, with Connor's friends cackling like hyenas, trying to encourage him to fight. Cathal and Foxy stood strong and silent. In a whirlwind of shouting and screaming, Mrs. Finnegan sprinted out the school gate.

"Mr. Sweeney! Mr. Fox, and Mr. Lowry! Inside, now," Mrs. Finnegan screamed.

Her face was curling as if she was trying to restrain emotion from something sour. Her shouting drew attention from all students and general passersby of the school. She lowered her voice but gritted her teeth and said, "My office now! If I hear one word back, I will have you expelled! Do you hear me?"

Cathal went to speak, but she cut him off again in anger, "Were you about to speak? Did you not hear what I just said?"

Cathal looked flustered and confused. Foxy placed a hand on his shoulder to console him, and then they walked alongside Mrs. Finnegan. Connor Sweeney skulked along beside them, his friends jeering as they walked by.

They followed Mrs Finnegan into the building and down into a small office. There were three chairs across from hers, which sat behind a standard office desk. She stormed into her seat and looked at the three boys, who were standing.

"Are you all that stupid?! Do I have to tell you to sit down?" she bellowed. The woman was seething with rage.

Foxy and Cathal tentatively sat down. Connor aggressively pulled out his chair and slumped into it. He dragged it as far away from the other two as he could and stretched out in the chair.

Mrs Finnegan stared a hole clean through him. He stared back, showing her complete disrespect.

"What's this rubbish about, Miss?" Connor Sweeney asked indignantly.

Mrs. Finnegan was askew with the disrespect, her eyes laser focused on Connor.

"This rubbish, Mr. Sweeney, is about a call I received late at night on Halloween, that there was a brawl with school students who were drinking, smoking, damaging property and having a full-on riot outside the restaurant like common hoodlums!" Mrs Finnegan roared.

"Ah, we were only messing around, Miss," said Connor.

"No we weren't," Foxy said quickly.

Connor looked at him, outraged, and said, "Ah, don't be a rat, man. Sure you know we were only messing around, don't you?" He then slapped Cathal on the back.

Cathal took the hit and kept looking forward. Mrs Finnegan's eyes turned to Foxy.

"Mr. Fox, the video of the event I saw…" she said, and Foxy's heart sank. He knew people had recorded it, but everything had been so hectic since then that he really hadn't thought about it.

She continued, "The video I saw did not show what happened before or after. All I can see is you two and Ms. Moone fighting this fool and his friends."

Connor rolled his eyes, and she turned back to the Foxy and Cathal. "What I need to know from you is exactly what happened and why this broke out."

Foxy went to speak, and he had every intention of telling her everything. He felt no code of conduct when it came to Connor Sweeney about not telling tales, but before he spoke Cathal interjected.

"It was just a misunderstanding. Everything was alright in the end," Cathal said lowly.

Mrs. Finnegan looked stunned at this reply, as did Connor.

"Mr. Lowry, are you telling me that this buffoon had no part in starting that whole fight?" she said, pointing at Connor.

Foxy's jaw dropped looking at Cathal. "That's right, Miss. It was just a misunderstanding between all of us, but it's over now."

Connor smiled.

"Right," said Mrs Finnegan. "You two, out, and I advise keeping your heads very much below the radar, or else this might become a more serious conversation."

Foxy and Cathal got up to leave. Connor Sweeney joined them.

"Sit down, Mr. Sweeney" she said.

Connor turned back in surprise. "You heard I did nothing?"

Mrs Finnegan's lip curled "That was in relation to the fighting, but in regards to drinking and smoking and more disrespectfully the way you spoke to me this morning, you are staying back to discuss a suspension!"

Foxy and Cathal left the room only to hear mumbled complaints from Connor.

"Why didn't you let me tell?" Foxy asked.

"He's my issue. He's been at me, and the whole thing in the restaurant started because he was at me, so I just want to let it die. If we tell on him, it'll be worse for me. You're big and strong; you can fight him off. One day, though, he'll get me by myself and, well, it won't be very fun," Cathal said solemnly.

Foxy understood where Cathal was coming from immediately, and once again was overcome with guilt. This was a feeling Foxy had felt a few times recently, when his decision could have come out poorly for someone else.

"I'm sorry, Cathal," Foxy said, "I wasn't really thinking about that."

"It's okay," Cathal said, cheering up. "If it's okay, I'd much rather forget about Connor Sweeney for a while and try and find Nuada! Let's focus on the clue"

Foxy was glad to see Cathal cheered up, and agreed that checking the clue was the best place to start.

The rest of the day went by uneventfully, and the walk home was pleasant, albeit cold. The conversation between Cathal and Foxy all day led them to finally understand that they had no idea about where to actually start looking for a clue.

"What about sad old people?" Cathal said as they approached the turn-off for the Sullivans' lane "Maybe Nuada looks like the Fomorian did on top of Cnoc Mor, and he's just an old man?"

Foxy pondered on this. "Maybe so, but there are a lot of old people in Tinree Island. How would we find out?"

"Beats me," Cathal exclaimed.

They agreed to explore the idea further tomorrow. Foxy went in and recounted his day to Naoise, who was most pleased to hear about Connor Sweeney's suspension.

That evening, Foxy, Linda and Naoise all worked together making a beef casserole while Macdara had an especially long sleep on the couch.

Foxy was amazed to see how much better Naoise had gotten at cooking in a single afternoon with Linda. There was a great buzz about Naoise again. The casserole went down a storm and they all had a nice, drama-free evening.

The next two days went by in a blink. Cathal and Foxy procrastinated on the clue and never really explored any ooptions other than he may be an old man. It wasn't until the walk home from school on Thursday that Foxy invited Cathal in for dinner. Naoise had been doing a lot better, and he reckoned she would be up for the company. Since the death of Naoise's parents, the whatsapp group had essentially been radio silence, so Cathal really wanted to speak to Naoise, and Foxy was sure the feeling was mutual.

When Cathal entered the house, Naoise saw him and greeted him with an immensely tight hug. He hugged her back.

"How are you Naoise?" he asked gently.

"Oh, I'm all the better for seeing you, my friend," Naoise said earnestly.

The three made their way into the sitting room. Macdara was outside working away, and Linda was preparing dinner. The three friends exchanged niceties and revelled in Connor Sweeney's suspension before getting down to business.

"So Cathal," said Naoise, "Foxy says you think Nuada may be an old man?"

Cathal nodded.

"It is possible," said Naoise, "209ut it's also possible that he's like Fallow or Morrigan, and could be any animal or insect!"

Foxy just realised he never thought about Fallow and Morrigan, so he asked, "What are they doing now?"

Naoise smiled. "Oh, Fallow is guarding Tryst Manor, and Morrigan has been here most evenings. She sits with me in my room."

Foxy was taken aback, he couldn't imagine Linda being pleased with a crow inside her house, never mind a crow that is actually an ancient being. However, Foxy knew that anything that was making Naoise feel better was a good thing.

"So there's no way of knowing what form Nuada is in?" Foxy asked.

"Not exactly," said Naoise.

"Is there any breed of animal that's known for being sad?" Cathal said perking the ears of the other two. "My auntie has a dog who's awfully depressed."

Foxy and Naoise shared a glance, and then smiled at each other.

"Cows look sad sometimes?" Foxy said, more so for feedback than as a statement.

"I suppose," Cathal said, unsure.

Naoise began to snigger. "I don't think we should be looking for sad animals, guys."

"But they do look sad sometimes?" Cathal quipped back.

This sent Naoise into convulsions of laughter. Cathal couldn't see what was so funny. Foxy thought it was a good suggestion, but his heart lifted from seeing Naoise laugh so much.

"How does a cow cry?" Naoise asked in hysterics.

Foxy thought this was the opening to a joke as opposed to a legitimate question and replied, "Moo hoo hoo, like instead of boo hoo hoo."

Naoise nearly fell out of the room laughing, Cathal was laughing now, too. Foxy was so pleased at his joke answer he was smiling ear to ear. Linda popped her head into the room then. She was wearing as honest a smile as a woman could.

"Hello dears, I don't mean to interrupt the fun, but dinner is ready." She gave Foxy a nod just for him as she left.

When she left, Naoise said, "Okay, instead of looking for sad cows, let's think about who may have heard rumours or other things. More clues."

Naoise's eyes then lit up "You know what you should do? You should ask Mr. Jordan some questions about the Tuath De Danann and try to lean towards Nuada to see if he has heard any rumours? He seems to be keen on them; he might have heard some weak rumour or something, and it might help us out to some extent?" she said.

"That's a good idea," said Foxy as a voice rang out through the house.

"Dinner's going cold," Linda called from the kitchen. The three of them quickly scurried to the kitchen and enjoyed a beautiful, hearty roast beef dinner with heavenly gravy and the toastiest roast potatoes they'd ever had.

That night, Naoise and Foxy both walked out to the end of the lane with Cathal as he was heading home.

"So tomorrow we'll ask Mr. Jordan if he has heard anything about Nuada?" Foxy said.

The other two both agreed. There was a car coming in the distance. "This is me," Cathal said.

Before the car got closer, Naoise looked at them both and said, "I want you both to know how much I appreciate you being there for me. I want to let you know I'll do everything I can to try and repay that."

"There's nothing to repay," said Cathal.

"Exactly," said Foxy. "That's what friends do."

Naoise accepted this and politely said goodbye to Cathal as he hopped into the car driven by his very short mother.

When Cathal left, Naoise and Foxy walked back towards the house. The evening was just about in full darkness. Naoise looked at Foxy who was beginning to feel the chill, you could see his breath appear as he exhaled.

"I am very grateful," said Naoise. "You know, since I met you everything has been wild. You have been there at every step; don't think I haven't noticed. I also appreciate what you are doing for my family and my parents."

Naoise looked saddened by what she had said. She also began to look cold – Foxy saw her hugging herself in the cold. He offered a sympathetic arm and placed a hand on her shoulder, she turned into him, hugging him closely. Their eyes locked in the cloudy moonlight. Foxy had a feeling that Naoise was going to lean in and kiss him, but her head never moved. He debated whether he should lean in and kiss her, but his head also never moved.

Then, simultaneously, both their faces were slightly closer together. They had moved at the same time; they both knew they had gone beyond the point of return. Just as they were about to kiss, a large squawk from a familiar sounding crow deterred them.

Both very flustered and no longer feeling the cold, they looked around for the bird when suddenly Morrigan landed on Naoise's shoulder. The bird cawed again loudly.

Naoise laughed. "I don't think Morrigan approves. Maybe it was for the best."

Foxy looked a little stung by this statement. He had fully intended to kiss her, and felt a little shortchanged by Morrigan. Naoise, noticing this look, continued, "Well I mean just until we find Nuada and things settle down."

Previous experiences had Foxy leaning towards prioritising others' feelings, and if Naoise felt the time wasn't best, then Foxy was on board with that.

"Yeah, you're right, Naoise," Foxy said, quickly changing the subject. "So how do you think we should go about asking Mr. Jordan?"

The two continued to chat as they walked back toward the house. Helped Linda clean up after dinner and then went to bed.
••
The following morning when Cathal and Foxy arrived at school, they attended their usual classes. Mrs. Finnegan had taken an aversion to both of them since the meeting with Connor Sweeney; she never asked them a question or looked at them in class. She was treating Cathal as if he didn't exist.

It was the last class of the day when they got to Mr. Jordan's English class. He was discussing a Seamus Heaney Poem, *Mid-Term Break*. Usually Foxy would tune out in Mr. Jordan's class, but the poem today had him firmly paying attention. Mr. Jordan stood in front of the class as he was reading the end of the poem.

"No gaudy scars, the bumper knocked him clear. A four-foot box, a foot for ever year," Mr. Jordan read aloud to a few gentle gasps from the class.

It was a haunting poem, Foxy thought to himself. The idea of death was popping up a lot lately. The ending of this poem gave Foxy chills, and, astoundingly, a sense of guilt. This feeling of guilt that kept encroaching on Foxy when decisions popped up. He couldn't comprehend why he felt guilty over a poem which was about the death of a person he had never even known existed.

213

Before he had time to really process these emotions, Mr. Jordan had called off class. "Right guys, enjoy your weekend. On Monday I want a two-page analysis on *Mid-Term Break*. What do we think the primary theme is?"

The class hustled and bustled quickly to their feet and scampered out the door to make the most of the winterly weekend. Cathal and Foxy looked across the room at each other and silently agreed to hold back. Mr. Jordan had turned around and was cleaning up the board, and didn't notice the two boys staying behind. When he turned around, Foxy and Cathal had snuck up on him and were standing right at his desk.

He was surprised to see the two of them standing there. "Hello boys?"

"Hello Mr. Jordan," Foxy said with a cough. "We were wondering if we could ask you a question?"

Mr. Jordan sat down into his chair behind the desk and replied, "Well of course, is something the matter?"

Foxy and Cathal both shook their heads. "No, nothing like that," Cathal said.

"Basically, since you've told the story of the Tuath De Danann, Cathal and I have become very interested in them," Foxy said.

Mr. Jordan's eyes lit up. "Ah, I'm so glad to hear that," he responded. "They're fascinating aren't they?"

Foxy and Cathal both agreed.

"So what do you want to ask about the Tuath De Danann?" Mr. Jordan said like a gameshow host.

214

Cathal and Foxy looked at each other and realised they should have planned more. Now they were going to have to improvise.

"Well, there's one character we're particularly interested in" Cathal said warily.

Foxy quickly caught on to the direction Cathal had intended, and when Cathal stuttered Foxy took over, "So basically Mr. Jordan, from all the reading we have done on the Tuath De Danann, we think Nuada is really interesting."

Mr. Jordan's face lit up with excitement. "Ah, the King," the teacher said. "A mighty warrior with a noble heart, the bravest of them all with the sword of light vanquishing all foes."

Mr. Jordan began to reenact swinging a sword with a nearby meter stick.

Cathal and Foxy felt slightly cringe for the man, but they were both fond of him, so they let him act out his pseudo-battle. Foxy quickly realised it was time to put an end to the sword swinging.

"So we can't find much specifically about Nuada. We were just wondering if you knew anything about unique about him?" Foxy said.

Mr. Jordan relaxed back into his chair, resting the meter stick across his lap as he put his feet up on the desk. This was a conspicuous attempt to appear cool to the two boys.

"So Nuada was the king of the Tuath De Danann, a brave and honest warrior," Mr. Jordan started. "His home was one of the four great ancient cities of Murias, Falias, Gorias or Findias. I've never read anything that confirmed which one."

"Falias," said Foxy.

Mr. Jordan looked surprised, and Foxy quickly corrected himself, "I mean I think it's Falias from what I read."

Mr. Jordan smiled. "I always thought Findias, but I guess Falias makes sense lore-wise."

"What do you think happened to the Tuath De Danann after they defeated Phartholòn? Did they leave Tinree Island?" Cathal asked.

Mr. Jordan replied, "Well, according to the story, they returned to the clouds they came down from. Once they had defeated Partholòn, the quest had been fulfilled, so they returned to the four cities I would assume."

Foxy and Cathal had gained nothing from this information, and Foxy realised that they would need more to get any level of progression in their own quest. Foxy pressed a little further.

"What if they didn't return?" he asked to Mr. Jordan's intrigue.

"Well, I mean, technically they didn't defeat Partholòn, did they?" Foxy continued, "Since they trapped him in Dagda's cauldron, if you think about it he's only been trapped, not defeated, because wouldn't he still be alive in the cauldron?"

"That's an interesting point, Mr. Fox. I suppose if that were true, then the Tuath De Danann would still be in Ireland," said Mr. Jordan.

Cathal felt that they had him on a path now where they could get some inspiration off him, and thought Mr. Jordan was fully convinced it was just story interest they were after. Cathal knew Foxy wouldn't approve of this gung-ho approach, but he committed to it.

"Mr. Jordan," said Cathal.

Both Mr. Jordan and Foxy looked at him, as he seemed unsure in what he was about to say.

"We were reading an old book about the Tuath De Danann recently, and there was a clue in it that we couldn't figure out," Cathal said.

Foxy leered at him. He suspected Cathal was just going to tell him that one of the core three Fomorians killed Naoise's parents and that they needed to find Nuada so the very real Partholòn wouldn't get brought back to power.

Before he could come up with a decent reason to interject, Cathal said,"The clue said to find Nuada we would have to follow the sadness. If they never left Tinree Island where do you think the sadness could be?"

Foxy was put somewhat at ease, and less worried about Cathal saying too much as he noticed Mr. Jordan was thinking deeply. Foxy now knew Cathal was right to press, and decided to double down on it himself.

"Yeah, like, if sadness was a person or animal, what would it look like?" Foxy said quickly, embellishing Cathal's question.

Mr. Jordan's eyes looked blank, as he was searching internally for answers.

"I'm sorry boys, I can't think of a concrete answer for where sadness might be. There are no really sad places in Tinree Island; it's a pretty happy place all in all," said Mr. Jordan.

Cathal and Foxy were both dejected by that answer. Mainly because it had been a week, and the only thing they had come up with was to ask Mr. Jordan, which led them to nothing.

"Anything else, lads?" Mr. Jordan asked in an effort to wrap up the conversation.

Foxy and Cathal, defeated, just said, "No, Sir," in unison, and gathered their things to leave the room.

As they were walking out, Mr. Jordan said, "Sorry I couldn't give a more concrete answer, lads. Remember, it's just a story. You can make up your part for what happened next." Mr. Jordan collected his briefcase and jacket and was just about to leave when the words he said shot off a wave of excitement within Foxy.

"I really don't know where you would find sadness here. Apart from the giant weeping willow at Cnor Mor, I don't know of any sadness here," Mr. Jordan said laughingly, and left the room between the two boys.

Foxy's mind was racing. Cathal wasn't sure what was happening, but he could tell Foxy was trying to process something.

"Everything okay, Foxy?" Cathal asked.

"You know the way Fallow and Morrigan became animals?" said Foxy. "What if Nuada became something else?"

Cathal raised his eyebrows at Foxy. "Something else, like what?"

218

"Well didn't you just hear Mr. Jordan? What if Nuada became a tree – more specifically the weeping willow? I've been there. It's just before Cnor Mor. So if Nuada really felt guilty about Dagda, he would have stayed there, no?"

Cathal's moment of realisation sank in. "We need to go that tree. But it's going to be dark soon, and we'll need Naoise," he said.

"Tomorrow," said Foxy. "You, Naoise and I will go first thing tomorrow morning."

Cathal nodded, and both boys left the school.

***

When Foxy got home, he found Naoise in the sitting room reading the newspaper by the fire. He quickly sat down and informed Naoise of the plan and she perked up with excitement.

"Well, I suppose if Morrigan and Fallow could morph to a deer and a crow, Nuada could have become a tree. That's crazy to think if it's true we sat there before going up Cnoc Mor for the first time" said Naoise.

Naoise then looked suddenly quite sad, and Foxy noticed straightaway.

"Is anything the matter, Naoise?" asked Foxy.

"Well," said Naoise, "It's just that if the weeping willow is Nuada, and we were there earlier. Had we figured it out sooner, he might have been around to save my parents."

Foxy sat beside Naoise and held her hand tightly. "We can't think like that, Naoise," he said, looking her softly in the eye.

"There's no way we could have known, and we still may be wrong. That's why we have to go tomorrow to find out."

Naoise wiped away an errant tear from her face and agreed. "You're right, Foxy, we have to find out. We promised Vincent we'd try."

Both of them then enjoyed an unusually light dinner from Linda – a chicken salad in winter was a strange choice, Foxy thought.

"Just trying to be a little good; I'm getting a bit roundy," said Linda sadly about the healthy dinner.

"You're in terrific shape," Naoise said defiantly.

Linda looked thrilled with the compliment and replied, "Oh thank you dear. A healthy meal every now and then does no harm, but you are very kind, Naoise."

They smiled at each other while Foxy picked through cherry tomatoes in his salad.

Both Foxy and Naoise slept soundly that night, and awoke the following morning eager and filled with determination. They met Cathal at the end of the lane at 9:00 am. They had told Linda they were going over to Cathal's house. Foxy felt bad about lying, and Linda knew they were lying, but all parties concerned thought it was best to let the lie be said.

Cathal, Foxy and Naoise felt like they were onto something significant as they marched towards the field where they had taken a path to Cnor Mor before.

The talk was light along the walk through the fields "It's nice to be walking beside you both instead of behind you like last time," said Cathal.

Naoise and Foxy smiled. "It's the same feeling for us," Naoise said pleasantly.

As they trapsed through the fields on the bright but cold December morning, the harsh cold of December was not long away. The dewy grass was getting their feet and bottom of their pants wet.

As they trekked across, Naoise said, "So much has happened since we did this last time."

"I know," said Foxy fully agreeing with the point. "And so much more to happen."

Naoise took this as a message of encouragement. The three of them marched on until they hopped a farmer's gate into the last field before Cnoc Mor. There, in the middle of the field, was a giant weeping willow tree.

The mass of branches cascaded down, with the eponymous drooping leaves. Foxy's face lit up with inspiration.

"There it is," he said ecstatically, and he started running toward the tree.

Naoise and Cathal looked a bit unimpressed, but began to jog beside him.

"What's going on?" Cathal asked.

"Don't you see it?" Foxy said.

Cathal shook his head. "See what? The big tree?"

Naoise also looked rather confused. "Sorry Foxy, I don't know what you're so excited about either?"

Foxy laughed loudly and heartily as they ran across the field. "Look again," said Foxy, "How many trees have their leaves in Winter?"

They had just reached the wide berth of the tree when Foxy said this. Both Cathal and Naoise had the same eureka moment Foxy had just moments ago. The three of them stared up at the giant tree and its sprawling branches. Indeeded they were covered in blooming deep green leaves that swung down from branch to branch.

"Wow," said Naoise.

"I've got a question," haid Cathal.

Both Naoise and Foxy looked at him

"What do we do now?" Cathal asked.

Foxy and Naoise now realized that none of them had a further plan on what to do now that they'd reached the tree. They all agreed that there was something unique about the tree, but none of them had any clue on how to possibly summon Nuada.

"We could talk to it?" said Cathal.

"Hello Nuada!" Naoise screamed beside Cathal and Foxy, causing them to wince.

The tree remained still, bar a few leaves blowing in a timid breeze.

"What if you use your power, Naoise?" said Foxy.

Naoise shrugged and began to whistle softly. A larger gust of wind blew up the tree's wide base, ruffling the leaves and branches. It had no effect either besides shaking the tree.

"Eh, guys," said Cathal, "I don't mean to bring anyone down, but maybe it's just a tree. Like, is it possible that it's just unique and it hasn't lost its leaves?"

Naoise seemed a little remiss over this statement. Foxy quickly jumped in.

"Well, let's spend the day here anyway, and see if we can think of anything. I mean we have food and water, so let's brainstorm a while."

This perked Naoise right up. "Yes, exactly," she said. "One of us will come up with something. Cathal sat down under the tree and began to set up their little picnic. They had small sandwiches, a flask of tea, and various biscuits.

As the morning rolled by into afternoon, the three of them switched between having a good time with friends, joking and laughing, to trying to interact with the tree in a multitude of ways. They climbed it, sang to it, pulled off some of its leaves, poured water on it. Cathal even tried kicking it, much to Naoise's dismay.

It was early in the afternoon, the three of them were sitting on a blanket, each enjoying a sandwich, when Naoise suddenly dropped hers and stood up facing out into the field. Foxy turned to see what she was facing. There was an enormous man making his way across the field. Foxy got to his feet, as did Cathal. Foxy recognised the face Naoise made; he hadn't seen it since the day atop Cnoc Mor.

A breeze blew past the giant man towards the tree. Cathal, Foxy and Naoise all caught the stench that was caught in the breeze from the man. The closer he got, Foxy could not comprehend his size. He was well clear of seven foot, and broad. He had long, volumonous black hair. He was wearing what looked to be a massive robe thrown over his huge shoulders. The robe was tattered and scarlet red.

As the giant man walked, Foxy and Cathal noticed that on the ground behind him there were large, grey, dusty spaces where the grass had once been. He was getting quite close to them now.

"What do we do, Naoise?" said Cathal, terrified.

Naoise's eyes never faltered from the approaching man, and she said through gritted teeth, "It's too late to run, I'll protect you."

Cathal and Foxy were frozen to the spot, feeling helpless. The man was very close now. He stopped walking a little distance away from the group. Foxy noticed the grass underneath him was actually dying and decomposing as he stood there. Any of the other grass that blew into him from the breeze decayed the moment it touched him.

"Hello," he said in a foul, deep voice.

Naoise, Cathal and Foxy remained silent.

"My apologies for interrupting your little picnic; I was trying to find a quiet path to Cnoc Mor. I truly didn't expect to meet anyone on my way."

The man looked closer at them, and noticed Cathal looking at the dying grass beneath him.

The man laughed. "Oh don't mind that. That's just the decay and rot. It gets everything eventually; I just speed it up a bit."

Cathal was petrified of this man. He had a different presence than the other Fomorian.

The man then looked at Naoise and his eyes lit up. "Ah," he muttered in a low voice,
"I know who you are. How fortuitous for me."

Naoise's lips were beginning to shape a whistle when the man laughed louder.

"Please, child, don't bother with your wind tricks. I'm afraid they won't help you when you're not on the top of a mountain with a cliff," he said.

Foxy and Cathal were stunned that this man knew so much but Naoise was not. She stared ardently forward.

"I know who you are, Ms. Moone. Do you know who I am?" he growled in his horrid voice

Naoise did not answer.

"You're a Fomorian!" Foxy called across the small patch of grass.

"Yes. My brother killed your parents, Ms. Moone," the man laughed. "Aengus Moone was a very powerful being; it would have taken one of us three to kill him and his incessant wife."

Naoise's fists curled in anger and Cathal gasped in fear.

"Three?" Cathal asked. "Do you mean he's one of the core three?"

The man smiled a wicked smile and spoke directly to Cathal, "That is correct, little man. My name is Conann. Some call me Conann the oppressed. If you know who I am, you must be descendants of the Tuath De Danann, too. I didn't expect to be the first one here, but here we are. I was trying to remain hidden until all three of us were here, but if you three are offering up your lives. I will have to take them."

It happened in a flash. Naoise let out a sharp whistle, which launched a mighty gust of wind towards Conann. His feet didn't move, but it blew his robes off to reveal a bare upper body that made Foxy shudder. Below Conann's neck, most of the massive body had decayed away. Foxy could see bare muscle and clear bits of flesh that had decayed. He was very gaunt around the midriff, with most of his stomach fat decomposed. A strong rib cage sat beneath broad shoulders and long, lanky arms which were missing bits of flesh along the way.

Naoise blew another sharp gust of wind, this one stronger, but Conann braced himself from the wind and stood his ground.

"You need to use the tornado," said Cathal.

"If I do that, I'll pass out," Naoise said. "Plus, there's no guarantee it'll work."

The man grinned "I told you that wind wouldn't work."

He placed his hand on the ground, and a shockwave raced along the ground toward the group. As it raced along the ground, there was a trail of decay and death for the flora it passed by.

The group all dived out of the way. When it reached their little picnic area, there was a small explosion from the ground. They had just managed to avoid it. Foxy looked in pure fear at the trail that was left. Then his eyes moved towards Conann, who placed his hand on the ground again, this time facing Foxy.

Another shockwave flew along the ground, killing all grass and plants above it until it burst out upwards near Foxy. This time he could not get all the way clear, and the force of the blast sent him flying away from the tree.

Conann did the same thing sending shockwaves at the group. He was toying with them.

"I expected more from the daughter of Aengus Moone!" he bellowed.

Every time Naoise tried to whistle, Conann would create a small explosion near her. In no time at all, nearly all the grass surrounding the tree was grey, ashy and dead. Naoise, Cathal and Foxy were all separated and exhausted.

Foxy was losing hope very quickly until he spotted something that filled him with faith. It was the same thing he'd noticed about the tree earlier. It still had its leaves. If everything Conann touched died, why was the tree still very much living? Every other plant in the area had since died. Foxy had an idea.

"The tree!" Foxy shouted.

Naoise and Cathal's heads turned around, both scared but hearing the call.

"Get behind the tree!" Foxy called as he made a break for it, sprinting towards the back of the weeping willow while small bursts from the ground tried to trip him along the way. The other two sprinted from their respective locations, and the three of them hid behind the girthy base of the tree.

"I think we've played long enough!" Conann shouted. "Let's call a halt to this. At least die with some dignity, Moone. Your Father died bravely. Are you telling me you're going to die hiding behind a tree?"

Naoise went to step out but Foxy held her back by grabbing her wrist tightly, she looked furious about that.

"Wait!" Foxy whispered. "I have a plan."

The three of them waited behind the tree. Explosions popped off around the area, causing them to flinch. Foxy got the attention of the other two. "When I say it, hug the tree as tight as you can."

Naoise and Cathal both looked confused, but Foxy didn't have time to explain. "Just do it!"

Both of them nodded

Conann shouted out, "Okay Moone, have it your way. What a feeble way to go."

Conann then placed both his hands on the ground, and the largest shockwave yet shot out at breakneck speed towards the tree.

Foxy heard the shockwave leave Conann's hands and knew it was heading right for them. Right under the tree.

"Now!" Shouted Foxy.

228

Without a moment's hesitation, Cathal, Naoise and Foxy and hugged the tree as tightly as they could, each giving it a broad, tight hug, with none of their arms reaching around it.

Naoise and Cathal both closed their eyes tightly, but Foxy kept his open. He felt the shockwave getting closer, but instead of travelling under the tree, he felt and saw the shockwave get absorbed by the tree. The shockwave travelled up the wide trunk and then carried out into each of the branches, ultimately giving out a celestial glow from the ends of the weeping willow leaves.

Then, in a moment Foxy couldn't believe, the light that had been emitted from the leaves was sucked back into them, and then it reverberated back through the leaves into the branches and down the trunk of the tree again. Once the reverberating light had reached the base of the tree, a wave of light shot out in every direction. This glowing wave of light left a stunning view in its place.

As the light passed through the field, all of the grass that had been decayed by Conann's shockwaves grew green and luscious again. The field was a bright, healthy, grassy place once more.

"I knew it!" Foxy screamed with excitement.

Cathal and Naoise looked around, stunned. They stepped out from behind the tree to see Conann looking astounded.

"I don't understand," he said in a gritty, truly surprised voice.

"What is this magic?" he continued, anger taking over the surprise. "I'll kill you all!" He screamed, and instead of using his hands he began to sprint towards the three teens. He stopped in his steps when the tree began to shake wildly, but there was no wind.

Conann stopped and looked up at it. "What is happening?" he muttered to himself.

The tree shook wildly, twisting and contorting its branches so hard that all the leaves were beginning to fall off. Cathal, Naoise and Foxy stepped out of the span of the branches as they were getting covered in so many leaves that they couldn't see.

Then, to everyone's amazement, including Conann's, the trunk of the tree began to shrink and change shape. The wide branches continued shaking and spinning with the drooping leaves which were now covering the trunk and middle of the tree. The centre of the tree shrank until it was entirely hidden by a mound of leaves.

The tree had completely disappeared. All that remained was a massive pile of weeping willow leaves.

"What a pointless trick," Conann cackled. "All style and no substance. Silly power. It's now time to say hello to your parents. Like the rest of this land, you will decay!"

Conann was advancing on them when a voice froze him in place. Cathal, Naoise and Foxy were all also stunned by this voice.

"Not so fast!" the voice said.

Foxy saw immediately that it was coming from the mound of leaves.

Conann grimaced as from the mound of leaves stood a man who was not as tall but just as broad as himself. The leaves of the weeping willow formed a cape, which attached around the neck of the man. He had long, thick, blonde hair. contrary to the story told by Mr Jordan. He was wearing a very old pair of pants and what looked like chainmail armour.

Foxy, Naoise and Cathal were in complete astonishment. They were right.

"Yes!" Cathal screamed.

Conann stood up firmly to assert his height over this man.

"I knew we'd find you!" Naoise squealed.

Foxy's jaw hung open. There was a palpable power radiating off this man. Then Foxy said, "You're Nuada, aren't you?"

The man turned to Foxy, smiled, and said in a powerful, commanding voice, "I haven't heard that name in a long time, but yes I was once Nuada, the king of the Tuath De Danann, the high warrior and saviour of the land" He turned his eyes toward Conann "And I can be so again!" Nuada roared.

Conann charged at Nuada, re-killing the grass with every step. As he pounced, Nuada struck him with a punch that caused a sonic boom, making Naoise, Foxy and Cathal flinch. The punch sent Conann tumbling across the field. He stood up quickly, relatively unfased.

"Where is it?" Nuada asked himself, looking around. Then he looked down at the remaining pile of leaves on the ground.

"Oh yes," he said, then reached down into the pile of leaves and pulled from it a long, impressive silver sword with a golden handle.

Conann for the first time looked terrified himself. "That sword," he said out loud breathlessly to himself.

He stared at the sword Nuada was holding and saw that the sword was giving off a white glow.

Chapter 15: *How the Mighty*

"I know who you are!" screamed Conann, puffing out his decomposing chest in defiance. The grass and plant life around him were fading and wisping away into dust as they came into contact with him.

Foxy was in optimal reverence from the presence of Nuada. There was an aura of power pulsating off him. An extremely calming presence washed over Foxy as Nuada faced Conann. Foxy looked over to see Cathal and Naoise both awestruck, eyes fixed on Nuada.

"And I know who you are, Fomorian," Nuada responded across the plain with his commanding voice. "What is one of the core three doing in Tinree Island? You were banished by the Tuath De Danann to the west."

Conann quickly stuck his hand to the ground, firing a shockwave toward Nuada, who deftly sidestepped out of the path of the ending explosion. When the ground shot up at the end of the shockwave, it made Nuada's long red hair fly back. Conann grinned while launching another two shockwaves, both of which Nuada easily dodged.

"Banished while the Tuath De Danann reigned, yes. However your kind has long been gone and dropping like flies," Conann growled as his eyes flicked to Naoise, whose heart sank.

"You've been gone for a long time, king," Conann spat.

"Yes," Nuada said, looking forlorn. "But now, I have returned!" he called triumphantly as he leapt from where he was standing and, in a flash, reached where Conann was standing. When he reached Conann, he swung down the blade of light in a lightning-quick strike. Conann was quick enough to shuffle back and get his arm up to defend himself, but his arm was quickly cut from his body.

The severed arm poured a black, acidic substance which melted and burned the grass below. Conann howled in pain as he moved away from Nuada. The Fomorian then collected a series of the acid blood in his remaining hand until it pooled up into a small pile. He then flung it all around Nuada in every direction. Nuada ducked as the bits of blood landed and sizzled away.

Conann stuck his severed stump to the ground, and all of a sudden where all the drops of blood had landed it began to rumble. Instantaneously from each drop of blood that circled Nuada, a shockwave fired out towards the centre where Nuada was standing. The Tuath De Danann king braced himself for impact. Foxy winced as he watched this happen.

A huge, deafening explosion went off, knocking Foxy back, he looked at Conann, who was laughing hysterically.

"I killed the king," he cackled, but then stumbled back over himself as his eyes drifted upwards.

Foxy followed Conann's gaze skywards to see Nuada flying in the air on his back. Although very quickly Foxy realised Nuada wasn't flying, and with the bang from the explosion fading from his ears, he could hear something. It was whistling.

He looked over to see Naoise whistling, then looking back at Nuada. Foxy realised that Nuada was laying on a bed of wind held aloft by Naoise's power.

Naoise's whistle faded out as Nuada was lowered safely back to the ground. He looked back toward Naoise and said, "Thank you, my child."

With his attention averted, Nuada was then sent stumbling backwards when Conann burst across the plain and delivered a significant blow to Nuada's stomach. This caused the sword of light to fall from his hand.

Foxy was feeling uneasy now. Moments ago Nuada had seemed like an untouchable god, but now, twice in quick succession, he had been saved and then struck. Nuada got up to his knee.

"I appear to be a little rusty." Nuada coughed.

"You can do it!" shouted Cathal from a very safe distance.

Conann, who was now invigorated with confidence, marched up to Nuada.

"Rusty? Or overhyped?!" Conann shouted, striking Nuada again and sending him flying across the grassy area where the weeping willow tree had once stood.

Nuada coughed and spat out blood in pain. Conann turned his attention to Naoise and walked towards her. Naoise then whistled loudly, and as hard as she could. A gale force began to rise up from the ground, then the gusts of wind forming into a tornado, and started violently circling Conann.

Foxy, Cathal and Nuada were all shot off in various directions. Naoise whistled with all her might, trying to create the strongest tornado possible. From a distance, Naoise heard Nuada shouting, "Stop! It's not working!"

However Naoise ignored him as she whistled. Inside her head, she started to feel light, and her whistle weakened. It was then that Naoise could see through the waning gusts that Conann was firmly and comfortable standing on the ground. Naoise then collapsed backwards, but remained conscious.

She gasped. "How?"

Conann laughed as he pointed to his feet with his good hand. Naoise could then see that Conann had decomposed the ground below him and amazingly fused to the earth with his feet. He had decomposed part of his feet to merge with the ground. Then, forcefully bursting his feet out of the ground, he created a shockwave that raced toward Naoise, hitting her cleanly.

The blow sent Naoise flying into the air and back down for a hard landing.

"Naoise!" Foxy screamed in severe concern as Conann walked intently towards her.

"It is always a pleasure to end a family's bloodline." Conann crouched down in front of Naoise, who trembled in fear facing the giant Fomorian. "Just like the earth and all living things, the Moone lineage shall die here, too."

Conann then started to move his decomposing grey hand towards Naoise's face. Naoise could feel the rot emanating off Conann's hand. Foxy began to run towards them, calling Naoise's name. Just before Conann placed his hand on Naoise's face, Nuada tackled Conann with distinct force. The Fomorian and Nuada rolled and stumbled away.

The two then rose quickly to their feet. Conann thrust his hand towards Nuada's face. Nuada grabbed Conann's wrist at the last moment, fighting him back. With his free hand, Nuada grabbed Conann's throat and squeezed. The two beings began to try out-muscling each other. Locked in a stalemate, the two were caught in a test of strength, with neither one giving an inch.

Conann's severed arm was dripping black, viscious blood on Nuada's arm, causing his skin to sizzle and burn.

Nuada looked around and made eye contact with Foxy.

"Boy," he called, "The sword!"

Nuada's eyes then darted towards the errant sword of light, which was laying a short distance away. Foxy quickly surveyed the area. Cathal might as well have been a world away, Naoise was frozen with fear and clearly shaken.

Foxy then quickly made up his mind and, filled with determination, raced towards the sword. Conann and Nuada were still locked in their stalemate with neither gaining the upper hand.

Foxy reached the sword of light and grabbed it without hesitation. He was very keenly aware of how heavy it was. He also noticed it was slightly warm. He lumbered the sword up into his hand and began running towards Conann's back.

Conann's eyes flicked away from Nuada, where they had been fixated. His pupils shot to the corner of his eyes as he heard Foxy running behind him. Conann quickly stamped one foot in the ground, and where Foxy was running was suddenly very soft.

Foxy began to slow and stumble as his legs sunk into the earth. Conann had composed chunks of the ground where Foxy was running. Foxy's sank up to his hips. He tried to continue running, but the ground was so dead it was basically mush, with the same consistency as quicksand.

Foxy then had an idea, and decided he had to act on it.

"NAOISE!" he screamed. "Remember your training!"

Naoise looked up from where she was sitting, feeling weak and tired. She looked deeply concerned at Foxy. She was also unsure of what he meant by training. Until she saw what he did. Sinking into the ground, Foxy raised the sword of light and grabbing the base of the hilt. He threw it forward. Under normal circumstances, the sword would have just travelled a few yards but Naoise understood Foxy's plan.

With what strength she had left, she whistled, and just like in training with the balloon she was able to create a bed of wind under the sword and control it. The sword maintained its position in the air.

"NOW!" Foxy shouted as he began to sink totally into the earth.

Naoise then whistled sharply

"Nuada, move!" Cathal shouted from a distance, having observed the entire situation clearly.

Nuada hearing Cathal's call and Naoise's whistle, and he quickly dived out of the way. Conann was confused for a moment, but a moment was all he had left.

As Naoise's whistled sharpened, Conann felt the wind blow past his ears. He felt a piercing cold in his chest. He looked down to see the full blade of the sword of light sticking through his chest. Naoise had carried the sword straight into his heart.

Conann began to fall, the grass dying at his knees. Kneeling down, Conann looked up with the sword sticking out of his chest. "Partholòn" he croaked with his final words.

"Partholòn, I came. The others are coming, too. The scourge will be unleashed."

Naoise then whistled sharply once more, and the sword completed its travel and cleaved its way entirely through Conann. The sword held its position in the air, dripping blood, until Naoise guided it to Nuada, who grabbed it and held its weight easily.

Holding the sword of light, Nuada first walked towards the mushy hole in the ground and easily lifted Foxy out of it one-handedly. Then Nuada walked up to Conann's back.

Nuada raised the sword, placed it to Conann's neck, and said, "Look away, children."

Foxy and Cathal turned their head, but Naoise continued to watch. Nuada looked her in the eye.

"I want to watch," she said through her tears.

Nuada looked sympathetically at her and said "Trust me, no, you don't. Now. I won't repeat myself. I told you to look away."

Naoise closed her eyes and turned around.

Foxy then heard a clean slice, followed by a heavy thud. Foxy then couldn't help himself; sneakily, he tried to turn his head around, but just saw in his own peripheral Nuada throw a ball shape and a body's shape into the hole where Foxy had been sinking.

"Now, children," Nuada said breathlessly. He was clearly exhausted.

"Let us speak."

Naoise, Cathal and Foxy all walked up to Nuada and faced the unusually tired being.

Nuada then collapsed to a knee, and the three rushed to his aid.

Chapter 16: *The Stone of Fal*

Nuada coughed up some blood, panting heavily. He then fell from his knee and layed completely on his side. Laying in the foetal position, Nuada gasped for air.

"What do we do?" Cathal said, severely panicked as nearby the remains of Conann The Oppressed decomposed rather quickly and the dust of his flesh drifted into the air.

"I don't know," Foxy said, also unsure. He looked at Naoise. "Naoise, what do we do?"

Naoise knelt down beside Nuada calmly. Placing a hand on Nuada's giant shoulder, she began to whistle a very gentle tune. A soft, quiet breeze rolled through the grass. It slowed Nuada's breathing, but the king of the Tuath De Danann still grimaced.

"Ancient power takes a heavy toll on the body," Naoise said, rubbing Nuada's arm.

"Remember when I collapsed on top of Cnoc Mor?"

Foxy and Cathal both nodded.

"This is the same thing. I nearly collapsed moments ago. Using power gifted by Danu is hard for a body to contain. It's why the little training we did was so tough. You have to train the power. Nuada had been asleep for a very long time; his body needs to get used to his own power again. At the start of the battle when he easily batted Conann away, that was the *real* power of Nuada. It must have been so difficult for him to hold him away. He really is amazing."

Nuada's eyes closed, and his breathing calmed.

"Is he dying?" Cathal asked, concerned.

"No," Naoise said sternly.

"He just needs to rest a while. We will have to stay with him while he rests."

Foxy also knelt down beside Nuada.

"If it wasn't for him, Conann would have killed us no doubt," said Foxy.

"How long will it take for him to rest? My parents will wonder where I am," said Cathal.

Naoise's eyes were fixed on Nuada as his chest swelled in and out with his eyes closed.

"Cathal, *you* can go home if you want, but I will stay. He saved our lives," said Naoise.

Cathal felt like a fool.

"Well obviously I'm grateful he saved our lives. I was just wondering. Obviously I'll stay," Cathal said sulkily.

"I'll text Linda and tell her we're staying at Cathal's. Cathal, you can tell your parents you are staying at the Sullivans'. We'll stay here as long as it takes," said Foxy.

This pleased Naoise greatly.

The three of them sat down around Nuada to rest their own bodies after the taxing experience with Conann. Being the time of year it was, the sun began to set around 4pm, and the dusky early moon crept into the sky. There was a moment as the sun was passing behind the distant mountains and the moon was blossoming that Foxy looked at the sky and then surveyed his surroundings. It was the first time it truly sank in how beautiful Tinree Island was, and Ireland by extension. He really felt that it was worth protecting.

Thankfully, Foxy and Naoise had brought plenty of food; there was more than enough to cover them throughout the night. Most unlike the three of them, they spoke very little as the evening trickled by into darkness and the cold began to set down upon them.

Each of them put on their jackets, and shared cups of tea from a flask to keep them warm. Naoise laid the picnic blanket over Nuada, who remained unconscious on the ground breathing in and out silently.

"Does it take long?" Cathal asked, taking a sip of tea.

"Does what take long?" Naoise responded.

"For the effects of using the power to wear off?" Cathal said.

Naoise herself took a sip of tea and let out a satisfied, visible breath of air.

"I'm not really sure, to be honest," said Naoise. "I was only out for a few hours, but Nuada has been asleep for a very, very long time."

Foxy didn't speak on the matter. His eyes were fixed upon Nuada. He had a sinking feeling, but hadn't yet asked the question.

"Guys?" said Foxy, drawing their attention.

Both of them gave a sound of acknowledgment, and they awaited the rest of his question.

"I was thinking, Nuada must have been extremely powerful in his day. I mean, we only saw a flash of his strength at the start, and he sent that Fomorian flying," said Foxy.

The others listened intently.

"Even Naoise's tornado couldn't move him, and he's only one of the core three, so we know how strong Nuada is. My main fear is how powerful is Partholòn?"

The words hung in the cold air. It was deathly silent, apart from Nuada's gentle breathing. Cathal and Naoise felt a certain twinge of fear from what Foxy was saying. It was the first time they had thought about it.

Foxy continued, "From what Aengus said, Nuada, Lugh and Dagda were easily defeated by Partholòn. Only with Dagda's sacrifice could they trap him. I mean, what if the other two or three succeed? What if Cethlenn and Tethra actually achieve what they're trying to do and they raise Partholòn? I mean, is there anything we can do?"

The three sat in silence, absorbing the reality that Foxy had presented them with. There was no reason to believe Cethlenn or Tethra were weaker than Conann. If they both arrived now, they would be done for, Foxy thought.

"We can stop them," Naoise said defiantly. "Although I agree. If Partholòn is brought back, we may not be able to defeat him, even with Nuada. That is why it is important to continue the task Vincent gave us. We found Nuada. He will succeed and find Lugh. Then we defend the mountain."

Cathal was just about to speak when he was interrupted by a loud noise from above. He looked up to see what it was. It was a large crow cawing.

Naoise looked up and gave a slight smile as Morrigan landed beside her.

The crow hopped around on the ground squawking loudly until the bird made its way right up to Naoise's face.

"Can you believe it, Morrigan?" said Naoise. "We found him."

Morrigan stopped cawing for a second to look at Naoise emotionlessly. Then, all of a sudden, the crow started screaming and pecking Nuada's head and face.

Panicked and surprised, Cathal and Foxy jumped to their feet.

"Morrigan!" called Naoise as she ran to shoo the bird away from Nuada's face. Morrigan then flew around and kept trying to get at Nuada but Naoise protected him.

In the standoff, Morrigan would trick Naoise with a mid-air juke and then get a peck in on Nuada.
"What is she doing?" Cathal asked amidst the panic.

Foxy was panicking too. He was unsure of whether to step in or not, as he had received a few of Morrigan's pecks before and was wary about getting another.

Before Naoise could answer Cathal, Nuada said, "She is trying to hurt me, and for good reason."

Nuada was laying still on the ground.

Morrigan landed swiftly on Naoise's shoulder and let out a large caw, while Nuada rolled onto his large back and looking at the sky. He took a deep breath and exhaled a mist of vapourised breath from the cold.

Morrigan then leapt from Naoise's shoulder to Nuada's chest. She flapped her wings wildly, looked at Nuada, and was about to peck again until he spoke.

"I'm sorry, Morrigan," he said in a powerfully sullen voice.

The crow leaned in very close to Nuada's face. He looked up at her and the stars.

"I am sorry; I should have never let Dagda do what he did. Partholòn was too strong for us, though. He saw everything we did before we even thought it. The only thing he didn't see was a sacrifice.".

Morrigan cawed back.

"We debated that. Lugh and I discussed raising Dagda and Partholòn again," said Nuada.

Morrigan started cawing loudly as Nuada began to look very remorseful. His lips frowned, and his eyes became glassy.

"We knew we couldn't defeat him. It was Ireland or Dagda. We made the decision to honour his sacrifice. It was not a decision made lightly."

What looked like a very light tear formed in the deep black eye of Morrigan. The bird then sat on Nuada's chest and laid its head on the Tuath king. Nuada gently petted Morrigan. He said through tears, "It's good to see you again, old friend."

Foxy inched closer to where Nuada lay on the ground and looked down on him.

"Are you alright?" Foxy asked.

Nuada then grunted and sat up while Morrigan hopped off him and back onto Naoise's shoulder.

"I think so, my young friend," Nuada said to Foxy.

He stood up then and towered over the three friends. He put his arms on Cathal and Foxy's shoulders while Naoise stood between them with Morrigan looking up at Nuada. His sprits seemed good, but all three of them were very aware of how sickly his face looked.

"It may take me a while to fully recover and gain my full strength back," Nuada said stretching his back.

"Mr. Nuada, Sir?" Cathal asked cautiously.

Nuada smiled and looked him. "Yes, my little brother?" Nuada replied, patting Cathal on the head.

"You said you debated bringing back Dagda and Partholòn. How exactly did you plan to do that?" Cathal asked.

Nuada lifted his arms over his head, stretching his back and neck and also showcasing his impressive large physique, and began to answer Cathal while Naoise, Foxy and even Morrigan listened intently.

"The power of the four treasures of the Tuath De Danann, one of which is Dagda's cauldron. They can be nullified by any of the others. They are paired, you see. My sword can falter Lugh's control of his spear, and his spear can block my sword's light. When Danu created the treasures, she did this in case one of the treasures was ever used for wrongdoings. So much like the sword and spear, Dagda's cauldron and the Stone of Fal are the same. The stone can break the cauldron, and vice versa the cauldron can trap the stone. So without the stone, a true king of Ireland can never be found. We had the Stone of Fal at the time; that was how we planned to break the cauldron, thus freeing Dagda and, by extension, Partholòn."

Naoise then thought heavily and said, "So without the stone, the other Fomorians can't free Partholòn?"

Nuada nodded. "I believe so, but they will be coming here to find it. If they get the stone to the cauldron, I believe this entire land will be in grave danger."

Foxy then raised his hand, for reasons he never knew why. Nuada looked at him, puzzled, and pointed at him, insinuating he was ready for a question.

"Do the Fomorians know where those treasures are?" Foxy asked.

"Well, they know where the cauldron is," said Nuada as his eyes darted towards the shadowy mountain of Cnoc Mor.

"This is why I waited here. My guilt over Dagda overcame me. I stayed here to protect his sacrifice. I fought off countless Fomorians over the ages. Eventually, though, they stopped coming, and in my wait I became a part of the land, as several Tuath De Danann did who became tired."

Nuada then placed a weighted hand on Foxy's shoulder and looked at Morrigan.

"You see, my young friend, we're so tired. We've been here so long. Home has been calling us. We cannot go, as to risk returning home is to risk the scourge of Ireland, which is what we were sent here to protect."

Cathal, now following Foxy's train of thought, raised his hand. Nuada let a small smile creep out and looked at Cathal, awaiting the question.

"So we know where the cauldron is, but where is the stone? As long as the Fomorians don't know where it is, are we safe?" Cathalasked.

Nuada's eyes flicked back towards Naoise.

"Yes. We kept it in Tinree Island, but in a safe location. It has been guarded there for a long time," said Nuada. He then looked at Naoise intently.

"If my assumptions are correct, you are a Moone, are you not" Nuada asked her.

"That is correct, Sir. Naoise Moone," she said as she placed her hand out.

Nuada shook her hand gently and said, "Well the Moones have guarded the stone for a long time, I'm sure your parents…"

Nuada could tell from the sharp reaction on Cathal's and Foxy's face, that something had transpired. Morrigan then cawed continuously.

"Is that so?" Nuada said.

249

Naoise's looked down. Nuada lifted her chin up gently, then gave her a tremendously tight hug.

"I never met your parents, but I vow to you, they did not die in vain. I will avenge them," Nuada said his as he clutched Naoise tightly.

Nuada then quickly picked up the sword of light, glared at it for a moment, then began to walk away from the battle site.

"Where are you going?" Foxy called after him.

"Come along, children" Nuada called back.

"What's wrong?" said Cathal.

Nuada stopped walking and turned around.

"If the Moone parents have passed on, then that means for the first time the stone is left unguarded. Morrigan tells me it was Tethra who killed your parents, Ms. Moone. She also tells me another ally is in search of Lugh. We will await them where the stone is held," Nuada said.

Foxy and Naoise then began walking. Cathal waited behind, still trying to add two and two together.

"So where is the stone?" Cathal asked, annoyed.

As they walked, Foxy turned round to shout back,"The stone is in Tryst Manor!"

The party then marched across the field away from Cnoc Mor back towards Tryst Manor.

Cathal, then feeling dumb for not being able to figure that out, picked up the picnic blanket and ran after the rest of them.

Morrigan flew on ahead into the deep dark night.

Chapter 17: *The Festive Reunion*

The dark sky covered the group as they walked through the fields and made their way back to the road, Cathal was feeling particularly exhausted from the battle against Conann and the amount of walking. Nuada appeared to be returning to strength, the effects of his collapse seeming to have waned. As they climbed over the fence out onto the road, Foxy raised a good point.

"How are we going to get back to Tryst Manor? It's a hell of a long walk from here," he said.

Nuada looked back at the mountain and then at the moon in an effort to gauge his location.

"I know where we are," said Nuada.

He then looked at the three teens and said, "You three go on home for the night. I will make my way to Tryst Manor. Trust me, I know the way. Morrigan tells me her and Dagda's son Fallow is there. I believe I also owe him an apology."

"Are you sure?" Naoise asked, concerned.

Nuada smiled. "Yes I am. You three are to arrive at Tryst tomorrow morning."

Then Nuada hiked up his boots, waved goodbye to the children, and began to jog away into the darkness, his weeping willow cape bouncing in the shadows. Then he was gone.

"What do we do now? I told my parents I was staying at yours'," asked Cathal.

"Then you might as well stay with us. The Sullivans' house is the closest anyway. Linda and Macdara won't mind," Foxy said.

The three then began to walk in the same direction Nuada had previously jogged off in.

"He's not as serious as I thought he would be," said Naoise.

"What did you expect?" replied Foxy.

"My parents had always painted Nuada as a selfish man, but I only felt kindness from him," she said.

"Me too," said Cathal. "When he speaks to me, I find it very calming."

"It's probably because of what happened to Dagda why your parents had a dislike against him" Foxy cleverly pointed out.

"You're probably right." Naoise then looked at the moon. "I wonder how Vincent is getting on?"

The three walked back to the Sullivans'. Being very late, they snuck in quietly without waking anyone. Naoise tip-toed into her room, while Foxy went to his bed and Cathal took the small couch in Foxy's room. It fit him perfectly.
***

The following morning, the three of them met in the kitchen and after a brief conversation with Linda explaining that Cathal's parents were feeling quite sick, and they thought it best to stay here. Linda didn't believe them for a moment, but she was content to let the lie slide as the three of them appeared happy and healthy that morn. Little did she know of the danger that the three teens were in a short while ago.

With a quick good morning to Macdara, they left the house and made their way towards Tryst Manor. It was a very sunny, yet cold, morning. The fresh air was crisp to the touch, and there wasn't a breeze in the air.

As they began to walk Foxy said, "It is such a long walk to the manor from here."

"It should only take two hours," Naoise replied happily, enjoying the morning.

"I agree with Foxy; it's a super long walk. I actually have an idea," Cathal said.

Foxy looked at him, wondering what idea he could have. In fact, it was the simplest idea there was.

"Oh yeah? What is that?" Foxy asked.

"Well, my parents are big into cycling. We have loads of bikes left around the house. We obviously can't use my parents', but I bet there are a few old ones we could take" said Cathal.

"Oh my god, that would be amazing," said Foxy. "We could cycle there in half an hour, and we have to walk by your house anyway Cathal so it works out perfect."

"Yeah it's ideal, and my parents won't be home. They'll be gone for a long ride on a Sunday morning, so we can just get the bikes and go. They'll never even notice them," said Cathal.

Foxy noticed that Naoise looked unhappy.

"I think we could just walk. It's really not that far," said Naoise.

"Are you mental, Naoise?" said Cathal. "We could be there in a quarter of the time."

Naoise was remiss at this comment.

"I just thought it was a nice morning, and we could walk together," she said.

"To be fair, Naoise," said Foxy, "we could be coming back and forth from Tryst Manor quite regularly. Having a bike would be really easy. It seems like a no-brainer to me. I mean, I wouldn't mind cycling to school instead of walking either, and we'll be back in school tomorrow. Cycling would be nice, especially if it's getting cold."

Naoise, who was overwhelmed by all the logical points, let out a loud 'ugh' noise and followed it up with a pouty expression.

"I can't ride a bike, okay?" she said, embarrassed.

Cathal's initial reaction was to laugh, but he fought desperately to stifle it. Foxy then saw Cathal tittering, and couldn't help but begin to laugh out loud at Naoise's lack of what seemed to be a basic skill.

Naoise pouted and said, "It's not funny! My parents never cycled, so they never taught me!"

Cathal now gave up trying to hide his laughter and broke into full-on hysterics. He and Foxy's laughter only grew as Naoise became bright red in the face.

"Stop!" she cried.

The two boys' laughter subsided.

"I just find it funny that you are basically a hero with ancient powers, but you don't know how to ride a bike," said Foxy.

Naoise's embarrassment quickly switched to a smile. "You think I'm a hero?" she said.

Foxy was aware of how pleased Naoise was hearing this comment.

"I mean yeah," said Foxy. "You've saved us twice now. In my mind that makes you a hero."

Naoise smiled at him sincerely.

"You *are* fairly amazing," Cathal said in a tone full of generosity. "Even if you can't ride a bike," he continued, which made Foxy laugh again.

Naoise was now semi-laughing with them, but still seething below the surface about the jabs.

"So, what do we do? I really can't ride a bike," Naoise said seriously.

"I think I have you covered for today anyway, until you learn how to ride a bike properly, Naoise" said Cathal.

The three arrived at Cathal's house, which was a quaint country house with a large shed to the side. The house looked similar enough on the outside to the Sullivans'. Foxy had noticed that most of the houses in Tinree Island – with the exception of Tryst Manor – looked relatively similar.

Just as Cathal had said, his parents were gone.

"Wait there a second, I think I have the best solution for this," Cathal said as he went into the large shed and wheeled out a familiar looking bike.

"That your bike? said Foxy.

Cathal nodded, and then went back into the shed.

Foxy and Naoise could hear grunts coming from Cathal and lots of metal clanging against itself. A few moments later, Cathal wheeled out a bike that took both Foxy and Naoise by total surprise. Cathal started wheeling out the bike and it just kept coming. Foxy laughed, recognising the type of bike it was. Naoise, however was mainly confused, as she had never seen one before.

"Why does the bike have two seats?" asked Naoise.

Cathal laughed while he shoved out the kickstand on the tandem bike.

"This is a tandem bike; it's for two people. So you can sit in the back and let Foxy do all the steering, and all you have to do is pedal," said Cathal.

Foxy smiled and looked at Naoise. "Well, do you think you can manage this?"

Naoise walked over and inspected the long red tandem bicycle. She gave a few contemplating hums as she walked around it. Finally, she turned back to Cathal and Foxy.

"I think it will do just perfect."

Cathal and Foxy were both delighted to hear this.

"Well alright, what are we waiting for? Let's make our way to Tryst Manor," Cathal exclaimed as the three of them wheeled the bikes out of Cathal's short driveway and faced the road towards Tryst Manor.

"Follow me!" Cathal shouted, hopping onto his bike and taking off. Cycling was an area where Cathal felt like he could lead the group.

Behind him, Foxy climbed onto the front of the tandem bike and grabbed hold of the handlebars.

"Only the front handlebars move, Naoise, so you get onto the back seat and hold onto those handlebars. They don't move. I'll steer," said Foxy.

Naoise gingerly sat atop the back seat of the bike and held onto the rigid handlebars.

"Okay, I think I'm ready Foxy," Naoise said nervously.

"Okay, I'm about to go. I'll push off and when I do you just start peddling. You ready?" Said Foxy

Foxy had already pushed off, to a scream from Naoise. Foxy peddled hard to get the heavier bike moving. He noticed it was quite difficult, then he looked behind him and saw that Naoise hadn't started peddling yet.

"You've got to peddle, Naoise!" Foxy shouted back, breathing hard.

"I'm scared," said Naoise.

"It's alright Naoise, I've got you," Foxy said, peddling hard and getting the bike moving.

His words calmed her, and she relaxed into the seat, got her feet on the peddles, and started peddling the back end of the tandem. The relief was instant for Foxy, the stress of peddling alone was gone, and now the cycling felt like a breeze.

They were moving comfortably with the cool breeze blowing against them. Naoise was shielded from the icy wind by Foxy's back.

"See Naoise! I knew it would work," shouted Cathal from a short distance ahead. He looked absolutely exuberant that the three of them were out for a ride.

When Cathal moved forward a little bit, Foxy said to Naoise, "I knew you could do it!"

"Thanks Foxy," Naoise said sincerely. "I want you to know that I've got you, too. You're something of a hero yourself."

Foxy's smiled beamed from ear to ear on the front of the bike, hidden from Naoise's eyesight. He had felt certain feelings for Naoise before, especially the night on the fence, but he was never sure if the feelings were reciprocated. This was the first time he felt that Naoise might like him, too.

The three friends cycled off into the sunny morning on the road to Tryst Manor. It was a moment of pure friendship.

When they arrived at the large gates, Naoise alighted from the tandem bike and reached her hand around the massive, iron-clad post holding the gate up. There seemed to be a release switch, which triggered the gates to start moving.

When the gates were fully opened, Noiase climbed back on the rear of the tandem bike. The three friends then cycled up the long drive. Foxy particularly liked the sound of the bike going over the crunchy, fallen, frozen leaves on the ground. They arrived up at the courtyard of Tryst Manor to a peculiar sight.

Morrigan was flying in circles above, cawing loudly, swooping up and down. Meanwhile below, Fallow the stag and Nuada were engaged in what appeared to be a wrestling match. Fallow had his head dipped and was charging, while Nuada was gripping his sprawling antlers and holding him back. Nuada forcefully pushed Fallow back, his hooves dragging in the loose gravel.

"Come on my boy, you must have more strength than that," Nuada bellowed across the courtyard.

Fallow then crouched really low, letting out a huff so deep the dust rose from the gravel. Then he began to charge down Nuada, who was still laughing. Nuada caught a glimpse of the friends as he laughed. He turned to them.

"Children! Hello, my dear friends!" he shouted.

Foxy saw Fallow's eyes light up when he saw that Nuada was no longer watching him. He increased to a full sprint and was just about to tackle Nuada, but then Fallow was stopped in his tracks immediately. While maintaining eye contact with Naoise and waving at them with one hand, Nuada casually put out his other hand and stopped Fallow dead in his tracks by putting his hand right on his forehead. Naoise, Foxy and Cathal were all jaws agape looking at this, especially since Fallow was a large deer, and he was moving exceedingly fast.

Nuada noticed their shock, and then turned to Fallow, laughing. He then got Fallow in a headlock and rubbed his forehead vigorously like a big brother harassing his younger sibling. Fallow did not look pleased. Morrigan then flew down, landing beside them and squawking loudly.

Nuada let go of Fallow. "We were only playing," he said, then turned his attention to Naoise.

"How did you sleep, child? A rest at Tryst Manor has revitalized me entirely. I haven't seen this place in such a long time."

"I slept fine," Naoise said politely.

"I slept well too," Cathal said enthusiastically.

Nuada looked at him, confused by the outburst, but gave a nod of encouragement. "Good man," he said.

Foxy layed down the tandem bike and walked further out into the courtyard. It was warm in the sun, but the chilly breeze remained.

"Did you find the stone?" Foxy asked.

Nuada's laughed ceased slightly. He gave Fallow a more sympathetic pat on the head.

"Come on out back; there is something I must show you," Nuada said, and he led the way out to the grassy area where their training had been cut short.

They reached the large green area surrounded by the high garden hills, and walked out into the centre of the area.

"I didn't want to show you until you were here. Children, please stand back," Nuada said sternly.

Fallow, Morrigan, Foxy, Cathal and Naoise all stood off the grass as Nuada made his way right out to the middle. He took out the sword of light, which was only radiating a dull glow at the moment. He placed it on the ground and held the handle. As he knelt down beside the blade, the glow began to brighten. The glow off the blade was getting stronger and stronger until it was getting so luminescent that Foxy couldn't look anymore and had to shield his eyes. Through his fingers, Foxy was able to see what was happening.

The brightness from the blade was actually removing the grass, but not in the way Conann had been decaying it. This effect was more so the entire sods of grass being pushed back. Foxy could barely make out what was being uncovered under the earth. Shortly after, a wide area of grass had been cleared.

Nuada called out to them, "Please come over, it is perfectly safe. Have a look."

Foxy and the rest walked over to see what looked like a large, circular, granite area, but when observed closer Foxy could see it was a series of circular stone rings, like the inner workings of a clock. In the middle of the stone rings was a smaller obsidian looking sphere. It was very black, and appeared to be wedged deep into the innermost stone circles.

There were lots of carvings on the stone circles. Foxy couldn't quite make out what they were. Naoise spotted Foxy looking at the carvings and she crouched beside them and traced her finger over them.

"They're Gaelic runes," Naoise said.

Nuada's eyes lit up. "Ah, correct young lady. Your parents taught you well."

"What is it?" Foxy asked.

"An ancient tomb," Nuada said sombrely. "A violent spirit's resting place. When Dagda and Partholòn were trapped, Lugh and I knew we had to hide the stone in a safe place. We knew that even the core three Fomorians wouldn't dare trespass into this tomb, so we placed the stone deep inside here. Then, to always keep a close eye, we began building Tryst Manor here."

Naoise looked stunned. "You built Tryst Manor?"

Nuada laughed "Well, it was no more than a cottage when Lugh and I built it, but it has grown over the centuries into the fine manor you see before you."

Foxy still remained puzzled. "Are we going into it?"

"The stone is safest in the tomb. However, the tomb can only be opened one day a year: the winter solstice – December 21st," Nuada said.

"That's two weeks from today!" Cathal said excitedly.

"Yes," Nuada said sternly.

"I believe the Fomorians now know its location. The descendants may not have the same fear of the spirit inside the tomb, and will most likely risk getting the stone. We cannot allow that to happen. On December 21st, the Fomorians will come. We must not allow them to get the stone."

"How does it open?" Foxy asked.

"See the black sphere in the middle?" Nuada said. "On the winter solstice, the sun shines directly through that at a certain angle, which opens the tomb. I believe the Fomorians may have gotten this knowledge through Naoise's parents before they killed them."

Nuada placed a warm hand on Naoise's shoulder as he spoke. "We must prepare for December 21st; two weeks is not a long time. If we can protect the tomb, without having to go into it, that would be our main goal. We should try avoid going into it at all costs."

Cathal raised his hand again, and Nuada pointed at him.

"Since nobody else is asking, who is the violent spirit in the tomb?" Cathal said worriedly.

Nuada's face lost all elements of friendliness as he looked closely at the obsidian sphere holding the tomb closed.

"A phantom born of pure pestilence. The Fear Gorta," he said with a cold voice.

Naoise looked frightened.

"The hungry man," she said with a chill. "My parents told me he was feared by Fomorians and Tuath De Danann alike."

"Yes," said Nuada. "The collective mourning of famines and unbearable pain created this vile spirit. Before we ever fought the Fomorians, it was Dagda who actually lured the Fear Gorta to the tomb. He had promised infinite food from his cauldron. Once the spirit entered the tomb, Dagda escaped and sealed it. The phantom has been in there since. When Lugh and I placed the stone down there, we never encountered him. Thankfully."

"It's going to be a wild two weeks, isn't it?" Cathal said.

"Wouldn't be the same if it wasn't," said Naoise, smiling.

Cathal feigned a smile back.

"So explain to me again how it opens?" Cathal said.

Nuada rolled his eyes and walked across the stone circles towards the sphere. With each step Nuada took, the stone emitted a gentle yellow glow. Every place Nuada's foot landed, a small glow would appear. Morrigan then landed beside Nuada, and the stone gave off a glow every time her small crow feet moved.

Fallow then walked out next, same as the two before him, and each step of a hoof produced a small glow.

Cathal winced with each step that they took. He had no idea what was happening.

"What's causing the glow?" he asked.

"These are ancient Tuath stones, gifted by Danu herself. They react with Tuath De Danann power. The glow is harmless; it just means a Tuath De Danann has stepped across," Nuada said.

Cathal responded enthusiastically, "So you mean we could have just walked across these stones to find out if we are Tuath De Danann rather than training?"

While Cathal was yelling, Naoise took a step out on the stone, and sure enough the large stone's clock-workings emitted a faint glow with each step. Naoise seemed pleased with herself, although she surely expected it.

Cathal and Foxy stood on the grassy edge of the stones, facing everyone else. Cathal looked scared.

Nuada spotted him wincing and chuckled.

"I assure you, young Cathal, these will not fall. Please join me," Nuada said

Cathal looked at Foxy, waiting for him to make the first move. Foxy looked back at Cathal and smiled.

"It's alright, Cathal, I'm sure it will be okay either way," said Foxy.

Then he took a step out onto the stones.

There was no light. Foxy looked down at his feet to be sure. He saw Naoise's face, and she looked extremely forlorn. Foxy took a few more steps to be sure, but alas, no soft glow emitted from the stones.

Nuada looked stoic as Foxy's heart sank. He now knew he was not the descendant of a Tuath De Danann.

Foxy's sadness was interrupted by sounds of cheering and excitement. He looked beside him to see Cathal stepping around madly.

"Look!" Cathal roared as he stepped around the circles, slowly, then quickly. Each step Cathal took gave off a bouncing yellow glow. His eyes met Foxy's and Cathal was slightly remiss noticing no glow off Foxy's feet.

"Bravo, young sir!" Nuada clapped.

Naoise smiled for Cathal, but Foxy could see that she was also disappointed for him.

"Does this mean I have a power?" Cathal said fervently.

"It does!" Nuada said. "We will discover it together over the next two weeks!"

Cathal jumped up and down, the glow from the stones rising each time he landed. Naoise walked over the Foxy and put her hand on his arm.

"You were the leader when we didn't know, and you're still the leader when we do know," she said to little comfort of Foxy.

Nuada saw Foxy's sadness and faced him.

"Foxy, you may not be a Tuath De Danann, but you have what cannot be taught: bravery and loyalty. I trust you will remain a vital member of this adventure. I sense your part is yet to be played," said Nuada.

Foxy smirked in order to break the awkwardness, but inside he was deeply sad.

"Let us eat," said Nuada, and then he made his way to the manor, followed by Morrigan and Fallow.

"I'm sorry," Cathal said when it was just the three of them. "I just got excited."

Foxy looked at him and smiled. "It's okay Cathal. I would have been excited too. Come on, let's go eat."

Cathal turned and excitedly raced off toward the manor. Foxy slumped behind him, with Naoise walking at his side. She softly held his hand as they walked.

***

Over dinner, they laid out their plans for the next two weeks. The plans were quite similar to the schedule before.

Foxy shared that they must attend school to avoid attention, so the three of them would attend school Monday through Friday, then return to Tryst Manor after school. Foxy feared being made fun of on the tandem bike, but then remembered Connor Sweeney had been suspended, so they should be okay.

They had hoped that Vincent would return before December 21st to aid the assumed battle against the Fomorians. Naoise stated that anytime she contacted him, there was never any response. Nuada reassured them to maintain hope, but that they would plan for the worst-case scenario.

Nuada told them that every day after school there would be training. They would develop Naoise's power, uncover Cathal's, and train Foxy physically. Nuada also told them he would need to train rigorously every day to regain his own strength.

Much to Foxy's surprise, Nuada told them that on December 20th there would be a Christmas party in the manor. He said it was always customary to have a feast before a battle. Regardless of the size of the battle, the feast would always be big.

Cathal, Naoise and Foxy would come up with their usual lie of sleepovers, and all agreed to stay in Tryst Manor the night before the winter solstice.

After a hearty meal cooked expertly by Nuada, the three friends saddled back up on their bikes and made their way home ready for school in the morning.

It would be Naoise's first return to school since the death of her parents, but Foxy was quite sure she would be fine.

Linda was sweeping the front of the house when Naoise and Foxy rode in on their tandem bicycle. She erupted with laughter and joy.

"Aren't you two a treat!" She squealed, calling Macdara to come outside.

He came out from the sitting room and also laughed and smiled. Naoise felt slightly embarrassed.

"A fine bike," Macdara said. "Remember, Linda, when we used to ride one round the island?" He then tickled her playfully.

"Oh, stop it!" she laughed.

Linda and Macdara, who were blinded by memories of their own tandem bike, never actually asked where Naoise and Foxy had gotten it from. The Sullivans, Foxy and Naoise then retired to the house, and not long after they all drifted off to bed.

***

The following morning, after a light breakfast and quick chat with Linda, Foxy and Naoise set off to school on their bike, meeting Cathal at the road.

They cycled on the gloomy morning, light specks of rain spitting against their faces.

"I have a concern," Cathal asked.

"Oh yeah?" said Foxy.

"I know we all kind of know it, but we've never really talked about it. What if we die?" Cathal said calmly.

"I have thought about it," said Foxy. "I just feel like it's something we have to do, you know? Like we have to stay on this path."

Naoise cleared her throat from the back of the bike.

"Let me put it this way, Cathal. If we die, that means we failed. If we fail, everyone is going to die anyway. Partholòn could be unstoppable," she said.

"I guess that makes sense," said Cathal. "It's still a scary thought, though."

"At least you have a power to defend yourself," Foxy said sullenly.

"I wonder what it will be," Cathal said. "I think I'd like a power like yours, Naoise. Controlling fire instead of wind, cause fire is cooler than wind, no offence."

Naoise smirked. "By definition Cathal, wind is cooler than fire." Then she gave a light whistle, and a slight breeze wobbled Cathal on his bike.

"Hey, stop that!" he shouted.

The three laughed as they wheeled down the road toward school.

When they arrived at school, the teachers faked sympathy for Naoise. Some of them were glad to see her back, but more so ambivalent towards her. Naoise was fairly quiet in class, and until Foxy came along she really embodied that loner persona so many thrust upon her.

Foxy, Naoise and Cathal had far bigger things to concern themselves with than basic trigonometry and dissecting sheep's hearts. Regardless, the three of them kept their heads down and struggled through their schoolwork on the first day, eager to see what Nuada had in store for them.

Throughout the day, Foxy was overcome with heavy feelings of being left out. He knew Cathal would be learning his descendancy power and Naoise would be growing hers. Foxy also knew Nuada's nature would be to make him feel important even if he had nothing to do. However, he felt so involved in the events that he knew he couldn't excuse himself.

Monday in school flowed by event-free, and afterwards the three of them cycled off towards Tryst Manor.

The winter air was dense now, and even gripping the handlebars was difficult with the limited dexterity of the frosty fingers they all had. When they arrived outside the Tryst Manor gate, Foxy had a deep, sickening feeling in his stomach. Naoise noticed something was the matter.

"Are you okay, Foxy? she asked while getting the release switch for the gate.

Foxy was a little stunned by this, as he wrongfully thought he was hiding his nerves.

"I'm fine. I guess I'm just a little worried about what I'm going to do," Foxy replied.

"I know what you're going to do," said Naoise.

"Me too," said Cathal.

Foxy looked at both of them, bemused.

"What's that?" asked Foxy.

"Your best," Naoise said, smiling.

"Exactly! You never do anything less!" Cathal reinforced her point.

Foxy tried his best to maintain his composure, but his nerves washed away and were replaced with a lump in his throat so large and filled with gratitude that he knew if he spoke he would cry. This was the last time Foxy felt that he may not be included, and he quickly returned to true form. He was keen to get back on board and find out what the next two weeks were going to be like.

Foxy eventually swallowed the frog in his throat and eked out the words, "Thank you, you guys."

The three shared a sombre moment before cycling up the path into the courtyard. They arrived in the yard, left the bikes, and walked towards the back area, where the Fear Gorta's tomb entrance was.

As they walked across the grass towards the large circular stones, they could see Nuada sitting cross-legged right in the middle, basking in the dying sunlight. The dark early evening would set in shortly. Foxy noticed that there was no sign of Morrigan or Fallow.

They approached Nuada, who looked extremely content as he faced the sky with his eyes closed. He heard them step onto the stones and gently opened his eyes. Cathal and Naoise's steps gave out a gentle, resplendent glow while Foxy's remained standard. Foxy was unfased by this and gave a friendly wave to Nuada, who responded with a wave, although he remained seated.

"Hello children," Nuada said in his usual, powerful yet friendly voice.

They all greeted him back.

"Why are you sitting out here? It's freezing," Cathal said.

Nuada laughed.

"Being able to feel cold is a sensation I've not had the privilege to feel in a very long time. Feelings are a privilege, children. Never forget that," Nuada said.

Foxy always remembered those words.

Nuada took one more gaze at the sun and stood up, towering over the three of them.

"Today, I am feeling very wonderful. We are approaching Christmas – Nollaig Shona. The history of Christmas is to celebrate it by hanging mistletoe and joining together to ward off evil spirits. You all being here has filled my heart with joy," Nuada said.

Foxy was aware that Nuada was being more sentimental than usual, and had a feeling that something was occurring.

"Anyway, enough time for festivities the night before the solstice. For now, we train. Young Cathal, come with me for today," Nuada said.

He then walked off towards one corner of the large grassy garden. The night was coming quick, but the evening floodlights from the house lit the area quite well.

Naoise and Foxy were confused as to why just Cathal was being taken away to train.

"What's going on?" Foxy whispered to Naoise.
Naoise, in total confusion, shouted after Nuada, "Hey! What are we supposed to do?'

It was at that moment that something flashed right in front of the two of them and landed in the gross just in front of the circle. The shockwave caused both of them fall backwards. The speed at which it landed made it impossible to see what it was at first.

Shortly after the dust settled from the impact, Foxy was able to see what had happened. A large spear was standing upright in the grass. Glowing, and silver the spear was long, and Foxy could see that it had similar Gaelic runes on it as the ones on the stones below it.

Foxy and Naoise's eyes were fixed on the spear when a tall man walked over to it and removed it from the ground. He twirled the spear around once impressively and looked at the two of them.

He had very long, straight, blonde hair, and was wearing a tunic and trousers that resembled Nuada's outfit. He had a series of medallions and chains hanging around his neck.

He smirked at the two friends, walked over to them, and reached a hand out to Naoise.

"Ms. Moone, I presume? I have heard a lot about you," the man said in a friendly voice.

Naoise took his strong hand and was instantly raised to her feet. Foxy sat there putting the pieces together.

"Who are you?" Naoise asked in quiet amazement.

Then a voice came from behind them. "That's Lugh, Ms. Moone" the voice said.

Foxy then saw a hand reach out to help him up. He looked up and his heart lifted. He reached out, took the proffered hand and stood up. Before Foxy got a chance to speak, Naoise had attacked the man with as tight an embrace as there could be. Foxy was ecstatic to see that she was hugging Vincent.

Chapter 18: *The Winter Solstice*

Naoise wouldn't let go of Vincent for a long time. She cried as she hugged him, and he squeezed her back, holding back any emotion of his own.

"I wasn't sure if you would ever come back," Naoise finally said, breaking the hug and wiping tears from her eyes.

"Neither was I," said Vincent.

Foxy and Vincent's eyes met. Vincent stuck his hand out to Foxy without hesitation.

"I see your half of the task is also completed," said Vincent, throwing a nod over to Nuada.

Foxy, not missing a beat, reached out and shook Vincent's hand sincerely.

"It's really good to see you," Foxy said earnestly

The two exchanged a look of shared respect. Just as they broke their handshake, Lugh walked over, placing his spear standing upright, and bowed in front of Foxy and Naoise. His long hair draped over his face and nearly touched the ground.

"I am Lugh. It is my utmost pleasure to meet you. Vincent here has told me all about you and the grave situation we are in," said Lugh as he turned specifically to Naoise.

"Ms. Moone, it is my vow to you that I will avenge your parents, and no harm will come to you. Nuada and I have spoken, and we are both in agreement that we will honour your parents' sacrifices."

Naoise felt quite awkward, but appreciated the sentiment.

"Thank you, sir. Together we will combat the Fomorians," she said.

Lugh stood tall in front of them.

"Vincent my friend, I owe you a great deal of thanks, too. I have not seen Tryst Manor in a very long time. I am glad you found me in the state I was in," said Lugh.

"What state were you in?" Foxy asked. "Nuada was a tree, Vincent; he was the weeping willow at the base of Cnoc Mor."

Vincent's face was pleasantly surprised, like someone who has solved a puzzle they were working on for a while.

"Interesting," said Vincent. "I wish Lugh had been as easy to find as a tree."

"What do you mean?" asked Foxy.

"This ancient gentleman had taken the form of a waterfall, which made finding him quite difficult" Vincent said.

"A waterfall? How does that work?" said Foxy.

Lugh picked up his spear and gave it another impressive twirl. Foxy got the impression that he was showing off at this point.

"I always had a certain flow to me. After Dagda became trapped, Nuada became so crestfallen there was no talking to him. The Fomorian numbers were almost gone, so I felt I had nothing to do. I wanted to wait peacefully, as I knew someday they would try and raise Partholòn again. I went to wait in a small pond in a forest, and I waited so long I became a waterfall."

"How did you get him to revert to his normal form? If it weren't for the Fomorian, we couldn't have changed Nuada back," said Foxy.

"You have to damage the life around them," said Vincent. "Once I had determined Lugh was a waterfall from stories and rumours I had read and heard, I poured a small bit of bleach in the pond, which woke him up. Aengus always told me above all else Tuath De Danann love nature."

Foxy's eyes lit up with realisation "Ah, that makes sense. Since Conann started decaying the earth around the tree, that's what spurred Nuada to wake."

"I believe he was killed, leaving the other two to deal with?" said Vincent. "I have little doubt they will attack on December 21st. Aengus and Aine had often told me of the tomb of the Fear Gorta and the stone of Fal. However, I never knew its exact location within the grounds. We must defend that stone with everything we have."

Lugh began to do unnecessary acrobatics, spinning his spear and using it as a vault to throw himself around the area.

"Now that I am here, we are safe. Do not worry, my friends. I have not yet met a Fomorian that could withstand my spear and I," said Lugh.

"Partholòn did," Naoise said indignantly.

Lugh continued performing his theatrics, creating a helicopter over his head with the spear.

"Partholòn isn't here, my child. It is just Tethra and Cethlinn. I could take them both down in one fell swoop, should I need to." Lugh now performed a handstand atop his spear.

"And the Fear Gorta?" Foxy said coldly.

Lugh stopped immediately, his sense of confidence and even playfulness immediately wiped away.

Foxy and Naoise were both shocked by the gravity that the Fear Gorta's name carried for someone like Lugh. Foxy remembered Nuada's seriousness when speaking of the spirit, too.

"The Fear Gorta is no Fomorian," said Lugh. "He is a being that caused almost as much damage to this beautiful land as Partholòn. Partholòn wants to burn the land and bring it closer to the otherworld so that the Fomorians may rule. He has an agenda. The Fear Gorta was born from pain in its purest form, and exists only to serve torture."

Lugh's voice went very cold. The man who was twirling his spear and boasting immunity a short while ago was long gone. "Have you ever gone hungry, children? Have you ever seen the ones you love go hungry? Not just hungry for food; hungry for affection, happiness, desire, or even the hunger to live?"

Naoise and Foxy were both very cold. Foxy's eyes were drawn to the obsidian sphere that kept the spirit locked away.

"I went into this tomb once before to hide the stone. I assure you I do not want to enter it again. That is why I will fight off every Fomorian who comes near it. The danger of the Fomorians with the stone that could free Partholòn is grave. However, if the Fear Gorta escapes, that is a scene I would rather not see."

"That will not happen," Vincent said confidently.

Cathal had seen the commotion from Lugh's spear and, spotting Vincent, began to run over. Nuada, who was slightly annoyed, followed back to the tomb's door.

"Vincent!" Cathal said, excitedly rushing over.

The two also shook hands. Cathal's eyes were drawn to Lugh, who quickly glanced at Cathal.

"I see you are a descendant, my small friend. What is your power?" said Lugh.

"I don't know; I'm waiting for Nuada to tell me," said Cathal.

Nuada walked over, grabbed Cathal by the scruff of his neck, and began dragging him back. Foxy and Naoise could hear Nuada talk as they walked away.

"Yes, it's great we're all together, but we must train, young sir, or you will be of no use in battle!" Nuada shouted.

"I agree," said Lugh. He once again picked up his spear and gave it a fancy spin, his move finished with the spearhead pointing at Naoise.

"I've been told, young lady, that you're quite the wind maestro. You and I will train together today. Follow me!" Lugh demanded as he cartwheeled his away across the lawn away from the centre and to the opposite side of Nuada and Cathal.

Naoise looked at Foxy, shrugged, and off she went, following the boasting gymnastics of Lugh. Foxy looked at Cathal in one direction and Naoise in another and began to feel that sadness creep back in until Vincent put a hand on his shoulder.

"You will be training with me, Mr. Fox," said Vincent. "Nuada told me you had no Tuath De Danann blood. That does not mean you are not integral to this operation. Come, we have a different type of training."

Foxy remembered that Vincent was also not a descendant of the Tuath De Danann, and didn't feel as alone anymore. After all, Vincent had seemed like a key player in everything so far. Vincent began to walk back towards the inside of the manor. Foxy followed him.

Following Vincent around the side of the manor and into the building itself, Foxy found himself back in the library where Aengus and Aine had told him all about the Tuath De Danann. The library seemed much bigger now.

"I trust you read that book Naoise gave you?" said Vincent.

Foxy was surprised at this statement. "How did you know she gave me that?"

Before Foxy could continue further, Vincent interrupted him. "I recommended that book. It's the same one Aengus had me read through when I was first exposed to this."

Foxy was beginning to feel a kinship with Vincent, which he found quite strange as before the death of Naoise's parents Foxy had always felt like Vincent had a strong dislike of him.

Maybe he still does, Foxy thought, *but the current matters are more important.*

He watched Vincent go to one of the shelves and, rather than pull out a book, he took out a large, rolled-up sheet.

On the table in the centre of the room, Vincent rolled out the sheet which was revealed to be a very large set of blueprints for the house. Foxy's eyes ran across the interjecting lines on the page and understood it to be a map of the whole grounds, not just the house itself.

"I had these made up recently, so they are quite accurate," Vincent said.

Foxy walked closer to the table and cast his eyes from side to the side. It was at this point he realised he had only been in a fraction of the manor. Looking at the blueprints, there were virtually entire wings of the house he had not been to yet.

"What are we doing with this?" asked Foxy.

"From what I've been told, Foxy, you are not a Tuath De Danann, the same as myself. Nuada told me this morning. Cathal only has a fraction of descendancy, and is not a true Tuath De Danann either. However, Nuada is confident he may be able to draw some power from the boy. You and I, Foxy, we have to work without ancient powers. Do you know how we do that?" asked Vincent.

Foxy looked at him, befuddled, trying to wrack his own brain for a clever answer. Then he saw Vincent playfully tap his head with his finger. Foxy then knew what he was going to say.

"We have to use our minds," said Vincent.

Foxy then placed his eyes back across the plans to the manor and grounds. "So what exactly do we do on December 21st when the Fomorians come?" asked Foxy.

Vincent then pulled out a drawer under the table, took out a series small figurines, and began to place them at different points across the map. Some at the main gate, one at the tomb entrance and some at various other locations on the map.

"Foxy, you have to think of it like this. Nuada, Lugh, Cathal and Naoise will be our soldiers. I will fight too, which makes you our general. We have to plan for this attack. There can't be that many Fomorians available to come. Any normal rank Fomorian, Lugh or Nuada will be able to easily deal with. I am even confident that Naoise could quite easily deal with some basic level enemies. Our main concern is if Cethlinn or Tethra arrive," said Vincent. "Trust me, Foxy, Aengus and Aine were powerful beings. If Tethra killed them both, he is extremely strong."

Foxy was quite quick on the uptake, and instantly grabbed a few of the figurines that Vincent had left out. He placed them all around the tomb.

Foxy spoke with a tone of authority "So we should prioritise the protection of the tomb? From what I believe, the Fear Gorta and the stone must be kept in there at all cost."

"True," replied Vincent, rearranging the figures, "but I would perhaps place Lugh at the front courtyard, as there is the most access points and he could take down the lower rank Fomorians. Then I was thinking of placing Naoise and myself at the far end of the garden where there is another access point. Then Nuada and Cathal will be placed at the tomb. If Cathal develops an ability, that is."

Foxy thought on this for a moment. He took the figures and placed them in different places.

"I know you haven't seen it yet, but Nuada got exhausted very quickly fighting Conann. Perhaps having him as the last line of defence is dangerous. Lugh seems much more vibrant. I would place Nuada and Cathal in the courtyard. Nuada's power can make up for Cathal's inexperience," said Foxy.

Vincent was looked intrigued as Foxy continued, "Then I agree on the far side of the garden, you and Naoise will be able to hold your own ground there."

Foxy then placed an extra figurine in the middle where the tomb is.

"Then at the tomb will be Lugh and myself."

Foxy could see that Vincent was clearly unimpressed with the idea of Foxy putting himself into battle.

"I can help" Foxy pleaded.

"Trust me, I was there when we fought Conann. I helped more than Cathal, trust me. Also, with Nuada's spear we can do long distance attacks while also protecting the tomb. This is the strategy. Trust me."

Vincent stared at the blueprint with the figurines around the board. A look of acceptance came over his face as he thought over the plan. He turned and nodded at Foxy.

Foxy took in Vincent's agreement and felt once again like an integral part of the team.

"Is there a plan B?" Foxy asked. "What if they do get the stone, and the Fear Gorta escapes?"

"If that happens, and we are still alive, we will have to head for Cnoc Mor and try to head off any attempts to raise Partholòn," Vincent said sharply.

"It won't happen!" Foxy said confidently.

Foxy saw a smile crack across Vincent's face for the first time.

"I concur," said Vincent. "Right, let's go over other possible entry strategies the Fomorians may use."

Foxy and Vincent went back to work on the blueprint.

The evening passed late into the night until it was time to cycle home. When Naoise, Foxy and Cathal all saw each other again, Foxy couldn't believe how exhausted his two friends looked. Naoise was pale as a ghost and looked as she was about to faint. Cathal, on the other hand, was covered in muck and breathing very heavily.

Foxy felt as he may actually be lucky to not have a power.

"Ready to cycle home?" Foxy asked jokingly.

"I am ready for wherever there is a bed," Cathal said breathlessly.

Nuada laughed loudly and patted Cathal hard on the back, which clearly shook him.

"We didn't find your power today, but tomorrow is a brand new adventure," Nuada bellowed

Cathal looked uneasy. Foxy was sure Naoise was just about to faint when she said, "I need sleep."

Lugh also laughed, and, seemingly true to character, performed a standing backflip beside Naoise just to accentuate how untired he was.

"You couldn't be tired, Ms. Moone. We did so little?" Lugh said condescendingly.

"Tomorrow, we rotate. I will take the girl, and Lugh, you take the boy," said Nuada.

Foxy saw that both Cathal and Naoise seemed glad to be swapping partners. Both were wondering how could it be worse than what they had gone through today.

"We will do some combat tomorrow too, Foxy," Vincent said as he wheeled over both Cathal's bike and the tandem.

Vincent turned up the little lights at the front of each bike, further telling the teens it was time to get going.

"You'd best head home, you lot. I have to cook a dinner to feed these," said Vincent.

Cathal threw himself up on his bike and pushed off to let the bike freewheel down the hill. Naoise sat on the rear of the bike and lay her head on the crossbars.

"Foxy, please do all the peddling," she said.

Foxy smiled, got on the front, and, copying Cathal, merely kicked off to let the bike roll downhill effortlessly.

***

After a peaceful nighttime cycle, they bade farewell to Cathal at the entrance to his house and both Naoise and Foxy made for the Sullivans'. When they arrived home, Foxy caught whiff of a familiar smell. It was the warm smell of the hearty stew he'd had the first day he met the Sullivans. He and Naoise quickly walked into the kitchen and, almost instantly after a quick greeting, Linda gave them each a bowl. They sat and horsed the food into them. Neither had realised the hunger that they'd actually been feeling.

"Busy studying?" Linda said in a coy voice.

Foxy was about to answer, then remembered what Macdara said about leaving well enough alone.

"Yes, we have Christmas exams next week," said Foxy

Naoise quickly realised the situation too. It was as if Linda just wanted to be sure that they would lie to her. After a quick cup of post-dinner tea, everyone headed to bed.

***

The rest of the week functioned the same as Monday. They would go to school, keep their heads down, get their work done, and after school cycle out in the frosty air back to Tryst Manor.

Connor Sweeney returned to school on Wednesday. He and Foxy shared a glance in the hall, but Connor didn't act. Foxy had heard from other students that he received a final warning, and would be expelled on the next offence. The beast had been tamed in Foxy's eyes. He wasn't stupid enough to get expelled, was he? Foxy thought to himself.

The training did not get any easier, either, as the week went on. Both Cathal and Naoise found that training with either Lugh or Nuada was just as difficult as the other. Vincent and Foxy practiced close-quarters combat each day, with Foxy using wooden daggers. Vincent's rationale for this was that Foxy wouldn't be able to keep the Fomorians at a distance, so when they got close he had to know how to defend himself.

Both Nuada and Lugh focused on using wind without feeling faint when training with Naoise, and with Cathal they focused on Vincent's earlier techniques of physical pressure, hoping it would lead to the discovery of a power.

It was on Friday that there was success.

Cathal was training with Nuada on the Friday. Foxy and Vincent were taking a well-deserved break in the middle of the tombstones. Foxy looked over at Cathal and Nuada in the corner. Nuada looked more frustrated than usual, and Foxy could hear him talking loudly.

"What else do we have to try?" Nuada said angrily, "We've tried every offensive thing and nothing is working. Your descendancy is weak, but you should have something!"

"I'm sorry," Foxy saw Cathal mouth.

Nuada picked up one of Vincent's wooden swords and was torturingly poking Cathal with it, who was seated in a painful-looking squatting position with his arms above his head.

"Don't apologise, look inside yourself. There is something there!" Nuada shouted and then, rather than poking Cathal, he swung the wooden sword down from above. Cathal put his arms over his head to protect himself. Then all Foxy saw was bits of splintered wood fly around all over the place.

Nuada stepped back, stunned. Foxy decided to go over to see what had happened. Cathal now stood up and expected to be hurt. He looked amazingly at his own arms, which should have been hurt by the wooden sword, but incredibly he was fine. When Cathal looked at his arms properly he nearly fainted himself. Foxy also saw what was making Cathal weak and Nuada smile. Cathal's forearms were rock solid. Literally.

Foxy looked at Cathal's forearms and hands, which had lost the texture of skin and were now looking like sheets of bright rock. His arms had morphed so that his skin was covered in literal rock. Cathal stared amazingly at his arms.

Nuada lifted him up in the air like a Father raising a boy then placed him back down.

"Amazing, young Cathal," said Nuada.

"What is this?" Cathal asked, amazed.

"Tuath powers are traditionally linked to elements. It appears to me, young Cathal, that you have a link to earth. I had been trying to find what offensive abilities you had, when all along you are a defensive being. I should have guessed," Said Nuada. "Let's try again."

And in a flash Nuada had thrown a punch at Cathal's stomach. Cathal winced in anticipation of pain, but all Foxy heard was a loud clunk. Nuada looked very pleased. He began to laugh loudly.

Cathal pulled up his training top to now see that his arms had reverted to normal, but across his belly was the same rocky texture that had just been on his arms. Cathal began to smile too, recognising what was happening.

"Can you believe it, Foxy?!" Cathal shouted patting his own rocky stomach.

Truthfully, Foxy couldn't believe it, but he was seeing it. Foxy swallowed a glimmer of that isolated feeling and forced himself to be enthusiastic for Cathal.

"That's amazing Cathal! It really is," Foxy said sincerely.

"Leave them to work," Vincent said, calling Foxy back to join him in the middle.

"Yes," said Nuada. "We must now harness this ability."

Cathal now looked enthused. "Let's do it! I'd like to see Connor Sweeney hit me now!" Cathal said, taking his squatting position again while Nuada cracked another wooden sword against Cathal's leg and it splintered into pieces like the first..

When Foxy reached Vincent again, he was offered a bottle of water, which he took. As he drank under the floodlights, Vincent said, "Be happy for him. His power will help us."

Foxy heard these words, but continued drinking the water. He then quickly got over his own selfishness.

"I am happy for him. Truly," Foxy said.

"Good," said Vincent and the two engaged in combat training once again.

***

The weekend of training flew by. Naoise and Cathal looked less exhausted each day, and it was clear that they were getting control of their powers. Foxy was happy for both of them, however, the weekend cycles where they discussed their powers and improvements were hard for him to listen to.

The 21st of December was set to fall on a Saturday. The following week repeated itself the same as the one before, except for Christmas exams, which culminated on December 20th. Foxy, Naoise and Cathal were all concerned with a far greater issue on the 21st, but they slogged through their exams. Sending the usual sleepover text so that they were all accounted for, they headed out to Tryst Manor on Friday evening. Foxy cast an eye into the Sullivans' drive as he rode by. He was aware of the danger tomorrow faced. Cathal did the same as they wheeled by his house. The reality of the Fomorian attack was setting in.

As they rode, Foxy reflected on his time since he moved to Tinree Island.

"Guys, if it weren't for you two. I don't know what I would have done," said Foxy.

"I'm not sure what tomorrow will bring, but I do know that these last few months have been some of the happiest in my life, Fomorians and all. I guess what I'm trying to say is, you guys are the best."

Naoise reached forward from behind his back and gave Foxy and a pat on the back.

"Had it not been for you two, I wouldn't have made it through my parents' deaths. I've never had friends before, so it really is a privilege to be here with you," said Naoise.

"Since we're all saying nice things, I just want to say how miserable I was before you two came along," said Cathal. "Every day I was afraid of going to school because of Connor Sweeney. Now at nighttime I can't wait for school, because it means I get to see you guys again."

They all shared a moment cycling in silence, absorbing the nice words they had all said.

"Just imagine how good it will be when we defeat the Fomorians. Imagine if we find a way to release Dagda and actually kill Partholòn. The three of us could go on a trip far away from Tinree Island. See the country that we saved," said Foxy.

Naoise was unusually quiet.

Cathal pumped his fist in the air as he cycled onwards.

***

It was just dark when they arrived at the manor. They dismounted their bikes and Cathal rushed himself into the manor, claiming that he needed to use the facilities. Naoise and Foxy looked at the manor together. As they started to walk towards the entrance steps, Foxy looked at Naoise and saw a speck of white land on the tip of her nose. She smiled when she saw him looking at her. Both their eyes lifted towards the sky to find to their own delight that it had just begun to snow.

They both raised their heads up as the snow gently fell across their faces. It was a very serene moment, mixed the floodlights of the manor and the dull moonlight. The snow was almost luminous as it begun to flurry down upon them.

They looked back down at each other and their eyes met. Both smiled at the snow on the other's face.

"I really did mean what I said; it is a privilege to know you," said Naoise, looking deeply into Foxy's eyes.

Having been in this situation once before, Foxy no longer hesitated. Figuring it may all end tomorrow anyway, he leaned in towards Naoise and kissed her on the lips. He felt the icy cold of her mouth first from the snow and breeze, but then he felt Naoise kiss him back.

The two embraced at the snowy base of the Tyrst Manor entrance steps. When the kiss finally broke, they smiled intently at each.

"I've been wanting to do that a long time," said Foxy.

"I know," said Naoise, laughing. "I've been waiting a long time."

Both of them smiled when the door burst open. It was Cathal. He looked extremely excited.

"Come quick, both of you have to see this!" Cathal shouted, and then he ran back inside the manor.

Foxy and Naoise ran up the stairs and into the main foyer. They couldn't believe their eyes. The entire house was decorated in the most beautiful Christmas decorations. Holly hung around the bannisters and windows. There was a large, decorated Christmas tree in the corner, and the fire place could be heard crackling in the distance.

As Foxy gazed around at the stunning decorations, Nuada walked through the foyer holding a very large turkey that looked like it was just out of the oven. It smelled delicious. Lugh then quickly followed behind holding two baskets, one filled with fresh baked bread rolls and the other an assortment of desserts.

"Good evening, children," said Nuada in a powerful voice, storming through the foyer towards a room Foxy had never been in.

As Foxy looked at Nuada entered the room, Vincent zoomed past him wearing oven mitts, which Foxy found very comical on Vincent. He was holding a very large bowl of steaming vegetables. Even with the mitts, they were clearly burning his hands.

"Please make your way to the dining room, Ms. Moone," Vincent said, hurrying into the same door Nuada had just gone through.

Cathal poked his head out of the same door.

"Guys, come on!" Cathal said, racing back into the room.

Naoise and Foxy looked at each other, shared a smile, then made their way into the room. When they walked in, Foxy saw that it was a dining room with a fireplace roaring in the corner. This room was also decked out in the finest Christmas decorations. In the middle of the long hall was a fine, big, circular dinner table with Christmas centrepieces. Turkey and bowls of food had been placed all around it. There were even Christmas crackers.

Nuada stood at the table and held his arms out.

"Children, brothers, friends, tomorrow is a grave day. The sun will rise early, the tomb will open, and the defence will begin. However, tonight we celebrate those we cherish. We toast to those we wish to see again, and remember those we cannot. Come, friends, let us eat."

They all sat down at the table and began to help themselves to the food. Cathal was filling his plate so much that Foxy could not believe such a short person could eat that much. Foxy then saw Nuada and Lugh split the wishbone between them, with Lugh winning and laughing uproariously. Vincent quietly and with dignity filled his own plate and began to eat. He had poured himself a glass of white wine.

Foxy and Naoise then prepared their own plates. Vincent poured Foxy and Naoise a small drop of white wine, and then gave a quiet smile and winked at them. He didn't pour one for Cathal, who was solely focused on eating.

They all ate their dinner happily, pulling Christmas crackers with one another and smiling genuinely. Nuada and Lugh were recounting tales of former feasts before battle. They spoke of a night where Dagda had eaten an entire pig by himself.

"I don't believe it!" said Cathal.

"That's because you haven't seen Dagda," Lugh replied comedically, and the whole table laughed.

The evening rolled by with nothing but hearty, positive vibes all around. Each of them were deathly aware of what the following day had in store for them, but they were able to enjoy the night for what it was.

The dinner rounded to a close as each of them finished their plate. To everyone's amazement, perhaps even his own, Cathal had finished his dinner. He was absolutely stuffed; he would have energy for days. As they all settled into their chairs, Lugh and Nuada picking at the remains of the turkey carcass. Foxy took his glass and stood up. Naoise looked at him in anticipation.

Foxy cleared his throat and got the attention of the room.

"I'd like to make a toast" He said nervously

Nuada hushed Lugh and listened intently. Vincent also looked on with great interest.

"This may be the last chance I get to say this, but since you all are the ones who will be doing the majority of the battling tomorrow, I just want to wish you all luck, and I want you to know that I believe that the people in this room can take down any enemy. So, thank you!"

Nuada then stood up and raised a glass to Foxy.

"Without you, Mr. Fox, none of this would be occurring. You are the ties that bind. You brought us all together. I toast to you, young sir," said Nuada.

Vincent then stood and raised a glass. "To Foxy."

The rest of the room stood up and also raised a glass. "To Foxy," they all said in unison.

His heart was very full at that moment. He nodded at them thankfully. Nuada looked out at the snow pelting down.

"Now we need a name for this little band of brave warriors. When they write songs of our battle, who shall they reference?" said Nuada, now with an air of tiredness in his voice.

Foxy thought about what to call the group, but Naoise spoke.

"The legends of old," she said.

Foxy was delighted to hear this, and he could see that Cathal was too. Their group chat name would now be the name including ancient warriors. It seemed very surreal to Foxy.

"A great name!" Lugh exclaimed.

"I agree," said Nuada.

"To the legends of old!" Foxy raised a glass again, and once more everyone toasted.

"I think it time for rest. We rise early to prepare," said Nuada, who excused himself from the table. Lugh did the same and bowed goodnight to the room.

Vincent was next.

"There are rooms made up on either side of yours, Naoise. Goodnight, Naoise," Vincent said. He then turned to Foxy and Cathal. "Goodnight to you, my friends."

Vincent smirked and left the room.

The three friends sat in the room around the table. The fire was still burning, and it was very warm. They moved from the dining table to the big armchairs that surrounded the room. Cathal was already drifting off; his chair was closest to the fire.

Foxy walked over and put some longs on the fire.

"You know, I think I'll just sleep here," said Foxy.

He looked at Cathal, who was already asleep now. Naoise smiled at Foxy.

"I'll do the same. It started with the three of us; we should spend the night together." Said Naoise.

Each of them sat down in their chairs, throwing an adjacent blanket over themselves. The room was warm and cozy, plus after the large feed it didn't take long for each of them to drift off. They each slept soundly until the rising sun woke them through the window. The winter solstice was here.

Chapter 19: *The Scourge Creeps*

It was an exceedingly bright sunrise. Foxy's eyes opened gently, he gazed out the window to see an auburn hue rise over the hills. Foxy usually loved looking at the sunrise, however this morning he was full of dread. There was a heavy kaleidoscope of butterflies in his stomach. He sat there in the warm chair, comfortable. He was very aware that when he got up, the day would begin. This was a day Foxy was not looking forward to.

Foxy had been told that the Fomorians would come the morning of the winter solstice to retrieve the Stone of Fal from the tomb. With that stone, they could counteract the Dagda's cauldron and release Partholòn.

The group assembled at Tryst Manor were there to defend the stone. The plan was twofold: they had to stop the Fomorians from accessing the tomb, but they also had to stop the spirit of the Fear Gorta from getting out.

Foxy knew today would be a day of grave events, either way. He decided to close his eyes, just for another five minutes. He made it about thirty seconds into his extra five-minute snooze when the door to the room they were sleeping in burst open with little regard for the sleeping parties.

"It's time," Vincent said loudly.

Cathal woke up with a shudder, looking confusedly around the room; he was amazed it was the morning already. Foxy glanced over at Naoise and saw that her eyes were already open. She had been awake a short while too.

"Now, let's get to our places," Vincent said as the three of them stood up and stretched to greet the ironically beautiful morning.

"Get to your places immediately. Naoise, with me. Cathal, go with Nuada. Foxy, get to the tomb centre with Lugh; he's already there. There are weapons there waiting for you."

Vincent then left the room swiftly. Foxy turned to both Naoise and Cathal.

"We can do this. Just imagine meeting back here after we win. Keep those good thoughts going. Use your powers and don't worry about me. I have full confidence in you both," said Foxy.

Naoise didn't speak; she just rushed over to Foxy and hugged him tightly. Cathal then somewhat awkwardly tried to join the hug from the outside. Foxy spotted him trying to get in on it and spared him an arm. The three friends embraced by the smouldering fire. They then made their way to their battle stations.

***

Cathal walked up beside Nuada, who was standing in the centre of the courtyard at the front of Tryst Manor. He had no indication of humour on his face. The friendliness was gone, and all that remained was a face that was very clearly ready for battle.

"Use that power defensively, young Cathal. Draw them to you; you won't take damage. Then I can get them from behind before they get a chance to hurt you," Nuada, drastically serious.

Nuada was holding the sword of light extremely tight; Cathal could see the whitening of Nuada's knuckles around the hilt. Cathal looked down at the weapon Vincent had left for him. It was a short sword. Cathal was extremely unimpressed with it. He thought it looked like a default starter weapon in an RPG game.

"How many will there be?" Cathal asked.

"I don't know," said Nuada with a wisp of concern in his voice.

The two of them stood there on the cold, yet bright, morning. Waiting.

Meanwhile on the other side of the manor, Vincent and Naoise stood side-by-side facing the wide-open fields that spilled off the back of the house. The sun made the tips of corn fields glitter like sparkles on the ocean. Vincent was holding two daggers in each hand, the handles of which had a unusual design, allowing him to place his fingers through the handles. This let the daggers also operate as a knuckleduster of sorts.

Vincent had also placed a series of daggers in front of both of them on the ground. There was a large amount of them all. These were not wooden like the ones Naoise had practiced using her wind on; they were very real.

"Use your wind like we practiced, Naoise," said Vincent.

He could tell Naoise was very frightened.

"How many are coming, Vincent?"

"I don't know," he replied sternly.

At the same time in the middle of the Tryst Manor grounds, standing atop the rounded stone tomb of the Fear Gorta and the location of the Stone of Fal, Foxy stood with Lugh. Long gone was Lugh's boasting, show-off nature flipping around the place. Instead, he was a very serious man standing tall with his spear by his side.

Foxy had been left a longsword as his weapon. He had used one in training, but the weight of this one felt unusually heavy. From where he was standing, he could see Naoise and Vincent on the hill facing west, while he could just see the edge of Nuada's shoulder on the east side in the courtyard.

With a light whoosh, Lugh's spear lifted off the ground without him touching it. Foxy had read that Lugh could control his spear, and that's why he had chosen Lugh to take the centre ground. His thinking was that he could use the spear remotely to take down targets at a distance. Foxy, like his two friends, was still mainly concerned about one thing.

"How many do you think are coming, Lugh?" asked Foxy.

The spear began to shoot around the tomb in a circle. It became so fast that it was like the blades of a fan. The wind from it made Foxy wince. Surely no one could pass that without being obliterated.

"I don't know, Mr. Fox. All I know is we must keep this tomb safe," replied Lugh.

It was at this time that Foxy looked down at the tomb. He'd presumed it was meant to open when the sun touched it, but it looked the same, although the obsidian sphere in the middle did look a little lighter.

"How does the tomb open?' Foxy asked curiously.

"You take out the sphere," said Lugh.

Foxy began to reach down towards the sphere, merely to examine it. In an instant, the circling spear stopped and pointed itself toward Foxy.

"Don't go near it, boy," Lugh said with no signs of friendship in his voice.

Foxy recoiled and reverted away from the sphere.

"I wasn't going to, I was just going to look," said Foxy.

Lugh looked extremely unimpressed.

"You wouldn't want to look, if you knew the evil down there. Now focus up, boy. They'll be here soon," Lugh said, casting his eyes from Vincent and Naoise to Nuada and Cathal.

They waited half an hour, but there was no sign of movement. In that half hour, neither Nuada, Vincent or Lugh changed their expressions. Cathal, Naoise and Foxy, however, were beginning to hope that perhaps the Fomorians weren't coming and they could go back to have a nice breakfast.

That hope dwindled very quickly.

"SIGHTING!" Vincent shouted.

Foxy and Lugh whipped around to look in their direction. Vincent turned around, and in the distance Foxy could see that he just held up one finger.

"What does that mean?" Foxy asked worried.

Lugh had an expression of complete confusion.

"It means there is only one coming on that side. Quick Foxy, run towards Nuada and Cathal. Tell me what you see. I'll send the spear alongside you so you're safe," said Lugh.

Without a moment of consideration, Foxy took off running towards the part of the grass where he could see Nuada and Cathal. He also saw something else. It was a woman emerging from the forest adjacent to the manor. He moved closer, the spear floating beside him. Foxy could see it was a young woman. A beautiful young woman, with shimmering sheets of long black hair draping almost down to her hip. She was wearing scarlet red robes and carried what looked like a very old staff.

Foxy could see Nuada step in front of Cathal, confronting the woman. It was at this time the back end of the spear gave Foxy a mid-air whack. That caused Foxy to turn toward Lugh, who was gesturing him back. Lugh dared not leave the tomb unguarded for a moment. Foxy rushed back to him.

"There's just one woman. No army, no masses just one woman," said Foxy.

Lugh's face dropped.

"It's just them," he said coldly.

"Foxy, I need you to run over to Naoise and Vincent. Tell me what you see," said Lugh.

Foxy turned again without hesitation and ran across the large clearing towards the hill where Naoise and Vincent were perched looking out. He got there breathing slightly heavily. He didn't even speak, standing between Naoise and Vincent. Foxy saw another individual making their way across the vast corn fields. It was most definitely only one person. Even from simply looking, Foxy got a much worse vibe from this individual than the woman.

Foxy couldn't make out what they looked like. The individual was wearing jet black robes with the hood pulled up. There was a dark hollow where the face would be. Foxy couldn't see any distinguishable features. The robes they were wearing had gold runes sewn into the front and back. The individual was slowly making their way through the fields.

The jet black ominous figure frightened Foxy to his core as they strode through the waist-high corn. As he got slightly closer, Foxy saw that they were carrying a large, regal orb in their hands. They were holding it with both hands. The hooded figure stopped walking and looked up. Foxy still couldn't make out a face. It appeared that Vincent had noticed the orb at the same time.

"Oh my god," said Vincent as his jaw dropped.

"What is it?" Naoise asked, concerned.

Foxy could hear Vincent's breath quickening.

"It's Tethra," said Vincent with fear in his voice. It was the first time Foxy had heard it from Vincent.

At this very moment Foxy could see Tethra's hands twist the orb so that it cracked in the middle and opened up. What spilled out of it was a whirlwind of blazing fire. The dark blue flames swept over the entire field in moments. The heat of the flames pushed Foxy, Vincent and Naoise back. Foxy sat on the ground looking out at what was once a cornfield. It was now simply scorched earth. Tethra stood amidst the flames, unfazed and simply began to walk forward. Foxy had never felt panic like it, the heat from the flames was scalding. He saw that once the chemical-looking flames had decimated the field, they returned to the orb.

Tethra gave the orb another twist, and the flames formed a funnel which shot directly towards where the three of them were standing. The flames were moving with impossible speed.

"Naoise!" yelled Vincent.

Over all the crackling and burning noises Foxy could hear a whistle. The funnel of fire that was making its way towards them was suddenly shifted ninety degrees upwards when Naoise created a wind wall, diverting the fire skywards. The fire then spun out and returned to the orb.

Tethra began to walk slowly towards them again.

"Vincent what do we do?!" Foxy shouted amid the chaos.

Vincent looked frozen in fear. His eyes gazed out at the burnt land. Tethra had done so much damage so quickly. He was stunned.

"VINCENT!" Screamed Foxy.

That jolted Vincent from his empty stare. He turned to Naoise and Foxy.

"Foxy, run and get Lugh!" said Vincent.

"But the tomb?" Foxy said worriedly.

"If you don't get Lugh, we're going to be burnt to a crisp!" Vincent shouted back.

Naoise was still whistling. She was using wind to blow out the remaining wisps of flame still burning the ground. Just before Foxy turned to run for Lugh, he saw Tethra raise his orb in the air over his hooded head. Once again the flames emerged and charged them down rapidly. Naoise began to redirect her wind, but the flames were up so high this time. They weren't heading for Vincent, Naoise and Foxy. The three of them looked at the flames fly over them from the safety behind a wind wall. The fire stream raged through the skies and then made its target clear. It collided with a corner of Tryst Manor, causing a huge impact and knocking down a corner of the second floor.

Naoise screamed loudly. Vincent grabbed her quickly.

"Naoise, the wind! Use it to put out the flames," Vincent said fervently.

Lugh saw the impact on the manor, but he was still glued to the tomb. It was evident he didn't want to leave.

"Naoise, come with me!" Foxy said, grabbing Naoise by the wrist and pulling her along with him.

"FOXY!" Vincent screamed as he ducked from the heat of the flames flying back overhead to Tethra's orb.

Naoise and Foxy were full-on sprinting across the grass towards the tomb lid in the centre of the wide garden. When they reached there, Lugh was looking very worried about what Foxy was about to say.

"Lugh, you need to go help Vincent. Naoise and I can guard the tomb," said Foxy.

"Boy…" Lugh said tentatively.

"Please, Lugh, we can't fight him. We need you. Naoise and I killed Conann, we can guard the tomb. I promise," pleaded Foxy.

"It's true," said Naoise. "I won't let anyone in here! It's just one, Tethra, on that side; you have to stop him!"

Lugh winced at the name Tethra.

"We've fought before," Lugh said enigmatically.

Very quickly, Lugh's spear turned sideways, he jumped on it like a surfboard, and *whoosh*, the spear took off. Foxy watched it fly over Vincent and out in the fiery field.

Foxy then turned to Naoise.

"Now Naoise, I need you to stay here. I have to see what's going on with the others," said Foxy.

"Foxy!" Naoise cried.

"Use your wind to make a whirlwind, and sit in the middle. If that's what Tethra can do, who knows what the other one can do," said Foxy. Then he ran off without giving Naoise time to debate.

When Foxy left the stones, he heard a whistle and looked back while he was running to see a windy cyclone encircling the tomb.

Foxy rounded the burnt side of the manor to find Cathal on the ground. His skin was rock solid, but he was barely conscious. Foxy quickly got down beside Cathal, trying to comfort him but being gentle. Foxy had received so much stimulus in the last five minutes that he thought he was going to collapse.

"Cathal, what happened?" asked Foxy.

"If it wasn't for this power, I'd be dead," Cathal said breathlessly. "The plan was a failure. We could have never prepared for what she can do."

"Nuada?" asked Foxy.

"He's fighting her now. Don't go, Foxy. You can't do anything to stop her," Cathal coughed.

Ignoring Cathal, Foxy looked down at the sword he was carrying and made his way towards the front of the manor. When he turned the corner he saw blood splattered all across the courtyard. Nuada was still standing in the middle of courtyard swinging his sword of light furiously.

Foxy then saw what he was swinging at. There were large icicles shooting at him from the woman's staff. They were manifesting right from the top of it. Large and jagged, they were shooting towards Nuada at lighting pace. Nuada was deflecting them as fast as they were forming, although Foxy could see deep cuts all along both of Nuada's arms. There were clearly some he hadn't deflected in enough time.

Cethlinn looked stoic. There was no emotion on her face as she shot the harsh-looking ice blades towards Nuada. Foxy's first thought was that it made sense that she would use ice if Tethra used fire. There was a moment of respite when Cethlinn stopped firing ice for a moment. In that split second, Nuada pounced towards her with the sword of light raised. Just as quick as Nuada pounced, Cethlinn produced a sprawling, large ice wall. When Nuada struck the wall with his sword, the ice wall exploded in every direction. Shards of ice flew everywhere. Foxy put his hands up to shield his face from the debris. When he lowered his hands, he saw that all the shards of ice were suspended mid-air, every single one of them now surrounding Nuada and pointing directly at him.

Nuada looked around, panicked.

"Nuada!" screamed Foxy, drawing the attention of Cethlinn.

That momentary distraction gave Nuada an opening, and he leapt toward Cethlinn at such speed that there was broken ground from where he'd been standing. She was only able to defend herself with her staff, which she turned into solid ice upon impact at the last moment. There was a deafening sonic boom from the collision. Nuada bounced back as Cethlinn slid back across the courtyard. Foxy could see that Nuada was breathing heavily.

Nuada turned toward Foxy.

"Run! Young Foxy, you must flee!" shouted Nuada.

Foxy looked at him with the greatest concern. He then saw Cethlinn look at him.

"There is no point in running boy. The scourge is upon us. The mighty Nuada is only a fraction of what he once was; he cannot hold. We will take the stone, and Partholòn will restore this land to its wretched state," Cethlinn said in an icy voice.

"Run to Lugh! Protect the tomb!" said Nuada with his eyes fixed on Cethlinn.

"He's fighting Tethra!" Foxy shouted back.

Nuada's eyes darted around quickly.

"Who's guarding the tomb?" said Nuada.

Foxy could see Cethlinn laugh.

"No one, it seems," she said with a smirk

With Nuada now distracted, Cethlinn unleashed a fierce flurry of ice on Nuada. Hundreds of ice clumps landed on him at the same time. He couldn't deflect them all off. They built and built around him, Nuada struggled in vain until he was completely covered in ice. Where he once stood was a large mound of ice. He was frozen solid.

Foxy began to run toward where Nuada was frozen, but stopped when he spotted a large ice ball heading his way. He just about got his sword up in time to protect himself. However, it collided directly with his chest, sending him flying across the courtyard. He was fighting to stay conscious; he was in pulsating pain. Through his flittering eyes he saw Cethlinn walk around the manor towards where Naoise was guarding the tomb. She didn't even look at Cathal as she walked past him.

Foxy knew he had to get up. He could see Nuada through the ice, but he was not moving.

Get up! Foxy thought to himself.*Get up! Naoise needs you!*

Then Foxy heard a distant female voice deep in the recesses of his mind.

"Your part is yet to be played, Foxy. You must get up," the voice said.

Just then, Foxy's eyes closed and he slipped into unconscious.

***

He quickly woke to find himself lying flat on his back in the lake of Falias. Sitting nonchalantly beside him, was the woman with fiery red hair whom he had spoken to several times before.

He looked at her as he sat up. All his pain had vanished.

"Am I dead?" he asked.

She looked at him gravely and took him by the hand.

"No, my child. You must free Nuada. All is not lost yet," she said.

Foxy looked at her. He felt defeated.

"What can I do? They're too powerful. If Nuada can't stop her, what can I do? I'm not even a Tuath De Danann," he said glumly.

The woman looked at Foxy sympathetically. She looked crestfallen herself.

"Dear Foxy, it is time to go back and listen to me very closely. Some of the bravest and strongest warriors in our history were not Tuath De Danann. Trust me. You have ancient blood in you. All will show itself in time. Now is not the time for sorrow and questions."

Foxy's eyes looked at the woman. He was infatuated by her kindness. Her presence made him feel like everything would be okay.

She continued, "Now is the time to fight. You feel like you are not needed. Naoise needs you. Nuada needs you. I need you."

Foxy stood up in the lake. The woman stood up beside him and placed her hands on his shoulders. They felt warm and calming.

"You may be the greatest of us all," the woman said as she gave Foxy a slight push down on his shoulders. Foxy fell through the water of the lake, then woke back up staring at the ice mound where Nuada was frozen.

"You may be the greatest of us all," the voice rang out again in his head.

Foxy mustered up the strength from deep down in his core and stood to his feet. All the pain from the blow was back. He looked over to see Cathal moving slightly. Foxy cast his eyes back towards Nuada, and he felt a surge of energy. The energy felt as if it was coming from his very core. He picked up his sword, sprinted towards the ice mound, and swung the sword at it.

The ice was so thick, Foxy's sword barely made a scratch. Foxy was crying intensely as he continued to swing the sword. His whole body ached, but he kept striking at the ice.

"Come on, Nuada!" Foxy screamed as he kept chopping at the ice.

With each hack and slash at the ice, Foxy's arms ached more and more, but his ferocity and pace never slowed.

"You have to break out, Nuada!" Foxy's face was covered in tears as he kept hacking.

"She said you needed me! But we all need you! I need you, Lugh needs you. Ireland needs you!"

Foxy then swung the sword high above his head and landed one impressive strike right where the rest of his blows had landed. Then, to his own amazement, he saw the smallest crack appear. Suddenly, the crack started to spread, and through sheer intuition he took a step backwards. The ice mound exploded with Nuada jumping skywards from the broken ice.

Foxy was still crying with the same intensity but now he was smiling ear to ear. Nuada turned to Foxy, his face holding a ferociousness Foxy had not seen before.

"I could hear you when I was in there, Foxy," said Nuada "Who was the 'she' you were referring to?"

Foxy looked back unsure at Nuada. He had never explained the dream to anyone before.

"The woman in the lake," Foxy said tentatively.

Nuada smirked through the intensity on his face.

"If Danu is speaking to you, then she must have faith in us," said Nuada.

Nuada then raised his sword and rushed towards the tomb, shouting back, "While we breathe, we fight!"

Nuada raced around the corner, and Foxy rushed after him. Foxy stopped to help Cathal get to his feet.

"I can't," Cathal said softly.

"Yes you can!" said Foxy.

Cathal winced in pain as Foxy lifted him.

"No Foxy, I can't! They don't need me. Even though I've got the power, it's you," Cathal said, shuddering in pain.

Foxy looked at him, concerned.

"It's always been you. This whole thing, you're at the centre! Go help them! Do what you always do!" Cathal said as Foxy let go of him. He slid back down the wall.

Foxy knew time was of the essence and didn't hesitate. He nodded at Cathal and then ran off. When he turned to face the grassy area, he saw a staggering sight. The first thing he spotted off on the side of the clearing was Vincent, who was barely moving. His clothes were smouldering with smoke. Then, in the middle of the clearing, Naoise's cyclone remained.

He then spotted Cethlinn flying through the air away from the tomb. Nuada was following her in the air, following up with another sword attack that Cethlinn braced for with her ice staff. The impact sent her spiralling into the ground. She recovered quickly and began shooting trails of ice back at Nuada. At the same time, Foxy saw Lugh soaring backwards from the field where Tethra had set the flames loose.

A torrent of flames followed Lugh as he held onto his spear, which was juking and swerving through the air in an attempt to avoid the flames. Then Tethra walked over the hill. The dark-hooded Fomorian carried his orb, recalling his flames as Lugh landed as close to the cyclone as he could.

Between Lugh defending the flames and Nuada defending the ice, they were both backed to either side of the cyclone.

"Defend the tomb!" Foxy could hear Nuada bellow.

In the midst of the fire and ice chaos, Foxy ran across the burning grass towards the tomb.

"Naoise!" Foxy roared as he neared the wind "Let me in!" he shouted

To his own surprise one side of the cyclone lifted up and Foxy was able to run under it. Just as quickly as it had risen it closed again. Foxy and Naoise were inside the wind. Naoise was whistling, but she was very pale and evidently weak. Foxy knew she did not have long left.

"You have to hold on, Naoise!" pleaded Foxy.

At the very top of the wind cone, Foxy now spied Tethra's flames above them, making their way down the funnel. Foxy knew that was it. He just covered himself over Naoise, who fainted at the same time, causing the cyclone to dissipate. The flames roared down towards the two friends. Foxy held Naoise tightly. He could feel the heat rising.

"I'm sorry, Naoise!" Foxy whispered what he thought were his last words.

Then there was a loud bang. Foxy looked up to see what had happened, as he'd expected his own death. He saw Lugh crash down beside them on the cindering grass. Lugh had sacrificed himself, taking the full brunt of the flames to protect Naoise and Foxy. His body was badly burned, and he wasn't moving.

"Lugh!" screamed Nuada, charging towards Tethra. But when he moved towards Tethra, Cethlinn got closer to the tomb. Nuada then stopped mid-attack to try press Cethlinn back. However, whenever Nuada battled Cethlinn, Tethra marched methodically towards the tomb.

Vincent was out. Cathal was out. Lugh was unconscious, as was Naoise. Foxy knew it was just him and Nuada left. Foxy saw Nuada was making moves towards Tethra, but before he could turn his attention back to Cethlinn, Foxy stood up, sword at the ready, and faced Cethlinn himself.

Cethlinn laughed heartily.

"You've lost, boy," she said.

"All is not lost!" Foxy shouted back.

From behind him, he heard Nuada breathing heavily.

"I'm afraid it is," said a deeply evil voice emanating from under the hood. "Enough, Cethlinn. Let us be rid of these once and for all"

For the first time, Tethra fully opened his orb, releasing an elysian wave of fire that made its way skywards, burning the air behind it. Cethlinn, at the same moment, drove her staff into the ground,ot down on her knees, and began what looked like praying. A steady stream of ice shot out of it and flew towards the air. The ice and fire met high in the air, forming a hellish helix of fire and ice, which began to spiral directly downwards toward the tomb, where Foxy stood alongside Naoise and Lugh's unconscious bodies.

"NO!" cried Nuada as he sprang towards them.

As fast as he could, he grabbed Naoise and Lugh's bodies and threw them out of the way sending them rolling far across the grass, not caring for the damage the throw might do to their bodies, but then there was no time. For the second time in a few moments Foxy was face-to-face with imminent death.

With a second left before impact, Nuada jumped on top of Foxy, holding him tightly and protecting him from the blast, which Nuada bore the entire severity of. Nuada roared in anguish. The impact was violent. The blast sent the limp bodies of Lugh and Naoise further across the grass. Foxy could then feel the massive weight of Nuada's body on him. He was about to pass out, too.

"We failed," Nuada said with his last breath before he closed his eyes.

Tethra walked over and shoved Nuada off Foxy with impressive ease.

"How the mighty…" Tethra said with a demonic voice.

Cethlinn looked at Foxy and feigned a pitying face.

"Shall I kill the two of them? The rest look like they're already dead," Cethlinn said coldly.

"No," Tethra said sternly.

"I gave my word to the girl's parents that I wouldn't kill her if they gave me the exact location of the stone and how to find it."

He walked over and with a deft clunk removed the obsidian sphere. Loud grinding noises of stone on stone echoed through the battleground as the circular stones began to lower themselves. The outermost stone lowered first, and then the rest followed, shifting and moving around and creating a black opening through which Foxy could see only darkness.

"Cethlinn, wait there. I won't be long," Tethra demanded. "I know where to go and how to do it safely."

Tethra walked into the dark void. The tomb was open. Foxy looked around at the devastation, he wondered why the woman in the lake had lied to him. Then he thought back to Nuada calling her Danu. Was it the mother goddess he'd been speaking to this whole time? Why would she lead me to this path? Foxy thought.

Cethlinn looked at Foxy.

"You'd better hope he lets me kill you. I know the alternative," said Cethlinn with a laugh.

Foxy didn't have the strength to respond.

After a short while, Tethra reemerged from the tomb.

"Did you see him? Was he down there?" Cethlinn asked curiously.

"He is there, but the girl's parents told me how to avoid him on the condition of no death if avoidable for her or her dear friends," Tethra said.

"So, did you get it?" Cethlinn asked excitedly.

Foxy could see Tethra holding his orb in one hand, and in the other hand he held a small stone no larger than an apple. It was golden.

"So it is time," said Cethlinn, grabbing her staff.

"Yes," replied Tethra. "The scourge is upon us."

Tethra and Cethlinn began to walk towards the field from which Tethra had arrived, but Tethra turned back. He placed both the orb and stone in his deep robe pockets. He grabbed Nuada and Foxy by the necks and lifted them both up with ease.

"I gave my word, death would not befall you if it could be avoided. However, there are fates worse than death," Tethra said in a shallow voice.

Then he threw both Nuada and Foxy into the dark opening of the tomb. He walked over to the opening. Foxy could only see the light, as inside the tomb was entirely pitch black. He saw Tethra's hooded face in the light.

"Goodbye," said Tethra. "Put the sphere back in."

Then he walked off.

Cethlinn had obviously put the sphere back in to close the tomb, as the loud stone grinding noise began again. The light was fading. Foxy quickly realised the entrance was closing. He scrambled to his feet, but he was in too much pain. He tried to get up, but when he finally did the lid was closed, and he was in complete and total darkness. The darkness was petrifying, and silence was heavy.

In the distance of the tomb, Foxy heard a chilling groan.

Chapter 20: *The Tomb of the Hungry Man*

The darkness was absolute. Foxy could not see his own hands in front of his face. The tomb had the coolness of a deep cave. Foxy reached blindly with his hands and eventually found a solid surface to steady himself against. The sheer darkness was disorientating.

"HELP!" shouted Foxy as panic began to set in. In response to Foxy's shout, he heard that awful groan again far in the distant echoey chambers of the tomb.

The groan had only been heard once, but he was sure he heard it. Foxy gingerly got down on his hands and knees and began to crawl around the floor blindly. He was as scared as he had ever been; his breathing was fast and shallow.

Foxy checked his pocket for his phone, which he found, but when he tried to turn it on, he found that the phone was smashed beyond repair. He placed it back in his pocket and began to quietly crawl on the floor. He didn't want to telegraph his location to anything that may be in the tomb. Foxy wasn't even thinking about the danger he and Nuada may have been in. He just knew he had to get out of the tomb as soon as possible to try and stop Cethlinn and Tethra.

"Nuada," Foxy said as softly as he could.

There was no response. Foxy began to scan the ground with his hands as he crawled trying to locate Nuada's body. In the total absence of light, Foxy foraged across the cold, stony ground for Nuada. Foxy had a creeping thought, but did not let it grow legs.

What if Nuada was dead? he briefly thought, but then in an instant quashed that idea from his head and continued his search.

Tethra had thrown them down there with force. Maybe Nuada was further away. However, it was so dark, Foxy was concerned that if he crawled too far he might be permanently lost from Nuada. When this thought crossed his mind, Foxy's hand landed on something metal on the ground. He blindly pawed across it and then realised what he was handling. It was the hilt of a sword. He felt the cold steel above the handle.

The situation then became a little less dire, for when Foxy's hand gripped the hilt, the blade began to emit a very dull, faint light.

With the light, Foxy could now get a faint look at his surroundings. He lifted the sword like a lit torch as he remained on his knees. He slowly moved it around to see that he was in a narrow passage with stony walls and a stone ceiling dripping the occasional bead of water. Foxy could see no semblance of where the entrance was on the ceiling, but when he did look down the dimly lit passage, he saw a body lying on the ground.

"Nuada!" he whispered.

There was no movement from the body. Foxy stood up and tip-toed along the passage to where Nuada lay motionless. He moved the sword closer to Nuada to see that his eyes were closed. Foxy's eyes quickly darted to Nuada's chest, which was rising and falling. Foxy let out a sigh of relief knowing he was alive.

Foxy placed a hand on Nuada's shoulder and shook him. Nuada did not wake.

"Come on, Nuada!" Foxy said, forgetting to whisper.

Foxy heard the groan once more. This time though it chilled him to his very bones. It felt and sounded like the groan had come from right over his shoulder; he heard it like someone right in his ear. He whipped around immediately to see no one was there.

Foxy turned back to Nuada, whose breath had become laboured. There were significant injuries and burns to his back from where he'd saved Foxy from certain death.

"They both saved me," Foxy said softly.

Which was true, both Lugh and Nuada had thrown themselves in the way of certainly fatal blasts for Foxy.

"Why save me?" Foxy said, feeling like all was lost.

He shook Nuada again harder. A small tear formed in Foxy's right eye.

"Wake up!" Foxy pleaded over Nuada's body.

"He is dying," said an ungodly voice from the end of the passage.

Foxy quickly turned to see the very faded outline of what appeared to be a man, but he was so far away it was hard to tell. Foxy just looked. He pointed the sword at the figure. The figure was still too far away to be seen clearly, but Foxy knew who it must be. Foxy was mustering bravery from deep within him. He raised the sword and had to force his legs to march towards the being.

"There is no need for that," the spectre said. "Follow me, if you want to save him as he has saved you."

The distant phantom walked off down a further chamber corridor. Foxy remained still with one hand holding onto Nuada's shoulder. He watched the figure walk away, and he could hear further wheezing from Nuada's breathing. Internally contemplating, Foxy was thinking about the fear in which the others spoke of the Fear Gorta. This must have been him, Foxy was thinking, but what if it was a different spirit? A decent one?

Foxy was discussing with his own mind. If he went with the individual, he might save Nuada, or the spirit could have ill intents. However, when Foxy looked at Nuada, he was sure he would die if he did nothing. Foxy considered for a moment, and then thought that more is lost through indecision than wrong decisions.

"I'll be back, I promise," Foxy said, and he slowly started walking along the corridor, illuminating the dark halls as he walked with the sword of light. Foxy reached the end of his passage, which had a left turn and a right turn. Both looked identical, but he clearly remembered the figure walking down the left passage, so Foxy followed that way.

When Foxy took one step left, the darkness of the tomb changed. He was baffled as he looked around to see that he was no longer looking at a damp and dark tomb. He was in the beautifully lit hallway of a house. Lightbulbs above illuminated the hall, and they bounced back off the shiny wooden floorboards.

Foxy looked behind him to see that the tomb was entirely gone. There was a simply a closed door directly behind him. He tried to open it, but it was locked. Foxy then heard a conversation coming from the other side of the house's hallway.

"Gerard, come down for dinner," a familiar female voice shouted through the halls.

"I'm coming, Ma," said a familiar child's voice.

Foxy took a precautious step forward as he saw a child run across the end of the hall, his shoes causing a soothing pitter patter along the wooden floor.

"There's my little man," a male voice said.

Foxy continued walking up the hall of the house until he reached an open door. He looked in to see a family eating dinner. A mother, father and a young son. Foxy's jaw dropped when he connected the dots. This was his family. That little boy was him. The feeling of nostalgia was overwhelming for Foxy, and tears started to flood his face.

"Mam, Dad," Foxy said softly.

He could smell the stew in the house. It was majestic. The smell was the very thing that made him feel at home when he first arrived in Tinree Island. Foxy's mother looked straight through the door. Foxy smiled, as he thought she was looking at him, but he quickly realised they could not see him when he heard a voice from the corner of the room.

"They cannot see you. This is a memory," said the voice.

Foxy looked to the corner of the room to see an impossibly thin, very elderly man sitting in an armchair. He was very well-dressed, wearing an old cotton suit. He was also wearing a flat cap that several elderly Irish men would wear. His face was extremely gaunt, his lips cut dry. He was sitting with his legs crossed and his hands folded across his lap.

"Who are you?" Foxy asked, also noticing that the memories could not hear him.

"You know who I am," said the figure, sitting still.

Foxy continued to stare at the old man sitting in the chair.

"You're the Fear Gorta," said Foxy strongly.

"Yes," said the man, standing up. "Or the hungry man, as the ignorant like to say. It is a shame what happened to our language."

He gestured to the happy family at the table.

"Take one last look, Mr. Fox; you may never see this memory again," said the Fear Gorta, walking out the room. He left a trailing hand for Foxy to follow him.

"How do you know who I am?" Foxy asked, slowly following the man out of the room.

"You prayed for me," said the Fear Gorta.

Foxy took one step outside of the happy warm auburn lit room. Then, suddenly, he was in a cold hospital wing. The bright ceiling lights blinded Foxy for a moment. He held up the sword of light to shield his eyes. He looked ahead down the hall to see another version of his younger self. This one was a little older, but still nothing more than a child.

There was a doctor crouched down beside him.

"I remember this," said Foxy.

"What is it?" asked the unseen Fear Gorta, a voice that was seemingly emanating from inside Foxy's head now.

Foxy moved slowly towards the doctor and the younger version of himself.

"This is the day my parents died," Foxy said blankly.

When Foxy reached the child, he could see in through the ward window. There were two hospital beds with bodies lying in them. They had sheets pulled up over them. In between the two beds, stood the Fear Gorta. He had a hand on each bed. He tutted while looking at them and shaking his head.

Foxy's jaw was agape while looking in through the window at the hospital beds.

"A terrible thing, disease. It kills without prejudice. Do you remember what you said that day?" asked the Fear Gorta.

Foxy looked down at the child and the doctor. The younger version of Foxy was crying inconsolably.

"Why did they have to die?" asked the young memory.

When the doctor spoke, though, there was no words. Just mumbled, distorted noises.

"If they're gone, then I want the whole world to die, not just them! It's not fair!" screamed the younger Foxy.

The doctor then looked up at Foxy, now showing the gaunt, twisted face of the Fear Gorta. He then stood up and began to walk away down the hall, turning into another corridor.

"You see, Foxy, you asked for the world to die. You spoke to me, and I listened," Hissed the phantom as he walked away.

Foxy took one last look in through the window at the hospital beds and then returned to following the Fear Gorta. This time when Foxy took a step around the corridor, he found himself sitting in a small van. The van was travelling through the Irish countryside. Foxy could see the other version of himself, at the same age, looking sadly out through the window.

"This is the day, I came to Tinree Island," said Foxy.

"Yes," replied the Fear Gorta, who was looking at Foxy from the rearview mirror. This time he was taking the position of the driver.

"Remember how miserable you were?" asked the Fear Gorta. "You thought it was the end of the world. You thought you'd be all alone again."

Foxy looked at himself and realised just how sad he looked at this moment.

Then a whisper came directly into Foxy's ear.

"All alone again," said the whisper, startling Foxy. The jolt from the whisper was accentuated by the fact the van was speeding up.

"You wanted to be all alone, though, didn't you?" said the driver. "I'm only giving you what you asked for."

The van then reached breakneck speed and swerved off the road down a steep hill. Foxy screamed, but upon impact he found that he was standing outside. He looked up to see he was standing on top of Cnoc Mor.

It was the exact moment when the first Fomorian had Cathal held by the neck.

"You felt helpless here, too, didn't you boy?" asked the Fear Gorta, who was standing directly next to the Fomorian.

Foxy looked at himself. Standing still, frozen, while Naoise was getting ready to save Cathal's life.

"I didn't know what to do," said Foxy, beginning to weep.

A smile came across the face of the hollow phantom.

"Let the tears out. Bask in them. Let the sadness overcome you," he said.

The Fear Gorta walked menacingly over to Foxy and held out his arms, Foxy once again didn't know what to do; he was frozen in place. Foxy then dropped the sword of light and began to start crying ferociously. The Fear Gorta placed his long, bony arms around Foxy and embraced him in a hug. Foxy continued to weep heavily.

"Why can't I help anyone," he wailed.

The Fear Gorta hugged him tighter.

"It's okay, child, I have you. I'll take the sadness away. I'll hold onto you," said the Fear Gorta.

Foxy could feel the sadness lifting, the overwhelming weight of the depression was being pulled off him. In a moment of pure vulnerability, Foxy hugged the Fear Gorta back. The man then leaned down to Foxy's ear.

"I'll take your sadness. I'll hold onto you forever," it whispered in his ear.

This frightened Foxy, who tried to pull away but couldn't. The Fear Gorta's arms were latched around him. He couldn't move an inch.

"What's happening?" Foxy shouted.

"I haven't tasted sweet misery in a very long time," moaned the spirit. He started cackling.

"We will stay embraced forever. I will nourish these horrid memories forever. You and I will be bonded for all eternity."

Foxy could see that the surroundings of the top of Cnoc Mor were beginning to fade, the light was diminishing. Then, in a swift transition Foxy found himself back in total darkness in the tomb. The pitch black was dreadful. Foxy wanted to scream, but the being was holding him so tight he couldn't open his mouth. The claustrophobic panic was settling in. All Foxy could hear was the horrendously evil laugh from the Fear Gorta. Foxy felt suffocated and couldn't breathe. He was locked into the horrid emotions writhing off the Fear Gorta.

Then, deep in the distance of the tomb, there wasn't total darkness. There was a light. Foxy opened his eyes fully against the pressing body of the Fear Gorta The blurry light shaped itself into a human – a woman, Foxy thought. Then he could see it was the woman from the lake. Her fiery red hair, and beautiful pale face radiated in the tunnel.

"Danu," Foxy barely croaked against the body of the Fear Gorta.

Danu just smiled at him from a distance. Then two other blurry light shapes appeared beside her. Foxy's eyes were flooding with tears, but through his misty vision he could see clearly who it was. His heart lifted, and thus he felt the grip from the Fear Gorta loosen.

It was his parents standing either side of Danu. Each of them were dressed as they were on that Christmas morning when he was a child. That was his fondest memory of them. They were smiling at him silently. Foxy's heart was overcome with love. It was a love he hadn't felt in a while, and it wasn't the love for someone else. He had felt so useless at times in his life, he had forgotten how deeply he was actually loved.

The Fear Gorta's arms were getting weaker. Foxy could push back an inch or so.

"Where's our little warrior?" said Foxy's mother.

"Yeah!" Said Foxy's father. "Where is the hero who is going to slay the foul beast?"

Foxy's soul soared.

"You must use powerful happy memories to overcome the sorrow," Danu said.

Foxy looked at his parents longingly. He thought fondly of the Christmases they spent together. The birthdays. Playing in the garden. Sitting on his father's shoulders watching hurling matches together. His mother hugging him goodnight. An image flashed into his mind, of both his parents hugging him outside their home before his first day of school. The love he felt for his parents was intense.

Then an image popped into his mind, of Linda showing him his room on the first day he arrived in Tinree Island. Himself, Linda and Macdara enjoying a warm stew on a wet rainy evening in the kitchen. Foxy saw himself working with Macdara on the farm, and having chats with Linda over cups of tea. Foxy felt more love in these memories, too. Linda and Macdara had loved him too.

Foxy had flashes of Cathal dressed as the wizard on Halloween. This made Foxy smile and begin to laugh, which appeared to weaken the Fear Gorta further. Then Foxy saw Nuada defending them against Conann and saving him from the blast that Tethra and Cethlinn had directed towards him. He even saw Lugh dancing and twirling his spear, showing off. Intermittent flashes of Vincent disliking him when they first met flooded to his mind. These evolved to Vincent shaking his hand and smiling at him when he returned. Had Vincent learned to love him, too, he thought.

Then, in a swirl of emotion and memory, Foxy saw Naoise. He was wet and nervous on his first day of school in Tinree Island. There she was, getting out of her car. She smiled at him straightaway. The following memories came at Foxy in a whirlwind of flashbacks.

He saw himself and Naoise eating soup that Vincent had prepared for them in Tryst Manor, the first time he visited there. He saw her whistling in English class. He had a fond memory of the two of them walking through the field on the way to Cnor Mor the first time. The warm sun glistened across the dewy grass. Then he remembered when he and Naoise sat out on the fence in the Sullivans' farm under the moonlight. They'd held hands for a moment. This memory quickly transitioned to Foxy and Naoise standing outside Tryst Manor in a light snowfall. He remembered them kissing, and then he felt a surge of collective love as all the memories cheered for him in unison.

He summoned unknown strength and was able to free his arms, Foxy could see the sword of light on the ground from the faint light of Danu. He was able to half crouch and grasp it with fingertips. He picked it up, and with almighty strength he shoved the sword of light straight into the Fear Gorta's back.

The Fear Gorta fell backwards onto the ground with a diabolical howl. Foxy could see the sword of light on the ground from the faint light of Danu. Foxy turned to look at his parents and Danu. They all smiled at him sincerely as their light began to fade. In a brief moment, they were gone.

Only the sword of light lighting the hall now, Foxy looked at the Fear Gorta on the ground. It now resembled a feeble, dying, old, emaciated man.

"Foxy!" a shout echoed through the chambers.

"Nuada!" Foxy shouted back.

"Stay where you are! I'll come to you," Nuada called back.

Foxy could hear footsteps slowly echo in the halls, and Nuada was blindly making his way through the passages. He eventually rounded a corner and saw the light from the sword.

"Foxy!" He said exuberantly and hurried his walk towards Foxy. He was very clearly hurt.

"I am so glad to see you're alright, my friend," said Nuada.

His eyes then cast to the Fear Gorta, who was laying on the ground holding his stomach. His emaciated features were only furthering as his body was collapsing in on itself as if there was a vacuum sucking the air from him.

"Foxy," Nuada said with a croak in his voice, as if he was about to cry.

Foxy looked down at the pathetic figure writing on the tomb floor. Foxy held the sword closer so they could get a brighter view of him.

"I stabbed him," said Foxy plainly.

"You must have summoned very powerful memories to physically strike him. Only pure love can overcome him," said Nuada.

"Will he die?" asked Foxy.

"He will now," said Nuada, grabbing the blade off Foxy and swinging it high above his head.

"Wait," wheezed the Fear Gorta.

"What is it, demon?" Nuada replied coldly.

"The boy," said the skeletal being on the floors "he is of ancient blood."

Foxy looked intrigued at the Fear Gorta, and as a matter of fact so did Nuada.

"Heed your lies, spirit," Nuada said strongly, "the boy is not Tuath De Danann."

"Correct," said the Fear Gorta. "He has a warrior's blood. If I tell you, will you kill me?"

Nuada looked at the spirit, puzzled.

"Let this world be rid of me, and me rid of it," spat the Fear Gorta.

"Speak your truth phantom," Nuada said lifting the sword aloft his head again.

The Fear Gorta clawed back to his knees. He was almost transparent now, he was so thin. Foxy looked at the situation, eagerly awaiting the response from the spirit.

"The boy," said the Fear Gorta, "the boy is a descendant of…"

Then the Fear Gorta paused, while Nuada swung the blade. Just before the blade connected with the neck of the hungry man, he whispered, "Setanta."

Then the blade struck the neck of the flattening being. His head fell off, but before it reached the ground the being of the Fear Gorta simply vanished with a whisp.

Foxy looked at Nuada, stunned.

"Who is Setanta?" asked Foxy.

———

"The bravest warrior ever who wasn't a Tuath De Danann," replied Nuada.

Foxy began to ask another question, but Nuada cut him off.

"My young friend, I will tell you everything. Firstly we need to escape from here. If my theory is correct," Nuada saidn but then he was cut off by a loud noise.

An echo rumbled through the halls of the tomb.

"I knew it," said Nuada.

"What is it?" asked Foxy, semi-panicking.

"With the stone taken and the Fear Gorta vanquished, the tomb has nothing left to guard, so the entrance with open. However, it will only open for a brief period before shutting itself permanently, having fulfilled its purpose," he said, beginning to run.

He led the way with the sword of light in his left hand and pulling Foxy with his right. The stones were grinding against each other making the same noise they made when the tomb first opened. Nuada and Foxy were running through the catacombs of passages, consistently hitting dead ends. They were trying to follow the sounds of the stones, but the echo of the halls made it hard to trace. Eventually as they ran around with the panic beginning to set in, the stones stopped making noise.

"They're fully open," Said Nuada with urgency. "We don't have long."

They continued chasing down pathways, but each of them looked the exact same. Plus, it was possible that in their urgency, that they got turned around on themselves.

"We must hurry!" Nuada said, seemingly losing control.

Foxy had a thought. When he was caught by the Fear Gorta, the further he walked forward with him the farther he went from himself.

We're going further in, Foxy thought. Then a sudden realisation hit him. "We have to go backwards!"

Nuada looked at him, clearly fretting about the situation.

"Hand me the sword," said Foxy, to Nuada's confusion. "Quick we don't have time!"

Nuada passed the sword to Foxy, who turned around and began to race back the path they had come. Following back the way they came seemed to have some results, as all of a sudden there was a blast of air that met them when they turned a corner.

"We must be close!" Cried Nuada as they sprinted through the halls.

Then suddenly they heard the grinding stone noise again.

"Its closing!" shouted Nuada.

They increased their pace. Foxy was at a full sprint and Nuada limped through his pain behind him as fast as he could.

"I spent an era as a tree; I am not getting stuck in one place again!" Nuada shouted as they tore through the halls.

The grinding stone noise was getting louder.

"We're nearly there," Foxy said.

Then they both heard a voice.

"Nuada!" The voice shouted and echoed.

"It's Lugh!" Nuada said to Foxy, "We have to nearly be there!"

"Where are you?!" Nuada and Foxy shouted

The grinding continued as they banged into a wall from taking the turn too fast. They didn't have time to focus on the pain, as they just kept running towards the sounds.

"Hurry up!" shouted Lugh.

Then another voice shouted through, which made Foxy run a little bit faster.

"It's closing! You have to hurry!" reverberated Naoise's voice through the tomb

Nuada and Foxy then turned one corner and saw some light deep in the distance.

"There!" shouted Foxy.

As they sprinted full tilt toward the light, turning the last corner they could see the exit finally. There was only a small gap, the stones were trying to close but hanging between the last two stones to close was Lugh. He had a hand on each stone holding it ajar while his body dangled below them.

"I can't hold it!" Lugh screamed in pain.

Foxy and Nuada made it to the exit, and Nuada lifted Foxy up. Foxy extended out a hand which was grabbed by Vincent, who pulled Foxy up out of the tomb and into the fresh bright air of the day.

Then with a painful gasp Lugh's arms slipped and he fell into the tomb alongside Nuada. The stones began to shut.

"No!" cried Foxy

The stones were amazingly held open. Foxy saw what was keeping them open. Cathal had stuck his arm in the stones. From elbow to wrist, he was keeping the stones open with his arm in rock solid form. From this small gap that Cathal had provided two hands appeared from underneath.

Foxy heard Naoise whistling, and then felt a mighty gust of wind blow by. The wind was directly targeted between the stones. it forced them back a few inches, allowing Nuada and Lugh's hands from below to clamber up a bit. Lugh was able to get his head through, and then his shoulders he was then able to push them back another little bit so Nuada could jump up and hang from the edge of the stones.

Lugh was able to squeeze himself out, and then started pushing the stones apart again. In one last-ditch effort, Nuada pulled himself and out. Cathal then fell backwards, clutching his arm in pain, Naoise fell weak and nearly fainted again. Nuada and Lugh both lay breathing heavily on the ground as the stones of the tomb lid shut themselves tightly. Forever.

"What happened down there?" asked Lugh. "The Fear Gorta?"

"He killed him," Nuada said genuinely nodding at Foxy.

340

Vincent, Naoise, Cathal and Lugh all stared at Foxy in awe.

"How?" Lugh asked, amazed.

Foxy looked around at all of them, his eyes then landing on Naoise.

"You all helped me," he said honestly.

"And he's going to help up defeat the Fomorians. You know why?" Nuada asked the group.

"Why?" Lugh said curiously.

"Because that boy, Foxy, is a descendant of Setanta" Said Nuada proudly.

Chapter 21: *All is Not Lost*

Everyone involved in the battle sat around the now-closed tomb, breathing heavily and attempting to nurse themselves into better conditions. While worse for wear, Cathal, Vincent, Naoise, Lugh, Nuada and Foxy were, for the most part, still able to continue. There were battle scars aplenty, but no fatal injuries.

"Morrigan has flown to Cnoc Mor. We will wait here until we hear news of Tethra's and Cethlinn's location," Vincent commanded the team.

Lugh was astounded at the news Nuada had just shared. Vincent's eyes were open wide with amazement. Naoise clapped her hands to her cheeks and squealed. As per usual, Cathal and Foxy were late to the knowledge party.

"I knew there was something special about you!" Naoise said, beaming. "Your bravery was beyond normal!"

Foxy was totally and utterly dumfounded.

"Are you sure of this, Nuada?" Lugh asked very seriously, surveying Foxy from head to toe.

"The Fear Gorta said it before he was killed. He was in the boy's mind," said Nuada.

Lugh took a step closer and looked very closely at Foxy's face. Foxy was still and quite unsure of how statuesque he should stay as Lugh looked at him.

"I guess he does look a bit like Deichtre *(Deck-Tir-A)*," said Lugh, beginning to smile.

Lugh took a step back, shook his own dismayed head, and began to laugh.

"Well I just can't believe it," said Lugh, then turning to Nuada. "This gives us a chance, which we badly need; we're so far out of practice. We couldn't keep up with Tethra and Cethlinn. I do apologise."

Lugh then bowed his head and spear to Foxy, who looked slightly embarrassed. Foxy's eyes glanced toward Naoise, who was still beaming with a flattering smile. Foxy gestured for Lugh to rise.

"Who is Setanta? And who is Deichtre?" Foxy asked with the greatest curiosity.

"Well, my boy," said Lugh, finding strength and confidence in his voice again, "Deichtre was a beautiful human woman. She was Irish as Irish could be – gorgeous hair, flawless skin and a sweet lilt in her accent like you wouldn't believe. I actually knew her for a short period of time."

Nuada stepped in, cutting off Lugh's unnecessary description of Deichtre.

"Deichtre had a son," Nuada said calmly with the full attention of everyone.

"That son's name was Setanta."

It seemed Nuada paused for dramatic effect. Foxy was quite literally ready to burst at the seams if he did not continue.

"Setanta grew up to become the fiercest warrior this land ever knew. His time was after the Fomorians, and when Partholòn was trapped. It was only for Setanta that the wicked Queen Maeve did not ruled this land, too. Setanta was not a Tuath De Danann, nor was he human. He had transcendent power. Power gifted to him by Danu," Nuada said, continuing his story.

"I saw Danu in the tomb," Foxy exclaimed.

Nuada's eyes narrowed at Foxy.

"You did?" Nuada said.

"Yes." Foxy looked down, remembering the awful hug that the Fear Gorta had placed on him.

"When I think about it, she saved me," said Foxy.

"Have you seen her before?" Nuada asked, interested.

"Yes, quite a few times actually. I speak to her in a lake sometimes in my dreams," said Foxy.

Lugh and Nuada looked at each other.

"Interesting," said Lugh scratching his chin.

"This all but confirms it," said Nuada.

Foxy looked even more confused by that.

"I've seen her too, once," Cathal interrupted, and all eyes swung to him.

"The night before we trained for the first time. I wasn't going to go, but then I saw her in the dream and she convinced me to go. Although, I couldn't speak to her, she only spoke to me. Does that mean I'm a descendant of Setanta too?" asked Cathal.

"I don't think so, my young friend," said Nuada. "I believe she knew Foxy would need friends like you. Tell me, Foxy, do you speak back to her?"

"A lot," said Foxy. "She showed me your home, Falias."

Nuada and Lugh gasped.

"I saw the giant castle, and the town being pulled along by the enormous chain," said Foxy.

"No one who isn't a Tuath De Danann or a direct descendant of Setanta could speak to Danu," Nuada said with shock.

"Then it is true," Lugh said.

"My goodness," Vincent said under his breath behind them all.

Foxy felt everyone's eyes on him, a feeling he didn't love.

"So who was Setanta?!" Foxy asked more intensely.

"Well, as I was just saying, he was a warrior like no other. Setanta was a member of the red branch knights in Ulster. They were engaged in a violent and bloody war against Queen Maeve's vicious Connacht army, who weren't much better than the Fomorians.

"There was one evening when the red branch knights were stationed around a small lake in Ulster. Setanta became quite bored at the thought of sitting around the campfire all evening. He was only eighteen; naturally he got bored quickly. So he picked up a hurley and sliotar and went off for a walk, pucking the ball around to himself," Nuada said, clearly gearing himself up for the full story. Foxy listened with fascination.

"While Setanta walked around the lake, hurling the ball to himself, he spotted a girl who was about the same age he was. She was sitting off a small pier, dangling her feet in the water. She had flaming red hair and skin as white as snow. Setanta was awestruck and approached the girl to talk to her. He introduced himself, and decided to sit beside the girl. He introduced himself as Setanta, and she as Aoife.

"They were speaking very friendly to each other when Setanta heard a rotten growling from behind him. When he and the girl turned to see what it was, there was a large, violent-looking hound seething at them from the trees. The dog's teeth were bare, and it was frothing at the mouth. The mighty dog charged them down, and the girl screamed. Setanta knew nought else to do, so he grabbed the hurley and struck the sliotar as hard as he could. At the very last moment no less, the dog's mouth had just opened to bite when Setanta drove the sliotar down his neck, killing the dog."

Foxy and Cathal were amazed by this story. From the faces on the others, it appeared that Vincent, Lugh and Naoise were very familiar with the story of Setanta.

Nuada continued, "With the dog dead, Setanta turned around to see that the girl was now hugging another woman who also had fiery red hair. She introduced herself as Danu, the mother of the girl. She thanked him for saving her daughter's life. Her daughter asked if she could stay with Setanta. Danu granted this request, but told Aoife that she would no longer be a Tuath De Danann. Aoife agreed.

"Danu blessed the two of them, and before she left she bestowed an ancient strength on Setanta – strength that only belongs to the brave and noble. Danu then left.

"Setanta was also known as Cu Chullain, the hound of Culann. It turned out the dog he killed belonged to a blacksmith for the red branch knights. Setanta swore himself to be the new guard dog for the blacksmith. So he became the hound of Chullain. Setanta and Aoife lived happy lives and eventually married and raised several children. Setanta's new power made his ferocious in battle. He helped defeat Queen Maeve's army in the war between Ulster and Connacht. He was a wild and passionate warrior."

"I'm related to Setanta?" Foxy said, puzzled

"Yes," said Nuada. "Like you, his bravery knows no bounds. There was never a man, nor Tuath De Danann, who was a warrior like Setanta. You have that power in you, Foxy!"

"How did he die?" Cathal asked.

"Ambush," Lugh said coldly.

"Aye," Nuada agreed. "When the war of Ulster and Connacht was over, Setanta and Aoife were walking through the countryside when the remainders of the Connacht army attacked. There was so many of them. Setanta fought them off fiercely to allow Aoife to flee. He struck down rebel after rebel. For hours he fought, but there was too many. Eventually they struck him down with a spear from afar.

"Even that didn't kill him. The Connacht rebels watched him as he was mortally wounded. Setanta crawled up the nearest hill, and, with his cloak, tied himself up against a tree. With his sword still drawn, he faced his enemies as he was dying. For three days, not one Connacht rebel dare approach him. It was only when a Raven landed on the shoulder of Setanta did they know he was dead," Nuada finished solemnly.

"Wow," said Foxy.

"Wow, indeed," said Cathal. "That's an amazing way to die."

Naoise punched Cathal in the arm for his offensive remark. He did not have his scaly skin implemented, so the punch hurt.

"You have shown the bravery of Setanta over and over again, young Foxy," said Nuada.

"We have been using you wrong," said Vincent. "I thought you should be in the back like me, but we need you up front. You are special, Foxy; I knew it the first time I saw you. I wouldn't expect my parents to gravitate towards you like they did if you weren't."

Foxy was moved by those words from Vincent. Then a thought crossed Foxy's mind.

"Nuada," he said, "what exactly does this mean? Like what changes just because I am a descendant of Setanta?"

"Throughout history, there have been various bloodline members of Setanta who can unlock the ancient power that had been bestowed on him by Danu. If the Mother Goddess is speaking to you, I believe that to be a clear sign that the power is in you. You overcame the Fear Gorta. We can defeat Tethra and Cethlinn before they raise Partholòn. Your power will be unlocked. I am sure of it," Nuada said proudly.

"Not to be that person," said Cathal, "But I feel like it has to be asked. What's our next move?"

"They may not move straightaway," said Lugh.

"True. Even though they won, it will have cost them a lot of energy to battle like that. We must regroup and wait until we hear from Morrigan. When they are seen, we will get the stone back." said Nuada.

"I want to go see Linda and Macdara," said Foxy.

"Me too!" said Naoise.

Then, in a moment of utter shock for Foxy, he heard, "Me too," From Vincent.

Both Naoise and Foxy looked at him. He looked back stoically.

"I believe I need to have an overdue conversation with them. It may be my last chance. I could have lost that opportunity today," Vincent said genuinely.

"That is wise. Let us rest ourselves. You will hear from us when it is time. Until then, please spend time with your loved ones," said Nuada.

Foxy, Naoise, Cathal and Vincent left the burnt battleground. Cathal began to mount his bicycle.

"I'll drive," said Vincent, walking over to his car, which had been damaged by the ice blasts at the front of the house but not beyond repair.

Naoise got into the front, and Cathal and Foxy painfully slotted themselves into the back. This was reminding Foxy of old times, although the mood in the car was very different. As they drove out of Tryst Manor, Foxy looked out the window. He kept replaying the story of Setanta over and over again in his mind.

***

Vincent dropped Cathal off at his house, then began to make for the Sullivans'. Both Naoise and Foxy were aware of the tenseness radiating off Vincent and the fact he was driving slower. After a brief period, they turned onto the lane leading up to the Sullivans' house. Vincent parked outside and slowly turned off the car.

Linda walked the out front door to see who it was.

Linda's eyes lit with worry as she saw Foxy and Naoise exit the car. Scrapes, bruises and even some burns adorned their young bodies.

"Oh my goodness! What on Earth happened???" Linda shrieked.

Then Vincent stepped out of the driver's door. Linda's eyes locked onto his battered body. The tension was palpable.

"Hello Ma, can we talk?" said Vincent.

At that moment, Macdara walked around the side of the house cleaning some oil off his hands with an old rag. Seeing Vincent, Foxy and Naoise's condition stopped him in his tracks. Foxy could sense the family drama about to emerge. Vincent had only spoken to his parents once in the last several years, and that was the night Naoise's parents were killed. Foxy figured he'd better leave them to talk.

"Da," Vincent said, nodding plainly at Macdara, who then looked at Foxy and Naoise.

"Why don't you two go inside for a while. Shower up," Macdara said, his eyes laser-locked on Vincent.

Foxy and Naoise were able to walk past Linda, who stayed as the third point in the family triangle. Foxy got behind her and closed the door.

"Best to let them talk in private for now," Foxy said.

Naoise agreed, and both of them went to their respective rooms. Foxy quickly got into the shower. The hot water stung against the wounds. It was the little nicks and cuts he couldn't even remember getting that stung the worst. He could hear incoherent mumbling coming from outside. To Foxy's delight, it didn't sound like a serious argument; it seemed more like a conversation. He tried his best to respect their privacy, and wanted to stay in the shower until the conversation stopped. He did not want to know what they said. Foxy firmly believed it was none of his business.

After a short while, the talking stopped and Foxy got out of the shower, dried himself off, and sat on his bed just taking a moment. A moment was all he had before Naoise knocked lightly and opened his door.

"They're at the table downstairs. I think we should go down," Naoise said shyly.

She did not want to go down. Neither did Foxy, really, as they both knew serious chats were to be had at the kitchen table. Foxy and Naoise also both knew they couldn't back out of the story yet. They had to stay with Nuada, Lugh, Vincent and Cathal until the end.

"Okay," said Foxy, standing up.

He and Naoise then walked down to the kitchen, where Vincent, Linda and Macdara were sitting around the table, each having a cup of tea. There were two unmanned cups with steam rising from them. Vincent looked at Foxy and Naoise. Macdara and Linda's eyes were firmly on their own mugs. Foxy and Naoise sat at either end of the table. Linda took a quick look at Foxy and whimpered.

"So," Macdara said coolly, "Setanta?"

Foxy felt like a deer in headlights. It was evident that Vincent had told them everything. Foxy couldn't believe how amicable Vincent and his parents were being. It felt like they were ganging up on him.

Linda whimpered again.

"I knew there was something about you from the moment we met," said Macdara. "I have had countless kids from the area help work the farm throughout the years. Not one of them ever finished ploughing the field with the drag harrow. I mean, we use tractors, I just wanted to see if they stuck it out. You were the only one."

Foxy's first reaction was betrayal. He remembered how hard it was pulling the drag harrow up and down the field on a damp September morning.

"Vincent brought us up to speed, or as much as he is capable of telling. Don't worry, we won't tell anyone," said Macdara.

"I'm sorry," Foxy said to everyone's surprise.

"Sorry for what?" responded Macdara.

"For all of this," Foxy bemoaned. "The danger, the death, the potential scourge. I'm just so sorry."

Linda whimpered loudly again, this time drawing the annoyed eyes of Macdara.

"Foxy, my boy," Macdara said simply and softly, "you are not the cause of all of this."

Foxy was very thankful for these words. Naoise looked at him, smiling, and was also very gracious of the kind words from Macdara that seemed to ease Foxy's worries.

"But you are the solution to it," said Macdara.

Foxy was stunned by this response. He felt as if there had been a massive weight placed on his shoulders.

"What do you mean?" he asked, stressing.

"Well, my son and I may never fully see eye to eye again, but I have to say that deep down I always somewhat admired him for sticking to his guns. I failed to trust him once, I don't intend to do it again." Macdara gave a fond look towards Vincent, who seemed to begrudgingly accept it.

"Vincent says that you, Foxy, are the key to defeating whatever evil is lurking. He has asked a favour of us," Macdara said to more whimpering from Linda. She sniffled and rubbed loose tears from her eyes.

"But what if it…" cried Linda, but she was cut off by Vincent.

"Ma, as I said before, if we don't try this, it could be curtains for everyone anyway," Vincent said softly and with authority.

"What's the favour?" Foxy asked, glancing between everyone.

"I've asked," Vincent said gently, "For you and Naoise to move back to Tryst Manor until this is all sorted."

"And Linda and I have agreed," added Macdara. Linda grimaced.

"It won't be long," said Vincent. "Tethra and Cethlinn will move shortly, but it is necessary that we all stay together."

Naoise was between emotions. She was happy to go back to Tryst Manor; that was her home after all. But she was sad to leave the Sullivans' house. She had really enjoyed her time there, and loved the warm family feeling that emanated through the house.

Foxy didn't really have time to process his emotions before Macdara stood up and faced the window out to the farmyard.

"Foxy, I have led a relatively simple life, but I love my life. I love my wife, I love my son," said Macdara giving the faintest glance to Vincent. "I also love my foster son, and his friend."

Naoise and Foxy smiled.

"I love all these things, and I love my little farm. While these things may seem small compared to the whole country, I believe these things are worth protecting. Won't you protect them for me?" Macdara asked Foxy sincerely.

Linda wiped the tears from her cheeks and looked at Foxy. She let out a painful sound of misery each time she looked at him.

Foxy looked from Naoise to Vincent, then from Linda to the back of Macdara's head, as he was still looking out the window. Foxy knew they were all waiting for his answer. He knew silence would reign until he answered Macdara. He briefly debated internally, but deep down he already knew his answer. The revelation that he had ancient blood hadn't actually changed too much for Foxy; he was always going to do everything he could to help.

"I'll protect them," Foxy said strongly. He then stood up and looked around at the room. "I'll protect everyone."

Naoise smiled and winked at Foxy from across the table, giving a silent applause. This made Foxy blush.

"Then what are we waiting for? Foxy, Naoise go pack some things and meet me in the car," said Vincent, but before Vincent left he walked over to his father. Outstretching his hand, and shook Macdara's hand firmly, maintaining eye contact.

"Thank you," Vincent mouthed to his father, who nodded back at him. Then Foxy saw Vincent walk over and give his Mother a tight hug. She returned it in kind. They whispered something to each other that Foxy could not make out. Vincent then walked out of the kitchen. Foxy wasn't certain, but he thought he saw a tear in Vincent's eye.

***

Foxy threw as many clothes into a bag as he could, then made for downstairs, where he arrived in the kitchen again. Naoise was already hugging Linda and Macdara goodbye. When Foxy entered, Naoise left and gave Foxy a light hand on the shoulder on the way out. Naoise knew this would be difficult for him.

Foxy walked into the kitchen, placed his bag on the table, and simply looked at Linda and Macdara. He was trying to find the right words to articulate how truly grateful he was and how much he loved staying there, and truly how much he loved them. A lump was rising in Foxy's throat, and he felt if he spoke tears might flow. He could see Linda wasn't far from crying either.

Foxy tried to speak, fighting back tears, "I just want to say…" Foxy lost the run of his voice. Hoarseness and shallow sounds now replaced his words. While Foxy couldn't get his words out, Linda finally spoke, also fighting tears.

"Foxy dear, anything you wish to say, do me a favour," she said, walking over to Foxy and taking him by the hand. "Keep those words in mind, and tell us when you come back when all this is over, okay?"

Foxy felt the weight of having to speak lift. He just smiled sincerely through watery eyes and hugged Linda tightly. Macdara, who was watching on, also didn't say any words, he just walked over and joined them in a hug. He placed his massive arms and hands around both of them. The three of them hugged in the kitchen in what would become a very fond memory of Foxy's.

***

After a short drive, Vincent, Foxy and Naoise spotted Cathal sitting out on his front wall on the road.

"There's Cathal!" Naoise said, urging Vincent to pull over.

Vincent slowed the car down and let the window down. Naoise spoke to Cathal from the car. Cathal looked ecstatic to see them, he lifted his hands to the sky in a 'finally' gesture.

"Cathal, what are you doing?" asked Naoise.

Cathal lifted up a bag from behind the wall and walked towards the car.

"Well when I got back to see my parents, there was a note left saying that they had gone on a cycling trip and wouldn't be back until after Christmas," Cathal said, putting the bag into the car.

"I texted you all, but you didn't answer, so I figured I'd wait for Vincent out front, but he took so long to drive back."

Naoise put a hand on Cathal's shoulder.

"I'm really sorry about your parents leaving, Cathal, that's not nice," Naoise said sincerely.

"That's okay," said Cathal, slightly unsure. "I'd rather be with you guys anyway."

"I'm glad you're here too, buddy," said Foxy.

The group was now whole again and ready. After a quick drive, they once again entered the mighty gates of Tryst Manor. When the car pulled into the courtyard, Foxy saw that Lugh and Nuada were both sitting on the ground with Fallow between them. It seemed they were resting. Nuada's eyes lit up to see the car return. Both Nuada and Lugh were becoming more and more pleased as each person got out of the car, until the entire party stood together out in the courtyard.

The day was slowly turning into night. Nuada walked towards the three friends and Vincent, towering over them.

"It lifts my heart to see us all back after a fierce battle ready to go again," said Nuada.

"Any word?" Vincent asked.

"Nothing yet," said Lugh. "Morrigan will update us as soon as she sees anything near Cnoc Mor, then we'll mobilize straightaway."

"Aye," said Nuada. "Until then, please, friends, let us go inside. We rest. We may not have long."

The entire group made their way inside Tryst Manor and went back to the dining room they had been in the night before. So much had changed in a day, Foxy thought. Each of them let their bodies rest, and more importantly let their minds be at ease. None of them spoke. Foxy could see that everyone actually had their eyes closed except for him and Naoise. They nodded at each other and quietly left the room without alerting anyone else.

Foxy and Naoise made their way out of the main front door of the manor and sat on the cold steps looking out at the dark evening over the forest.

"So, Setanta?" Naoise said in a joking voice. "You're basically royalty."

Foxy smirked back. He playfully pushed her away.

"It's crazy if you think about it, isn't it?" asked Naoise.

"Tell me one thing about any of this that isn't crazy," Foxy joked back.

"That's true."

"I'm telling you, Naoise, once this is all over – once we win! – you, me and Cathal, we're going to get a car or a train and see this entire country. Let's travel the entire land. We can see it all," said Foxy.

A quiet, solemn "hmmm," was all that Naoise responded with.

"Next Summer, we can even go abroad; go see the whole world. Who knows what's out there? I can't wait to do it all with you by my side," Foxy said, full of young love

Naoise turned and smiled at him. It appeared to Foxy that she was withholding something, but he didn't press her. She scooted closer to him on the steps and simply laid her head on his shoulder. Foxy put his arm around her, and the two stared in silence for a moment. Then, in the distance, they heard a caw. Through the fog of the dark night, both of them saw a crow flying towards them.

Chapter 22: *Once More Dear Friends*

The crow swooped down towards them and then quickly about-faced and flew sharply off in the same direction it ha comeme. Foxy was perplexed to what had happened.

"Is it time, Naoise?" Foxy asked nervously.

"No sighting," said Naoise "I'd better tell the others."

Naoise went back inside. Foxy was thinking on her response to his proposal of travel. She had seemed reluctant. He then got that feeling that he had said the wrong thing. Perhaps he had come on too strong. Things had been so chaotic the last while, and Foxy was now wondering if had he romanticised he and Naoise's relationship too much.

He sat on the stoop replaying the scenario over and over in his head. He assured himself he was correct in his assumption that Naoise had seemed off with him and he wasn't overreacting. His internal conversation lasted a while before he rejoined the others inside. He entered the large hall, where they were all congregated mid-conversation.

"So with no new information, what's the plan?" asked Lugh.

Nuada looked around the room, and without speaking just began to walk upstairs. Lugh looked shocked at this action.

"Nuada, what do we do?" he asked again.

Through fierce exhaustion, Nuada mumbled back, "We rest," as he continued up the stairs and out of sight.

Cathal looked as happy as Foxy as ever had seen him. He grabbed his bag of clothes and whatnots, looking at Vincent.

"Can I stay in any empty room?" asked Cathal.

Vincent actually cracked a genuine smile and gave him an out of character thumbs up.

"I think I'll call it a day too, then; it's been one for the ages," Lugh said, cracking his back over his spear, then, very gingerly, he too walked upstairs.

Vincent, Naoise and Foxy were the only ones left downstairs now. Foxy was hoping Vincent would leave so he could ask Naoise what her problem was. Even now, Foxy could sense that she was off with him. He still couldn't figure out why.

"Your room is ready as you left it Ms. Moone," Vincent said plainly.

"Wonderful, Vincent, thank you!" Naoise replied. And then, to Foxy's dismay, Naoise quickly jaunted up the stairs and out of sight too.

Foxy gawked at the stairs Naoise had just darted away to. She was mad at him, he was sure of it now. That in turn made him mad at her, because he firmly believe he'd done nothing wrong. He was just about to go after her to talk when a voice hammered home how tired he was.

"Foxy, you must be shattered. Please, a room is made up down here," Vincent said politely.

Foxy was just inkling to run up after Naoise and confront her, but he decided a sleep could maybe solve all his problems. The room Vincent led him to was neat and warm. Foxy thought he would have a very hard time sleeping, as Naoise's reaction was playing on repeat in his mind. However, the opposite was true, as he fell asleep quite quickly.

Momentarily, before he nodded off, he hoped he would wake in the lake of Falias. Not to ask about Setanta, or ancient power, but simply to ask for advice about what he had done to offend Naoise.

***

Foxy did not wake up in the lake of Falias. He woke up in Tryst Manor, and his first through was *Where's Naoise?*

While mentally he was still under duress, Foxy felt tremendously well-rested physically. He'd had a wonderfully deep, dreamless sleep. When he left his room to head towards the kitchen, he noticed lots of noise. The closer he got, he realised it was a mix of banging, clanging and conversation. He poked his head into the kitchen door to realise that he was the last one out of bed.

Foxy's eyes flicked around the room, and he spotted Naoise and Vincent cooking. Cathal, Lugh and Nuada were sitting at the table having a conversation. Foxy wondered what the three of them were discussing. Vincent spotted Foxy as he walked in and acknowledged him.

"Ah, good morning Foxy. Have a seat; good lad," said Vincent with a certain pep in his step.

Foxy didn't answer back as all he noticed was that Naoise did not turn around to look at him. Foxy went to speak and ask Naoise what was going on, but was interrupted by Nuada.

"Sit down, blood of Setanta. We were regaling each other with war stories. Young Cathal here was giving us another example of your bravery – fighting a wicked foe on Halloween night!" Nuada said, chewing on burnt food clearly cooked by Naoise.

Foxy sat down as their conversation continued.

"I was once in a fierce battle myself on Halloween night," Lugh said. "Against the Dullahan. Wicked creature; never got the end of him. But some day!"

A plate was then forcefully thrown down in front of Foxy. It had all the makings of a breakfast except everything was either very burnt or undercooked. Naoise didn't say a word as she threw the plate in front of him.

"Thanks," Foxy said sarcastically. This drew a scowl from Naoise.

Foxy couldn't believe no one else was commenting on her odd behaviour. He looked around to see if anyone would comment on it, but everyone continued with their breakfast.

"What's the plan today, then?" Cathal asked as he ate, which looked well-cooked.

"Same as yesterday," Nuada said calmly. "The battle was lost, but the war continues. We merely await the next battle. Morrigan will update us on any sightings."

"Are we training today?" Cathal asked nervously.

Nuada laughed loudly. "I don't think so, my young friend. Let us rest until we are called once more unto the breach. Let us enjoy the morning."

After breakfast, Naoise left the kitchen so quickly Foxy did not get a chance to speak to her. Vincent began to clean up by himself. Foxy and Cathal offered to do it and Vincent allowed them. He then left the room alongside Nuada and Lugh.

"I fancy a bit of training, myself," Lugh said, grabbing his spear.

Cathal and Foxy took to scrubbing the large mess left by Naoise's cooking.

"Well, did you see that?" asked Foxy.

"See what?" Cathal responded earnestly.

"Oh don't be stupid, Cathal, the way Naoise was treating me," snapped Foxy.

Cathal looked astounded and giggled.

"Honestly, what way? I literally didn't see anything. I was listening to Lugh and Nuada's stories. They're pretty amazing guys, did you know once—" Cathal began, but he was cut off by Foxy.

"What could I have done to make Naoise mad?" Foxy demanded to know, brushing and scrubbing plates.

Cathal was clearly annoyed, a personality trait seen very little out of him.

"Sure, how am I supposed to know?" Cathal quipped back. "Why don't you go and ask her?"

A lightbulb went off in Foxy's mind and his eyes lit up.

"I'll do just that," Foxy said, storming out of the room and leaving Cathal to do all the washing up.

"Oh grand, I'll just do all the washing up," Cathal said in the distance as Foxy stormed out of the kitchen, into the foyer and headed straight for Naoise's room. Thundering up the marble stairs, his heart was lifting.

Now a little bit of doubt creeped into his mind. What if Foxy confronted Naoise and she said she hated him when he asked what was wrong? Maybe everything she'd said was all a lie, and she never even liked him at all. Foxy didn't think he would be able to hear that, but then he thought of all the positives with Naoise.

Actually, when he thought about it, everything had incredible since their very first meeting, bar the last twelve hours. His rational side kicked in and found that there must be a logical reason for her anger. He knew which room was Naoise's, as there was a pair of female converse left outside it. Curiosity overrode his fear, and standing outside Naoise's room he knocked on the door. There was no answer.

Foxy looked up and down the hall and then knocked again, louder. There was still no answer. Cautiously he pressed down on the handle and opened the door very slowly. He poked his head in the door to see that the room was empty. He gave the room a full look around to make sure Naoise wasn't in any corner. She wasn't.

Quite like Naoise, the room was elegant and quirky. Everything was neat and tidy, but the room had an unusual décor of jet black and deep pink. The colours were quite harsh on the eyes, but for certain it was her room. He quietly walked into the room and closed the door behind him. He figured she would be back momentarily. He glanced around the room, then decided it would be more mannerly to wait outside her room rather than it.

Just as Foxy was about to leave the room, he spotted a book on her desk with a distinguishable title on the leather-bound cover. Foxy looked and saw that the book clearly read, 'DIARY'.

He instantly told himself he shouldn't read it, but as he internally expressed this thought he caught his hand reaching out for the book. Foxy had to stop himself from grabbing the book. He went to leave the room, made it to the door, then stopped. Looking back at the book, Foxy thought that if he read it, perhaps he would know why Naoise was upset. That way he could remedy the issue without having to confront her. While he quantified his upcoming actions, he knew deep down it was sheer undeniable curiosity that led him to walk back to the book and open it.

He flicked open the first few pages. He saw that Naoise had been keeping this diary since she was a child. Foxy could spot the handwriting improve as he flicked forward through the pages. He saw various page titles such as 'My first day of school', 'Travels with Dad' and 'Why was Mam angry?'

Each chapter of the diary was lengthy and seemed to go into quite a bit of detail. The further he scanned through the book, he saw more of the same until he landed on a chapter that caught his eye. The title read 'The new boy at school'. Foxy read down through the page until he realised that the chapter must be discussing him.

"I met this new boy today. He was soaking wet, but he looked so brave. I can't imagine how scary it is going to a new school, especially in a weird little rural town like this. There's something about him. I wanted to speak to him, and when I did he spoke back as a friend, not making fun like the other boys in school. P.S., he's not bad on the eyes either!" The diary read.

Foxy smiled reading this passage, he flicked through the rest of this as it recounted the first day of school where he had met Naoise. Flicking through the next pages he saw all the previous events accounted for. 'A fight after school' discussed how impressed Naoise had been when she saw Foxy stand up for Cathal against Connor Sweeney.

'Lunch with Foxy' talked about how much fun Naoise had the day her and Foxy ate lunch together at Tryst Manor. That was the day they she had given him the book.

'Mam & Dad' was a sad read, as Naoise expressed her inexplicable pain over the loss of her parents. She spoke at great length about how grateful she was to Foxy and the Sullivans for their support. Foxy now realised Naoise must have brought this book to the Sullivans', as there were entries made while she was living there recounting her love of Linda's food and her happy conversations with Macdara.

Foxy then found exactly what he was looking for. It was a diary entry dated today, December 22nd. Once again Foxy checked his surroundings to make sure no one was coming up the hall before diving into the chapter. The title was ominously labelled, 'How do I tell him?'

The first few paragraphs quickly chronicled the events of the battle that took place the previous morning. Foxy actually thought that if anyone found the book, the short description of the battle would do it no service. It was the second half of the entry that caught Foxy's eye. He began to read her diary again.

"The battle will begin again soon. I am was scared today, although Foxy was beyond brave, as he always is. It's really no surprise he is a descendant of Setanta! I knew he was special from the first time I saw him.

"I have to admit I am frightened; those two Fomorians are so powerful. I find myself caught between a rock and a hard place. Naturally, I am scared of what will happen if we lose again. They already have the stone, so the outcome of them raising Partholòn is very scary, but I am also worried about what happens if we win. What comes next? What will Foxy do? I worry about him so much; it's so dangerous. I really don't know what I'd do. If something happens, how could I say goodbye?

"Last night, he spoke about what we would do after I knew what I'd have to do. It's one of the hardest decisions I've ever made. I decided I am going to try and push him away. I think if he likes me less, the loss won't be as bad or something, if what I think is going to happen happens. Maybe that's me being pessimistic, but I can't help but see any other outcome. It'll be really hard, but I think it might work. After all, how much could he like me? No one ever really liked me. So that's what I'll do, because there's no way I can tell him about…"

Then the chapter ended unfinished. Foxy frantically flicked to the next page, but to his own dismay, they were blank. He now knew he had done nothing wrong. It was actually Naoise's concern for Foxy that was causing her to be mean. This did not smooth all tides with Foxy, as now he felt a madness at Naoise because he found her idea particularly dumb.

He stood there thinking, but then he heard distinct footsteps across the hallway. He sharply closed the diary and placed it back exactly where he had found it, then stood very still. The footsteps grow louder and louder until they were right outside the door, then faded away down the rest of the hall. He could hear the voices of Vincent and Nuada talking about something. When the voices had fully disappeared, Foxy looked back outside the room, checked thatthe coast was clear, and then left.

Foxy was incensed; he couldn't get on board with Naoise's rationale.

She was going to be mean to me on the off-chance that I die? Foxy thought to himself.

It made him feel as if she didn't believe in him. Turning the corner, Foxy made his way back down the stairs and into the kitchen. Cathal had made very little progress with the washing up. Foxy started to help again by grabbing the plate Cathal was doing a morose job of washing and doing it properly.

"Well, what did she say?" asked Cathal.

Foxy was about to tell Cathal what he'd read, but then knew he would be incriminating himself for reading her diary, which he knew was a morally wrong thing to do.

"I couldn't find her," he said coldly.

"Ah. I'm sure she'll be back later on." Cathal replied, relaxed.

***

The day floated by, and when dinnertime came and there was still no sign of Naoise, Vincent to his own annoyance had to come and basically clean everything again before he started cooking dinner.

Lugh had come back in from what seemed like consistent training all day. Foxy and Cathal had seen him flipping around and fighting his own spear throughout the day when they went on walks of the grounds to combat boredom. Nuada walked the halls of the manor all day, stopping to admire portraits and paintings. He told Foxy and Cathal long stories about the pople in the paintings. On any other day, Foxy would be ecstatic to listen to these stories, but Naoise was the only thought on his mind.

When Vincent served dinner that evening, it was almost as if he knew she was coming. Like a routine, Naoise had just entered the room as Vincent plopped a plate of roast beef in front of her.

"Good evening, Ms. Moone," he said.

"Evening, Vincent!" Naoise replied cheerfully.

Her eyes never moved toward Foxy, and Foxy – who was now feeling anger towards Naoise – did his best to not let his eyes move toward her.

"Where have you spent the day, young Moone?" Nuada asked, tucking into his large-portioned dinner.

"Just walking in the woods with Fallow," said Naoise. "I haven't really spent any time with him in a while, so we just spent the day in the woods."
"A day well spent!" Nuada replied powerfully. "A day in nature is a day at peace!"

Naoise smiled back at Nuada as if nothing was the matter.

"How is Fallow?" asked Cathal.

"He's great! He's a bit lonely with Morrigan gone scouting all the time."

When Naoise looked at Cathal, her eyes were blind to Foxy, who was sitting right beside Cathal. Once again, to Foxy's bewilderment, it appeared no one could see the tension between the two of them. They all stayed there and ate their dinner. Naoise was the life of the party.

When dinner had ended, before anyone had gotten a chance to even clear their plates, Naoise said, "I think I'll go to bed. I walked a lot today; I am pretty tired." She yawned.

"Goodnight then, Ms. Moone," Nuada said sharply. Then, turning his head to Foxy, he said, "Now Foxy, let me tell you another story of Setanta in battle. Oh he was fierce!"

The words coming from Nuada's mouth melted to nothing more than a dull drone in Foxy's ears as he watched Naoise leave the room. He then filtered back to Nuada's story just at the very end of it.

"And there wasn't a single scratch on him! Can you believe that?!" bellowed Nuada.

***

Later that night, they all went to bed. Foxy once again debated just going to Naoise's room and confronting her, but he let stubbornness win and chose to stay in bed. If she didn't want to talk to him, then maybe he wasn't going to talk to her.

***

The next day repeated almost identically, a nice warm breakfast was merged with a cold shoulder from Naoise. Then she disappeared for the morning and afternoon, not appearing until dinner. Once again, she announced her early bedtime. Foxy scowled at her as she left the room. She simply ignored him.

Foxy and Cathal were landed with dinner clean-up, too. It was late at night as they cleaned, when Vincent re-entered the kitchen.

"I promise we are doing a better job," said Cathal.

"I believe you," said Vincent in a friendly manner.

"Cathal, could I have a word with Foxy?" asked Vincent.

Foxy was unsure, but eager to know what this was about. Cathal was just happy to get away from the washing up for a while, and happily left the room. Then it was just Foxy and Vincent in the room.

"You and Naoise haven't spoke at a meal in two days," said Vincent.

Foxy remained silent, playing it off as nothing.

"That's not like you two at all," Vincent continued as he got himself a glass of water from the sink.

"It's nothing," Foxy lied.

"I never said it was something," Vincent said softly.

Vincent then went to leave the room with his water.

"If I may, Foxy," said Vincent, "Take it from someone who spent a long time not saying what he wanted to say to those who mattered. If it *is* something, which I'm not saying it is, it doesn't matter in the end. If you care about someone, you should let them know."

Vincent then left the words for Foxy to digest and left the room. Foxy finished the last bit of the washing and made his way to bed. He tossed and turned in his sleep, waking in and out of consciousness. He kept thinking on Vincent's words.

Foxy figured now he would not get back to sleep. He checked the clock to see it was 6 am on Christmas Eve morning. Lying there in bed staring at the ceiling, he was filled with motivation. He no longer wanted to play this game of silence. He was going to go to Naoise's room to speak to her. He didn't care what time it was. He got dressed and walked out of his room quietly, so as not to wake the others, and walked through the chilly hallways. However, when he reached the stairs he was met with a shocking sight.

Sitting there on the stairs, fully dressed and wide awake, was Naoise. Their eyes met.

"Naoise," said Foxy.

She shushed him.

"What are you doing up?" he asked.

She shushed him again and gestured towards the front door. She tip-toed towards it. Softly as she could, she opened it and made her way outside. Foxy followed and quietly closed the door behind him. They both wrapped their arms around themselves on the icy cold morning porch. There was thick, clear vapour when they exhaled.

"So, what are you doing up?" Foxy asked again.

Naoise looked upset, and was fighting tears.

"I was coming to talk to you," she said.

"About what?" Foxy said playing dumb.

"Oh don't be stupid, Foxy. You know we've been off the last two days. I hated it. I hated not talking to you. Come to think of it now, what are you doing up?" she quizzed.

"To be honest, I was coming to talk to you," said Foxy.

"About what?" said Naoise.

Foxy smiled and said, "as you said, don't be stupid."

They both laughed, and almost like that, things were back to normal.

"I'm sorry Foxy. Really. I wasn't thinking, and I really hated having us not talking. I mean, you're my best friend," said Naoise through tears.

Foxy smiled and relished in the nice moment, as he feared what he was about to say may undo the positive reconnection just made.

"What is it you can't tell me?" asked Foxy tentatively.

Naoise's eyes sharpened immediately, and she took a step back from Foxy.

"Foxy," said Naoise accusingly.

"I went to talk to you the day before yesterday, and well…" Foxy took a deep breath. "Well, I read your diary."

Naoise's jaw dropped. She looked absolutely disgusted.

"How dare you?!" She snapped.

"How dare *me*?" Retorted Foxy. "How dare *you* try to push me away because you think I'm going to die?"

Naoise was stunned. She gasped and went to speak, but the words didn't come right away.

"That's not what I meant, I meant…" Naoise started to reply, but cut herself off.

"Then what? I know it was wrong to read your diary, I really am sorry, but you just stopped speaking to me out of nowhere, so what was I meant to do?"

Naoise wiped the few falling tears from her eyes.

"You weren't meant to read that, Foxy. That was a really lousy thing to do," Naoise said strongly.

Then she composed herself and looked out at the dark nights sky.

"But I forgive you," she said sincerely.

Foxy was now the one who was stunned.

"So, what is it, you can't tell me?" he quizzed again.

Naoise turned to Foxy and hugged him tightly. He hugged her back instantly. Engaging with the embrace, he felt Naoise sob lightly against his chest.

"Please Foxy, stop. I forgive you, but please don't pry further. Please," pleaded Naoise.

Foxy said nothing for a moment, then hugged her a little tighter.

"Okay," he said lowly.

His own thinking was that he would rather Naoise have a secret and be back on speaking terms with him than to have the two of them at odds. Even though Naoise had said it first, Foxy also hated the fact that they hadn't been talking the last two days.

"So, we're good?" asked Foxy, moving back from the hug to look at Naoise's doughy, sad eyes.

She smiled back at him, flashing her white teeth, which seemed to look extra white in the dark morning.

"Yes, we're good. After all, Christmas is not a time for fighting," she laughed.

The two hugged again on the front steps of Tryst Manor, and just as they had heard a few days before, there was a shape flying in from the distance. Once again, Foxy could discern it was a crow.

"Morrigan," whispered Naoise.

The bird was cawing frantically and loudly. Naoise looked panicked. She reached for Foxy's hand and gripped it tightly. Foxy and Naoise stood up on the stoop of the manor as the crow landed just beside them. The bird was squawking very loudly now. This naturally called the attention of the other occupants of the manor. Nuada opened the door first and walked out to the frosty winter air.

"Morrigan," he said in a half daze, "What word have you?"

Morrigan screeched and cawed again, Foxy had no idea what the crow was saying, but it appeared that Nuada and Naoise could understand quite clearly. Lugh, Cathal and Vincent followed shortly behind Nuada. Lugh was invigorated, seeing the bird.

"Is it time?" said Lugh holding his spear tightly.

Chapter 23: *The Cave Below*

Nuada looked at Lugh coldly. Scanning the other members, Foxy, Vincent and Cathal all looked at Nuada with bated breath.

"We go again. Tethra and Cethlinn are making their way to the mountain. They are walking. We need to leave, now," said Nuada, racing inside to grab his sword.

"Get ready, we leave in two minutes!" shouted Vincent, who also ran back inside.

Nuada was already back outside the manor. Foxy couldn't believe how quickly he had grabbed his sword. He must have had it behind the door, Foxy thought.

"Lugh, you and I will run. We'll be there in no time. Vincent, you bring the children! Meet us there as soon as you can!" Nuada shouted into the manor, and in a flash he and Lugh were running off down the driveway.

In a wild mad panic of running around, Vincent emerged with the weapons Cathal and Foxy had used in the previous battle. Vincent had gotten himself dressed and ready awfully quick, too. Foxy thought it strange that none of them were wearing any armour or anything, but figured it would have played against them, as it would have been way too heavy.

Like children fleeing a burning building, Vincent hurriedly moved Foxy, Cathal and Naoise into the car. Naoise sat in the front, and Cathal and Foxy in the back. The tires on the car spun, causing dirt and stones to rise and spray as the car sped down the lane. On the way down, Foxy spotted Fallow running in the woods behind the car.

The gates were already open when they reached the bottom of the driveway, and Vincent – without a moments consideration that there may have been another car passing by – interjected himself onto the road. Foxy also saw now that Fallow had run through the gates behind them and was running down the road too. Morrigan was flying beside the charging stag.

The car's speed was immense, and Vincent took corners so fast it caused Foxy and Cathal to fly around the back of the car. The morning was jet dark, but there was a glimmer of a sunrise emerging near Cnoc Mor. Foxy's heart was beating incredibly fast. He and Cathal exchanged a look in the backseat of the car. This was it.

They arrived a short while later at the tourists' car park near the base of Cnoc Mor. The car screeched to a halt, and they exited. Foxy gazed at the giant, silhouetted mountain. They could hear the waves splashing against it from the abyss of the dark sea. The sunrise was merely a sparkle currently. Vincent looked around and saw a blinding light from the other side of the trail, where Foxy, Naoise and Cathal had started their ascent the time they hiked the mountain. The light had a heavy hue of red and blue, and Foxy had a sinking feeling. He had seen that light before.

"Let's go," Vincent demanded as they all ran towards the light.

As they ran, a thought crossed Foxy's mind. What could they do to stop them? He knew this light to be Tethra and Cethlinn's merged power. Even if he was a descendant of Setanta, which as of now Foxy thought didn't actually mean anything, how could they stop them?

Foxy, Vincent, Cathal and Naoise rounded the corner, and sure enough they spotted a large, dark, fire and ice spiral helix firing at something. Foxy looked closer and saw Tethra's horrible hooded figure shooting fire from his orb while Cethlinn stood upright holding her staff out forwards. They were shooting it at the base of the mountain. Foxy couldn't actually figure out what was happening.

"They're trying to dig into it!" Vincent shouted, and it was clear that they were doing quite a job of it. They had left a large impression of the base of the towering mountain, where they were targeting their attacks.

Just at that moment, the tunnelling beam was interrupted by a spear soaring through the dark air and colliding with Tethra. The spear went straight through him from behind his chest, quickly turned 180 degrees and then flew through Cethlinn beside him. This caused the fire and ice beam to stop, but otherwise the wounds seemed to be no great bother to them.

With the sunrise now lighting the area a little more, Foxy could see Lugh catch his spear after recalling it to him. Tethra and Cethlinn turned around to face Lugh. Tethra reached for his orb to open it, but Nuada pounced from seemingly nowhere and swiped at Tethra with his sword. The Fomorian chief moved swiftly at the last second, harrowingly avoiding the sword. Nuada quickly readjusted himself and began to swing at Tethra again, who amazingly dodged the sword attacks.

At the same time, Lugh had taken the battle to Cethlinn, who was shooting her ice shards at him. Lugh moved out their direction with ease. The two Fomorians didn't seem as powerful now as they did at Tryst Manor.

"Using that beam tires them," said Foxy.

"You're right," said Vincent. "Now's the time"

Foxy summoned his courage, which he found quite easily, and charged towards the battle. Vincent followed behind him, then, like a fork in the road, Foxy turned towards Nuada and Tethra while Vincent ran towards Cethlinn and Lugh.

Tethra was struggling to find time to open the orb, as Nuada was relentless with his attacks. A vital blow came, when Foxy reached them and dived at the Tethra's feet, wrapping his arms around them and causing the Fomorian to be unable to dodge for a moment. Nuada landed a clear blow on Tethra, who couldn't dodge and only managed to get an arm up to block. The sword of light swiped straight through Tethra's defending arm, and it fell on the ground. He roared in pain.

"Now run," said Nuada to Foxy, who listened immediately.

Scrambling back to his feet, Foxy moved safely away from Tethra, who had become enraged and now rather than dodging was striking back at Nuada with his remaining arm – the arm that was holding the orb. Trails of flame came out of the attacking orb, and Nuada blocked every one of them.

Vincent had been less successful on the other side. when he reached Cethlinn, she had spotted him coming and struck him with a large ball of ice that collided with Vincent's chest and sent him flailing across the ground. However, at that point Cethlinn was sent twirling and flying through the air.

Foxy could see Cethlinn corralling through the air, flipping wildly upside down and landing harshly on the ground. Foxy then saw exactly what had happened. Cethlinn had also been hit by a large ball in the chest and simultaneously Lugh had sent his spear horizontally behind Cethlinn's legs, causing her to rotate up into the air. To Foxy's amazement, he then saw the ball that hit Cethlinn move and stand up.

It had been Cathal, and he had been propelled by Naoise, who Foxy could hear whistling. Cathal had curled himself into a ball, hardened his skin, and was torpedoed into Cethlinn. She was beginning to make her way back to her feet when Lugh hurled his spear towards her. Cethlinn was able to defend this with a sprouting ice wall. it sprawled high and wide and fully surrounded her. Lugh's spear was hyperactively charging into the ice, chipping away at it bit by bit. Every time the ice would get chipped away, Cethlinn would regenerate it.

Foxy locked eyes with Nuada across the field.

"She's defending!" roared Lugh, "Go help Nuada."

Lugh continued breaking down the ice wall as it was being generated. He tried to attack Cethlinn from above, but she covered the top with ice, too.

Cathal ran towards where Vincent had been launched. He was in pain but alright. Cathal conveyed this through a thumbs up back to Foxy.

Naoise had run up to Foxy, who was watching Tethra continue to attack Nuada with his flaming orb. Nuada was comfortably dodging the attacks.

"This seems too easy," said Foxy.

"Let's not complain about that," said Naoise, who then began to start whistling.

A small, circular tornado began to surround Tethra. The flames were caught by the wind, and Tethra was surrounded by a whirlwind of flames. Nuada leapt backwards to allow room for him to once again pounce forward. With Tethra's vision blinded from the tornado of fire, Nuada sprinted through the flames at blistering speed, grabbing Tethra with his non-sword-carrying hand. Nuada then spun himself around in an effort to build momentum, and then he launched Tethra into the air like an Olympic hammer thrower.

"Now, young Moone!" roared Nuada, louder than Foxy had ever hear him shout before.

Naoise now whistled strongly and sharply causing another whirlwind to materialize underneath the now skyward bound Tethra. The wind caught hold of him, and at a supreme force launched Tethra into the side of the mountain. He actually landed with a terrible crack and skidded down the jagged side ointo the makings of a hole they had carved earlier. It appeared he was down for the count.

"Well done, Ms. Moone!" Nuada barked.

"Yes!" Naoise said to herself.

Foxy still seemed dubious. This couldn't have been their whole plan, he thought to himself. They'd appeared invincible a few days ago, but now they were both bested seemingly without too much ease. Had things just worked out ideally for once?

In the cold morning air, the sun was beginning to rise now, illuminating just how much damage had been done to Tethra. He looked broken. Foxy saw him attempting to scramble to his feet. One of his legs was broken, and his robes were in tatters. His hood was ripped, and Foxy caught a glimpse of his awful face underneath. His face was one that had been extremely burned. His melted skin was deep red all over his face, and Foxy could see that the exposed parts of his body were also horribly burnt.

Foxy's worst suspicions were then brought to life. It had been too easy. He heard noise coming from Tethra. Lugh even stopped attacking the ice wall for a moment to look at Tethra. Nuada walked towards where Foxy and Naoise were standing. Across the field, Cathal and Vincent stood up to face Tethra, too. Foxy could then figure out what the noise was.

It was laughter. Tethra was laughing.

"You did exactly what we wanted," Tethra gurgled.

There was a sense of urgent panic sweeping over the rest of the group. Foxy had been feeling it since they arrived.

"What do you mean, demon?" asked Nuada.

"We would never be able to tunnel into the mountain and fight you at the same time. Plus, we were exhausted from the battle the other day. We were just waiting to get into position." laughed Tethra.

"Position for what?" Foxy asked under his breath.

"Position for what?" Nuada asked much louder, walking towards Tethra.

"For this."

Tethra grinned. He was still holding the orb with his one remaining arm. Suddenly, he lit the orb ablaze and pushed it towards his own stomach. He forced the orb through his stomach, burning aside his skin until the orb was inside him. The flames spread throughout his body, and began to burn him intently.

"Now, Cethlinn!" Tethra screamed.

As the flames engulfed Tethra, there was a blinding and staggering flash. The sound was deafening, and the force knocked everyone off their feet in a prodigious explosion. Tethra had blown himself up.

Foxy's ears were ringing and his eyes were stinging from the blistering light of the explosion. He looked up from the ground to see that the explosion hadn't only forced outwards. Where Tethra had stood, there was only remains of his robes, and in the side of the mountain a large gaping hole. The giant hole in the side of Cnoc Mor had been opened from the explosion.

Foxy scanned the remains of the explosion and saw that Vincent, Nuada, Naoise, Lugh and Cathal were all scattered around the ground trying to recompose themselves. Foxy could see the massive cave entrance. He also saw a woman now running into it. Foxy's eyes quickly darted back to Lugh on the ground. The explosion had destroyed Cethlinn's ice wall, but that the ice had protected her from the blast, leaving her unharmed for a head start into the cave.

"Stop her," Nuada said, fighting back to his feet. He had taken the brunt of the blast. Lugh was also in a bad state; he'd been hit with all the ice exploding outwards at him while Cethlinn was safe inside the ice wall. Cethlinn had now totally disappeared into the cave.

"Anyone who can go, go!" Shouted Nuada, who attempted to walk towards the cave holding his ribs, but he was nursing severe injuries.

Lugh had yet to get back up; he was groaning in pain. Vincent was back on his feet. After being launched by Cethlinn, he had actually been the furthest from the blast. Foxy quickly gave his own body a quick check, and amazingly he felt okay. Before he knew it, he was running towards the cave.

Foxy hadn't really had the thought process to start running and then do the activity, it just happened very naturally. Foxy began to run faster as he was approaching Nuada, who was barely back to his knees. Nuada held out an arm.

"Take this, young Fox," said Nuada, holding out the sword of light and calmy flipping it so the handle was facing Foxy.

Without breaking stride, Foxy gripped the sword tightly and continued at pace.

"Go ahead, young Fox! I'll catch up!" claimed Nuada.

Foxy spotted Vincent across the field, who was also running towards the cave entrance. Vincent was also wincing in pain with each step, but there was an expression of determination on his face. Foxy was happy to see that Cathal was also running behind him, much slower, but doing his best to keep up.

"We can do this!" a voice said behind Foxy as he ran. He turned to see Naoise running behind him too. Far behind her, Nuada was limping towards the cave, and on the other side Lugh was just making it back to his feet.

"Let's go!" shouted Foxy, increasing his run to a sprint. He was matched in pace by Naoise. They conjoined with Cathal and Vincent's run just outside the cave, each of them holding their respective swords. Like an army storming the battlefield, they ran. Then, from the bright light of the morn, each of them was plunged back into growing darkness as they entered the wide cavern opening.

The cave was a long, wide-berthing tunnel. The group traversed it as far as they could until the natural daylight that had breached the cavern opening dissipated. They were then thankful for the light that glowed from Nuada's sword, which was held by Foxy. The sword lit up the tunnel more than enough for them to continue into it.

The cave went down and down. They had to slow their walk to traverse it safely. The decline had become so steep at times that they had to slow their urgent run to a trepidatious walk.

They descended further and further into the cavern. The air was getting cooler and thinner.

"Shush," said Foxy.

They all stood still and listened. There was a distinct noise a short distance ahead of them.

"Footsteps," whispered Vincent. "Let's go, quick!"

They hurried their steps down the steep descent, which levelled out. It appeared they were at the bottom. They had descended so far so quickly that Foxy felt a little dizzy. They speedily made their way along the flat tunnel now, getting closer to the footsteps. Turning a corner, they caught a glimpse of Cethlinn's back. She was clearly hurt from the collision of Cathal and Lugh's spear. They noticed a bright amber light illuminating from around the corner Cethlinn had just turned.

"Stop!" shouted Vincent.

Once again running at a full sprint, they chased her. When they rounded the final corner; the party was met with a wide-open cavern. To everyone's surprise, the cavernous room was exceedingly bright. Foxy saw that on the far side of the wet, stony floor where Cethlinn was heading, there was a jagged rocky plinth. Sitting on top of the plinth was the source of the light – a small, glowing object about the size of a tennis ball.

It was round, and produced an impressively powerful amber glow. Foxy looked closer and was able to see it was, in fact, a very small cauldron.

"Dagda's cauldron!" said Foxy.

Cethlinn was limping towards it as the group chased her. The room was extremely spacious, with high stalactite laden ceilings, the chasing footsteps echoed throughout the room.

Cethlinn was nearly at the cauldron when Foxy made a last-ditch effort and threw his sword at her. He fell over with the combination of his sprint and the force with which he'd thrown it.

"Same as last time, Naoise!" called Foxy as he fell to the ground hard.

Naoise let out a sharp whistle and a gust of wind caught the sword and sailed it right towards Cethlinn. The sword pierced through her back, causing Cethlinn to stop in her tracks. She gasped as the air left her body. However, she didn't fall over. She continued to stumble towards the glowing cauldron.

"I am coming," she groaned as she moved towards the cauldron; the hilt of the sword still visible in her back.

She was now using her staff as a crutch, hobbling across the cavern floor. She turned and launched a shower of icicle shards. Cathal turned his skin to rock, and while he was knocked back, he was left unharmed from the ice blasts. One of the icicle shards struck Naoise in the shoulder, causing her to scream in pain and fall back.

"Naoise!" shouted Foxy with the greatest concern.

Foxy then saw Vincent running directly towards Cethlinn. He too had an icicle shard protruding from his shoulder, but it wasn't deterring him. With the greatest intensity, Cethlinn swung her staff again but only wisps of ice came out.

"She's dying," said Cathal, lowly.

Foxy thought the same, her power seemed to have waned massively. The ice shards that she produced now were small and slow. They did little to deter Vincent as he finally caught up to her and stuck his sword right into her belly.

Cethlinn now had two swords stuck in her torso. She coughed up blood, and her gaunt face went paler than usual. She made one more gargantuan swipe with her staff, a small beam of ice emitted from the end, knocking Vincent backwards. Cethlinn then reached into her own robe and pulled out a familiar looking stone. Foxy recognised it straightaway as the stone of Fal.

"The stone!" screamed Foxy.

Cethlinn held up the stone and screamed in anguish, fountains of ice flying around the room. She was in a rage. Huge pillars and beams of ice caked the room in ice. The amber light from the object was reflecting against the ice that filled the edges of the cave. She held the stone high above her head, letting out one last painful scream. Then collapsed to the ground.

Foxy and Vincent walked over to her as she lay on her side bleeding and gasping for air. Each of them pulled their respective swords out of her.

"I think it's time for you to die," Vincent said calmly.

"I agree," wheezed Cethlinn, "for our death means his return."

Vincent and Foxy paused for a moment. Foxy looked back at Naoise, who was holding her shoulder with had a melting shard of ice still stuck in it.

"What do you mean, demon?" demanded Vincent, who hoisted his sword high above his head.

"You're too late," gasped Cethlinn as her entire body covered with ice. Freezing ice encompassed her entire body, her icy statuette lay dead on the ground. Her face held an odd smile.

"No second chances," said Vincent, who swung his sword down on the ice figure, breaking it into pieces and ensuring her demise.

Although, when the frozen Cethlinn shattered, the stone seemed to roll by itself along the floor. Vincent did not see it, but Foxy did. The stone was rolling by itself, almost as if it were pulled by a magnet closer to the cauldron on the plinth. "The stone!" screamed Foxy as he shoved Vincent out of the way and dove towards the stone. He managed to get one hand on the stone, but he couldn't contain its position. The stone was still being drawn to the cauldron, only now the force of it was pulling Foxy along the ground, too.

"Help!" shouted Foxy.

Vincent ran over to him and tried to hold onto Foxy, but the draw between the stone and the cauldron was so great it was now pulling the two of them across the ground. The pull from the stone became so painful that Foxy's hand eventually gave out, and then the stone shot towards the small glowing cauldron on the plinth.

They collided.

The flash from the collision was blazingly bright; a crystal white light filled the room. The amount of ice left in the cavern only reflected it around, making it brighter. Foxy and the others all had to shield their eyes. Foxy heard a loud thud.

After a moment, Foxy was able to flitter his eyes open a fraction. He spied across the room an enormous man laying prone on the ground. Foxy was staggered by his colossal size. He was about the same size as Nuada, but twice the width, and he had a great big belly. Foxy tried to open his eyes further. The room that was filled with amber light was now brimming with a deep red hue.

"Dagda?" Foxy said out loud to himself.

Foxy then looked to his left and saw Naoise staring at the plinth. Her eyes were sunken in her head with fear. They were immobile.

"What's wrong?" said Foxy.

Naoise didn't reply, because her eyes and sight were firmly fixed where the plinth was. Foxy turned to look.

Beside the plinth was now a huge cauldron which had turned on its side. Sitting cross-legged on the plinth was a man. The man was wearing very long and very tattered robes; they almost looked like worn bandages. Across his lap he held a long sickle, which was glowing the deep red colour.

The man stroked his finger along the sharp edge of the blade. He had long, shaggy hair that draped down over his greying face. Foxy couldn't see his face clearly, but he could easily distinguish he was wearing a smile. The man on the plinth looked at the broken icy pieces of Cethlinn on the ground. He tutted audibly.

Foxy stood up, as did Naoise, followed by Vincent and Cathal. Each of them froze in place. No one moved, and no one said a word. The man sat there, continuing to run his finger along the edge of the blade. Foxy saw that he had actually cut his finger on the sickle, but continued to trace the edge, deepening the wound. Foxy also heard him humming an ominous tune quietly to himself.

At that moment, there were more footsteps that entered the cavern. Foxy quickly turned around to see Nuada holding up Lugh at the corner back to the tunnel. Lugh held out his arm, and then in a rapid bullet motion, his spear came flying into the room faster than Foxy had ever seen it. The spear transcended across the room directly at the man who was sitting on the plinth.

Without so much as raising his head, the man on the plinth used one hand and calmly reached up. In an astounding feat, he caught the spear dead in its track mere inches from his head. He continued humming and tracing his other hand along the sickle.

"Impossible," Lugh muttered in complete astonishment.

The man now ceased humming, and simply tossed the spear to the side. He looked up, revealing a heavily battle-scarred face and one eye covered with a blood-stained bandage. He looked at each of them in the room.

"I... see... all," Partholòn said in bated breath.

Chapter 24: *All Is Lost*

The cavern was void of noise. There was no response to Partholòn's resurrection. Nuada, Lugh were aghast, staring as the villain they had fought eons ago. Naoise, Cathal and Vincent were also statuesque as they eyed the being sitting on the platform whose sight in turn was fixed on them.

Foxy wasn't sure what he was feeling. There an indescribable pressure in the room; the air was heavier. He couldn't quite place his finger on the exact cause of the change in the atmosphere, he simply attributed it to tangible power literally emanating off of Partholòn. Partholòn never blinked from his one exposed eye.

Partholòn's vision then flicked over to the impressively large man on the floor, who had begun to stir. Foxy looked over at him too. It did not take him long to realise that this giant of a man must be Dagda. He was slowly coming to life on the ground, grunting and rolling to his side. Partholòn's face morphed into sheer disgust seeing Dagda on the ground.

"How long have we been trapped due to your filthy actions?" snarled Partholòn "The last thing I remember was your disgusting, fat body holding me, and being dragged into that damned cauldron."

His eye then flicked back to the shards of Cethlinn that remained on the ground. Once again he tutted.

"Poor Cethlinn." He looked longingly at the ground "Tell me Nuada, where are my other two core Fomorians?"

Nuada puffed himself up and stepped forward, leaving Lugh to balance himself against the wall.

"They're dead! We have vanquished them, and we will vanquish you shortly!" Shouted Nuada with great passion.

"Hmm," Partholòn grunted quickly. "I have seen what is to come, I don't think those events are to pass. I see a different future – one where the scourge happens and Fomorians rise from beneath to claim this land and rid it of its ingrateful inhabitants."

Dagda made it to one knee, breathing very heavy. In a manner similar to how Lugh controlled his spear, Foxy then saw Partholòn's long sickle rise from his lap and fly towards Dagda's back. Dagda, it seemed, had no idea on earth what was actually happening.

There was a clash of metal on metal that rang out through the hollow clearing as the sickle was spinning its way in the direction of Dagda. Nuada had pounced in the sickle's way. He made an X shape with his arms and blocked the sickle with his bracers. The sickle spun out to the side, then reverted to Partholòn, who caught it coolly.

"Nuada," panted a breathless Dagda.

"Rest, Brother," replied Nuada. "I will protect you."

"You were stopped once, Partholòn, and you will be stopped again!" yelled Nuada, who charged at Partholòn.

Fist raised, Nuada closed in on Partholòn, who sedately leaned back just enough for Nuada's strike missed his face by mere millimetres. Nuada's momentum caused him to stumble past Partholòn's seated position. When Nuada had gone beyond Partholòn, the sickle was raised in the Fomorian's hand, and it struck down along Nuada's back. This caused blood to splatter across the floor and skid along the ice shards.

Nuada grunted from the blow and quickly turned around to defend himself from another blow from the sickle. Partholòn's weapon bounced away again and flew back to his hand. Nuada was hurt, from both this blow and the explosion Tethra created. There was a culmination of pain building within him.

At the same time, Lugh's spear had made another attempt at Partholòn, this time from the side as opposed to straight-on. Partholòn now leaned forward, avoiding the spear, which continued on its path. Right in the direction of Nuada. He was stunned by the appearance of the spear and was unable to move and simply faced the spear head-on. The spear was deflected away at the last second by the sword of light.

Foxy was standing there, once again, like when he ran for the cavern, he had moved instinctively. Without thought, Foxy raced across the room to deflect the sword, saving Nuada from a grave encounter. Partholòn raised an inquisitive eyebrow at the boy, who was standing there holding the sword of light. There was a meshing of the red glow from his sickle and the bright silver gleam from the sword Foxy was holding.

"I did not see that," Partholòn said calmly.

Foxy was breathing heavily, his chest feeling the pressure that was pulsating from Partholòn. It was only now that Partholòn stood up off the plinth. His feet floated slowly to the ground below.

"Why did I not see that boy?" asked Partholòn with more venom in his voice that before.

Foxy did not respond. Partholòn took one step towards him. Nuada rushed at Partholòn with another punching blow. The evil being raised his sickle in defence and absorbed the full blow of Nuada's punch with the flat side of the blade. A small sonic boom erupted throughout the cave. Then, in a rush of madness, Foxy once again charged the ancient being and swung at him with the sword of light. Partholòn was just barely able to get his sickle across to block it.

Even so, Partholòn's defence was a fraction late. Some of the blade from Foxy's swing had breached the block and had struck Partholòn's forearm. The blade was about half an inch buried in his arm. Partholòn looked incensed as his good eye glared at the wound on his arm.

"Why can't I see your actions, boy?!" growled Partholòn, and he struck Foxy in the chest with his free hand.

All the air was knocked from Foxy's body as he flew back. He was totally winded. While clawing for his breath, Partholòn and Nuada, in a test of strength, tried to push one and other back and forth.

Nuada attempted to hit Partholòn again, but was met with a vicious swipe of the sickle across his chest. Partholòn didn't have time to deliver another blow as a giant, meaty fist swung just where his head was. Nuada was barely able to dodge in time.

Foxy now saw Dagda behind Partholòn for the true size he was. The man was simply colossal. Nimble for his size, Dagda threw a number of punches at Partholòn, with the Fomorian dodging each one with millimetre precision. His dodging became more intensified as Lugh, foregoing his spear, decided to attack also. Through laboured pain, Lugh struck at Partholòn from one side, Dagda from another, and now, rising again, an invigorated Nuada joined in his Tuath De Dannan brethren's attack too.

Each of them launched a myriad of strikes at Partholòn. Occasionally, Dagda's fist would collide with Nuada, and Lugh's kicks would hit Dagda, but each of them would continue striking even though there was an odd slip on the ice sheets that scattered the cave floor.

"Don't stop!" roared Nuada. "Don't give him a chance!"

They maintained their pressure. Foxy's chest muscles finally relaxed, and he was able to take a much-needed breath of air. He saw the flurry of fists and feet from the three ancient warriors. Although he could see clearly, not one of them had landed a hit on Partholòn.

"Wind!" screamed Lugh. "We need wind, Ms. Moone!"

Naoise's tonally whistle filled the cavern, and a dense, powerful cyclone of wind formed right in front of Naoise. The cyclone quickly accelerated and launched towards Partholòn and the three warriors. On the cyclone's impact, Nuada, Dagda and Lugh each took a step back and allowed the wind tunnel to collide flatly with Partholòn. The cyclone surrounded him, and Naoise maintained the whistle for as long as she could. The gale force wind hurled and twisted around Partholòn, who now shot up to the ceiling with wind's pressure, and there was a loud bang that rang throughout the room.

"Yes!" shouted Naoise.

"Save your celebrations," Vincent said coldly.

The wind cyclone dissipated, and to Naoise's grave disappointment the bang hand't been Partholòn hitting the ceiling. It was his sickle, which he had stuck into the roof. He hung relaxed from the sickle with one hand. High in the air, his hair and robes dangled above Nuada, Lugh and Dagda.

"What now?" asked Dagda, breathing like a man who'd just ran a marathon.

'Brace!" Nuada commanded.

Foxy saw Partholòn's sickle leave the ceiling, and the Fomorian leader fell at an increasing pace. He lifted his sickle and swung it high over his head. there were large pieces of the ceiling falling down behind him, and as he came to impact with the ground he brought the sickle down into the ground between Nuada, Lugh and Dagda with a crashing might.

There was a seismic blast that catapulted the three of them into the far reaches of the cave. A blinding dust cloud hung around where Partholòn had landed. Nuada, Lugh and Dagda were all lying motionless. Foxy looked left and saw Naoise staring at him. She nodded at him and titled her eyes towards the dust cloud.

Foxy knew Partholòn could not foresee his movements like everyone else, and he knew his vision was obscured by the dust and silt floating in the air. He knew this was it; this was his chance. So he ran, at full velocity. Foxy ran towards the cloudy centre of the cave.

The sword of light cocked in a stabbing motion. Foxy's insides were alight with fear and a wild mix of other emotions. He neared the centre just as the dust began to settle. Foxy saw him, just rising back to a stand was Partholòn. As predicted, he did not see Foxy. He turned to Foxy's side and was met with a sickening blow to his stomach. The sword of light glistened in the stomach of Partholòn as the blood seeped around it.

Foxy's eyes moved from the wound he had caused up to Partholòn's face, which did not show any signs of pain. If anything, Foxy thought he looked merely inconvenienced. Partholòn's one clear eye started back at Foxy.

"There is something about you, boy," said Partholòn.

Nuada and the rest were rising back to their feet and began to race towards Partholòn again.

"But I do not have time to find out what it is. The scourge must happen now!" said Partholòn through gritted teeth.

He shoved Foxy backwards and looked around to see the Tuath De Danann faithful approaching on him. Naoise's whistle also began again.

"The scourge is upon us!" roared Partholòn, "I'll see you at the top, if you make it there."

Then, in a fiery red blaze, he held his sickle directly above his head. With a morose *whoosh*, he shot straight up like a bullet. He collided with the ceiling sickle-first, broke through the rock, and continued straight into the core of mountain. Up he went. Bits and rock and rubble fell from the wide, cylindrical hole made in the roof where Partholòn had ascended. A beam of daylight came in through the hole in.

"He's gone to the top!" Foxy shouted to the rest of the group. "We have to get to the top!"

Cathal was the first to turn and run back out of the cavern they had just entered, but he ran into something. He stood back from whatever he had run into to see it was a person. He looked again. Not a person, a Fomorian. A grey, decaying, ragged-clothed Fomorian stood in his way, blocking the exit of the cave.

Cathal stumbled backwards and tripped over a stone. The Fomorian approached. Cathal's eyes rose. As quickly as Cathal looked at the rotting head of the demon, the being was squashed against the wall. Like a pesky fly, he had been swatted. Foxy had seen exactly what happened. Dagda had swung his now-large cauldron like an Olympian hammer thrower and flattened the Fomorian against the wall.

The gargantuan man walked over and helped Cathal up.

"Thank you," Cathal said in awe.

"Hate these Fomorians. Every last rotten one of them," said Dagda.

Then, to everyone's concern, around the corner of the tunnel walked at least another dozen Fomorians. They slowly turned and began to make their way towards the group. The one in front was a female with long, shredded robes.

"We knew he would come back," she said.

Nuada stepped forward. "Let us rid these demons together. Foxy, hand me my sword," he said.

"Let him hold onto it a bit longer" Dagda moaned as he stretched his back, picking his cauldron back up, which was attached by a thick, mossy chain. The large, black cauldron had sporadic thick, brown roots growing around it.

"I think I could do with some loosening. Jump in if I'm in trouble," said Dagda, walking to the forefront of the group. Foxy went to join him, but was held back by Lugh.

"Watch," Lugh said. Foxy stayed behind and did as he was told and watched.

Dagda hurled his massive cauldron over his shoulder by the chain and began to trot towards the Fomorian offense. This was not a quick run, but for the size of the man it looked fast. Each of the Fomorians now burst into a run towards Dagda. The cauldron then began to swing in the air. Dagda turned 360 degrees to increase the momentum, and then let go of the cauldron, which collided with the Fomorian masses. It was like a strike in bowling – the otherworld beings were splatted and launched around the cavern. Dagda continued to chase them down, powerfully clobbering and beating anything that moved.

He was far more vicious that the stories Foxy had heard of the jolly old Dagda. He was very happy Dagda was on his side. Foxy ducked as one smaller Fomorian went flying over his head. Clearly thrown at a mighty force, the Fomorian crashed into the wall behind Foxy.

It was over very quickly, the initial wave had been neutralised momentarily by Dagda. He walked back, dusting off his hands.

"Silly beings have gotten weaker," Dagda said with a laugh.

Dagda then looked at Nuada and Lugh, nodding. "Boys," he said.

Both Lugh and Nuada bowed their heads and in unison said, "Forgive us."

"We wanted to honour your sacrifice," Nuada continued alone.

Dagda laughed heartily.

"There is nothing to forgive, brothers. I made the sacrifice. Would have been pretty senseless for you to free me and waste the sacrifice. Now is the time to not let it be in vain. We cannot allow the scourge to happen," said Dagda.

"Right!" said Lugh.

Nuada then turned to Foxy and looked at him sympathetically. Foxy knew he was going to say something Foxy wouldn't like.

"It's you, young Foxy," said Nuada.

Foxy looked back, puzzled.

"Don't you see? You're the one to stop him," Nuada continued.

"It's always been you, Foxy!" Naoise chirped in. Foxy was very happy to hear her words.

All eyes were on Foxy as he asked a very important question. "Why can't he see what I'm doing?"

The rest all pondered for a moment. Nuada looked as if he was about to speak, but couldn't find the words.

"Bravery," said Naoise.

Nuada snapped his fingers in a eureka moment.

"Quite right, Ms. Moone!" he said.

"Partholòn couldn't see Dagda's sacrifice because it was a truly selfless brave act," said Nuada.

"But you attacked him too. That's brave," said Foxy.

"Yes," said Lugh, now quickening on the uptake, "but we are powerful warriors. There's a difference between someone sacrificing thousands of years in a cauldron or a boy attacking an all-powerful being for the greater good. Don't you see, your weakness is your strength!"

"Not exactly how I would put it," said Dagda, "but he is right, I believe."

"We could be wrong," said Nuada. "But we know he can't see your future. You have to be the one, Foxy. He couldn't see your bravery now; you have the blood of the bravest warrior ever to grace these lands in you! Prove you are Setanta's descendant!"

"You can do it!" Cheered Cathal from the back.

"Yes," said Vincent, "the one to end this all."

Each of them looked at Foxy and gave him nods of affirmation. It was then that Foxy and Naoise's eyes met. She smiled wide at him and mouthed the words, "You're a hero," at him.

Foxy looked back at each of them, then down at the sword of light. He felt revitalized, Foxy thought to himself. For lack of a better term, he felt powerful. He raised his head and looked at the group.

"No more waiting, then! Let's get to the top!" Foxy said powerfully.

There was a raucous cheer as they turned to run out of the cavern. They could hear more footsteps. Leading the way, Foxy's sword lit the path once more as they now ascended the steep road on the journey out.

After the first incline had been completed, they encountered a series of four Fomorians, each of whom were sharply taken out of Lugh's spear. Further on the path, there were three more, for which Naoise whistled a gust of wind to raise each of them. When they fell, a revitalized Nuada struck them with a ferocious punch each.

They were closing on the end of the tunnel; they could see the daylight breaching the corners. Just at the clearance the incline subsided, and the group reached daylight again. The fresh air was invigorating. However, when they reached the field again, they stopped in their tracks when they were met by a haunting sight. There was a wall of people walking towards them.

Foxy estimated at least fifty more Fomorians making their way across the field from various directions. They looked astounded at the mound of Fomorian forces that marched towards them. Foxy then looked behind him. High above, there was smoke billowing from the top of Cnoc Mor.

"Fire?" asked Foxy.

"He is starting the scourge!" replied Nuada.

Dagda placed his cauldron on the ground, grunted, and then reached deep into the seemingly bottomless pot.

"Nuada, you take them to the top," said Dagda as his arm re-emerged from the cauldron holding a weapon. The weapon was breathtaking to Foxy.

Cathal literally said, "Woah," when Dagda took it out.

It was a giant stone hammer, almost the length of Dagda himself. Like the cauldron, the hammer was encased in growing roots all along the long handle and anvil-like top. He threw the heavy hammer up over his shoulder.

"Lugh and I can handle things here, I believe," said Dagda, to which once again Lugh did an unnecessary spear twirl.

Nuada reached out his arm, Dagda reached back, and the two shook hands.

"Good luck, brother," said Nuada. Dagda nodded.

Foxy, Nuada, Cathal, Naoise and Vincent turned to run up the mountain. Foxy looked back once to see Lugh and his spear cascading around the field and Fomorians dropping with a great quickness. He also managed to spot Dagda standing still, waiting for a swarm of Fomorians to come to him before knocking them blank with a mighty, circular swing.

"Eyes forward Foxy," said Nuada. "This won't be easy."

Chapter 25: *The Final Climb*

Foxy could see smoke billowing from the top of Cnoc Mor. The group simply couldn't maintain a run up the mountain, as it was far too steep. They had reduced their ascent to a speedy walk, which was still quite taxing on their bodies.

Cathal and Vincent in particular were finding the physical effects the hardest. Cathal's physical fitness was leaving him dragging; he was blowing hard and couldn't catch his breath. Meanwhile, Vincent was struggling with the combined effect of injuries and damage taken. Foxy, Naoise and Nuada were, in fact, hitting their stride and gliding up the mountain. Foxy stopped to look at Cathal and Vincent, who were visibly in strife.

The day was fully in bloom now; the bright Christmas sun shone across the mountain side. While it was cold, the direct sunlight forced the group to squint, which – although miniscule – was taking extra effort for a couple already depleted party members.

"Come on guys, we can't stop now," Foxy pleaded.

"Please," panted Cathal, "go on ahead, we're slowing you down."

Foxy looked at Nuada, who was glancing down at the now ant-size battle below, in which it still looked like Dagda and Lugh were creating havoc. Foxy didn't know whether to leave them or not.

"Go," said Vincent. "It's the right thing to do, we will catch up. You have to go now!"

Foxy waited another beat before Naoise dragged his arm. He looked back at Cathal and Vincent one last time before ascending.

"We'll be fine! I know you can do it, Foxy! I've never been more certain of anything!" said Cathal.

Foxy gave Cathal an empathetic smile as his short friend gasped for air.

"Foxy, let's go! We haven't got time!" Naoise said hurriedly.

"She's right, we press on to the summit," Said Nuada.

Cathal and Vincent had to stop entirely and breathe while Foxy, Naoise and Nuada continued trudging up the climb. They had breached a little over the halfway point, and fatigue was now beginning to set in for Foxy and Naoise. Nuada was also beginning to feel a continued effect from his injuries but played a brave face.

"Look over there!" said Naoise with more energy that she had possessed since entering the cave beneath.

Foxy's tired eyes glanced over to see her pointing at a jagged rock.

"What is it, Naoise?" asked Foxy, eager to continue the climb. The smoke rising from the top of the mountain was becoming more dense and spreading widely.

"The bags!" Cried Naoise, rushing over to the jagged rocks.

Then, to Foxy's amazement, there they were – the bags they had left there the first time they climbed Cnoc Mor.

"Oh my god, you're right!" said Foxy.

Nuada began to look frustrated.

"Children, we do not have time to tarry. Partholòn is trying to cast the scourge. What is in these bags?" Nuada asked angrily.

"Water!" Foxy gushed as he ran over the bags, ripping one open and pulling out a bottle of water.

He broke the top open and began to devour the shade-chilled water inside. Naoise was doing the same thing with her bag she that she'd opened. Foxy walked over to Nuada with half the bottle of water left and offered it to him.

"Drink, Nuada," said Foxy.

Nuada took the bottle and drank the water down. The look of a thirst quenched on his face was immaculate.

"Ah," said Nuada, satisfied. "Young Ms. Moone, bring the water for the rest of the climb. It will aid us."

Naoise emptied out all the rubbish from one bag and shoved the remaining water bottles into it. She then threw the bag on her back and began to climb. They hurried up the next portion of the mountain at a rejuvenated pace. They were closing in on the summit, with one more inclined section to go. They paused for a moment to look back down. They could no longer see Cathal and Vincent, and the ground was so far away it resembled a landscape painting. Just as they began their upwards hike again, there was an earth shattering BANG!

Foxy, Naoise and Nuada all stumbled over. They knew it came from the top of the mountain. Foxy looked up to see specks of red sparking and spouting through the smoke at the summit.

"He is getting ready to unleash the scourge. We must hurry. We can stop him!" Nuada shouted, turning to Foxy. "You will need to search deep down and find the deepest roots of bravery you possess. That is the true power Setanta left you. Bravery can't be learned, it can't be taught! It is inside you. You must realise that before we reach the top!"

Foxy's stared at the now flowing fire that was emerging from the top, a small tremble of fear sneaking into his heart.

"Nuada," said Foxy.

"What is it young sir?" Said Nuada knowingly under pressure for time.

"I think I'm scared," said Foxy, unsure.

Nuada looked displeased and somewhat annoyed, while Naoise looked truly frightened.

"Well of course you're scared!" scolded Nuada, much to Foxy and Naoise's surprise.

"I'm asking you to be brave, my friend. One cannot be brave if they aren't scared in the first place. Do you not think Setanta was scared when that vicious hound attacked him? Or when he was fighting the soldiers of Queen Maebh? Do you not think he was scared as he bled out facing death with his enemies staring at him? Of course he was scared! That's the secret, Foxy; we're all scared! All of the time. But how we act in those situations is what makes warriors out of us!" Nuada said empoweringly.

Those words caused Foxy to think back on his own actions during his time in Tinree Island. He was scared on his first day of school, but he went in anyway. He was scared when he saw Conor Sweeney attacking Cathal in the school yard, yet he still intervened. He was scared the day Conann had found them at Nuada's tree. When he thought back on all the events, he realised he was scared during pretty much all of them. Truthfully, no more scared than he was now. That gave him a lurch of confidence in his stomach. He stood up strong again, grabbing the sword of light tightly.

"Let's go to the summit!" Foxy said calmly yet emphatically.

"Huzzah!" bellowed Nuada, and Naoise clasped her hands to her cheeks with pride.

Collectively, the three of them surged up the final flight of Cnoc Mor to the awaiting Partholòn seated atop the holy mountain.

As they approached the flat summit, the thick, dense wall of smoke that surrounded the top looked almost like one of Naoise's whirlwinds. Except rather than wind, it was heavy, black smoke, almost a solid, it was that vicious.

They approached it.

"Careful," said Nuada. "Ms. Moone, can you clear a path?"

Naoise took a deep inhale and began to whistle gently. A much smaller whirlwind formed and made its way to the towering black smoke. Naoise's wind created a small clearing when the two collided.

"Are we ready? This may be our final battle," Nuada said.

"I'm ready. Are you, Naoise?" Foxy said, turning his head to Naoise.

She didn't say anything, instead maintaining her light whistle.

"It could all be over after this, then we can have normal lives!" Foxy joked.

However, Naoise did not look amused. She feigned a smile, continued whistling, and gestured for the group to walk through the small clearing. Nuada, Foxy and Naoise walked through the clearing Naoise had made, but they still could not see. The black smoke was far thicker than they expected, with their process now more like they were walking through a long tunnel, protected by Naoise's wind. Eventually they breached the far side of the black smoke. Before them was a horrifying sight.

The top of Cnor Mor in Foxy's memory was a lush, green, flat surface with large, mossy rocks all around it, accompanied by a staggering view of the sea. Now in the centre of the smoking hurricane, there was scorched black and red earth with bubbling pools of fire scattered around sporadically.

Foxy surveyed his surroundings. It was dark and bleak inside the smoke. There was very little daylight breaking in. Far across the summit of Cnoc Mor there was a familiar red glow, and there, sitting on a rock surrounding by an ominous red glow with his one good eye closed and his sickle across his lap was Partholòn. He was chanting some words very lowly. Foxy could not discern what he was saying.

"Partholòn!" shouted Nuada

Partholòn's one eye flicked open. Instantly, he looked incensed with rage.

"The scourge is here, Nuada. This smoke will soon spread to entire Country! Everything within it shall burn!" snarled Partholòn.

He continued sitting, closed his eye, and returned to chanting once again. The smoke began to increase its swirling speed, and it became thicker.

"That won't happen!" shouted Foxy, taking a step forward and holding the sword of light.

Without a beat Partholòn's sickle raised from his lap and spun across the fiery clearing towards Foxy, who ducked at the last moment. Nuada was amazingly able to catch the sickle. He looked stunned to see he had done it.

Partholòn's eye flicked open.

"I did not see that," snapped the wicked fomorian, floating down off his rock to a standing position. Pools of fire bubbled and burst around him.

Partholòn attempted to call his sickle back to him. The weapon glowed red in Nuada's hands and tried to return, but Nuada did not let go.

"What is this?" asked Partholòn, becoming more enraged.

"Foxy," said Nuada, "he cannot see your actions. He didn't know you would duck, so therefore didn't know I would catch it!"

Foxy looked in awe at Nuada holding the sickle, and then with a sickening crack, Nuada brought his leg speedily to the sickle and broke it straight across his knee. A harrowing grunt emerged from Partholòn when this happened.

"Foxy, as long as you lead in front and we act after you, he can't see what we're going to do!" Naoise said delightedly.

Nuada now also began to look thrilled as he realised this way to defeat Partholòn was valid.

"That won't matter an ounce when the boy is dead!" growled Partholòn. Then he floated a small bit off the ground, maybe a foot or two.

In a blink, Partholòn transcended across the scorched earth and grabbed Foxy by the throat. He stared at the boy for a moment, his wretched eye and horrid face was millimetres from Foxy's. Foxy could smell his breath; it smelled of burnt paper.

Partholòn soared upwards, holding Foxy. His hand wrapped around young Foxy's throat, squeezing impossibly tight. The higher and higher they flew, Foxy couldn't muster a word or a breath. His ears began to pop. They rose so high that Foxy gripped Partholòn's wrist with his left hand. Partholòn was ravaging with rage right in front of his face. With his right hand he raised the sword of light as if to strike, but before he could swing the sword, Partholòn gripped Foxy's sword-bearing wrist. He gripped so tightly that Foxy felt the blood stop reaching his hand.

The pair continued to fly skywards, moving further and further from the ashy crimson ground into the smoking silo. When they had reached an abnormal height, Partholòn stopped ascending and held Foxy mid-air.

"With you gone boy, I will see, and this land will know scourge!" said Partholòn with the greatest venom. Foxy's throat was still squeezed too tightly to respond.

Then Partholòn squeezed the hand holding the sword even tighter, and Foxy felt a searing pain. Where Partholòn's hand clasped Foxy's wrist, steam and smoke was beginning to rise. He was burning his wrist. Foxy held on as long as he could until his hand sprang open and down fell the sword of light. Partholòn released his hand from Foxy's wrist and revealed a red burn mark imprinted on his forearm.

"Now, boy, you too will burn!" screeched Partholòn.

Foxy now used both hands to try and wrench Partholòn's hand off his neck. He moved it but an inch so he could inhale a delicious breath of air. It also allowed him to speak.

"Even if I die, I promise this land will always be here! The land survives all!" shouted Foxy in pain.

The burning pain he'd felt on his wrist was now reappearing on his neck. He knew this was the end, and closed his eyes. He was prepared for it; there was no fear. The burning intensified. Making peace with himself, he blocked out all surrounding sounds. He had a moment of complete silence.

 Until one familiar sound broke through his barrier. It was unmistakable. It was a sound that had saved him before. A sound that made him happy. A sound that he truly loved. Deep, deep in the distance, far below where he and Partholòn had soared to, he heard a faint whistle.

Foxy re-opened his eyes. Partholòn had not heard this sound. Foxy was never as sure of anything in his life. He heard the whistle, but they were so high up. Naoise must have been whistling so loud, he thought. Foxy's eyes glanced downwards to see the falling sword of light, but when he looked closer it was not falling; it was rising.

Emerging through the smoke was a resplendent powerful glow of light beaming from the sword. The black, fiery smoke was now being pushed back by clear wind, Foxy saw. Cascading skywards through the smoke holding the sword of light was Nuada. He was being supported by a cyclone of Naoise's wind. Partholòn looked down to see Nuada rising, but he showed no surprise.

"I saw this come to pass," said Partholòn as he dodged the sword of light with ease while Nuada flew higher than Partholòn and Foxy's position. Then the wind from Naoise dissipated.

"I know you did," Nuada said with a grin.

For a moment, Nuada floated in the air high above them before he began to fall again. Partholòn's eyes flicked back to Foxy.

"But did you see this?" said Foxy powerfully.

Mere seconds before Foxy said this, Nuada let go of the sword of light. Foxy held out his burnt right arm and miraculously caught the sword. Foxy summoned all the strength he had, and right at the depths of his soul there was a sudden emergence of strength he had never felt before.

He saw one fleeting vision of a man fighting a what looked like a hundred soldiers on a battlefield. There was no chance of winning, and with each swing this soldier and his sword were putting all their might into the attack. Foxy felt he could summon the collective power from these swings. Then the ephemeral vision passed.

With one deft thrust of the sword, Foxy drove the first treasure of the Tuath De Danann – the sword of light – right through the heart of Partholòn.

With one breathless yelp Partholòn now gasped for air.

"I did not see that." Partholòn exhaled.

Nuada was now falling beside them. His speed accelerated immensely quick, and he descended away from them back towards the summit of Cnoc Mor. Partholòn was awestruck, his violent, pale face now losing all colour entirely. The black smoke that surrounded them was evaporating and washing away into nothingness.

Foxy and Partholòn floated in mid-air, embraced. Partholòn's hand was still wrapped around Foxy's neck, and Foxy's hand still held the hilt of the sword that had pierced the heart of the ancient evil. The surrounding smoke was now entirely washed away. The clear blue sky of a radiant Christmas Eve was dominating the landscape. Foxy could now see the ridiculous height Partholòn had flown him up to. The summit of Cnoc Mor looked miles away.

Partholòn's eye looked directly at Foxy's face.

"Bravery is the fool's achievement," said Partholòn as something amazing began to happen to him.

His body was decaying mid-air. Dust sized particles of him began to fade and float away out to the sea. The remnants of his face and body still held tangible. He and Foxy had not moved an inch. Foxy could now see that fragments of Partholòn's hand were beginning to dissolve into nothingness. Dark floating particles travelled from the body of Partholòn like dark ashes from a rotting fire.

"Bravery defeated you!" Foxy quipped back.

Partholòn smirked while his body was now less than more. Sections of him had become entirely see-through. Foxy could feel the grip on his throat truly loosen.

"The scourge will always happen, boy. Death is but a distant memory for me. I welcome it. Your bravery has achieved you nothing. Death awaits you, too," said Partholòn before he vanished entirely into the bright sunrise.

Instantly, Foxy began to fall.

Foxy didn't reach out to the ground as he fell. There was no fear; certainly no fear of death. He had made his peace with that possible reality on the ascent. Falling towards the earth, Foxy simply closed his eyes and thought back on happy times. His mind transcended back to his parents, the Sullivans, Cathal, Vincent, Lugh, Nuada and finally Naoise. While the young man fell through the sky, bound for impact, a beautiful smile made its way across the face of Gerard Fox.

Chapter 26: *Slan Go Foíll*

Foxy barrelled downwards, eyes closed, fully prepared for the impact and the ultimate consequences of it. He thought he had hit the ground, because he felt something on his back. His breath was instant, and his eyes opened. Staring up he could only see the sun. On his back, though, he felt pressure.

He looked over his shoulder to see a particularly mucky Nuada had grabbed his torso with his right arm.

"Nuada," said Foxy, stunned.

Nuada turned and looked at Foxy with the greatest smile Foxy had ever seen on his face.

"You did it, my friend," said Nuada, beaming with pride. "No, my brother!"

Foxy then saw in the right hand of Nuada was Lugh's spear. It was flying upwards, holding Nuada. Once Nuada had made the safe capture of Foxy, the spear began to lower again. The closer they got to the summit, Foxy could see Cathal, who was jumping around the scorched ground with joy. Vincent was clapping with exuberant cheer. Lugh looked as if he had been beaten to an inch of his life, but was smiling nonetheless as he controlled the spear. Dagda was also there beaming and clapping loudly. Foxy kept looking, scanning the ground. The spear that was holding Nuada and Foxy finally touched back down on the summit of Cnoc Mor safely.

Just as they landed, Cathal ran over to Foxy, hugging him tightly.

"You did it Foxy! You did it!" roared Cathal with tremendous excitement.

"Bravo Foxy." said Vincent "You were always special, now you have proven it."

"We were under pressure, but we managed to defeat all the Fomorians below," said Lugh, trying to hold himself up.

"Well," said Dagda, "I did most of the heavy lifting, I'd say. But nevertheless, a boy defeating Partholòn for good. Songs and stories will be told, and this event will go down as legend."

A bird also squawked overhead at this point and swooped down rapidly. Morrigan landed right at the feet of Dagda. The bird titled her head towards Dagda, who looked back at the bird and almost instantly said, "Morrigan?"

The bird cawed again. Dagda fell to his knees.

"I am so sorry, my love, I will never leave again," cried Dagda, his big belly resting on the ground when he leaned over, bowing on the ground.

The bird called loudly, and simply hopped on Dagda's shoulder.

"And I you, my love," said the giant man, wiping a tear from his eye. At that same moment, from the trail emerged a large stag, who was panting heavily. Dagda's eyes saw the deer and he immediately ran over to him.

"Fallow my boy! You're here, I wouldn't have left without you!" said Dagda, embracing the stag around its wide neck. Fallow nuzzled his giant head around Dagda's back, while Morrigan sat perched on his shoulder.

420

"This reunion is possible because of this young boy here!" said Dagda.

However, all these kind words fell on deaf ears, as Foxy's eyes continued to dart around the summit. He was starting to panic.

"Where is she?" asked Foxy.

Nuada took hold of Foxy and looked at him bracingly.

"She's unconscious, Foxy," Nuada said politely. "She used the last of her powers to save me from the fall. Then the others arrived."

"Is she alive?" asked Foxy.

"Yes," said Nuada. "But we may not have long."

"Long for what?" asked Foxy, now with legitimate concern.

"For a goodbye," said Nuada sadly.

Foxy gasped, his stomach dropping. He then saw across the way a small bit near where Fallow had emerged. There was a thriving patch of dense green grass there where Naoise lay. Foxy ran over and stumbled to her side.

"Naoise!" He pleaded gently, taking her by the shoulder and shaking her softly. Tears began to form in his eyes.

"Please, Naoise wake up; you can't be dead!" cried Foxy as he hugged her limp body.

"She is not dead, Foxy," said a warm, familiar voice.

Foxy turned around and rubbed the tears out of his eyes to see a woman. This was a woman he had seen before. It was Danu – the woman from the lake. There she stood just across the clearing atop the summit of Cnoc Mor. The morning sun shone like a halo around her. She was wearing her beautiful blue waterfall dress, and her crimson red hair fell like soft satin curtains over her shoulders. Danu began to walk towards Foxy and Naoise.

With each barefoot step she took across the burnt mountain top, the scorched, ashy earth beneath was overtaken by luscious flora. Sprouting blades of emerald-green grass, daisies, dandelions and daffodils all emerged from wherever her foot touched the earth. Every footstep created life. As she walked, a trail of heavenly meadow followed her.

When she passed Lugh, he bowed while making as little noise as possible. She walked further, and Vincent also bowed, following Lugh's lead. Vincent elbowed Cathal and forced him to bow too. Danu was wearing a warm smile as she crossed.

When she passed Nuada, there was a small smile exchanged between them as Nuada also then bowed. Approaching Dagda, Morrgian and Fallow, each of them also bowed their heads. Morrigan was still perched on Dagda's shoulder.

Danu now reached Foxy, who was on his knees beside Naoise, who was still lying unconscious.

"Danu?" asked Foxy.

She smiled at him, and crouched beside them. She looked at Naoise's face.

"You know I really did enjoy our chats, Foxy. I know you had a part to play," said Danu, her inviting face now looked at Foxy. "And you played it so well. I am so proud."

"Danu," Asked Foxy "Can you help her?"

"She does not need help." Said Danu who then placed a warm hand on Naoise's unconscious shoulder. Suddenly, Naoise's eyes flicked open.

"Naoise!" shouted Foxy with immeasurable relief. "Are you okay?"

Naoise's fluttering eyes darted from Danu to Foxy.

"I think so," said Naoise, visibly confused.

Foxy reached over, grabbed her, and hugged so tight he wasn't sure if he would ever let go. Foxy was bursting with glee. This was everything he'd wanted. They had defeated the evil, and everyone was okay. He turned to Nuada almost boastfully.

"See Nuada, she's fine! There's no need for a goodbye," Foxy cheered.

Cathal was also cheering in the background.

"Now Naoise, everything will be okay!" Foxy smiled.

Naoise, however, looked sullen. Her eyes fell, not looking at Foxy.

"I'm afraid, my very dear friend," said Danu, "There is a need for a goodbye."

Foxy felt like he had taken a gut punch. Turning to Danu, he asked, "What do you mean?"

Danu stood up and began walking back across the clearing very slowly, creating as much foliage as she could.

"My friend, the prophecy is complete. It is time for the Tuath De Danann to come home," Danu said with some sadness in her voice.

Foxy was so stunned he couldn't speak.

Then Danu walked to the edge of the cliff, right where Cathal, Foxy and Naoise had sat before. She stared out at the glistening water, then she took a step off the cliff. Foxy shuddered for a moment, but Danu remained still. She took another step. Each footprint left a small trace of bright blue particles in the sky, as if there was an invisible bridge off the edge of the cliff.

Danu then turned once more to Foxy and the rest.

"Foxy, I owe you all my gratitude," she said. Her eyes then moved to Cathal and Vincent. "And of course you two also"

Both of them bowed their heads again. Then a groan and grunting came from Cathal. Particles of light began to emerge from him, it was like every pore on his body suddenly expunged a single light particle. The formation of light particles surrounding Cathal then floated over towards Danu above her, then vanished out to the sea.

"What was that?" asked Cathal.

"My dear friend, you are a brave warrior indeed, but not a full Tuath De Danann. You are not foretold to return to Falias, but your power has now transcended this world."

Cathal looked at his skin. He tried hardening it again, but nothing happened. He looked devastated. Vincent put an arm around him in an effort to cheer him up.

"Still the hardest man I know," Vincent said supportively.

Dagda, with Morrigan perched on his shoulder, walked over to Foxy and extended a hand.

"My friend, I will always remember you for reuniting my family," said Dagda.

Instinctively, Foxy stuck his hand out from his kneeling position and shook Dagda's hand. Morrigan cawed, then they walked towards the cliff edge where Danu was standing in air. Before joining them, Fallow walked over to Foxy, dipped his massive head, and exhaled a noise of sadness. Then the stag made his way over to Dagda and Morrigan.

"Wait, I still don't understand what's happening," Foxy wept.

Foxy then looked back to Danu. He saw Dagda now walking along the invisible bridge out towards the sunrise, except instead of a deer and a crow by his side. Dagda was walking hand-in-hand with a gorgeous, dark-haired, heavy-set woman and a strapping young man on his other side. Foxy watched as the family walked across the air. When they passed Danu, much like Cathal's power each of them evaporated into particles of gorgeous baby blue lights. Just like that, they were gone.

"Where did they go?" asked Foxy, wanting someone to explain explicitly to him what was happening. Naoise's eyes were still askew from Foxy's.

Foxy then saw Lugh limp to Cathal and Vincent. He faced them, leaning on his spear and attempting to make himself as tall as possible. He nodded to them.

"Boys, it's been a pleasure," Lugh said with a smirk. Cathal and Vincent smiled back.

Lugh then limped his way over to Foxy and Naoise.

"Ms. Moone, I will see you shortly," Lugh said to Naoise. Then he turned to Foxy. "My goodness, Foxy, you are some warrior!" he said genuinely.

Then as Lugh limped towards Danu he spoke again, "Some warrior indeed."

Then, just like Dagda and his family moments before, Lugh stepped out over the sea and vanished into the morning breeze.

"Naoise, what's happening?!" Foxy pleaded with all his might.

Finally, Naoise looked at Foxy with a pouting lip. She was about to burst into tears.

"It's time," Nuada said strongly. "On your feet, both of you, now. Come on."

Nuada helped them both back to their feet. He turned to Naoise.

"Naoise, perhaps you should go have a word with the others first. Let me chat with my friend for a moment. I have already said my goodbyes to them," said Nuada.

Naoise jogged over to Cathal and Vincent. Foxy's eyes followed her, but Nuada's soft hand on his shoulder regained his attention.

"What's happening, Nuada?" Foxy asked calmly.

"This is as the prophecy foretold, my friend. When Partholòn and the Fomorians are defeated, we are to return to home. Our home. We have fulfilled this land's need for us. It is time for us to rest," Said Nuada.

Foxy's eyes welled up again.

"Does Naoise have to go?" He asked with a croak in his voice.

"I'm afraid she does, Foxy," said Nuada.

Foxy could feel the tears coming. He was trying to fight them. One snuck out and he quickly wiped it from his face, feeling embarrassed.

Nuada spotted this and then looked Foxy in the eyes.

"Tears are nothing to be ashamed of, dear Foxy. Tears let us know something is important, and whenever a tear is shed we know there is a powerful emotion at play. To show a tear is sometimes an act of bravery; something you know all too well," said Nuada. "But now, Foxy —" Nuada placed both hands on Foxy's shoulders, " — it is my time to leave. This beautiful land has been my sanctuary for a very long time. I will miss it, and I will also miss you. Be strong for her, will you?"

Nuada hugged Foxy.

Foxy hugged him back, and then Nuada broke from the hug. Before he turned, Foxy saw one solitary tear streaming down Nuada's face.

"Farewell, Foxy," Nuada said, turning to walk to Danu.

"Farewell, Nuada," Foxy replied, gaining strength back in his voice.

Nuada then scooped the sword of light up from the ground and examined it for a moment. Then he walked honourably across the flourishing grassy summit. He paused before stepping off the edge.

"Slan go Foill Eire," Nuada said. Then he walked off the cliff-face, took a few steps further out, and in a beautiful series of moving particles he too vanished.

Foxy looked over to see Naoise being embraced by both Cathal and Vincent. When their hug ended, Vincent placed an arm around Cathal. It seemed more so to support himself, as Foxy could clearly see Vincent was crying, heavily.

Naoise walked over to Foxy, and the two looked at each other. Their eyes met as if for the first time.

"This is what I couldn't tell you," Naoise said, trying to smile.

"Why didn't you tell me?" asked Foxy.

"Because if you knew we would all vanish when Partholòn was defeated you never would have done so. If he stayed trapped, we would have been able to stay here, but I always knew this was a possibility."

Foxy didn't speak for a moment. He just looked at her.

"I'm sorry," she said. "I'm sorry we can't go travel and explore with you. I would love that, but sometimes…" She began to weep. "Sometimes paths just go in different directions."

Foxy was about to cry also, but remembered Nuada's request to be strong for Naoise. Foxy hugged her tight, and she squeezed him back lovingly. Foxy had never fought as hard to speak without tears in his life.

"Just because paths go in different directions doesn't mean it wasn't a wonderful journey while they were together," Foxy said confidently.

Naoise pulled away from the hug, and their eyes met once again. The two kissed on the top of the mountain. The kiss evolved into an even tighter hug than the one before.

"I love you, Foxy," she whispered into his ear.

"I love you too!" Foxy replied, now unable to fight his tears.

When they pulled back from the hug slightly, Foxy could see that particles of Naoise were beginning to float towards where Danu stood on the edge of the cliff-face. However, Danu simply looked, she did not rush.

Naoise now stood back and looked at her own body, which was evolving into light particles and floating away.

"It's time for me to go home," Naoise said with bulbous tears in her eyes. "Goodbye Foxy."

"Goodbye, Naoise," Foxy said longingly.

She began to make her way towards Danu, specs of light transcending off her and making their way out to sea. Naoise paused at the edge of the cliff, and Foxy made his way over to Cathal and Vincent. Each of them held very emotional faces, with tears aplenty between them.

Naoise stood on the cliff-face. She went to take a step off, then shuddered.

"I'm scared!" she cried.

Foxy ran towards her. Naoise heard him coming and turned around, but then Foxy saw something that made him stop running. The sight he saw filled him with a sense of peace, as heartbroken as he may have felt. This was the right thing for Naoise.

"You'll be okay, Naoise. I promise," said Foxy.

Cathal and Vincent had also seen this sight and were too in awe.

Naoise still looked too frightened to step out. Then she felt someone grab her hands. She turned to see what Foxy had saw. It was her parents, or rather visions of her parents. Aine, her Mother was holding her left hand and smiling at her, while her imposing Father, Aengus, held her right hand. Standing behind them was also her stunning older sister. Both parents looked at Foxy and empathically nodded at him.

Naoise was overwhelmed with emotion. One final time, she looked behind at Foxy, Cathal and Vincent. Smiled her usual gorgeous quirky smile. Then Naoise faced Danu and walked hand-in-hand with her parents and sister out across the air towards the incandescent sun. Danu turned and walked beside them. In a graceful, stunning whirlwind of particles, each of them with one final concluding step departed the land of Ireland.

Epilogue

Crestfallen, Foxy, Vincent and Cathal began to slowly make their way down the mountain. Unbelievably, the descent was now harder than the climb. Each of them were emotionally distraught, physically exhausted and even spiritually spent. There was virtually nothing said between them as they slowly made their way down. They approached the bottom, legs heavy and hearts heavier. Scattered all around the ground were decaying patches of grass from where the remaining Fomorians had been defeated. The three remaining members of the legends of old stood there and looked for a moment. Foxy's eyes glanced at the giant hole leading to the cavern in the side of the mountain.

Cathal's ears perked up. They could hear sirens in the distance.

"Let us leave here before it gets tricky," said Vincent.

They increased their walking pace to just below a jog. Incredibly, when they made it back to Vincent's car, the car had been left untouched from all the chaos surrounding the mountain. They got into the car – Vincent in the driver's seat and the other two lads in the back. There was a moment of silence. A breath was enjoyed by each of them, it was over. The sirens were growing louder.

"Where are we going?" Foxy asked, devoid of emotion.

Vincent was caught off-guard by this question. He did not reply.

"What will happen to Tryst manor?" asked Cathal.

Vincent looked at Cathal in the rear-view mirror.

"My promise will remain. I vowed to protect that place, and so I shall," said Vincent.

Cathal looked out the window, seemingly unimpressed by the answer.

"Is it okay if I stay there until my parents come back?" Cathal asked stoically.

A smile crept its way onto Vincent's battle-hardened face.

"That would be just fine" said Vincent.

Vincent's eyes then flicked to Foxy, who was still staring at the top of the mountain.

"But first," said Vincent, "let's get out of here."

The car pulled out and exited towards the road heading away from Cnoc Mor. Vincent drove onto the road as a team of fire engines sped their way towards the mountain. As the car drove away, Foxy's eyes were glued to the ever-decreasing summit of Cnoc Mor until they turned a corner and it faded from view.

***

A short moment later, they arrived back at the Sullivans' house. When the car pulled in, Linda rushed to the front door. She looked beyond worried. In a flash, Macdara had emerged from the nearby yard. They both looked eager and frightened.

"We heard there was a volcano on Cnoc Mor?!" Linda screeched.

Vincent was the first to get out of the car and shook his head, disregarding the rumour. A partial wave of relief washed over them. Then Cathal got out to add to the partial relief, and then Foxy got out and looked at both Linda and Macdara. Linda and Macdara waited a moment. They were waiting for someone else, but she was no longer there.

Linda's face looked utterly heartbroken. She clasped her hand over her mouth, and Macdara bowed his head. Foxy speedily walked over to both of them and hugged them tightly. Foxy now began to weep again. Linda held him warmly.

Vincent made his way over to them. He looked at Foxy.

"This young man did more today than we could ever possibly thank him for," said Vincent.

Foxy looked back at him and extended a handshake. Vincent swiftly stuck his hand out and shook Foxy's firmly.

Cathal now limped over to Foxy, and hugged him. Foxy was unprepared for this, and quietly hugged him back. The two didn't speak a word, they just smiled at each other. Cathal and Vincent limped back to the car.

"Vincent!" Macdara called just before they were about to get into the car.

Vincent turned and his eyes caught Macdara's.

"I know it's not the best time, but tomorrow is still Christmas day. If yourself and this young man want to join us for dinner, it would really mean the world to me, and your Mother," Macdara said.

Vincent smiled.

"I would love that. I'll see you tomorrow, Da."

Macdara and Vincent shook hands. Then Cathal and his new roommate got into the car and left the property.

Linda was still hugging Foxy. Macdara walked back over. It was back to just the three of them. It had been a long time.

"Foxy, my boy," said Macdara, "what I reckon you need is rest."

Foxy wiped away the errant tears that remained on his face.

"Perhaps you're right," he said.

Linda went to usher the young man inside, but Foxy stopped for a moment.

"Linda," he asked to her astonishment, "is there anything to eat?"

She leaned into him and hugged him tightly.

***

The three of them ate a poetic meal, as Linda cooked the same stew she had made the first day Foxy arrived. As she cooked, Foxy took the longest shower of his life. He had cried so much that he just let the hot water flow over him.

The meal they ate was bittersweet. Macdara and Linda were thrilled to see Foxy and Vincent safe, but beyond grief that Naoise had not returned. They had not asked explicitly what happened, as they did not need to. After dinner, the sun had fully set. Macdara made his way to the living room and was enjoying an evening snooze.

Foxy offered to help Linda clean up after dinner.

"Don't be silly, Foxy. It's Christmas Eve. I can do it. You go up to your room and take it easy," she said.

Foxy obeyed, made his way up the stairs, and lay on his bed. A thousand thoughts raced through his head. One recurring image was Naoise with her family. This eased him.

The evening rolled by, and Foxy was just about to fall asleep when there was a knock on the door.

"Yeah?" asked Foxy, sitting up in bed.

Linda opened the door and crept in.

"Sorry Foxy dear, I just thought that maybe you'd want this," she said.

Foxy could see she was holding a letter.

"What is it?"

Linda held up the letter and looked at it.

"Well, it's a Christmas present," said Linda. "From Naoise."

Foxy's eyes lit up.

"What did you say?" he asked.

Linda walked closer to Foxy and sat on the side of the bed.

"She gave this to me and asked me to give it to you on Christmas morning if she didn't return. Since it's basically Christmas now, and I just think whatever is in there might help you sleep better, I'll leave you alone with it. I'll see you in the morning. Happy Christmas, Foxy," Linda said as she went to leave.

Foxy's eyes were so glued to the letter, he almost forgot to say it back.

"Happy Christmas to you too, Linda," Foxy said with more character in his voice than he had all day.

Linda looked back and smiled, then exited the room. Foxy sat up on the bed and looked at the crimson envelope, addressed to 'Foxy' and written in neat handwriting. He took a deep inhale and opened the letter. His eyes scanned the letter. It read:

"Dear Foxy,

If this letter has made its way to you, then Partholòn has been defeated and myself and the other Tuath De Danann have returned to Falias. All I ask of you, Foxy, is please do not weep for me. I am home, with my family. I am not in a position to be wept for. I hope you are having a wonderful Christmas morning. I had planned to get you a bike for Christmas, but sadly that never came to fruition. A lot of things I would have liked to happen never came to fruition, but also a lot of them did. I always dreamed of meeting someone like you. Someone who's funny, brave, kind and loyal. You will never know how much the last few months meant to me. The time I spent with you and Cathal will hold a treasured place in my heart for eternity. I hope you live your life to the fullest, leave no stone unturned, never slow down, and always stay looking for adventure.

With love, your fellow Legend of Old,

Naoise"

Foxy fell back on the bed clutching the letter to his chest. He almost felt like he was choking holding the tears back. Eventually he just let them out, but he was smiling. No longer was he weeping for her departure; he was happy for her to be at her true home with her family. Foxy re-read the letter over and over again, until eventually his eyes gave out and he drifted off to sleep.

***

Foxy's eyes reopened a short while later, but he was not at the Sullivans' house in Tinree Island. He was in his bed, which was once again positioned in the beautiful still lake of Falias. Foxy sat up in the bed and felt that majestic cool breeze roll across his face again. All of the physical pain had been lifted from his body while in the lake; the lack of pain was wonderful.

He looked around the lake to see if he could spot Danu, he could not. Something about the lake felt different this time. The water felt denser, and the sun warmer. Foxy inhaled the lifting light air deep into his lungs.

Foxy began to walk away from his bed as he had done several times before in the lake of Falias. He walked for a very long time and never saw anything resembling Danu or Falias itself. Foxy realised he would wake up soon. This may be the last time he ever visited the lake, he thought to himself.

He decided to sit and wait in the warm, still water to wake up. He trailed his hand slowly across the water surface, creating a series of ripples back and forth. He was very much at peace. Then his head faced a direction opposite from where he had walked.

He stood up and was certain he could not see anything. The horizon was as blue as the sky, and there was definitely nothing there, but he was sure he had heard something. He paused in the water, making himself statuesque not moving an inch so as to discern what the noise was.

Foxy turned his ear towards the direction he thought he heard the noise, and deep, deep in the distance carried a soft breeze. He heard a faint whistle.

The End

Printed in Great Britain
by Amazon

29222372R00249